THE MAN FROM BLOOD GULCH

WILLIAM W. JOHNSTONE

AND J. A. JOHNSTONE

PINNACLE BOOKS
Kensington Publishing Corp.
kensingtonbooks.com

PROLOGUE

Gunshots and the wild hollering of the bandits echoed throughout the gulch, the thunderous stampede of hooves not quite drowning out the screams and shouts of the terrified settlers. A dozen families lived in Parson's Gulch—forty-seven people along with chickens, hogs, dogs, cows, mules, and horses. There'd never been any trouble.

Until recently.

Twelve-year-old Garret McCoy splashed through the shallow stream, dragging along eight-year-old Mary Jane Potts, an iron grip on her thin wrist, her corn-yellow pigtails flapping in the breeze. It was like dragging along an anvil; Mary Jane fought him all the way.

McCoy reckoned he couldn't blame her. After all, most folks in their right mind wouldn't run *toward* all the shooting and screaming, which is exactly what McCoy was doing.

"I'm scared!" Mary Jane shouted.

"We've got to know what's happening." McCoy kept pulling, not willing to admit he was frightened too.

They came around Bill Wilder's barn, squatting at the corner to peek around and watch the chaos unfolding along the dirt road which led into and out of the gulch, houses and barns and sheds and chicken coops on either side. McCoy stared wide-eyed as two score bandits rode through the gulch, blasting away with their six-guns at anything that moved.

Doris Manning, who did the sewing for so many folks, tried to dart into the imagined safety of her clapboard home. She made it up three of the five steps to her front porch when one of the bandits squeezed off a shot and blood bloomed wet and red between her shoulder blades. She fell forward then slipped back down the stairs.

McCoy flinched at the sound of the gunshot.

More people were killed, men and women indiscriminately.

Jasper Jenkins, the old man who whittled down by the stream while fishing and smoking his pipe, was shot in the face. Paul Branson, father of three, new to Parson's Gulch, chased his three children out of the way of the galloping horses only to be ridden down himself and trampled bloody into the mud. Claude Irving, the community blacksmith, came storming from his forge, rifle clutched in his meaty hands, but he never got off a shot. Three bandits peppered him with multiple blasts, spinning the big man away. Old Lady Callahan, who was always so happy to babysit the young ones, tripped and went sprawling in the mud. As she tried to get up, a horse hoof caught her in the forehead. Her eyes rolled white and that was all she wrote.

McCoy was terrified but found he could not turn

away from the carnage, his eyes wide with morbid fascination. A desperate bleating sound drew his attention. He turned and saw Mary Jane behind him, sitting on the ground, knees pulled up against her chest, eyes squeezed tightly shut, hands over her ears to block out the horror.

He opened his mouth to tell her . . .

. . . what?

That it would be okay? That he'd keep her safe?

Lies.

The marauders broke off into twos and threes, weaved in between the buildings, flushing out anyone trying to hide. Guns blazed and bodies fell over one another into the mud. Three grim riders broke off from the main body, galloping hard for the Wilder barn. McCoy's eyes went big.

He grabbed Mary Jane's wrist again, yanking her to her feet. "Come on!"

They ran around to the back of the barn and followed the narrow footpath behind the houses until they came to Mary Jane's home, a small and rickety shack that always surprised McCoy to still be standing. Mary Jane tried to run for the dilapidated staircase going up to her backdoor.

"No!" McCoy held on to her, tight.

He'd seen the men kicking in doors, pulling people out of their homes. The gunfire had waned, but the screaming and shouting had increased.

"Under here!"

McCoy pulled her down to her hands and knees, and then both went flat to their bellies. They wriggled under the house. McCoy kept scooting forward, inches at a time, until he was right behind the house's front steps. He glanced back often to make sure Mary Jane was still with him. She'd gone to pick berries, and McCoy's father—who was pals with Mary Jane's father—told him to go with her since she was too young to be wandering the woods alone.

Watch over that little girl. His father's last words to him. *She's your responsibility*.

McCoy peered through the gaps in the steps. He didn't want to be caught, but he was desperate to see what was happening. From his hiding place behind the steps, he could see his small house across the street, but that's not what firmly had McCoy's attention at the moment.

In the middle of the muddy road, McCoy's father was on his knees. One of the marauders stood behind him, a six-gun pointed at the back of his head. The marauder was a porky fellow with a greasy sneer. McCoy gasped, eyes widening with growing fear. There was blood on his father's face, at the corners of his mouth, one eye swollen closed, black and blue. His father didn't even look frightened, McCoy thought, just tired, head hanging, shoulders slumped.

Another stranger paced back and forth in front of his father, sharp featured, thin but straight, a sneering expression on his face. McCoy had seen the man before. The patch over his left eye had made him memorable. He'd been through Parson's Gulch about a week ago, and McCoy had seen him having heated words with his father, some dire dispute, although McCoy hadn't been close enough to hear the words.

Now the man was back with a bunch of marauders,

roaring through the gulch to murder and terrorize. Why these men had singled out his father, McCoy couldn't guess unless it was the fact that his father was a sort of unofficial leader in the community. A few of the folks in Parson's Gulch even called him *mayor* . . . half joke, half sign of respect.

"You didn't want to do this the easy way, Warren," the man in the eye patch said. "Now you see what happens. Now you see how serious my employer is about this land."

McCoy flinched at the man saying *Warren*—his father's first name. To McCoy, he was *Pa*, and to everyone else in the gulch he was *McCoy*. When McCoy's mother had been alive, she was the only one who'd called McCoy's father Warren. It seemed a cruel presumption for this nasty stranger to call McCoy's pa by his first name.

Warren McCoy spit, a mix of blood and saliva. "There ain't gold in that stream, I'm telling ya. Old Pete found a couple small nuggets, and the rest of us swarmed all over that stream, panning our hearts out. Came up with nothing, so we all just went back to our normal lives. Folks just live here now regular like. We ain't doing nothing to nobody. Just living."

"And that's too much," said the man with the eye-patch. "Bart, send him on his way."

The porky marauder lifted his six-shooter and shot Warren McCoy in the back.

People screamed.

Garret McCoy's mouth fell open. *No.*

The world seemed to slow, his father pitching forward, eyes rolling up, until he finally landed face-first in the mud, instantly immobile like a cold slab of beef. McCoy felt dizzy, unable to rip his eyes away from the scene, like he just witnessed something impossible, like if he just kept looking, wide-eyed and slack-jawed, his father would get up again.

Then the yelling—pure anger and hatred, words smashed together in one, long animal sound of pure fury.

It was McCoy's older brother Danny, a fifteen-year-old walking, talking grudge against the world. He stormed down the steps of the house across the road, clutching his father's double-barreled shotgun, eyes wild with rage, face twisted.

The porky one called Bart turned and raised his gun, but he was too slow.

Danny jerked the triggers, and both barrels belched fire. Bart's head vanished in a blur of red mist. More screams. The corpse toppled onto his father's.

Danny didn't live one more second after that. The man with the eyepatch along with a half dozen more of the marauders drew and blazed away at the boy.

All the onlookers kept screaming and screaming and screaming.

McCoy felt his chest tighten, his gut convulse.

Danny took a few sideways steps, lead slamming into him from every direction, fresh blooms splashing red across his chest, belly, and thighs. He took a couple more halting steps, almost like a drunken dance which would have been comical if not for the horror of it. The teen fell forward into the mud and never got up again.

McCoy tried to move without thinking, there was no reason to it, nothing that could be done, but the urge was overwhelming to crawl out from under the house and go to them.

Something kept him from moving forward.

He looked back. Mary Jane had both hands latched onto him, her thin fingers wrapped around his arm, pulling him back with everything she had. The plea in her eye couldn't have been any plainer if she'd said it out loud. *Don't go. Don't go. Don't go. Don't—*

The last words of McCoy's father floated back to him. *Keep watch on the girl.*

"Now, listen up, you people," the man in the eye-patch shouted. "Just forget about this place. When we come back, you'd better be gone. If you're still here . . . well, I reckon you know what happens."

The marauders mounted their horses and rode away.

For a long moment nobody moved. The gulch had gone dead quiet save for the sniffles and sobs of the few overcome with emotion.

McCoy felt Mary Jane let go of him.

He crawled out from under the house, movements leaden, a strange, dizzy feeling separating him from the rest of the world like it was all happening behind glass. He had a vague awareness of others, folks hugging and crying, some drifting back into their homes. He had the notion somebody might be talking to him, a muted voice, like someone trying to speak to him underwater. He ignored it.

In his peripheral vision, he saw Mary Jane run into her mother's arms. Good. One less obligation to weigh him down.

He paused to look at his father and brother. They didn't look real. Just cold meat stuffed into familiar clothing, now shot through with lead. He walked on and into the house, aware there were still folks calling his name.

McCoy went through the little house quickly. They didn't own much, and he barely filled the canvas sack. He grabbed the saddle and went to the small barn out back and saddled the old splotchy gelding. The animal still had a few good years in it. He mounted up. Where would he go? Kansas, maybe. Hadn't his pa mentioned a sister there?

He'd figure it out one way or another.

Less than twenty minutes after his father and brother had been ruthlessly cut down in the muddy road, Garret McCoy rode out of Parson's Gulch.

And he never went back.

EIGHTEEN YEARS LATER . . .

CHAPTER 1

The Colt Peacemaker felt strange on his hip.

Not bad, just new. He'd carried the Colt Navy for years, and it was a hard thing to give up something that had worked so well for so long. The Peacemaker's cartridge was bigger, and he liked that. He liked the way it bucked in his hand. Felt like power. But so far, he'd only shot tin cans and bottles with it.

Now it was time to shoot men.

The town of Black Oak was like any of a hundred others across Texas, and that meant there was at least one saloon. It was a hot summer day, and men would be piling into the place for a cold beer or a shot of whiskey.

The two outlaws on the saloon's front porch looked smug and overconfident. Probably because of the rifleman in the window across the street. They'd heard he was coming for them, so they'd put a man in the window and thought it was their little secret.

But Garret McCoy had spotted him, in the hotel window, second floor all the way on the left. He'd always had good luck sniffing out men who were trying to kill him, a natural instinct honed by far more practice and experience than any man should see in a lifetime. He'd joined up with a bunch of other dumb, wide-eyed Kansas boys right after Fort Sumter. They'd show those Confederates a thing or two.

The bravado had faded fast at Wilson's Creek.

Evan at the raw age of eighteen, it was plain that McCoy was good at war, could ride and fight and handle guns. By Elkhorn Tavern, he had three stripes on his arm, in no small part because most of the boys he'd joined with had gotten killed.

By the Wilderness, he'd been plucked from his regiment to join a special raiding unit. He learned to ride hard and strike fast, and he was even better with a pistol than with a rifle.

And then one day the war was over, and all McCoy had learned was how to kill.

He needn't have worried, for the West always had a use for men with that exact skill. And some men were worth just as much dead as alive. McCoy didn't relish killing, but he'd seen enough to get numb to it.

Not that he was eager for his own. He'd lived this long because he was smart and careful and patient. Patience was key. If he turned up at the front steps to the saloon porch right now to face the outlaws, it would put his back to the rifleman across the street. There was no rule that said he had to face the outlaws this very minute just because they were smirking at him. He wasn't obliged to walk into their trap.

He turned abruptly to circle behind the saloon, catching the outlaws' surprised look from the side of his eye.

When he was out of sight, he touched his guns to make sure they were still there. Of course they were, but it was a fidgety habit. Two fingers on the butt of the Peacemaker on his hip, then a thumb along the cool metal of the hammer on the Colt Navy in its new place, holstered under his stomach at the belt line. If he spent all the lead in the Peacemaker and still needed to shoot, he could drop it and draw the Navy crossways. It was a comfortable setup for him. He'd been too nostalgic for the Navy to give it up completely, and it was good to have the old friend ready as backup.

He entered the saloon through the back door, went down a short hall, taking it slow to give his eyes a chance to adjust. He emerged from the hallway into the front part of the saloon, a highly polished bar off to his right with an enormous oil painting on the wall behind it depicting a woman sprawled on a divan. She wasn't exactly dressed for cold weather.

The place was crowded for an afternoon, folks swilling beers and tossing back shots of whiskey, lively conversation and a few hands of poker at scattered tables. McCoy went to the bar, flagged down a harried looking fella in a dirty apron, and asked for whiskey.

He stood there a while sipping from the glass, turning around to lean back against the bar and keep an eye on the front door. They'd get curious and come in soon enough.

What happened after that remained to be seen.

They entered the saloon sooner than he thought they would, stopping just inside the door, casting about, obviously trying to spot him. A second later, they did. One elbowed the other, and they traded whispers, and in the next moment took a table across the room, backs to the wall, both watching him while McCoy watched them right back.

McCoy could just about read their minds. He hadn't stumbled into their obvious trap, and they were trying to figure what to do next. If they were smart, they'd mount up and get gone.

They were almost never smart.

The town's sheriff—a fella named Bryson Tate— was pretty good about rounding up drunks on a Saturday night and keeping the peace in a general way, but when it came to outlaw killers, he hadn't been much help. So that's when a trio of anxious men from the town council had approached McCoy. If the law couldn't rid the town of these men, then let a hired gun do it is what they figured. Tate simply didn't have the grit for it, and furthermore, it was suspected he took bribes from the outlaws to look the other way.

McCoy had put that to the test, letting it leak to Tate he would be headed to the saloon soon to take the outlaws dead or alive. Sure enough, word got to the outlaws, and it could only have been Tate who'd tipped them off.

Now McCoy's plan was to wait them out. They'd get impatient and make a mistake. Or the rifleman across the street would get impatient and come over to see what was going on, and then McCoy would have all three of them together. Not ideal, but better than having a sniper across the street taking potshots at him.

"Dirty" Dave Dunbar and Shane "Snake" Delany weren't the most ruthless killers McCoy had ever hunted, but they weren't model citizens by any measurement.

Delany got the nickname "Snake" because he had a tattoo of a sidewinder down his shooting arm and told everyone who'd listen he was as fast on the draw as a striking snake. Dunbar was called "Dirty" because . . . well, McCoy didn't know. Maybe the man didn't bathe.

By process of elimination, that meant the man across the street with the rifle must have been Larry Prince, who evidently didn't feel the need to bother with a nickname. Maybe he felt being called Prince was enough.

The saloon doors swung inward as a newcomer entered, a man hunched over in a long, gray cloak, head down and hat pulled low. There was nothing remarkable about him except the way he walked, a slow, deliberate gait like he was weary but determined, or drunk but pretending to be sober. Nobody took much notice of him, but McCoy watched the man with curiosity as he shambled across the saloon.

When the stranger drew even with the table where Dunbar and Delany sat, he suddenly threw off his cloak, stood straight, and drew a pair of gleaming, nickel-plated Peacemakers, leveling one at each outlaw.

"Don't move," the stranger said. "Get them hands on the table."

The outlaws complied, everyone in the saloon turning to get a load of what was happening.

McCoy realized he knew the man.

Bob Baily was another bounty hunter. He and McCoy had crossed paths before, which often happened when two hunters trailed the same prey. He wore a blue, bib-front shirt, and black pants with yellow stripes down the sides. A bushy mustache that drooped down each side of his wide mouth.

"I like your new Peacemakers, Bob," McCoy said. "Real flashy."

Bob's eyes flashed to McCoy quickly, then back to the outlaws. "That you, Garret?"

"It's me."

"Ain't seen you since Wichita."

McCoy shrugged. "I been around."

"Well, I reckon I know why you're here, and I'm just telling you to stand back," Bob told him. "I got the drop on these boys fair and square. You wanted them, you should've made a move sooner. My play, my reward."

"I guess that's about right," McCoy agreed.

"Okay then." Bob waved his six-shooters at the two outlaws. "You two get up and head out that front door and no funny business. I like to take my prisoners in alive, unlike some folks I could mention, but we can do it dead if that's how you want it."

Dunbar and Delany stood slowly, hands in the air, and moved toward the front door, Bob following.

McCoy cleared his throat. "I need to warn you, Bob—"

"Warn me what?" Bob shot back. "You going to take my prisoners from me? You just stay at the bar and enjoy your drink and keep your hand away from that shooter on your hip."

"Dang it, Bob, you need to listen to me for your own good."

"You don't give me orders, so don't get all tough with me, Ghost McCoy." Bob licked his lips nervously.

McCoy's eyes narrowed. "I don't much fancy that nickname."

"Never mind that," Bob said. "You just mind your business, and I'll mind mine."

The outlaws left the saloon, and Bob Baily followed.

The unmistakable crack of a rifle shot split the air.

Bob flew back into the saloon, hat spinning away, fancy shooting irons drooping from his hands. He landed hard with a *wham* on the rough floorboards. Blood dripped down one side of his nose from a neat hole in the center of his forehead.

Yells, panic, curiosity, excitement, fear, all mixed together from everyone in the saloon, some standing to get a better look at the show, others diving under tables for cover.

McCoy was already moving sideways from the bar, his Peacemaker flashing into his hand. Snake Delany burst back through the swinging saloon doors first, Colt Walker in his hand, blazing away where McCoy had been standing at the bar a split second ago, whiskey bottles exploding in a rain of glass and amber liquid.

McCoy fanned the hammer of his Peacemaker twice, catching Snake in the chest and knocking him back into Dirty Dave, who was trying to enter. Both men went down in a heap.

Dirty Dave recovered quickly, coming up to one knee and lifting his pistol, but he wasn't fast enough.

McCoy fired.

The shot caught Dirty Dave in the throat, and he dropped his pistol and flopped over, making a heart-breaking gurgling sound.

McCoy rushed to the front door but stood off to the

side, trying to peek around the corner into the street without exposing himself to the rifleman. He took a couple of quick looks. The hotel window across the street was empty, but that didn't mean much. The shooter could have been hiding off to the side of the window just as McCoy was doing, waiting for his chance to shoot again.

Dirty Dave hadn't finished dying yet. He squirmed on the ground, kicking and twitching, both hands at his throat, blood seeping wet and red between his fingers.

McCoy took a longer look this time, but he didn't see anyone in the hotel windows, and nobody took a shot at him.

Dirty Dave stopped twitching.

McCoy heard a horse whinny, then galloping hooves. He went out the front door, stepping over the corpses of the two outlaws, and saw Larry Prince riding out of town as if the devil himself was on his tail.

McCoy put two fingers in his mouth and whistled sharp and shrill.

A boy came around the corner leading McCoy's horse by the reins. The animal was a huge black mare. A good bit of horse flesh. The boy was a young Mexican, maybe fifteen, bucktoothed. Dark eyes. He handed McCoy the reins.

"Stayed out of sight until you whistled," the boy said. "Just like you told me."

"Good man." McCoy dipped into his vest pocket and came out with a coin. He flipped it to the boy.

McCoy mounted his horse and frowned as he saw Sheriff Tate huffing and puffing toward him, face red.

"Where do you think you're going?" Tate demanded. "You can't just shoot up my town and ride off."

"I didn't start the shooting. I finished it." McCoy pointed at the two bodies in front of the saloon. "Those are my kills, you hear? I'm coming back for my money."

Tate frowned and snarled but didn't contradict him. He didn't have his outlaws backing him up anymore.

"You'll get your bounty," Tate said. "Nobody here's going to cheat you."

"Not if they know what's good for 'em, they won't."

McCoy clicked his tongue, and the big black horse took off like a shot after Larry Prince.

CHAPTER 2

Larry Prince fled across Texas.

And Garret "Ghost" McCoy pursued.

His big black mare was a strong animal, and McCoy slowly gained on the outlaw. Prince surely knew the situation and would have to decide if and when he'd turn and fight. Or maybe he was trying to make it to some hideout where he could hole up. Or maybe Prince was hoping to stay ahead of McCoy just long enough for nightfall, and maybe the outlaw would try to lose McCoy in the darkness.

They came to a river, wide and shallow, and McCoy reined in the horse at the bank. He'd watched as Prince had easily forded the river and rode on. McCoy recognized this area, the dry grassland and scattered copses of scrub oak. If he crossed the river and kept heading south, he'd get to a place he hadn't been to since he was a boy, a place he swore he'd never visit again. If that's where Prince was going, then McCoy was forced to wonder if he really wanted the reward for the outlaw that badly.

McCoy dithered a moment, considering. It had already been a good payday. He could turn back and collect on the corpses of Snake and Dirty Dave. There was no desperate reason to chase after Prince . . . except, of course, that McCoy never liked that feeling of leaving something unfinished.

He was just about to turn back when he saw Prince veer east, following the lazy path of the river.

McCoy thought about it another moment and then spurred his horse forward, splashing through the river to the other side. Prince's changing directions had decided him. Garret would see the job finished one way or another, bringing Prince back dead or alive.

But in the time it took McCoy to decide, Prince had stretched his head start. He didn't want to lose the outlaw in the darkness and would need to ride hard to catch up before nightfall. He spurred his horse to a full gallop.

Soon dusk began gathering around him, and not long after that the sunset plunged him into night. He eased his horse back to a trot. If the animal put a hoof wrong or stepped in a gopher hole, she could break a leg, and then McCoy would be stuck walking. He mumbled a curse at himself for letting this situation develop. In the darkness, Prince could veer off in any direction, even cross the river to the other side again or—

Something caught his attention ahead. Twinkling lights. A village or a small town.

McCoy slowed the horse to a walk and headed for the lights. If he was guessing wrong, if Prince had doubled back, then McCoy had lost the man and that was all she wrote.

But if the town ahead was Prince's destination all along, then McCoy would sniff him out.

A half hour later, McCoy found himself walking down the town's main street, one and two story buildings rising up on either side. The town wasn't much. It went another street or two to either side of him, and he could see the end of the street and more Texas beyond, a hundred yards down, maybe more. He passed a livery stable and a few shops. The first place with lights on in the windows was a saloon with rooms upstairs, a typical setup from the look of it. He dismounted and looped the horse's reins over the hitching post and paused to listen before going inside. Talk, laughter, the clink of glasses. Nothing out of the ordinary.

He looked up and read the sign over the door. *The Thirsty Coyote.*

McCoy went inside.

Men playing cards, drinking at the bar, saloon gals batting eyelashes in an attempt to drum up business. An upright piano against one wall and nobody playing it. A big mirror behind the bar that nobody had washed since the Millard Fillmore administration.

All eyes were on McCoy as he crossed the room to the bar, but in the next moment, everyone had gone back to their business. The bar was manned by a nervous-looking little bald man with a sweaty face. He came over to stand in front of McCoy, eyebrows raised into a question.

"Whiskey," McCoy said.

The bartender's eyes shifted to the left.

Three men down the bar turned to face McCoy, none

of them looking much like church folk. The two in back looked like typical bruisers, broad shoulders, scowling faces, six-guns on their hips. McCoy couldn't decide if the one in front looked better or worse.

He leaned against the bar, a smirk coming easy to his face, a black vest over a purple shirt. Black hat with a band of worked, silver discs. More silver on his gun belt, big buckle. Black pants and boots that looked like they might be snakeskin. Angular face, clean shaved. Dark, glittering eyes like polished river stones.

"This is a private club, friend," purple shirt said.

Nobody had his hand near his gun, but the tension was there. McCoy kept things polite.

He shrugged. "Beg pardon. I didn't know. Looked like any other saloon. I'm looking for a man named Larry Prince, who maybe just rode into town. If you happen to know where he might be, I'll be on my way."

"You the law?" purple shirt asked.

McCoy noticed the room had gone silent, everyone especially interested in the answer to this last question.

"I don't carry a badge, if that's what you're asking," McCoy said.

Purple shirt snorted. "That's a funny way to answer a *yes or no* question. I'm thinking that's a bounty hunter answer."

"Let's just say I'm interested in Prince." McCoy looked around the room at everyone watching him. "And nobody else. That ease your mind?"

"My mind don't need to be eased," purple shirt said. "Because, like I said, this is a private club, and you're going to be leaving now. You can find the door, or I can show it to you if you'd prefer—"

Someone cleared his throat. Loudly.

All eyes turned to the man sitting at the corner table. McCoy took a long look at him. The man in the corner looked part slicker, part two-bit politician, and part riverboat gambler. A new blue suit with a garish paisley waistcoat. Rings on his fingers. Dark hair slicked back. And a well-trimmed mustache. A long, thin cigar smoldered in the corner of his mouth.

"Now, Gerald, let's show some hospitality," said the man in the corner. "We don't get a lot of visitors here in Coyote Flats. This gentleman might go away with the impression we're not friendly, and give the town a bad name."

Purple shirt straightened up. Apparently, this was Gerald. "You're the boss, Mr. Jericho."

"So you're looking for Larry Prince," said the one called Jericho. "I thought my eyes had deceived me when I saw him riding through town earlier. Seems he's back. I can't say that pleases me, no, not at all."

"If his presence offends you, I happen to be in a position to rectify that situation," McCoy said.

"Is he still running around with those two lowlifes, Snake and Dirty Dave?" Jericho asked.

"Them two fellas won't be running around with anyone ever again."

A devilish smile quirked to Jericho's lips. "Yes, I see. Hmmmm. Tempting, yes, very tempting indeed. It's decided then. I want to see this."

Jericho stood and pulled on a pair of black leather

gloves. He plopped a bowler hat on his head and grabbed a walking stick topped with a silver ram's head. "What is your name, sir?"

"Garret McCoy."

"Walk with me, Mr. McCoy. I daresay I have a fair guess where Mr. Prince might be keeping himself."

They left the saloon and walked toward the other end of town. McCoy glanced back and saw Gerald and his two sidekicks following at a respectful distance.

"Where are we going?" McCoy asked.

"To see . . . ah, how shall I put it?" Jericho wondered out loud. "To see a business rival. Yes, that's a civilized way to put it." As they walked—more of a stroll really, as if Jericho was simply out to take the night air—Jericho gestured to a two-story building off to his right. "That's Carmen's Place, sort of neutral ground here in Coyote Flats. If you still want that drink of whiskey later, then that would be your best bet."

McCoy could hear music and laughter emanating from within as they passed.

They reached the other side of town, not a long walk—and Jericho led him to a squat-looking adobe building with a red tile roof.

Jericho paused and looked back at Gerald. "Best if you and the boys wait here, Gerald. If you hear anything untoward, you can come rushing to the rescue."

Gerald touched the brim of his hat. "Anything you say, Mr. Jericho."

"Come, Mr. McCoy," Jericho said. "Into the lion's den."

They entered.

The ceiling was low, the lighting dim, the atmosphere

smoky with tobacco. Dour men hunched over their drinks at a half-dozen tables. They all looked up as McCoy and Jericho entered, their demeanor hostile and unwelcoming.

Jericho leaned toward McCoy and said in a low voice, "Not a cheerful sort of place, is it? You'll find the company is more of the same."

A big man stood up from one of the tables in back, thinning black hair on his melon head, ruddy cheeks, huge, bushy mustache curled and oiled at the ends. His sleeves were rolled up, revealing massive forearms covered with rough hair.

"I think you might be in the wrong place, Jericho."

Jericho smiled warmly. "Big Mike, you are a sight for sore eyes. Don't alarm yourself. I'm here on business. Fetch Mortimer, would you?"

Mike narrowed his eyes. "I don't fetch. But I'm sure Mr. Lorenzo will be curious why you've decided to pay a visit. Wait here."

Big Mike vanished into the back room.

McCoy stood still and let his eyeballs roam the room. Like in the Thirsty Coyote, these men were all hard types, the difference being those here seemed entirely bereft of good humor. When Big Mike had left to find this Lorenzo character, they hadn't gone back to their own conversations. They simply sat and stared at McCoy and Jericho, faces dour, eyes piercing, as if willing the two interlopers to try something.

Jericho seemed perfectly at ease. But McCoy kept one thumb hooked into his belt, not quite threatening but very ready.

Big Mike returned a moment later with another man

in tow. He was as tall as Big Mike, but with lean, sharp features, nose and cheekbones with a beard carefully trimmed to a point at the tip of his chin, gray at the corners of his mouth. More gray streaked through the black hair at each temple.

McCoy assumed this was Lorenzo.

Lorenzo looked from Jericho to McCoy. There was something odd about his gaze, almost as if he was looking right at you, but pretending not to. McCoy found it off-putting.

"Something you want from me, dandy?" Lorenzo asked Jericho.

Jericho's smile didn't touch his eyes. "Such hospitality. I understand Larry Prince has returned to Coyote Flats."

Lorenzo frowned. "What makes you say that?"

"A little birdy told me," Jericho said. "Now, you do understand that as part of our little agreement, Prince was supposed to get lost and never come back. I'm sure you remember. We are still honoring the truce, aren't we?"

Lorenzo shrugged. "That depends. Another part of the truce is you don't bring your hired guns into my place. Or do I misremember?"

"Not at all." Jericho gestured to McCoy. "This gentleman is not in my employ. He's the one looking for Prince."

Lorenzo's odd gaze shifted to McCoy. "Oh? And why should I care about that?"

"Whether or not you care is immaterial to me," McCoy told Lorenzo. "There's a bounty on Larry

Prince. He ran. I chased him. I never even heard of Coyote Flats before an hour ago."

Lorenzo put his hands on his hips and made a grumbling sort of growl in his throat.

"Come now, Mortimer," Jericho chided. "Surely this is a tolerable compromise. Prince gets dealt with, which I'll find satisfying. But you're not giving up your man to me, so your pride won't be too terribly offended. McCoy here is an outside third party, not one of my people."

Lorenzo growled a bit more, sighed, and then said, "Don't let anyone say it was me that broke the truce. Mike, go bring Larry in here."

Big Mike frowned but did as he was told.

A moment later, he came back with Larry Prince in tow. Prince's nervous eyes went around the room and landed on McCoy. He blinked and swallowed hard, knowing right away he'd landed in hot soup.

Prince looked at his boss, eyes pleading. "Mr. Lorenzo?"

"Sorry, Larry," Lorenzo said. "I got to give you up."

Prince went pale. "Mr. Lorenzo, I came back so you could protect me."

Lorenzo shook his head and *tsked*. "Well, that's the problem, Larry. You weren't supposed to come back. That was the understanding."

"Mr. Lorenzo—"

"It's out of my hands, Larry."

"Don't turn me over to this fella, Mr. Lorenzo."

"Well, see, that's where you've misunderstood," Lorenzo explained. "I'm not turning you over to this man. I'm just not stopping him from taking you. That gives you a chance. You can draw, or you can run. You can try. That's something anyway. It's a chance."

Prince swallowed hard.

McCoy didn't move. He just fixed his eyes on Prince, thumb still hooked into his gun belt.

Prince licked his lips, glancing at the front door then back at McCoy, probably trying to figure his best chance.

The men near Prince pushed back from their tables, stood, and moved away from him.

McCoy simply waited. He already knew how this was going to go.

The room had gone dead quiet.

Prince very subtly leaned toward the door like he was about to make a run for it.

Then his hand dropped to his gun.

McCoy drew and fired, the Peacemaker's thunder shaking the room.

Prince took the shot high in the shoulder and stumbled back into a table, glasses tumbling off and shattering on the floor. The expression on his face was a heart-breaking mix of anger and bewilderment as he kept trying to fumble for his six-shooter.

McCoy cocked the hammer back on his Peacemaker with a thumb, took careful aim, and fired again.

Prince took it square in the chest. He wilted into an awkward heap, one arm twisted under his body, legs akimbo. Smoke hung in the air. Nobody said anything for a long moment.

Jericho gave McCoy a friendly slap on the shoulder. "Well, that's taken care of then. If you get that whiskey at Carmen's Place, tell her the first one is on me."

CHAPTER 3

McCoy was pleased to find that Carmen's Place wasn't populated entirely by gunmen.

Crowded, shopkeepers and cowhands and regular folk, although here and there he spied a few hard men with guns slung low, but at least they didn't seem to be looking for trouble. A short man with a cigar was going at an upright piano with enough vigor to make it behave, the cigar puffing more smoke than a locomotive.

He found a spot at the crowded bar and politely asked the men there if he could squeeze in. They didn't object.

The bartender was short, fat, and sweaty, but had an open, affable face and a friendly demeanor.

He smiled at McCoy. "Ain't seen you in here before."

McCoy smiled back. "But I can still be thirsty, right?"

"If you are, I got what can cure it."

McCoy put a coin on the bar. "Whiskey."

The barkeep brought the whiskey. McCoy leaned against the bar and sipped, listening to the music and taking in the friendly atmosphere. He made himself breathe in and out, trying to get calm. He'd killed men in the war. Too many men. Each time, he thought it would get easier, but it never did. He didn't blame himself. It wasn't a matter of guilt. But it was a serious thing ending another man forever. He supposed if he ever got used to it, then that would signal he'd lost something inside himself.

Maybe.

Who could say?

He sipped his whiskey and waited for the tension to leak away and everything to go back to normal inside him.

"You must be McCoy."

McCoy looked up.

The woman behind the bar almost knocked both his eyes out. The neckline of her black dress fell off her shoulders revealing a lot of smooth, light brown skin, a graceful throat. Thorny-stemmed red roses were embroidered into the dress's material. High cheekbones and deep brown eyes. Lips stained a red so dark they were almost black. Her hair, glossy and as black as midnight, was pulled back into a tight bun, giving her beauty a severe edge.

She was looking at him, and McCoy felt her piercing eyes straight down to the bottom of his gut.

"You have to be Carmen."

"I don't have to be." She smiled, straight white teeth. "I get to be."

"You run this place?" he asked.

"Run it. Own it. Curse it on the bad days," Carmen said. "Being boss isn't always a bed of roses. But I don't like working for anyone else. Jericho says to buy you a drink."

"Already bought one."

She set the bottle on the bar next to his shot glass. "Then have the next one on the house. Or the next three. Whatever you like."

"I don't want to take advantage," McCoy told her. "I can pay."

"You need a room for the night? You can pay for that," she said. "Or if you want company in the room, you can pay for that too. Cherry seems your type." Carmen lifted her chin, indicating a woman at the other end of the bar talking to a pair of cowboys. Buxom. Lots of red hair spilling down over white skin.

McCoy grinned. "And how would you know my type?"

"Cherry's every man's type." Carmen refilled his glass for him.

"I'll take the room," McCoy said. "I'll pass on the company."

Carmen *tsked*, a sly smile quirking to her lips. "Oh, no. You'll hurt Cherry's feelings."

"I'm easy to get over."

She narrowed her eyes, giving McCoy a good hard look. "Why do I feel that's never really been put to the test?"

"Maybe because I'm never in one place for too long," McCoy admitted.

He had no home, drifting here and there after the next bounty. It had earned him the nickname *Ghost*. There one minute, gone the next. He didn't care for the nickname but figured he'd earned it.

"Maybe Coyote Flats will grow on you," Carmen suggested.

McCoy was keen to change the subject. He threw back the shot of whiskey, set the glass back on the bar, and Carmen filled it again.

"What did Prince do so bad that a man could earn a bottle of booze killing him?" McCoy asked.

"He made a play for the wrong lady," Carmen said. "Jericho didn't like it."

"Must have been some special lady."

"Very special indeed, Mr. McCoy."

"Who is she?" He asked.

"She's me," Carmen said.

Ah.

"I'll see that your room is made ready for you." And she left.

McCoy watched her go, wishing he didn't like what he was looking at so much.

"You're asking for trouble, Ghost," said a voice behind him. "You don't want to end up like Prince."

McCoy turned his head to see the lean newcomer take the spot at the bar next to him. He sighed and said, "How've you been, Dwight?"

Dwight Combs took his hat off and set it on the bar. He had rough features from bad skin as a youth and thin blond hair, eyes so pale blue they looked like ice. He wore a black leather vest over a cream-colored shirt. A huge Walker Colt hung from his hip on the left side.

"You should ditch that Walker and get modern," McCoy advised. "Get yourself a Peacemaker."

"I'm too used to the way the Walker feels in my hand," Combs said. "That bottle all for you?"

"Help yourself."

Combs reached behind the bar and plucked a shot glass from the stack, grabbed McCoy's bottle and filled it. "Thanks."

"You can return the favor someday."

"I heard about Bob Baily." Combs sipped whiskey and smacked his lips. "That was you?"

"I was there, but it wasn't me," McCoy said. "His own stupid pigheadedness killed him."

"That's been known to happen."

"What brings you to Coyote Flats?" McCoy asked.

"Tracked the Vargas brothers here," Combs said. "Missed 'em by two days. Trail's gone cold now."

"I thought Fester Schultz killed them in El Paso."

"He killed the older two," Combs said. "The youngest two are still running around. I don't care. Tired of chasing them."

"So you're hanging your hat in Coyote Flats? What for?" As far as McCoy was concerned, he'd swallow a cup of coffee at first light and get gone. It wasn't much of a town, and there was nothing here for him.

Although when he thought about Carmen's deep, brown eyes and those dark red lips . . .

"I heard one of the factions might be hiring on more guns. Paying good too," Combs said. "Then some truce happened. Just my luck."

"Don't know much about it," McCoy said.

"Ain't that why you're here?"

"I tracked Larry Prince here," McCoy explained. "Took him down at Lorenzo's place."

"That explains the shooting then," Combs said. "I thought something was going on. Anyway, that's one faction. This Jericho fella is leader of the other."

"How'd that develop?"

"Who knows?" Combs said. "But it was bloody for a bit until the truce. Hey, wouldn't that be a hoot if one side hired you, and the other side hired me."

McCoy refilled his glass. "You gonna shoot me, Dwight?"

"Not for free, I'm not," said the other gunman. "Damn truce isn't making any money for anyone."

"Dwight Combs!" shouted someone from across the room.

The conversation within the saloon died away, and the piano player stopped. Everyone looked at the man standing just inside the doorway, hand hovering over is six-gun . . . although *man* was a stretch, as the boy was barely eighteen maybe. Dark hair, clean brown skin that had probably never seen a razor.

"Who the hell's that?" McCoy asked.

Combs shrugged. "Do I know?"

"Well, he seems to know you."

"Dwight Combs!" the kid repeated. "I'm calling you out."

"Calling me out?" Combs frowned. "For what?"

The kid looked confused for a moment, then scowled. "You know for what. What it always means to call a man out."

"You want to shoot me?"

"Yes!"

"Well, I don't want to go out," Combs said. "I'm having a drink."

"Then I'll shoot you in here," the kid insisted.

Combs gestured around the room. "But everyone's having such a good time."

"In here or outside," the kid said. "You choose."

"Well, who in the hell are you?" Combs demanded. "I don't want to be shot by a stranger."

"I am Enrique Vargas," the kid announced. "You killed two of my brothers and are after the other two."

"Good Lord, a fifth Vargas brother," Combs said. "It was Fester Schultz killed your brothers, you idiot. I was after the others, but I gave that up."

"I'm still calling you out."

"Well, what the . . ." Combs was incredulous. "There's no point."

"I will kill you and then I will find Fester Schultz and kill him too," Vargas said.

"Could you move a few steps away?" McCoy asked Combs. "I don't want your blood splattering on me."

"Very funny, Ghost," Combs said. "This kid is serious."

McCoy shrugged.

Combs sighed. "Well, you're gonna have to get closer, kid."

Vargas frowned. "What?"

"You can't shoot anyone from clear over there," Combs said. "Ain't you never been in a gunfight before?"

Vargas frowned. "Of course, I have!"

"Then you know it's an up-close thing. It's personal," Combs said seriously. "You've got to look the man you're going to kill right in the eye."

Vargas looked around at everyone else in the saloon, suddenly unsure of himself. McCoy could guess what the kid was thinking, wondering if he was being made into the object of some joke.

Combs stepped away from the bar, squared his shoulders, and motioned for the kid to walk toward him. "Come on then. Nice and close. We won't start until you're ready."

Everyone in the saloon cleared out of the kid's path. He approached Combs slowly, eyes narrowed with suspicion. When they were standing close to one another, Combs held up his hand for Vargas to stop.

"Okay, now I'm going to count three," Combs said.

"Wait, this is too close!" The kid was visibly nervous now, beads of sweat on his upper lip and forehead.

"That's so we don't miss," Combs said. "One of us wins. One of us dies. You ready or not?"

The kid's eyes darted around the interior saloon. He was suddenly aware that every eye in the place was on him.

"I said are you ready?" Combs prompted.

"I'm ready!" Vargas snapped.

Combs held out his hand, let it hover above his Walker. "One!"

He'd barked the word so loudly, it made Vargas flinch.

The whole saloon held its collective breath.

"Two!"

Combs's hand was steady as a rock over the six-shooter, ready to draw in an instant.

Vargas was clearly nervous to the point of passing out, or at least that's what it looked like to McCoy. The kid was probably wondering how he'd got himself into this mess. It wasn't McCoy's business. He drank his whiskey and watched.

But Combs never shouted *three*.

Instead, his hand flashed out faster than lightning and snatched the six-shooter from Vargas's holster. The kid's hand went to his holster, gabbing at nothing but air. His eyes shot wide.

Combs swung the kid's pistol, and smacked Vargas on the side of his head just above the ear. The kid's eyes rolled up and he went down like a sack of potatoes. Everyone in the saloon let out a collective gasp, which transitioned into nervous laughter. A moment later, the piano player started up again as if nothing had happened, and everyone went about his business.

McCoy shook his head and chuckled. "You're always good for a laugh, Dwight."

CHAPTER 4

Garret McCoy sat at a table off to the side in Carmen's Place, forking scrambled eggs, salted pork, and biscuits into his mouth, morning sunlight streaming through the dirty windows. The place was empty except for the old Mexican gal who drifted through periodically to refill McCoy's coffee cup. Carmen's didn't usually serve breakfast—it was a saloon after all, not a hash house—but she'd told McCoy she didn't want him to go on an empty stomach.

He pushed his plate away, belched, and wiped his mouth with a napkin. One more cup of coffee and then he'd head out. He'd slept well and had had a few more drinks with Dwight Combs the night before after that Vargas business. Carmen had been a hospitable hostess, but having taken Larry Prince, there was no longer a reason for McCoy to hang around Coyote Flats. As soon as he'd drained his coffee cup, he'd get his horse out of the stable behind Carmen's Place and go.

The saloon door swung upon, harsh morning light spilling through, followed by a young man rubbing his eyes, then the side of his head. It was Vargas. He had

straw in his black hair. McCoy recalled that a few of
Smitty's boys—McCoy had learned that the fat barkeep
was called Smitty—had carried the unconscious lad out
of the saloon after Dwight Combs had knocked him unconscious. They must have dumped him on a pile of hay
in the stable out back.

Since there was nobody else in the place, Vargas
walked straight up to McCoy's table. "Where is Combs?"

"I wouldn't be in a hurry for a second go at him,"
McCoy said. "Didn't work out so well the first time."

"He humiliated me." Vargas rubbed the side of his
head again. "He hurt me. I owe him payback."

"He could have killed you ten times over," McCoy
said. "Your life. That's what you owe him."

Vargas grumbled something in Spanish.

Smitty appeared behind the bar, wiping everything
down. He spotted Vargas and frowned. "It's too early in
the morning for more trouble."

Vargas shook his head and groaned. He looked at
McCoy's cup. "Is there more coffee?"

Smitty glanced at McCoy, and McCoy nodded.

"I'll tell Consuela."

Smitty waddled away, and a minute later, the Mexican
lady appeared with a pot of coffee and another cup. She
filled a cup for Vargas, then topped off McCoy's too.
Why not? He wasn't in a hurry.

"Why'd you go after Dwight, anyway?" McCoy asked.
"Messing around with dangerous men is a good way to
shorten your lifespan right quick."

Vargas sipped coffee and shrugged. "They are my
brothers."

"Half of every knife in somebody's back is held by a

brother," McCoy said. "You never heard of Cain and Abel?"

"I do not know them well," Vargas admitted. "I was a child when my brothers left home. But last night they returned. My mother's house is on the edge of town. My brothers said they could not stay long because a bounty killer was after them. I decided I would help my brothers. My family. Family must stick together."

"I reckon there's something in what you're saying," McCoy told the kid. "Family is family, but let me ask you this. When's the last time your brothers acted like family toward you and your ma? When was the last time they visited home that they didn't need something, a place to lay low or a quick meal. If I had bounty hunters chasing after me, I wouldn't lead them to my mother's house. I don't know you or your kin. I'm just talking in general. My two cents. Think on it maybe."

Vargas stared into his coffee cup. "*Madre*—Mother— always said the two brothers who came last night were not so bad as everyone said. That they hadn't committed the crimes you see on the wanted posters. That they were misunderstood." A shrug. "But I suppose that is what mothers always say about their sons. Good boys. Just misunderstood."

McCoy didn't have anything to say to that. He hadn't known his mother as long as he would have liked.

Smitty appeared behind the bar again. "Mr. McCoy, Carmen will be along directly. She's hoping to say goodbye before you leave."

"Okay," McCoy said. "I can sip coffee and wait."

"Where is my revolver?" Vargas asked.

Smitty frowned, hesitated, then reached under the bar

and came out with the kid's six-shooter. He set it on the polished wood in front of him. "It ain't loaded. See that it stays that way."

Vargas retrieved the gun and slid it into his holster. He sat back down and picked up his coffee cup again. "The old woman makes good coffee."

"They usually do."

Carmen walked in and crossed the saloon toward McCoy's table. Instead of the attractive black dress she wore the previous night, Carmen wore a red and white checkered shirt buttoned up to her throat and a gray skirt, split for riding. Her black hair hung in a long braid down her back.

"Good morning, gentlemen." Her smile showed off those perfect white teeth. "Mr. McCoy, I hope you found your accommodations comfortable."

"As good as any hotel," McCoy said. "Slept like a baby."

She turned to Vargas, eyes narrowing, and the two exchanged words in Spanish.

McCoy wasn't much good at Spanish, but he thought he caught the gist. Something along the lines of *Go home to your mother. She's worried about you.* The kid looked embarrassed and stood, turned to leave the saloon.

He paused at the door and looked back. "I'll keep in mind what you said, Mr. McCoy. About family."

And then he left.

"He's not a bad boy," Carmen said. "Just mixed up about things like honor and duty. May I join you?"

"It's your place."

Carmen took the chair where Vargas had been a

moment before. "Mortimer Lorenzo will be along in a moment to speak to you."

McCoy frowned. "He sent you to tell me this?"

"Not at all."

"So how do you know?"

A sly grin. "This is Carmen's Place, and I am Carmen. Any whisper that leaves a person's lips passes by me before it reaches another person's ears."

"Sounds like a fancy way of saying you're nosey."

Carmen laughed, and it surprised them both, her face suddenly less mysterious, more open, a glimpse of innocence and youth.

"Perhaps I am nosey," she admitted. "After all, gossip is one of a saloon keeper's leading commodities after whiskey and women."

"So Lorenzo wants to see me, and you're telling me, why?" McCoy asked.

McCoy had recently shot a man in Lorenzo's place. Larry Prince had been one of Lorenzo's men. Could be that Lorenzo had had a change of heart, felt slighted about it, and now wanted McCoy to pay for his transgression.

"I do hear most every whisper, but I can't read minds," Carmen said. "I only ask this. If he makes you some offer, don't say yes or no right away. Speak to me first."

"Now, you've got my curiosity going," McCoy said.

"Most men are curious about me." She grinned and stood. "Few actually have their curiosity satisfied."

"I'll take that as a challenge."

"Take it anyway you like," Carmen said. "Perhaps I will see you again, Mr. McCoy."

She left.

McCoy sat in the empty saloon. His coffee had gone cold. He waited.

Well, he was under no obligation to sit there all day waiting for Lorenzo to show up. He'd only entertained the notion because Carmen had intrigued him. She was a good-looking woman, no doubt, but it had been McCoy's observation that the world was full of attractive ladies. A woman needed another quality to really stand out, and whatever that mysterious quality might be, Carmen had it in spades.

McCoy suspected she was also the kind of woman that could land a man in a mess of trouble.

He stood, looked around the empty saloon, and decided he'd had enough. He left out the back way and went into the stable and saddled his horse. A moment later, he was riding out of the stable, Larry Prince's corpse draped across the horse behind him, wrapped in burlap.

Wanted dead or alive, the posters said. It never failed to surprise McCoy how many outlaws chose death.

He spurred his horse to a fast walk, rounded the corner back to Main Street, and saw Mortimer Lorenzo standing in front of Carmen's Place, hands on hips. Big Mike and another of Lorenzo's gunmen stood several feet away from him, leaning on the railing of the saloon's front porch.

Lorenzo pushed his hat back on his head and squinted up at McCoy with that odd gaze of his. "I was looking for you, McCoy."

"I'm right here."

"Come down from that horse, and let's have a chinwag," Lorenzo suggested.

"I'm on my way out of town," McCoy said.

"I won't keep you long," Lorenzo promised. "But I don't like looking up at a man while I'm talking to him. Gives me a crick in the neck."

"You're not the first person to call me a pain in the neck." McCoy dismounted and looped his horse's reins around the hitching post in front of Carmen's Place. "Got a dead body here that's gonna start getting ripe soon, so talk fast."

"Direct to the point. I like that," Lorenzo said. "Fine. I'll be direct too. I want you to work for me."

McCoy frowned. "Doing what?"

"What do you think? Washing dishes and sweeping up?" Lorenzo grinned. "I saw you gun Larry Prince. You're fast and cold blooded and cool under pressure. I need more like you."

"Why would you need anybody like me?" McCoy asked. "I thought you and Jericho had a truce."

"Oh, we do, indeed, we do." Lorenzo put his hands in his back pockets and turned slowly, looking up and down the street as if curious who might be out and about. "But things change. Two bosses in a town . . . well, like two cooks in the kitchen, ain't it? Sooner or later . . . something's got to give."

"Makes sense, I guess."

"So if you know change is coming sooner or later, what's the smart thing to do?" Lorenzo said. "Wait and let the change roll over you and hope it all works out? Or guide the change in the best direction you can? I prefer to be ready. I prefer to be master of my own destiny. Better than taking a chance with fate and hoping for the best."

McCoy shrugged. "That makes sense too, I guess."

"So how about coming on my payroll?" Lorenzo asked.

"I don't know, Mr. Lorenzo. A man gets used to being his own boss," McCoy said. "Have you tried Dwight Combs? I don't know where he's got to, but he was hanging around Carmen's last night. He might be your man."

"Don't worry, he's on my list to talk to next," Lorenzo said. "Right now, I'm talking to you."

Carmen's words came back to McCoy. *I only ask this. If he makes you some offer, don't say yes or no right away. Speak to me first.* Did Carmen know something McCoy didn't? Probably. What was her stake in all this? Jericho had called Carmen's Place neutral ground, but McCoy wondered. Was she taking sides? Forming her own side?

"I'll need to think on it, Mr. Lorenzo," McCoy told him.

Lorenzo scratched a spot behind his ear, nodding. "I can understand that. Where are you taking Larry?"

"Back to Black Oak, I reckon," McCoy said. "I'll turn him over to the sheriff there and put in for the bounty."

"You might want to take him to the marshal in Austin," Lorenzo suggested.

McCoy frowned. "That's five days by horseback."

"Might be worth it," Lorenzo said. "Might be there's a man there I'd like to see shot . . . or at least behind bars."

"I don't work for you yet, Mr. Lorenzo."

"You don't have to work for me." Lorenzo handed McCoy a folded piece of paper. "That's a wanted poster. The man in Austin done me wrong, but he's not exactly in good standing with the state of Texas either. You take care of him, you're just chasing a bounty like you usually do, and it's only by coincidence it's a good turn for me. Who knows? Maybe when you come back through, I'll feel obliged to give you my own reward on top of what Texas is willing to pay. Leastways, it'll give you time to think about coming to work for me."

McCoy unfolded the poster and read. A five-hundred-dollar reward. His eyes went to the name.

McCoy knew the man.

He mounted, refolded the poster and shoved it into his vest pocket. "I'll think on it, Mr. Lorenzo."

He spurred his horse and rode out of town.

CHAPTER 5

The first two nights were uneventful. The terrain had gone dry and rough, and he camped between the high walls of a deep arroyo the first night. The second night he slept in a copse of cedar elms atop a low hill. He made campfires, ate beans, brewed coffee each morning, then moved on.

By the third day, Larry Prince began to stink, and by the time McCoy reached Austin, he would have gladly rid himself of the body even without the promise of the bounty payment. He found the federal marshal and traded Prince's stinking corpse for a voucher.

"Take that to the bank, and you'll get your money," the marshal said.

McCoy unfolded the wanted poster Lorenzo had given him and handed it to the marshal.

The marshal frowned at the hand-drawn likeness on the poster. His eyes deepened when his eyes slid to the name. "I thought this was one of you fellas."

"I thought so too," McCoy said. "I guess the Territory of Wyoming sees it different."

"No offense to you, but it's a fine line between what

you do and the law." He thumbed the star on his vest. "I wear one of these. It's no wonder more of your kind don't go bad."

McCoy almost told him that a tin star didn't necessarily keep a man from going bad, but then thought better of it. No sense antagonizing the law. "You seen him around?"

"Ain't seen him," the marshal said. "Don't mean he ain't around."

"Appreciate your time, Marshal."

McCoy left the marshal's office and considered what to do next. There was just enough time to take his voucher to the bank and get his money before they closed.

The day was sliding toward evening, and he decided to mix business with pleasure. He visited a couple of saloons, sipping beer and showing around the wanted poster. Nobody had seen his prey.

Maybe it was a wasted effort. He only had Lorenzo's word that the man he was after was even in Austin at all. He was tired and ready for bed and kept an eye out for a decent hotel, someplace clean. He'd be sleeping on the ground again on his way back to Coyote Flats and wanted at least one night in a soft bed.

He asked around and was told the Benford Arms was a reputable establishment about two blocks down, and it was affordable . . . not that McCoy was short of money, but he didn't like needlessly throwing it around either. He headed for the hotel, but saw another saloon on the way, and decided to give it one more try.

McCoy entered the Laughing Bronco and nearly turned around and walked back out again. The saloon was a dank and uninviting place. Sad men hunched over their drinks, looking glum, and dim lanterns cast a dreary, yellow pall over the room. A dreary place for defeated men to drown their sorrows.

Well, I've come this far. Might as well show the wanted poster to the barkeep.

He crossed the room to the bar and ordered a beer. Before he could show the wanted poster to the barkeep, a haggard-looking saloon gal sidled up next to him, intent on drumming up some business. It wasn't that she was bad looking. Just tired, McCoy thought, lines in her face and dark circles under her eyes. In another time or place, she'd have been handsome enough.

But it wasn't another time or place, and McCoy told her as politely as possible he wasn't interested. She shrugged and told the barkeep she wanted a whiskey.

McCoy sipped his beer.

The next two men who came into the saloon caught his attention. A tall, skinny one with a face like a rat and a floppy battered hat. The other was chubby and shorter and wore a threadbare top hat with a turkey feather in the band. Both wore six-guns on their hips. They'd only caught McCoy's eye because he'd seen them in the last saloon he'd been in. McCoy tried to remember if he'd seen them in saloons before that.

They took a table and sat, and McCoy put them out of his mind.

McCoy finished his beer just as the barkeep returned.

"Get you another?"

"No thanks." McCoy unfolded the wanted poster and set it on the bar. "Seen this fella around, by any chance?"

The barkeep squinted at the poster, giving it careful consideration. "I don't rightly know. A pretty common-looking face."

"What about the name?"

The barkeep shook his head. "Don't ring a bell."

From his peripheral vision, McCoy saw the saloon gal glance at the poster, go rigid, then turn away.

McCoy dropped a coin on the bar for the beer. "Thanks anyway."

"Good luck to you." The barkeep left to attend to other customers.

McCoy turned back to the saloon gal. "How about you?"

She looked at him as if just remembering he was there. "How about me what?"

"Seen this man?"

She didn't even bother to look at the poster. "No."

"I'm Garret. What's your name?"

She hesitated. "Maddy."

"Maddy, it's important that I find this fella," McCoy told her. "Maybe take a closer look."

She sighed, looked quickly at the poster, then shook her head. "Lots of men come through here. All the faces look the same after a while. Excuse me now. I have to powder my nose."

Maddy turned away from him abruptly and left at a fast walk. Then she took a quick turn down a back hall-way.

McCoy slowly counted to thirty, then followed.

He didn't consider himself an expert on women—not by a country mile—but he had a fair sense of when somebody wasn't being straight with him. He walked down the hall to a back door, went through it, and found himself in a dark, narrow alley.

The sound of hollow footfalls going up wooded steps. He glanced left just in time to catch the billowing hem of a woman's dress vanish up a narrow flight of steps going up the side of the building across the alley. McCoy looked the other way and saw a shadowed doorway. He stood in it and waited.

And waited.

He was hungry and tired and was just about to call it quits when he heard the footfalls again coming down the stairs. McCoy sank back into the doorway, the shadows closing around him.

Maddy reached the bottom of the stairs, hair looking slightly mussed. She paused to straighten herself, looking up and down the alley, then crossed to the Laughing Bronco and entered through the back door.

McCoy counted to sixty before emerging from the shadows.

He crept down the alley and paused at the foot of the stairs, held his breath, listened.

Nothing.

He headed up the stairs slowly, wincing as each step creaked under his weight. It took forever to reach the top, stepping gingerly, but he didn't want to alert whoever might be up there that he was coming.

McCoy reached the top landing and faced a door with peeled paint. There was just enough room to stand off to the side. It wouldn't be the first time somebody had shot at him through a closed door.

He knocked.

The door swung inward immediately.

"I was hoping you'd come back so we could . . . oh."

He'd obviously been expecting Maddy and not Garret McCoy pointing a Colt Peacemaker directly at his nose.

"Hey, Rufus," McCoy said. "I was a might surprised to see your face on that wanted poster."

The likeness on the poster had been pretty accurate. The bent nose from so many punches in the face. The receding black hairline. The square jaw. But in the many months since McCoy had last seen Rufus Lee, the man had made a point to look different. He'd grown his hair down to his shoulders. A wild and bushy beard covered up that square jaw.

But McCoy had known the man well, and from this distance, there could be no mistake about his identity.

"Would it do any good to say I'm not guilty?" Lee asked.

"Normally, no. That's what they all say." McCoy eased the Peacemaker's hammer down with his thumb. "But since you saved my life in Laramie . . . and then again in Cheyenne . . . I suppose I can hear you out."

"Don't forget you saved my life in Denver," Lee reminded him.

"That still leaves you one up on me. I owe you." McCoy's gaze shifted briefly to the six-shooter on Lee's hip. "You'll behave yourself?"

"You've got my word."

McCoy thought about it a moment, then lowered his gun and let it drop into the holster. "Okay, then maybe we better go inside and talk about it."

"Not in there," Lee said. "It's just a storage area

Maddy fixed up for me. A narrow cot and a chamber pot. Nothing worth a look, trust me. Let's go back to the Bronco. I'll get us a bottle."

They crossed the alley back into the saloon and took a table in a shadowy corner so folks couldn't get a good look at Lee. Maddy appeared a moment later with a bottle and two shot glasses. She set them on the table and looked at Lee with a concerned expression.

"It's okay," Lee told her.

She nodded and went away.

McCoy took a quick look around to make sure nobody was paying attention to them, then slid the wanted poster across the table to Lee. "Okay, let's hear the story."

Lee unfolded the poster and looked at it. "I thought growing the beard and letting my hair grow would throw people off."

"Not folks that know you."

"I reckon not." Lee's eyes went back and forth on the words under the likeness.

McCoy knew what he was reading by heart. *Rufus Lee, bounty hunter. Wanted for the murder of a U.S. Marshal. 500 Dollar reward.*

McCoy pulled the cork out of the bottle and filled both glasses.

Lee sighed, folded the poster, and gave it back to McCoy.

They drank.

McCoy filled the glasses again. "Well?"

"Well what?"

"Start telling me about how you didn't do it," McCoy said.

"Wish I could," Lee told him. "But I did it. I shot the hell out of him."

McCoy's eyes narrowed. "Then what are we discussing here?"

"I didn't say I didn't do it," Lee said. "I just said I wasn't guilty, not of murder anyway."

McCoy threw back his whiskey and filled his glass again. It was going to be one of those nights. "Go on then."

Lee sipped his whiskey slower. "I was after the Hitch Morgan Gang."

"Never heard of them."

"They started up after you'd already left Wyoming," Lee said. "Small timers but mean. I cornered them, shot Hitch and another fella. That took the fight out of them right quick. Mean, yeah, but cowardly. I was about to bring in the other three alive when the U.S. Marshal showed up. I thought he was there to help, but he drew on me. I was faster. Seems he'd been taking bribes. He took a chunk of whatever Hitch and his boys robbed. I guess they don't pay U.S. Marshals enough."

"Didn't you tell them he was crooked?"

Lee shrugged. "Tell who? His deputies who'd been working for the man for years? Either they were crooked too or wouldn't believe me."

"So you ran for it."

"Just as fast as I could."

McCoy poured himself another one. It was definitely going to be one of those nights. He sighed and looked around the room, saw the saloon gal watching them from the bar.

"Maddy your girl?" McCoy asked.

Another shrug. "I don't pay her if that's what you mean."

"Right." McCoy filled Lee's glass. The bottle would be gone fast if they kept it up.

"Here's the thing," McCoy said. "Somebody sent me after you specific."

"Another marshal?"

McCoy shook his head. "Private citizen."

Lee frowned. "What for?"

"I was hoping you could tell me," McCoy said. "A man named Mortimer Lorenzo."

Lee sat back in his chair. "Oh?"

"Name rings a bell?"

"I told you I shot Hitch Morgan and another fella in his gang," Lee said. "The other fella's name was Mortimer Lorenzo . . . Junior."

McCoy shook his head and mumbled a curse. "Might be we're going to need another bottle."

"I guess we can put two and two together and figure I killed the man's son," Lee said. "Guess I don't blame him for wanting my blood."

McCoy thought about it, if someone had killed his kin. Yeah. He could understand it.

"So I guess you could shoot me," Lee said. "That's five hundred bucks. Plus whatever revenge money you might get out of Lorenzo."

McCoy rolled his eyes. "I ain't shooting you, Rufus. I think you know that. Now let's just put our heads together and figure this thing out. Maybe if we—"

The unmistakable sound of a pistol's hammer being

cocked back brought McCoy up short. He and Lee both turned their heads to see the two men McCoy had spotted earlier stranding there. The one with a rat face pointed his pistol right at Lee's chest. The one with the turkey feather in his hat pointed his six-shooter at McCoy.

Nobody moved for a long second. The place had gone stone quiet, the few scattered patrons in the Laughing Bronco all turning to gawk.

"Well?" McCoy said finally. "What do you two mangy critters want?"

Rat Face grinned. He had two teeth missing on one side. "We been tracking this skunk Rufus Lee for weeks, and now that five hundred is ours. We didn't recognize him with the beard, but we followed you around after we saw you showing that wanted poster to folks."

"Then you'll understand you're too late," McCoy said. "I've already got him in my custody."

"Don't look like no custody to me," Feather Hat said. "Looks like a couple fellas having a drink."

"Who the blazes are you anyway?" McCoy asked. "I know most of the bounty hunters who work Texas and Oklahoma."

"That just shows you don't know squat," Rat Face said. "Now get those guns out nice and slow and put them on the table."

Lee put his on the table.

McCoy pulled out his Peacemaker slowly and set it on the table next to Lee's gun, but from where he was sitting, the two grungy bounty hunters couldn't see the Colt Navy across his belly.

"We don't got no quarrel with you," Rat Face told McCoy. "You just sit tight while we march Rufus Lee down to the jailhouse and nobody needs to get a quick dose of lead if you take my meaning."

From McCoy's vantage, he could see Maddy reach behind the bar, and he braced himself, knowing what was about to happen.

Rat Face shook his pistol at Lee for emphasis. "Now you just stand up nice and slow and don't make no sudden—"

The room shook with the thunder of the double-barreled shotgun in Maddy's hands.

She wasn't the best shot.

She hit Rat Face but only with a smattering of pellets down his right arm. He dropped his pistol, stumbling back, screaming bloody murder.

Everyone in the place dove to the floor.

Except for McCoy.

He stood and flipped the table over in one smooth motion, his other hand drawing the Colt Navy and cocking the hammer back with a thumb.

Feather Hat blinked his dumb eyes, confused and startled by the shotgun blast. He gathered his wits and turned his six-shooter on Maddy.

McCoy fired and caught Feather Hat in the neck.

Feather Hat stumbled back, one hand clamping over his neck, blood oozing red between his fingers.

McCoy fired again, caught him in the chest. His top hat flew away as he spun around, took one halting step, then collapsed to the floor with a thud.

Rat Face had crawled back to his own six-shooter, grabbed it and aimed at McCoy.

Rufus Lee stepped forward and kicked the pistol out of Rat Face's hand.

Rat Face reached into his vest, came out with a little .32 revolver and leveled it at Lee.

McCoy fired again, caught him in the forehead just above his left eye. He twitched and went down.

Everyone in the saloon froze. Gunsmoke hung in the air.

When it became clear the shooting was over, patrons rose from the floor. Chatter rose, everyone wanting to talk about his personal view of what just happened. McCoy and Lee picked their guns up off the floor.

McCoy called Lee and Maddy into a huddle.

"It won't take long for the law to get here," McCoy said.

Lee shook his head. "That ain't good."

"I'll stay and tell them some story," McCoy said. "I'll say I was trying to apprehend you, and then these two interfered."

Lee looked at Maddy. Maddy nodded.

"Okay then," Lee said. "I'd best saddle my horse and go."

Maddy looked alarmed. "Go where?"

"I have an idea about that." McCoy told them his plan, and they all agreed.

Lee grabbed Maddy, kissed her hard, and was out the back door in the next instant.

"I'll make sure the barkeep knows what our story is," Maddy said, and left.

McCoy picked up the whiskey bottle from the floor. Most of the contents had spilled, but there was still a swallow left. He titled the bottle back and drank.

Definitely going to be one of those nights.

CHAPTER 6

Enrique Vargas went out into the night to fetch water from the well. He hauled up the bucket and filled the earthenware pitcher. He paused before going back inside to look up at the stars. This far away from the lights of Coyote Flats, the twinkling stars glittered against a vast black velvet blanket.

The sight made Vargas feel small, but not in a bad way.

Not like his failure with Dwight Combs.

Ah, but it had been foolish anyway. Was there anything so ridiculous as a boy trying so hard to prove he's a man? It was one thing to have pride. It was another to be stupid. Time to grow up.

He took the pitcher of water back into the small house and set it on the table.

His mother brought food to the table—beans, rice, tortillas.

She looked a lot older than she was, face lined, eyes always sad. She'd given birth to six boys and had been a good and faithful wife until Vargas's father had died nine years ago. With his brothers gone, Enrique Vargas had felt obligated to stay home and look after his aging mother.

An obligation he sometimes resented.

And then the resentment would make him feel guilty.

It was a simple life, even good if he'd been his mother's age, a quiet life suited for a person's waning years. Goats and a small herd of cows. Chickens that laid eggs to take to market. His father had worked hard to give them this small, simple life. Simple, but safe, and not especially uncomfortable.

But for a young man looking to take on the world . . .

Vargas shook his head. He was thinking the same useless thoughts around and around again in circles. He spooned beans into his mouth and tried to think of something else.

He and his mother ate in silence for a few minutes.

"You are quiet tonight, *flaco*," his mother said finally.

Vargas rolled his eyes. "Don't call me that. It's embarrassing."

"Then eat more," she said. "Anyway, nobody is here but us, so why be embarrassed?"

"Okay, okay."

"You want to go into town again."

Vargas shrugged.

"I know how it is," she said. "You are young. There is a girl in town?"

"Nothing like that, Madre."

"Well, if you go into town, don't wear your gun."

He rolled his eyes again. "A man wears a gun."

"Stop rolling your eyes."

"*Lo siento mucho.*"

"And a gun does not make a man," she said. "Your father worked hard for many years for me and you and your brothers. He never asked to be thanked. He did it for love and duty. That was a man."

Enrique Vargas knew this, understood it, but was too stubborn to say so out loud. He ate and said nothing.

"Is there a girl?" his mother asked. "Someone in town?"

"No."

"Then stay here."

"Okay."

But he tasted the lie even as it left his mouth. He would return to Coyote Flats.

And he'd be wearing his gun.

Carmen Espinoza's days were long, and she was always tired. To most, she seemed some regal queen, aloofly ruling from lofty heights, but running a saloon and a brothel was *work*. She'd set the barkeeps to watch each other to keep them from skimming, and herding the girls was so exhausting. So much sniping, a catfight ready to break out at any moment. Young girls were always a handful. She wasn't that much older than them, but with so much experience, so much she'd lived through and fought for, it seemed like decades.

All she wanted now was a long, undisturbed night's sleep.

Carmen wore a black silk nightgown that clung to her figure. It was held up by two impossibly thin straps over her shoulders and flowed down to her ankles, a slit up one side to show off plenty of leg when she moved just right. The garment had come all the way from Paris and would have caused an uproar among proper, church-going ladies. The nightgown had a much different effect on men, and Carmen was no stranger to what a man liked.

But that's not why she wore the gown, not tonight. The gown was thin and light, and the heat of the day lingered into the evening. She threw her windows open, hoping for a breeze.

A knock at the door.

Carmen frowned, recognizing the harsh rap. The metal ram's head of Jericho's walking stick.

She closed her eyes and held her breath, waiting. Maybe if she stayed quiet he'd think her asleep and go away, but, of course, that was foolish. Her lamps were on, and he'd be able to see the light under the door.

The knock came again.

She sighed out the breath she'd been holding, smoothed her gown, went to the door, pausing to put on her most convincing smile, and opened it.

"Señor Jericho," she said. "What a pleasant surprise."

"Pleasant, I hope," Jericho said. "But surely not a surprise."

Carmen stepped aside and gestured for him to come in, which he would have done anyway. Jericho twirled his walking stick as he sauntered into the room.

"Such a fetching frock," he said. "Aren't you going to offer me a drink?"

She went to the sideboard and poured him a whiskey from a glass decanter, then gave it to him. Jericho tossed it back in one go and smacked his lips. "That hits the spot."

"Another?"

"No thank you." Jericho set the glass aside.

Then he ran his hand down one of her arms, his fingertips and palms smooth for a man, but that hardly surprised Carmen. Jericho wasn't the sort to do any kind of hard work, not honest labor. He paid others for that.

And anyway, she'd felt his touch before.

"You know why I'm here?"

Carmen smiled knowingly. She was in no mood for anyone's company, let alone Jericho's, but it was her lot in life to pretend. "Why would any man be here?"

"I hope you don't let just any man up here." Jericho smiled when he said it, but there was an edge to his voice. "I'm sure you remember what happened to our good friend Larry Prince."

Carmen's smile widened as she allowed herself to be drawn into Jericho's embrace. "You think I encouraged him?"

"I know you know better." Then he let her go. "But I'm here about that other matter."

"Ah." She nodded. "McCoy."

"You told him to come speak to you before making any rash decisions, yes?"

"I told him," Carmen said. "Nobody has seen McCoy. He rode away and has not returned."

Jericho rubbed the back of his neck as he thought about that. "That might be just as good. As long as he doesn't go to work for that mouth-breathing cretin Lorenzo. This truce won't last, Carmen, and everyone knows it. The only reason we're not at each other right now, is that neither of us really has an advantage. If he hires a few more guns, or I do . . . if one of us feels stronger . . . well, neither of us are the sort of men to hesitate. I'll strike hard and fast. I know he'd do the same."

"Why not just leave things the way they are?" she asked.

He *tsked* and shook his head. "My dear Carmen, that's simply not the natural order of things. A wolf pack has but one leader. Power isn't shared. Even if we agreed to leave things as they were, I would always be waiting for him to double-cross me. No, my darling, I'm afraid Lorenzo has to go. And when the time is right, and I've built my strength sufficiently, then I shall fall on him so hard, he won't know what hit him."

Jericho was a sly one, and Carmen had no doubt he could and would carry out his threat, but Lorenzo was tough and mean. He wouldn't allow himself to be brushed aside so easily. Blood and violence were coming to Coyote Flats, maybe not tonight or tomorrow, but sooner than most people expected, in Carmen's opinion. She'd survived so far, and she'd need to play it smart if she wanted to go on surviving.

"That really is quite a gown you're wearing." Jericho shrugged out of his jacket and pulled his string tie loose. "I suppose as long as I'm here . . ."

Her smile widened. Carmen had learned quickly to lie with that smile, to make any man believe she was nothing but delighted by his attention. Boring bankers, dour undertakers, timid farmers, sweaty, smelly cowboys . . . they were all the same when boiled down to their basic, obvious needs.

But it had been Carmen's job to make each of those men feel they were special, the only man in the world.

She hooked her thumbs into the thin straps holding up her gown and slid them off her shoulders.

Jericho was not the only one hatching schemes and biding his time. Carmen had slowly been devising a plan to rid herself of this arrogant man.

But tonight she would smile.

And pretend.

"I don't think he's coming back," Big Mike said.

"A shame." Lorenzo reached across the table for the salt and spread some on his mashed potatoes. "He's good with a gun. We could have used him."

"There's plenty more like him," Mike said.

Lorenzo shrugged. "Maybe."

Lorenzo and his boys sat around their private club, eating, drinking, some playing cards.

Then Hank Blevins walked through the front door.

Lorenzo looked up and smiled. "There we go. I was wondering if we'd see Hank sooner or later."

Big Mike frowned. "I don't know him."

"You don't know lots of stuff," Lorenzo said. "I got people I use sometimes. For jobs on the sly, the fewer people who know the better."

And for a job on the sly, Hank Blevins fit the bill. He was the most forgettable man Lorenzo had ever met, average height, average build, average clothes. Bland, brown hair. A face like a bowl of mashed potatoes, white and formless, no distinguishing lines, nothing a man could make a memory out of. Hank Blevins was a walking talking nothing, and that was useful when you needed a man followed but didn't want the one following to be seen.

Blevins approached the table, and Lorenzo motioned for him to take a chair.

Lorenzo raised an eyebrow. "Well?"

"McCoy tried to do the job," Blevins said. "Didn't work out."

Lorenzo frowned. "What do you mean?"

Hank Blevins told Lorenzo the story in a straightforward manner without embellishments. McCoy's first stop had been to the marshal, just as Lorenzo had predicted. That's where Blevins had picked him up and began following him. It became clear soon enough McCoy was looking around for Rufus Lee, just like Lorenzo wanted.

"I lost McCoy for a bit," Blevins admitted. "But I got there at the end and heard the whole thing."

"What do you mean you got there at the end?" Lorenzo asked.

"Big shootout at a saloon called the Laughing Bronco," Blevins said. "Turns out that's where McCoy found Rufus Lee. Had him dead to rights by all accounts, but a couple of small-timers stuck their noses in where they wasn't wanted. McCoy gunned the other bounty hunters, but Rufus got away. I got there too late to see the shooting, but I snuck in close in my own quiet way and heard McCoy and the marshal talking, so that's how I know what happened."

Lorenzo *tsked*. "I was hoping you'd tell me McCoy shot Rufus right through the heart, but he tried at least, so that's good."

"How does McCoy trying and failing do us any good?" Big Mike asked.

"I don't know Ghost McCoy from Adam," Lorenzo said. "But I've known men *like* him all my life. You can't just start giving them orders. You can't tell them how it's going to be. That'll just get his hackles up. You push, and he'll push back twice as hard. No, you gotta make a suggestion. Then if he takes the suggestion, he's not following an order, but he's still doing what you told him to do. If he'd killed Rufus and collected the reward, then it would have worked out for him. It would have given him the feeling that my suggestions ain't so bad, and after a time, the suggestions start sounding a little more like orders and before you know it, he's calling me boss."

Big Mike filled his shot glass with whiskey and shook his head, letting out a long sigh. "I guess that's why you're the boss, Mr. Lorenzo. You got a long-term way of thinking."

"Short-term thinking leads to short-term living is what I've observed." Lorenzo turned back to Blevins. "So McCoy's back in Coyote Flats?"

Blevins shook his head. "Nope. I heard McCoy tell the marshal in Austin he was on his way back to Black Oak. He's got some money to collect there. I just stopped off here to let you know."

"Best get after him then," Lorenzo said. "He'll either come back here or move on, but I want to know. You keep following him. Mike, pick somebody to go with him."

Mike turned in his chair. "Duane, tell Rusty to get out here."

The old, bald man who'd been sitting in the corner and whittling on a chunk of wood stood immediately. "You got it, Mike." And he disappeared into the back room.

"You don't think I can handle it?" Blevins asked Lorenzo.

"You can handle it," Lorenzo said. "Just somebody to watch your back . . . unless you've got some objection."

Blevins shrugged. "You're the boss."

Duane came out of the back room a moment later with Rusty Calhoun in tow.

Rusty was an odd duck, with a shock of red hair that refused to be combed and buck horse teeth with a gap between the front two. He was prone to fits of giggling—which Lorenzo found annoying—and the most unlikely things would set him off. But he was a quick lefthander and did everything Lorenzo or Big Mike told him to without question.

"Rusty, this is Hank Blevins. He's been keeping an eye on that McCoy character for me," Lorenzo explained. "All you need to do is watch Hank's back."

"I can sure as heck do that, Mr. Lorenzo," Rusty assured him. "Don't have to worry about that at all. I'm on the job."

"Good." Lorenzo looked back at Blevins. "Hank, I want you back on McCoy's tail right away, but we can at least get a hot meal into you first. Duane, take him in back and feed him whatever we've got."

Blevins pushed back from the table and stood. "Obliged for that, Mr. Lorenzo." Blevins followed Duane out of the room.

Before Rusty could walk away, Lorenzo latched onto

his arm and pulled him close, pitched his voice low. "I've asked McCoy to join us. We can use every gun when we eventually make our move against Jericho, but . . . well, you know how I hate loose ends. If it looks like McCoy won't throw in with us, find a quiet, dark place where nobody can see and put a bullet in him."

Rusty grinned. "My pleasure."

CHAPTER 7

Whatever excitement Garret McCoy might have caused his first time through Black Oak, it was all over now, the town going about its routine like so many other towns just like it in this part of Texas.

"I'll take your horse from you, *señor*." White teeth smiling out of a brown face, the young boy might have been twelve years old. "I work for the old man at the livery stable. Brush and feed and water your horse. I will do it all. No trouble for you."

McCoy eyed the boy and asked, "Where's the older one?"

"That is my brother Pedro. He's helping Padre with the goats today," the boy told him. "I am called Jorge."

McCoy handed the boy the reins. "That's a lot of horse. Can you handle her, Jorge?"

"Oh, yes. I am very good with horses," Jorge assured him.

McCoy dipped into a pocket, came out with a coin, and flipped it to the boy. "Thanks. I'll be along to check on her later."

Jorge led McCoy's horse away down the street.

72   *William W. Johnstone and J.A. Johnstone*

McCoy hooked his thumbs into his gun belt and took a leisurely stroll toward the sheriff's office. He considered walking straight in but knocked instead.

"Come on then," came a voice from within.

McCoy pushed the door open and entered.

It was like any of a hundred other small-town sheriff offices McCoy had seen. A desk and a couple chairs, two empty cells along the back wall. A gun rack on the wall off to the side with a couple rifles and a shotgun. A narrow hallway to a back room maybe, and a back door.

Bryson Tate looked up from the papers he'd been shuffling on his desk and frowned. "Oh, it's you."

"I said I'd be back."

"I know." Tate opened the desk's thin middle drawer and took out a piece of paper, slid it across the desk to Tate. "There's your voucher. All legal."

McCoy took the paper, folded it, and stashed it in his vest pocket. "Just so I know, we're not going to have a problem, are we?"

Tate's eyes narrowed. "Not sure what you mean."

"A little bird told me those men I killed were paying you off. That's money out of your pocket," McCoy said. "Might be you hold a grudge. I'd hate to think if I had to come back through town someday in the future that I wouldn't be welcome."

An expression crossed Tate's face halfway between embarrassed and annoyed. "You'll be exactly as welcome as you are now. No more. No less." He sighed and rubbed his face like he was suddenly dog-tired. "Look, sit down a minute, will you?"

McCoy hesitated, then took the chair across from Tate.

The sheriff opened the deep desk drawer to his left and fished out a whiskey bottle and two glasses. He filled the glasses and pushed one toward McCoy.

McCoy didn't take it.

Tate drank his then refilled the glass. "You think I wanted those stinking rats crawling around my town? Not a chance. But we're not all like you. You shoot a man and collect a reward, and then you're on your way. I have to live here. My sister and her kids live here too. Something happens to them because I get high-and-mighty, then what?"

"That doesn't mean you have to take payoffs."

"If I'm not doing my job anyway, I might as well make something. Takes the sting out of it." Tate sipped his whiskey. "I'm not proud of it. I told myself it was better than having the town all shot up. You look at this tin star on my chest, and maybe you think that means I'm invincible. Well, I ain't bulletproof. Try going around this town and getting some help when it's time to strap on a six-shooter. Everyone points at the tin star and says *That's your job.* So you can go it alone and maybe get all shot up, or you can try to invent some kind of peace. Not a perfect solution, but what's perfect in this world? Anyway, that's my story. I'm glad they're gone, and if you don't cause any trouble for me, then I won't cause any for you. What do you say?"

"Not much." McCoy reached for the shot gloss. "But I won't let the whiskey go to waste at least."

He drank.

Tate refilled the glasses.

"How'd you get to be sheriff?" McCoy asked out of the blue.

"Me? Ran for it, and nobody ran against me. I know why now. A thankless job with lousy pay."

"Ever heard of a town called Coyote Flats?" McCoy asked. "They don't have a sheriff."

"That's because Coyote Flats ain't a town," Tate said. "Oh, it is in all the normal ways, people living there and such, but it's not an official town in the eyes of Texas. In such cases, sometimes the people get together and hire or elect a man to be sheriff, or they handle things their own way without the law."

"How does a town get to be official?"

"That's a little out of my ken," Tate admitted. "I guess eventually the town wants the benefits of being recognized on the map, so to speak, and so when the town gets big enough or loud enough, they get incorporated or some such."

McCoy sipped his whiskey and thought about that. "Any reason *not* to get incorporated . . . or some such?"

Tate shrugged. "I suppose if a town preferred to keep things the way they were. Maybe they don't want outsiders telling them what laws they have to follow. Maybe they don't want to pay taxes to no bureaucrat in Austin."

"Huh." McCoy stood and set the empty shot glass on Tate's desk. "Thanks for the drink."

"What now?" the sheriff asked.

"Not sure. The Gil Morgan gang's been cutting a swath through Kansas. Might have a go at them," McCoy said.

"But it's too late to start anywhere now. Might see if the hotel has a room."

"Good luck to you then," Tate said.

McCoy left the sheriff's office and decided to visit the livery stable before strolling over to the hotel. It wasn't that he didn't trust the kid to take care of his horse, but he always liked to verify things with his own eyes. McCoy hadn't gotten through the war by taking people's word for things.

On the way into the stable, McCoy spotted two men coming out, both Mexicans.

They were a few years younger than McCoy, but still a couple of hard-looking types with stern faces and a strong family resemblance. Both wore sombreros back on their heads and serapes of thin, rough wool thrown over their shoulders.

At first glance, the one with the beard looked slightly older, but it was fairly spare as beards went, with a smooth, youthful face underneath. He wore a two-gun rig, a heavy Colt Army on each hip.

The other wore only a single revolver, a shiny new Smith & Wesson Model 3, although McCoy guessed it might not be his first choice of weapon since he cradled a Henry rifle in one arm almost lovingly. Two bandoleers crisscrossed his chest with cartridges for the Henry.

They eyed McCoy as he and the two Mexicans passed one another, but nothing came of it, and McCoy entered the stable, pausing only a moment to look back at the two men, wondering why they seemed familiar. Some faces just looked like others, McCoy supposed.

Inside the stable McCoy found Jorge brushing down

his horse, the animal's coat looking rich and glossy, the boy taking his time to give the mare his full attention.

"Looks like you're taking good care of her," McCoy said.

"But of course, *señor*," Jorge told him. "I am very good with horses. I give them the best care."

McCoy smiled. "Good work. I can see you're the man for the job. I'm going to leave her overnight, so make sure to—"

He turned his head abruptly, eyes tracking the two Mexicans as they walked away from the livery stable. McCoy realized now that he did recognize them, but not because he'd met them before. He'd seen their faces on a wanted poster.

The Vargas brothers!

"Is something the matter, *señor*?"

"Everything's fine, Jorge," McCoy told him. "Do you know those two men who just left?"

"I never seen them before today," the boy said. "They brought their horses to the stable, and that's all I know."

"Listen, Jorge, do you know who I am?" McCoy asked. "Do you understand what I do?"

The boy nodded. "Oh, yes. You are the bounty hunter man. My brother Pedro, he told me."

"Those men out there are dangerous sorts," McCoy said. "And I need to find out about them. You'd like to make some money, yes?"

Jorge's eyes widened. "Oh, yes, *señor*."

"I need you to follow them and see where they go," McCoy said. "I need you to try to get close and listen to what they're saying. Can you do that?"

"I think so."

McCoy put a hand on the boy's shoulder. "But you have to be careful. Men like that don't mess around. If you can't do it, or you think you might be putting yourself in harm's way, then just forget it, okay?"

"I understand. I will be careful."

"Good. I'll either be at the saloon or the hotel if you need to find me."

McCoy left the stable, wondering if he was doing the right thing. Normally, if he saw a man's face on a wanted poster, that was good enough. It didn't matter *why.* Asking too many questions was a waste of time. McCoy would give the man a chance to come quietly.

But if he had to do it the hard way, then so be it.

This time was different. Enrique Vargas had piqued McCoy's curiosity. The young hothead seemed to think his brothers were not the evil men that the law was making them out to be.

Maybe.

Maybe not.

McCoy went to the saloon where he'd recently shot "Dirty" Dave Dunbar and Shane "Snake" Delany. Since he was going in the front door this time, he saw the sign on his way in. *Herman's Saloon.* Not the catchiest name for a watering hole, but whiskey was whiskey.

McCoy sauntered in and claimed a spot at the bar. The barkeep gave him the stink eye, obviously recognizing the bounty hunter, and probably wondering if McCoy was going to shoot anybody today.

McCoy held up a hand. "Peace. I just want a bottle."

The barkeep didn't look convinced but brought McCoy the bottle. McCoy drank and minded his own business except for occasionally glancing around to see who might be coming or going.

That's when he spotted the man at the far end of the bar.

He was so dull and inconspicuous that McCoy nearly looked right through him, but there was something about the man's bland face that seemed familiar. Or maybe that was some sort of trick of the mind. The Vargas brothers had looked familiar, and now maybe he was expecting to see familiar faces everywhere he looked.

But the man at the end of the bar was hard to pin down. McCoy couldn't imagine him in any context, couldn't picture where the two of them might have been in the same place at the same time. McCoy put the man out of his mind. There was no sense getting paranoid. Strangers came and went in saloons, and there was no point wasting thought on it.

A moment later, Sheriff Tate took a spot at the bar right next to him and ordered a beer.

"Should have known I'd find you at Herman's," Tate said. "No place else to go really, not in a town this small."

"Don't worry, Sheriff, I ain't shot anyone," McCoy assured him. "Yet."

"You already gunned our local outlaws," Tate said. "Nobody left worth shooting."

Either Tate didn't know the Vargas brothers were in town or he was playing dumb. McCoy figured the sheriff didn't know. There were plenty of faces on plenty of wanted posters, and he doubted Tate had taken the time to memorize him on the thousand-to-one chance some outlaw might just happen to pass through.

McCoy considered mentioning the brothers but then thought better of it. Tate might panic and do something dumb. Let the Vargas brothers think they were safe until McCoy found out more about them. Then he'd take them in his own time and in his own way.

"So did you decide to head for Kansas?" Tate asked. "Or are you headed back to Coyote Flats after all?"

Maybe it was because the man had a few drinks in him, but he seemed like he wanted to talk, not for any particular reason, just to be amiable.

McCoy thought he knew the answer but found himself thinking about it. Coyote Flats? No. What for? But then Carmen's face hovered in front of his mind's eye, those deep dark eyes drawing him in.

But no. Texas was full of women. So was the whole world. It was no time for McCoy to start getting foolish over a pretty face.

"I reckon there's nothing for me in Coyote Flats," McCoy said. "I'll head north sooner or later."

And then what after Kansas? McCoy didn't have an answer. Ghost McCoy. There one minute. Gone the next.

He poured himself another whiskey.

"Probably too quiet around here now for a fella in your line of work." Tate finished his beer, then wiped his mouth with the back of his hand. "Good luck to you."

Tate left the saloon, and McCoy watched him go. The sheriff seemed in a better mood. Maybe because McCoy said he'd be leaving Black Oak. McCoy understood. What did bounty hunters ever bring to a town but blood and death?

But what else did McCoy know? What else could he do to make his way in the world?

"You're McCoy."

McCoy turned abruptly. The dull-faced man who'd been at the far end of the bar was suddenly right next to him. He'd come upon McCoy without so much as a whisper.

And they call me *Ghost.*

"Yeah, I'm McCoy," McCoy said. "Who are you?"

"Hank."

"Hank who?"

"Just Hank," the bland fella said. "I got some information you might like to hear."

McCoy had to stop himself from rolling his eyes. "Well, you tell me the information. I'll tell you if I liked hearing it or not."

"Not here," Hank said. "Too many eyes and ears. I'm not eager to stick my neck out quite that far."

"Why stick your neck out at all?"

"Because I like money just as much as the next man," Hank told him. "I'm hoping you'll find the information useful and pay me."

"Pay you what?" McCoy asked. "What if I don't like the price? What if I don't like the information?"

"This information might save your life," Hank said. "I'll let you decide what that's worth. I've been talking to you too long already. I don't want us seen together."

"Where then?"

"There's an abandoned ranch house about six miles east of town." Hank gave McCoy the directions. "Meet me there at midnight."

McCoy shook his head. "What have you got to say in the darkness that you can't say in daylight?"

Hank grimaced. "Fine. How about an hour before sundown?"

"Okay then."

Hank tossed back the last of his drink, then turned and walked out without another word.

McCoy stood at the bar a moment, staring down into his shot glass. He didn't like Hank's story. There was a very specific kind of stink to it. You don't lure a man six miles out of town to whisper in his ear.

Garret was going, of course. If there was someone out there trying to lure him into a trap, then McCoy wanted to know who and why.

He thought about it for five more minutes, threw back another shot of whiskey, and then he had his plan.

CHAPTER 8

McCoy spotted the old ranch house while still a mile away, down a little-used dirt trail in the middle of an expanse of flat ground dotted with scrub oaks. Details came into focus as he drew nearer. The house was sizable enough for a large family, a big covered porch stretching across the front, the roof caved in on one side. A number of little outbuildings—chicken coop, smokehouse, smithy, and so on. A large barn with faded, flaking paint stood in direct line-of-sight to the house's front porch. A wooden fence circled the building and formed corrals out back, but there were so many gaps, it was hard to call it a fence anymore. Even from a distance, it was obvious nobody had lived in the place for years.

McCoy spotted Hank as he passed through the remains of a gate. Hank sat on a porch bench near the house's front door—or at least the gaping, dark opening where the door had been once upon a time. Hank's horse was tethered to a post off to the side.

McCoy squinted at the sky. Just about an hour of good daylight left.

"Glad you could make it," called Hank.

THE MAN FROM BLOOD GULCH

McCoy dismounted. He didn't bother tying up his horse. It was a good animal and wouldn't wander. His eyes narrowed, looking everywhere, into every corner and shadowed nook. He walked slowly toward the front porch. In his peripheral vision, he thought he caught movement in the hayloft window over the barn doors.

Maybe somebody was up there. Maybe not.

McCoy stopped at the short stairs leading up to the porch, put one foot onto the first step. "Okay, I'm here. Now talk."

Hank stood with a grunt, smacked the dust off his trousers. "Good of you to show. I guess you know a man named Mortimer Lorenzo."

McCoy's face hardened. "I know him."

"I believe he made you an offer of employment."

"He made it," McCoy said. "I didn't accept it."

Hank nodded. "So I heard. I believe you told the sheriff you're off to Kansas maybe."

"First, congratulations on your excellent eaves-dropping skills," McCoy said. "Second, where I go is my own business."

"I see."

"Do you?" McCoy said flatly. "That's good, but in case you don't see quite clear enough, I'll spell it out. I work for one person. Myself. Lorenzo doesn't have a thing to say about it."

A sudden, mad giggling came from within the ruined ranch house.

McCoy tensed, ready to go for his Peacemaker.

A man strolled from the house onto the porch, no hat, a shock of red hair, green kerchief loose around his neck. He had a smirk on his face, and McCoy felt even if he'd met this man under other circumstances, he would have disliked him instantly. The gap in his teeth made him look like a simpleton, but he had the posture of an experienced gunman. His wore his six-gun rigged for a left-handed draw, and that gave McCoy pause. There was always something just a little trickier about going up against a left-hander.

"I'm called Rusty." And the man giggled again.

"Nobody's going to call you much of anything soon," McCoy said, a warning tone in his voice.

That just got more giggling.

Hank frowned at the redhead. "You were supposed to come out shooting."

"Where's the fun in that?" Rusty asked.

"Fun don't enter into it," Hank said.

"Sure it does," Rusty insisted. "Because bad men like this walk around thinking nobody can touch them. I say different. I say it'll be big fun teaching him a lesson."

"Teach it faster," Hank said.

"Rusty, if you touch that pistol, you die," McCoy said. "And that's a plain fact."

A pause, Rusty's eyes widening slowly, like it had never occurred to him before he could get in over his head.

Then he threw his head back, laughing like a braying mule.

When his head came back down again, his face had gone hard and his hand fell to his gun.

Rusty was fast, and his six-shooter cleared leather.

McCoy was forced to rush his shot, and the Peacemaker bucked in his hand and spat fire. The shot caught Rusty low on the side. He got off his own shot, but it whizzed past McCoy's ear. Rusty tried to bring his pistol around again but staggered from the wound in his side.

McCoy fired again, catching him square in the chest.

Rusty's eyes rolled back and he went down hard, rattling the porch's floorboards.

The whole time, McCoy had watched Hank in his peripheral vision. Hank went for his own gun. He was no gunman, slow on the draw, but McCoy's attention had been all on Rusty.

Hank raised his pistol, pointed it at McCoy.

The crack of a rifle shot from the barn's hayloft window.

Hank's hat flew off, and his eyes shot wide. He ducked through the ranch house's front door just as McCoy fanned the hammer of his six-shooter twice, the bullets missing Hank and gouging splinters from the doorframe.

"Get around back!" McCoy shouted at the barn.

Then he entered the house, crouching, Peacemaker up and ready. His eyes squinted as he looked one way then another. The hallway to the left was blocked by fallen ceiling beams, the waning daylight filtering down through the ruined roof, igniting floating dust motes in the air.

McCoy cocked his head and listened.

Silence.

Nothing through the archway to his right, a large room bereft of furnishings, cobwebs telling a tale of abandonment.

A long hall stretched in front of him, going all the way to the back of the house, a blur of light at the end. McCoy moved forward, six-shooter up and cocked. He passed empty rooms, eyes and ears open, then paused at the end of the hallway. He peeked around the corner.

A wide kitchen. A rusty potbellied stove in the corner, chimney pipe fallen. A half-rotted hutch stood in the middle of the kitchen, no dishes or crockery, just mouse droppings and cobwebs.

Across the kitchen, a shredded screen door hung open on one hinge, Texas flatland beyond. McCoy paused. Had Hank made it out the back door? If he escaped to warn Lorenzo, then McCoy's plan would be ruined. But rushing forward without caution was a good way to get himself killed.

He paused one more moment to listen.

Then steps, someone coming close from outside.

In the next second, Sheriff Tate appeared in the doorway, a Spencer carbine tight in his grip. "I didn't see him come out back. He must still be—"

Hank emerged from behind the hutch, lifted his six-shooter, and fired.

Tate screamed and dropped the carbine, one shoulder jerking back as blood sprayed from his upper arm. He stumbled back out the door and went down.

McCoy aimed his Peacemaker and squeezed the trigger. The six-shooter belched fire, and a chunk of Hank's head above his left ear exploded bloody. He went down and hit the floor hard.

McCoy stood over him, cocked the pistol and aimed it at Hank, but the man was gone. McCoy eased the hammer back down and holstered the weapon.

Outside, Tate lay sprawled on the ground. As McCoy approached, the sheriff sat up, groaning, and clutching his shoulder.

"You got lead in you?" McCoy asked.

Tate shook his head. "No, but it took a chunk on the way through."

"I got stuff in my saddle bags," McCoy said. "I'll patch you up."

McCoy fetched his horse and took it to the back of the house. He took a flask of strong whiskey and a roll of bandages from his saddle bag and went to Tate, who was still sitting on the ground.

"Do you care if I cut that sleeve off?" McCoy asked.

"It's ruined anyway," Tate said.

There was a rip where the bullet had passed through, and the upper part of the sleeve was soaked in blood. McCoy pulled a knife from his boot and carefully cut away the sleeve. Tate hissed when McCoy doused the wound in whiskey.

"It wouldn't do for word to get out I killed these men," McCoy said.

"It was self-defense," Tate said. "I'll vouch for it."

McCoy wrapped the bandage around the sheriff's arm. "That's not what I mean. I'm going after the man who sent them. I don't want him to know what happened. It'll already be bad enough when these fellas don't turn up. But without bodies or news of what happened to them . . . well, who's to say what happened. Maybe they got bored and wandered off."

Tate thought about that. "If I go by the rules, I need to report this."

"I guess that's right."

"So you can see how it is, then," Tate said. "Sometimes there are . . . circumstances. Sometimes even the folks on the side of the law don't always go by the book."

"I guess that's right too." McCoy didn't think his situation and what the sheriff had done quite amounted to the same thing, but maybe Tate had a point about circumstances.

"You didn't have to back me up, but you did," McCoy said. "Thanks."

"I'm just trying to get on the right side of things again. I saw a shovel in the barn. You could bury these fellas, I guess. I'd help but . . ." Tate gestured to his wounded arm.

"I'll handle it," McCoy said. "If there's a doctor in Black Oak, you might have him look at that arm. I make no claims about being a medical man."

"Right."

Tate's horse was in the barn. McCoy fetched it for him and helped him climb on.

"Good luck in Coyote Flats," Sheriff Tate said. "I got a feeling you're going to need it."

McCoy watched for a moment as the sheriff rode away.

Then he went to the barn, got the shovel, and went to work digging two graves, finishing most of his chore by lantern light. The dead men's guns might have brought a few dollars, but McCoy didn't want to risk any of the men's possessions being recognized. He put their saddles in the barn and gave each of their horses a slap on the rump, sending them trotting into the night.

Finally, he mounted his own horse and rode back to the hotel in Black Oak. He put his horse up in the stable, threw his saddlebags over his shoulder, then shuffled into the hotel lobby, realizing he was matted with dirt and sweat.

"Too late for a bath?" he asked the desk clerk.

"Mabel ain't asleep yet," he said. "I'll get her started on the hot water. Bathroom's down the hall, last door on the left."

The bathroom wasn't much. A big wooden tub. A stool. Hooks on the wall. McCoy hung up his guns and dropped his saddlebags on the floor. Then he sat on the stool and pulled off his boots. He was sore all over. Funny how a man could wear himself out just digging a couple holes, muscles he hadn't used in a long time.

An old woman—Mabel, he presumed—came in with a steaming bucket in each hand. She might have been a hundred years old or a thousand.

"You need help with that?" McCoy asked.

"The day I can't haul water from the kitchen to this here tub, I'll be in the cold, cold ground," she said.

Fair enough.

Mabel poured the buckets into the tub. "Best get in before it goes cold."

McCoy started to unbutton his shirt, then paused, looking at her.

"You ain't got nothing I'm interested in seeing," she said. "And too old to do anything about it even if I was interested."

She left with the buckets for more water.

McCoy undressed and got into the tub, and by the time Mabel finished filling it, the water was up to his shoulders. McCoy had to admit the old woman knew her business—the water was hot but not so hot he couldn't stand it, and soon his muscles eased. He soaped himself all over.

Mabel gathered his dirty clothes off the floor. "You want me to launder these filthy things?"

"I reckon that's best."

She grunted and left with the dirty clothes.

McCoy bathed and felt like a new man, put on fresh clothes from his saddlebags, and went up to his room. He crawled in between cool sheets and was so tired, he figured he'd be asleep before his head hit the pillow.

But thoughts of what was going to happen next kept him awake. He meant to confront Lorenzo. There'd never been a question about that. A man sends killers after you, well, that just won't stand. McCoy's first instinct had been to be straightforward about it—ride into Coyote Flats, call the man out, and then shoot him right between the eyes.

But the more McCoy thought about it, the more something nagged at him, a little, itchy something he couldn't quite put his finger on. Something about Lorenzo bothered him, and suddenly it wasn't enough that the man had to die. McCoy wanted answers.

Knowing all his questions would still be there in the morning, he finally let himself drift off into deep, dreamless sleep.

McCoy splashed water in his face the next morning, strapped on his guns, grabbed his saddlebags, and went downstairs.

The desk clerk handed him his laundry, wrapped up in brown paper and tied with string. "Cleaned and ironed. I added it to your bill."

"Obliged." McCoy settled up, left the hotel, and went to the livery stable.

Jorge found him before McCoy could saddle his horse.

"*Señor*, I have information about those two men," the boy told him.

McCoy had completely forgotten he'd set Jorge the task of spying on the Vargas brothers.

"What did you find out?" McCoy asked.

"I followed them, *señor*," Jorge reported. "They went to the saloon and got very drunk. I was not allowed in, but I watched through the window. When they came out, they each had a bottle. They didn't see me. I stayed close, so I could hear them talking."

"Did they say anything worth hearing?"

"Not at first," Jorge said. "They complained about not having any money left and could not stay at the hotel. They went to the corral out back and flopped into a haystack to finish their bottles of whiskey. That's when they said many interesting things, *señor*."

McCoy's hand went into his pocket, but he didn't come out with any money for the boy, not yet. "Tell me what they said. I'll judge if it's interesting or not."

"They were debating on whether or not to go to the sheriff and turn themselves in," Jorge explained. "Juan said they needed to explain they had not killed anyone, but the other one—his name was Carlos—said they would go before a judge and get hanged, that nobody would listen to a couple of Mexicans."

McCoy thought about that, then asked, "Anything else?"

"Nothing much, *señor*. Just that they seemed confused what to do next."

"Are they still out there?"

"*Sí, señor.*"

McCoy handed the boy a dollar.

Jorge's eyes shot wide. "*Muchas gracias!*"

McCoy dropped his saddlebags and headed out through the stable's back door. He spotted them immediately, the two men snoring up against a haystack, boots off and flung carelessly to the side, empty bottles lying next to them, the Henry rifle leaning within arm's reach of one of them.

With as much stealth as he could muster, McCoy eased over to the rifle, grabbed it, then took five big steps back and cleared his throat loudly.

They kept snoring, one snorting and waving a fly away from his nose.

"Wake up, ya lazy bums," McCoy said loudly.

The two Mexicans twitched and came awake, one rubbing his eyes. The other one saw McCoy and reached for the Henry that wasn't there.

McCoy leveled the rifle at them. "Sit still and listen."

They froze, looking at him.

"Which one of you is Juan?" McCoy asked.

The one who'd reached for the Henry raised his hand.

"I heard you want to turn yourselves in to the sheriff."

The two brothers looked at each other and then Juan asked, "How did you know—"

"I'm asking the questions," McCoy interrupted. "You're both wanted dead or alive. I can shoot you right now and collect the reward. The law won't even blink. So which is it? Do we have a nice, civilized conversation . . . or do I play a tune for you on this Henry rifle."

"We didn't kill nobody," Juan said. "I thought if we explained to the sheriff—"

Juan's brother started letting him have it in Spanish.

"Hey, hey, hey, English please," McCoy said with heat. "I'm losing patience."

"The sheriff won't listen," said the other brother— Carlos. "Nor will the judge. It's pointless. I'd rather be shot than hung."

"I want to hear the story from the beginning." McCoy pointed the rifle at Juan. "You tell it."

"We didn't want to say anything before because we didn't want to talk against our two older brothers, but they are dead now," Juan said. "I do not like being on the run all the time. Always hiding. Our faces are everywhere on wanted posters for killing, but we killed *nobody*! It is the truth, I swear!"

"Convince me."

"Our brothers said to come into town with them," Juan explained. "This was in El Paso. They said they had a deal for how we could all make some money. I asked in what way, but they just smiled and said we would see soon enough. They were our brothers, so we trusted them. They took us to an alley behind a notorious brothel. This was very early in the morning. They went inside and told us to watch the horses and not let anyone come in the door behind them."

"And this didn't seem suspicious to you?" McCoy asked.

Juan nodded. "*Sí*, of course, but it was too late. We were there. We couldn't just ride off and leave our brothers."

"Keep talking."

"They knew when to hit the brothel," Juan explained. "There had been soldiers in town the night before, and the brothel had done much business. Louis—that's my oldest brother—knew where they kept the strongbox. He went in to take it, but then . . . shooting. Screaming. They came out with the money, and we all rode away fast. They'd killed three men while stealing the money." Juan shook his head and looked away, probably ashamed at the memory.

"Louis told us that we were part of the gang now," Carlos said. "That they had other jobs planned and we would help, but we said *no*. And then Juan and I left them."

"But it didn't matter," Juan said. "We were already branded as part of the gang. Everything our brothers did left a stain on *us*."

McCoy sighed. "Well, that's quite a story."

"What do you care?" Carlos said. "All men like you care about is collecting your bounty. Shoot us now and be done with it."

"I talked to your little brother," McCoy told them. "Enrique. Didn't seem like such a bad kid."

Carlos and Juan looked at each other, their demeanors softening slightly.

"My brother Carlos can be hotheaded, *señor*," Juan said. "I'm sure I speak for both of us when I say that if there is some way to get out of this *without* getting shot, then I'm sure we would be happy to listen."

McCoy lowered the Henry. "I currently find myself in a . . . situation. Maybe we can help each other."

"If our mother was here she would tell you, *señor*," Juan said. "We can be very helpful fellows."

CHAPTER 9

Gerald Muldoon liked his hat.

It was a gorgeous black hat with Mexican silver all around, gleaming discs that matched well with the silverwork in his gun belt. He gave it the once-over with a handheld whisk broom. The silver would be due for a polish soon, but not today.

He liked his boots too. Rattlesnake skin. He bent down and gave them a wipe with a soft cloth.

Gerald was of the opinion that if you had a good hat up top and some swanky boots at the bottom, then everything in between would fall into place. He looked at himself in the mirror. A shirt of deep scarlet, and a black vest. Snug-fitting black pants with red lines down the side matching the shirt.

Maybe he'd head to Carmen's Place later and give all the saloon gals a chance to swoon at him.

He headed downstairs into the smoky environs of the Thirsty Coyote. The place was nearly deserted, but it was still early. Two men hunched at the bar, conversing in hushed tones. Porky Rosenthal sat at the corner table reading the newspaper. His lips moved as he read.

Gerald didn't care for the nickname *Porky*, not because it was insulting to the beefy man, but because it struck Gerald as unoriginal.

Still, everyone called him Porky, so . . .

"What's the latest news, Porky?" Gerald asked.

Porky looked up from his paper. "They captured them Indians that attacked the corn train."

"How old's that paper?"

Porky looked at the front. "A few months. Fella left it here last week."

"Uh-huh." Gerald glanced around the interior of the saloon again, hoping to see someone better to talk to. "You seen the boss?"

"Front porch," Porky said. "Taking the air."

"Thanks."

Gerald found Jericho out front. He sat with his chair tilted back, foot up on the railing, gray smoke leaking from a long, thin cigar in the corner of his mouth. His bowler hat perched on his head at a jaunty angle.

"Restless, Gerald?" Jericho asked.

"I guess it's been pretty quiet lately," Gerald said. "Waiting gets me itchy."

Jericho puffed his cigar. "The calm before the storm, my friend. Enjoy it while you can. Things may heat up sooner than you think."

"Maybe." Gerald hooked his thumbs into his gun belt and looked up and down the empty street. It didn't look to him like anything much was about to heat up except maybe the sun coming down to give Coyote Flats a good afternoon baking. "It's hot enough, I reckon."

"I can't argue with that," Jericho said. "Be a good fellow and grab us a couple of beers."

Gerald went back inside. There was nobody behind the bar, so he drew the beers himself and took them back outside. He handed one to his boss.

Jericho drank deeply, then smacked his lips. "That hits the spot."

Gerald drank his too. It didn't hit the spot as much as a shot of whiskey would have, but the boss said beer, so Gerald got beer.

Gerald looked around, made sure nobody was nearby, then pitched his voice low and said, "Mr. Jericho, I could round up the boys right now, take them over to Lorenzo's and be done with this right quick. Or tonight after they got some drinks in them. You'd be in charge of this town by tomorrow morning."

"Perhaps." Jericho grabbed his walking stick, ran a thumb over the cool, smooth metal of the ram's head. "But not quite yet."

"You don't think we're ready?"

"Let's say . . . ninety-nine percent ready."

Gerald had no idea how the boss could put a number to such a thing, but the boss was the boss. "If it was dice or cards, I'd take those odds."

"But it isn't dice or cards," Jericho said. "It's your life, and more importantly, mine as well. We'll only get one crack at this, Gerald, and it's going to be done exactly right when we're one hundred percent certain of success. It will be done under my terms to guarantee the best outcome."

Gerald kept silent, but Jericho read that silence exactly right.

"You weren't here when Benson Crowley was boss."

Gerald shook his head. "No sir. I came right after."

"Benson Crowley did a respectable job of running Coyote Flats," Jericho said. "I was his right-hand man, and Lorenzo was his left . . . although it's the other way around if you ask Lorenzo."

Gerald nodded. "That's pretty much the way I heard it."

"I collected from the merchants and tradesmen . . . the in-town folk," Jericho said. "A sort of safety tax. They pay us weekly, and we see their businesses don't burn to the ground. That sort of thing."

Gerald knew that already. He went along on a number of the collections each week.

"Lorenzo collected from the ranchers and farmers," Jericho said. "People on the outskirts. A couple of prospectors too, if I remember correctly. A rougher sort of folk. Lorenzo's type. It was a good system and worked well for a long time."

Gerald knew what happened next in the story. "Until Crowley died."

Jericho *tsked*. "A shame really. Just dropped dead one day throwing a stick for his dog to fetch. A beautiful golden retriever. The doc said Benson's heart gave out. He wasn't even that old, not really."

"And that's when all hell broke loose," Gerald said.

Jericho shook his head. "Actually, no. There were a few uneasy days while everyone wondered what was going to happen. Looking back, I suppose I should have done something right then, called Lorenzo into a dimly lit back room to have a drink and work everything out and then simply stabbed him in the back. But we let it go on too long, and he gathered his people around him, and I gathered mine, and it got bloody for a while, each of us thinking he was Crowley's natural heir. And then we both noticed the same thing at the same time."

Gerald raised an eyebrow, curious. For once, he didn't know what was coming next in the story. "What was that?"

"Nobody was paying," Jericho said. "Not the in-town folks, and not the people on the outskirts. They were all waiting out the war, hoping Lorenzo and I killed each other. That's when Lorenzo and I decided to call the truce, and that's where we are today. Another reason that when I finally do make my move, it has to be the right time and in the right way. Transitions of power can be smooth, or they can be bloody. I prefer smooth."

"But what if it has to be bloody?" Gerald asked.

"Don't be so eager, Gerald. Lorenzo has some hard men working for him. Do you really want to go up against Big Mike?"

Gerald frowned. "Big Mike's no faster than me."

"He's good with his fists," Jericho said. "I've seen him take on two men at once, beat them right into the dust."

"Guns beat fists."

"I suppose that's true," Jericho said. "But I still want to proceed with caution. When the time is right, we can . . . oh, my. Look at this."

Gerald followed Jericho's gaze. A man on a black horse came down the street. Gerald didn't see why the boss would find it so interesting that a man on a horse—

McCoy.

Gerald had completely forgotten about the bounty hunter who'd come looking for Larry Prince.

"What's he doing back?"

"An excellent question," Jericho said. "I rather thought we'd seen the last of Ghost McCoy."

McCoy glanced over as he rode by, face blank, offering a curt nod.

Jericho returned the nod with an equal lack of warmth.

Gerald grunted. "Don't look like such a hard man to me."

"Never underestimate an opponent, Gerald," Jericho told him. "I have a feeling things are about to get interesting."

McCoy had to admit that Jericho was one cool customer He returned McCoy's nod, but there was no telling if he was surprised or upset or anything. McCoy rode on. If Jericho was going to be a problem, then he was a problem for later.

He dismounted in front of Carmen's Place, looped the horse's reins around the hitching post, and went inside.

A few ragged derelicts haunted the bar, but otherwise, the saloon wasn't seeing much business. No surprise. It was still early. McCoy went to the bar and waited.

A few minutes later, a man in an apron came out of the back room. It was a different barkeep than when McCoy had been here before. This guy was tall, with plenty of shoulders, and five days' growth on a chin you might break your knuckles on.

"Sorry," he said. "Didn't know anyone was here. Get you something?"

"Can you tell Carmen I'm here?"

"Why? You somebody special?"

"Name's McCoy."

"So what?"

"So tell her."

"Mister, I don't run and fetch the boss lady just because someone asks," the barkeep told him. "That's why she's the boss lady. She don't talk to just anyone."

McCoy sighed. "Look, I get it. You're doing your job. But I promise she'll want to talk to me. We have business."

"Do I have to come around this bar and toss you out on your ear?"

McCoy's face went hard. "You come around this bar, and you'll be picking up teeth."

The barkeep made a low growl in his throat, and McCoy saw the muscles in his neck flex. "You asked for it, mister."

He made the long walk around the bar, not hurrying, maybe hoping McCoy would come to his senses and leave. McCoy waited and let him come.

When the barkeep got to McCoy, he reached for him as if to get a fistful of McCoy's shirt, probably intending to drag him out.

McCoy let the barkeep extend his arm, then swung upward, hitting the barkeep on the point of his elbow with a hard knuckle. The barkeep hissed, his eyes going wide, and McCoy knew he felt the harsh, numbing tingle through his arm.

McCoy spun the man around, grabbed a fistful of hair, then slammed his face down on the bar hard. He heard the barkeep's nose crack, and the man howled in pain.

"Someone in the hospitality business should be more affable," McCoy said.

He kept pushing his face into the bar, smearing blood on the polished wood.

"Stop it! Stop it!" the barkeep shouted. "You're killing me!"

"Stop shouting, Joseph, you're embarrassing yourself."

Both men looked up to see that Carmen had entered the room. She looked as stunning as the last time McCoy had seen her. She wore a red blouse and black pants tucked into high leather riding boots, a flat-brimmed gaucho hat on her head, glossy black hair in a long braid down her back.

"Let him go, McCoy," she said. "You'll behave, won't you, Joseph?"

"Yes, ma'am," the barkeep said.

McCoy let him go.

Joseph stood slowly, rubbing his arm. Blood ran down his face from both nostrils. He had a bewildered expression, as if unable to comprehend what had just happened.

"Go see Doc Meyer down the street," Carmen told him. Tell him to send me the bill. I'll have Roy cover the bar."

"Yes, ma'am." Joseph turned to slink out of the saloon.

Carmen turned her attention to the bounty hunter, her sly smile somehow accusatory and amused at the same time. "You play too rough, Mr. McCoy."

"It's a rough world."

"We'd all thought you'd gone away," Carmen said. "What brings you back to Coyote Flats?"

"Maybe I missed you."

"Flattering if true," she said, "but somehow I think there's more to your being here."

"That's because you're not just a pretty face. Smart too. I want to talk to you."

"So talk."

"Over a drink would be better," McCoy said. "And in private."

"You understand I'm not to be had like the other girls in my employ," Carmen said in a warning tone.

"I wouldn't be interested then."

"Then let's have a drink," Carmen said. "As long as we understand it is just a *drink*."

"Lead the way."

She took him to an office in back which was everything she wasn't—drab, sparsely furnished, and strictly functional. A desk. A window looking out onto a side street. A bookshelf. A scratched and battered desk with a plain chair on each side.

McCoy looked around. "Not what I expected."

"And what did you expect?" Carmen asked. "Velvet drapes floor to ceiling? A tapestry depicting the Emperor Charlemagne? A desk of rich mahogany? Usually no one comes in here. I don't spend money on something nobody's going to see anyway."

"Practical."

"One often has to be practical in my line of work, but that doesn't mean I don't indulge myself on occasion." She reached into a desk drawer, came out with a bell and rang it, a high-pitched tinkle.

Two seconds later, an old Mexican woman entered. "*Sí, señora?*"

"A bottle of champagne and two glasses," Carmen told her.

"I usually drink whiskey," McCoy said.

"I usually don't," Carmen replied.

The old woman left, and it took her a little longer than expected to come back with the champagne and glasses.

"Do the honors, will you, Mr. McCoy?" Carmen asked, and dismissed the old woman.

McCoy took the champagne in a tight grip and popped the cork with his thumbs. It bounced off the far wall. He poured some into each glass, watched it fizz. "What shall we drink to?"

"Opportunities," Carmen suggested.

"Opportunities," McCoy echoed.

They clinked glasses.

They drank.

McCoy was surprised to find the champagne cold. He told Carmen as much. "I doubt Coyote Flats is big enough for an icehouse."

"We're not," she said. "But there is a well in the cellar, a deep one. I always keep a bucket at the bottom with a few bottles to chill."

"Lucky there was water down there."

Carmen shrugged. "Not my luck. Another man's, and he did not seem very lucky in any other way. He chose the spot for a hotel, thinking the railroad would come through. It didn't. He sold the place at a loss, and the next owner thought he could make money with girls and whiskey. He was right, and I was one of those girls."

"And now you're the owner."

"As you pointed out earlier, I'm more than just a pretty face."

McCoy sipped his champagne, mulling the woman

in front of him, and her place in a town like Coyote Flats. "You must be pulling off some kind of balancing act. Lorenzo on one side and Jericho on the other."

"It's worked out well for me, actually," Carmen said. "My place is neutral ground . . . neutral ground that happens to provide spirits and companionship to anyone with the money to pay for it. Business has been quite good."

"But your bread isn't buttered evenly on both sides," McCoy pointed out. "Sooner or later, Lorenzo and Jericho are going to lock horns. If Jericho comes out the loser, where does that put you?"

Carmen sipped champagne, then set the glass on the desk. "Do you think Jericho the sort of man to allow that to happen?"

"I guess that's what I'm supposed to find out," McCoy said. "I'm guessing you think I should talk to Jericho before accepting any kind of offer from Lorenzo. Does that still go?"

"So that's why you're here." Carman absently ran a slender finger around the rim of her champagne glass. "And I thought it was because you missed me."

"It can be two things."

"Yes, go and see him," Carmen said.

"I will. In the morning. You still got a room I can rent?"

"Absolutely. More champagne?"

McCoy stood. "No thanks. It gives me heartburn."

"Going so soon?"

"I'm going to put my horse up at the stable," McCoy told her. "Then I might have a look around Coyote Flats. I didn't see much last time I was here."

"It won't take you long."

He went to the door to show himself out, paused, looked back at her. "You and Jericho. Is that strictly a business arrangement? Or is he your type?"

That sly smile again, a little wan this time. "Does it matter?"

CHAPTER 10

McCoy stabled his horse, then began his slow stroll around Coyote Flats. He wasn't sure what he was looking for. Maybe he just wanted to get the feel of the place. He passed a tanner, a cartwright, and a grocer, doing more or less what tanners, cartwrights, and grocers did anywhere else.

He stopped at a victualling house for an early supper, where he ate a steak that was like chewing an old boot served with lumpy mashed potatoes and cold beans. He hoped there was another place in town to get a meal.

McCoy felt eyes on him as he walked the streets of Coyote Flats. Hard men leaning against porch railings, hats pulled low over narrowed eyes. Maybe Jericho's men. Maybe Lorenzo's. Probably both. Did they eyeball all newcomers that way? Or had they been told to keep tabs on Garret McCoy specifically? It didn't matter. McCoy was going about his own business and didn't need to explain himself to anybody.

He paused in front of a dry goods store called Miller's and ran his hand along his jaw. Five days' worth of stubble, and he was fresh out of shaving soap. He went inside to see what they had.

The man behind the counter looked as if he'd just finished being middle-aged and was deciding to give old a try. A bald and spotted pate, gray on the sides just above the ears, and an equally gray, bushy mustache that hung over his upper lip.

He looked up from his ledger and saw McCoy. "Help you, young fella?"

"Shave soap?"

The old man took a bar down from the shelf behind him. "This sells well enough. Has a pleasant aroma."

"Nothing too sweet, I hope," McCoy said.

"No, no, not for a gentleman such as yourself," the old man said. "This has a subtle musk with a hint of evergreen."

"A hint of evergreen, huh?"

"That's right."

"Okay, keep it here on the counter while I look around."

"As you like, sir, and please let me know if I can be of further assistance."

"Says *Miller's* on the sign," McCoy said. "That you?"

"I'm Walt Miller, yes, sir," the old man confirmed.

"Good to meet you, Mr. Miller. I'll have a look around your store."

"By all means."

McCoy didn't really need anything more than the shave soap, but he was in no particular hurry and was still trying to get a feel for the town and the folks in it.

He wandered along, glancing at the dry goods on the shelves.

The shop's front door creaked open again, and three men entered.

McCoy immediately recognized them from the Thirsty Coyote—Jericho's men, the one with the fancy silver around his hat and a couple of bruisers to back him up. The bruisers stood by the door, but fancy-pants went straight to the counter, leaned on it, snarling at the old man.

"Where were you yesterday, Miller?"

"Sorry, Gerald, Sarah was ill, so I didn't open the shop. She's not as young as she used to be, you know?"

"That's sad," Gerald said. "But yesterday was collection day, and as I recall, last time on collection day, you couldn't be found either. Do you think we're stupid, Miller?"

"Now, well, Gerald, I assure you that was just a coincidence." There was a nervous edge to Miller's voice. "I would never try to cheat Mr. Jericho out of his money. You know that."

"I hear you, Walt, I really do, but I can't help but think a gentle reminder might be in order, so you don't forget next time." Gerald nodded at the two bruisers.

One swept his arm along a shelf of lanterns which were knocked to the floor, glass breaking. The other tipped over a shelf of crockery which smashed on the floor. They laughed while they did it.

Gerald nodded his approval. "I think when you're sweeping that up, Walt, it'll sink in that you need to make yourself available on collection days. I'd hate to have to come back with the boys and really do a number on this store. Consider yourself lucky we didn't—"

Gerald broke off, head turning as he noticed McCoy for the first time.

"You looking at something, mister?"

"Just here for some shave soap," McCoy said.

Gerald squinted. "Oh . . . it's you. I heard you might be coming around to see Mr. Jericho."

"Word travels fast."

"It's a small town," Gerald said. "You want some advice?"

"Not especially."

"You're getting it anyway," Gerald told him. "Stay on Mr. Jericho's good side."

McCoy shrugged. "I'm just here for shaving soap."

"And I'm just here to collect." Gerald reached over the counter, grabbed a small metal box, opened it, and emptied the money onto the counter. "Your payment . . . plus interest for not being here yesterday."

Gerald scooped up all the money, then nodded to the bruisers. "Come on, boys. We're done here."

And they left.

Miller let out a heavy sigh.

"You okay?"

"I will be," Miller said. "I'm sorry you had to see that. I feel ashamed, I guess, letting myself get pushed around like that. I'm just an old man."

"Three men with guns," McCoy said. "Hard to stand up to that, whatever your age."

"I've thought about getting out, but Sarah and I are too old to pack up and start over somewhere else," Miller said. "And she hasn't been well lately. You'd think maybe we'd all band together and stand up to Jericho and his men, but if Jericho got wind of it, that would go hard for us. Easier just to pay, I suppose. Trying times indeed, but never mind me. You didn't come in here to listen to me bellyache about my woes."

"I reckon a man has a right to bellyache some if the woes are bad enough."

"Well, I thank you for that," Miller said. "Is there anything I can do for you before I get to cleaning up?"

"Just the shaving soap." McCoy handed him a dollar.

"I'm afraid you've caught me at an awkward moment," Miller said. "I'm unable to make change."

"Keep it." McCoy took the soap from the counter.

A wan smile from Miller. "Very kind, sir. Very kind indeed."

McCoy went back to the stable, grabbed his saddlebags from his horse, and went to Carmen's Place.

There were a few more people in the saloon now, drinking and sharing casual conversation. The big barkeep called Joseph wiped down the bar with a rag. He had a bandage across his nose, dark circles under his eyes. He looked up as McCoy approached.

"I apologize for our earlier misunderstanding." Joseph didn't sound too earnest about it, but at least there was no hostility in his voice.

"Forget it," McCoy said. "Carmen said I could get a room."

"She told me. I can't leave the bar, now that customers are coming in, but I'll get one of the girls to show you." He scanned the room quickly. "Cherry, get over here, will ya?"

Cherry bounced over. To McCoy, she seemed everything Carmen wasn't. All smiles and brightness; whereas, Carmen was dark and mysterious.

"Cherry, show Mr. McCoy to his room." Joseph handed her the key.

She took the key, beamed her smile at McCoy, and grabbed his hand, pulling him along. "Come on, Mr. McCoy. I'll show you."

Cherry led McCoy upstairs and down a short hall, then unlocked the room for him and took him inside.

"Thanks." McCoy tossed his saddlebags onto the bed.

Cherry went to the window and spread the curtains. "This is a good room. You can see down the street all the way to the Thirsty Coyote."

There was a vanity with a ceramic basin and matching pitcher. McCoy checked the pitcher. Fresh water. He went to his saddlebags and took out his straight razor. He went back to the vanity, poured some water into the basin.

Cherry pointed through the window. "And across the street is the bakery. It smells so good in the morning when they do the bread."

McCoy started to unbutton his shirt, paused, and looked sideways at Cherry. "I was going to have a shave."

"Go ahead. I don't mind." She plopped down onto the bed, belly first, chin resting in her hands, legs kicking behind her. "I like to watch a man shave."

"I appreciate you're in business," McCoy said. "But I'm not here for that."

"I know," Cherry said. "That's why it's nice just to hang around and chat. I don't get to do that with too many men, just talk without him wanting to get at me."

McCoy shrugged. He took off his shirt and draped it over the back of a chair. He sloshed the soap around in the basin a bit and then rubbed it on his face.

"Where you from, Mr. McCoy?"

"Call me Garret if you want."

"Where you from, Garret?"

McCoy considered how to answer, rubbing the lather up and down each jaw, along his chin, under his nose. "Not from anywhere, I guess. Move around a lot. There's no place I go back to, if that's what you mean. Where you from?"

"Here, now, I guess," Cherry said. "But I was born in a little place just outside Fort Worth."

"How'd you end up in Coyote Flats?"

"My ma and pa died." She said it matter-of-factly, as if any sadness connected to the event had long faded. "They ran a boarding house. I guess I was supposed to inherit it, but I was too young or something. I don't know. My uncle did all the talking to the lawyer, and then my uncle sold it and kept the money, and I guess he sort of sold me too and I ended up here."

"That doesn't seem like a very family thing to do," McCoy said.

"I didn't even know I had an uncle until he showed up and took everything," Cherry said. "But it could be a lot worse. At least I work for Miss Carmen. I wouldn't care to do this kind of thing working for a man. Carmen at least has been there and knows how it is, if you catch my meaning."

"Yeah, I think I understand."

"What's that?"

"What's what?"

"Down low on your back almost to the waist," she said. "To the left a little."

McCoy understood what she meant, an old, puckered scar of pink flesh. "There's where a surgeon dug a Confederate musket ball out of me."

"Did it hurt?"

"Like the dickens."

McCoy made long, easy scrapes down one side of his jaw and then the other, shaved until his whole face was smooth. He took the pitcher, splashed water into one hand, then slapped it on his face to wash away the excess soap. A clean towel hung from a bar on the side of the vanity. He used it to pat himself dry.

He turned to Cherry. "How's that?"

She hopped up from the bed and ran two fingers down his jawline. "Nice. You're handsome."

"Thanks. I've been practicing."

That made her laugh.

"Well, I need to get back downstairs, I guess." She went to the door, opened it, paused and looked back. "I meant what I said about it being nice to talk to a man without nothing happening but talk. Thanks. But if you did . . . I mean, if you changed your mind . . .?"

McCoy smiled. "I know where to find you."

She smiled back and closed the door as she left.

McCoy went to the window. Just as Cherry had told him, the Thirsty Coyote was in plain sight. McCoy would need to go there tomorrow to pay Jericho a visit, not because he especially needed to hear what the man had to say—although he was curious—but because

Carmen had asked him to, and he didn't want Jericho taking it out on her if he didn't show.

But that was tomorrow.

Tonight he wanted a couple drinks and maybe some friendly talk with some local folks as if he were a regular person and not some tough-skinned bounty hunter. Maybe he'd even get a late supper, something decent to wipe away the memory of the chewy steak earlier.

It wouldn't last, of course. Garret "Ghost" McCoy wasn't a regular person. Sooner or later, he'd have to be the bounty hunter again.

And that would mean blood.

CHAPTER 11

Night fell, and Carmen's Place quickly began to fill. There was something in the air, an extra rowdiness, some unexplained festive spirit that could carry through into the wee hours, a long, boisterous night of cheerful fellowship. Or that same spirit could turn sour with too much drink, too many losing hands at cards, too many men and too few women to meet the demand.

Cherry had seen it go both ways. Already a half dozen men had promised to come find her after they tossed back a few drinks with the boys. Even odds they'd all get drunk and forget. Or they'd all remember at once and there'd be a fight. Mostly everyone behaved. Carmen didn't like trouble in her place.

But every now and then there was just one of those nights.

And Cherry could feel that tension getting tighter and tighter as each hour passed. She hoped she was mistaken. She hoped so.

The saloon filled with bodies and smoke, and it got that smell it always did on crowded nights, sweat and tobacco and whiskey and beer, all of it combining into an oppressive cloud until once or twice an hour she had to go outside and breathe in a big lungful of cool night air.

Cherry stood out there a little longer than usual, knowing she needed to get back but not quite able to make herself relinquish the cool solitude of the back alley. The muffled revelry reached her from the saloon, but it was subdued and far away and like it had nothing to do with her.

But it had plenty to do with her, especially since they were a girl short, Doris being down hard with cramps from her monthlies. She sighed and almost turned to go back inside when—

Movement across the alley, someone in the shadows.

Cherry gasped. "Is somebody there?"

"*Lo siento mucho*." A young man stepped into the light, hands up in a *no problem here* gesture. "I did not mean to startle you."

She paused, curious, but leaned toward the door behind her in case she suddenly needed to dart back inside, her posture like a tense rabbit's ready to flee. "Who are you?"

He smiled. "I am called Enrique. Enrique Vargas."

Cherry thought him handsome and eased the tension in her limbs, not moving toward him, but no longer ready to run. He was her age, maybe a year older, but certainly no more than that. "What are you doing, skulking around in the dark, Enrique?"

His smile wilted a little. "I want to go inside, but I am embarrassed. I do not think I would be welcome."

"Oh?" Was it because he was Mexican? Cherry had seen Mexicans in the saloon on occasion, but not too many. Anyway, that didn't make sense. Miss Carmen was Mexican, and she owned the whole dang place.

"I caused trouble the last time I was inside," Enrique admitted. "I was foolish."

"You seem nice to me," Cherry said. "If you did come inside, you could buy me a drink, and I could keep you company."

Enrique's smile returned with renewed enthusiasm. "Maybe that is the final courage I will need. Thank you."

Cherry went back inside, pausing to look back and smile at the young man one last time.

The saloon had become more crowded in the short time she'd been out back. Joseph frowned at her from behind the bar. She was supposed to be working the room. She waved sheepishly and headed into the crowd of men, smiling and batting eyelashes, a light touch on the arm here, bump of the hip there. Appreciative smiles or leering looks from the men, but so far no takers.

Cherry ran into Claudia in the middle of the crowded saloon floor, a lanky brunette with long, long legs.

"They're not drunk enough yet," Claudia said. "Give them a couple more hours."

Cherry frowned. She supposed that could be good or bad, either one. Drunker men meant she was more likely to land some business. On the other hand, you could never tell what some fella might do, especially with a few extra drinks in him.

"Where's Missy?" Cherry asked.

Claudia rolled her eyes. "Upstairs, of course."

Cherry nodded. That just figured. Missy never had trouble getting business. She was about the most gorgeous thing on two legs with a big pile of corn-yellow hair on top of her head and a curvy figure. It could be a slow Sunday afternoon in the middle of a winter blizzard, and Missy would still find a way to land a client.

Cherry waded back into the crowd, flirting and waiting for the men to drink more.

She looked up and saw Garret McCoy slowly coming down the stairs. He wore a new, clean shirt, and it struck Cherry again that he was a handsome man, and he seemed nice. She liked him, and she was pretty sure he liked her too, although in a big brother sort of way. Cherry wouldn't be getting any business out of him tonight.

And that was fine too, really. It was a good thing to be able to look at a man now and then without having to wonder what it would take to part him from his money.

Cherry went to the bar and tried unsuccessfully to strike up a conversation with a few men, although truth be told, she didn't try very hard.

Then she felt a tap on her shoulder.

Cherry turned, saw him, her grin nearly splitting her face in two. "Enrique!"

He stood sheepishly, a foolish, lopsided grin, holding his sombrero in front of him with both hands. "Nobody seems to mind that I'm here."

Cherry looked around. Nobody paid them any attention. What was one more fella in a crowded bar? "I'm glad you came inside."

"I suppose . . . I mean I would be honored to buy you . . . I mean if you're not busy or anything. You'd mentioned before about a drink or . . . but only if . . ."

She laughed. "You can buy me a drink. I'd like that."

"Okay, yes, of course, uh, yes," he stammered, as if surprised she hadn't sent him away.

But why would she? He was handsome and shy, which she liked, and anyway the girls were encouraged to get men to buy drinks for them. She wouldn't make as much as she would if she took him upstairs, but maybe that would happen later.

Or maybe not at all, and they could just chat nicely like normal folks while sipping whiskey.

Enrique turned to the crowded bar but couldn't see how to get close.

"Let me." Never a bashful girl, Cherry pushed in between two men at the bar, waving a slender, pale hand in the air. "Joseph! Two whiskeys."

Enrique gave her the money, and she traded it to Joseph for the whiskey. They found a spot near the far wall off to the side where the crowd didn't press in on them so closely, and smiled at each other over their drinks.

"I'm glad you came inside," Cherry told him.

"I came here for other reasons," Enrique said. "But now that I am talking to you, I forget what those other reasons are."

"Oh?" Cherry raised an eyebrow, her smile going impish and quirky. "I can't really be that interesting, can I?"

"Outside, your smile seemed so friendly," Enrique said. "You seemed a very warm and friendly person to me."

Cherry felt her cheeks go pink. Men had complimented her looks—hair, legs, backside—so many times that the compliments had become meaningless. *Warm* was new. That somebody might think her friendly was such a simple thing, it might have been the nicest thing anyone had ever said to her.

They sipped their drinks, just looking at each other,

both feeling a strange buzz of excitement they'd never felt before. Cherry had the sudden wish to stretch this moment into two or three or all night, to make it last.

But, of course, it didn't.

"Cherry, I been looking for you everywhere."

She turned her head, saw who it was, and her smile fell hard, landed in little pieces at her feet. She recovered quickly, bringing the smile back wider, with more teeth, but it felt like such a lie on her face, it was almost painful. "Gerald. Hello."

"Come on, doll, let's you and me go upstairs." Gerald took her by the arm.

Enrique bristled. His face went from shy and friendly to hard and angry so quickly, it almost made Cherry flinch. All the girls had to handle situations like this. It was one of the first things Cherry learned after coming to Carmen's Place.

She put a hand gently on Gerald's forearm. "I just need to finish my drink with this gentleman. Just give me a few minutes, and I'll be along."

Cherry didn't want to see Gerald in a few minutes, but it was her job, and suddenly she thought that was the saddest thing in the world. She felt leaden and queasy, and it was more that the hot, smoky, close feeling of the saloon's interior.

Gerald looked at Enrique. "You've had your drink. Go on now."

The whiskey on Gerald's breath was like a slap in the face to Cherry.

"I'll go when the lady says," Enrique told him.

Cherry could see the muscles in Enrique's jaw working, his whole body going tense.

"You'll go when I say." Gerald let go of Cherry and took a step toward Enrique. The two men were nearly nose to nose now. "If you don't like it, I'm happy to make you go."

And just like that, it was no longer about her. Cherry had seen it a hundred times. She took a step back.

"Sir, you are rude and drunk," Enrique said. "I suggest it is you who should go on your way."

Two men pushed past Cherry to stand behind Gerald. She recognized them as more of Jericho's muscle. Carmen's Place was supposed to be neutral ground, but this wasn't a dispute between Jericho and Lorenzo. This was a fight over a woman . . . except that wasn't really true either. It was about who was going to back down, and from what Cherry knew of Gerald, he wouldn't hesitate to let his friends do some of the fighting for him.

Enrique saw what was happening and scowled. "Big man. You need your boys here to help you?"

"I need you gone," Gerald said. "How it happens is nothing but details."

Cherry turned away and pushed through the crowd toward the bar. There would be a little more tough talk, but then one of three things would probably happen, at least according to her prior experience. One of the men might back down and slink away, but Cherry had a feeling that wasn't going to be an option this time. Or the two men involved could start throwing fists, not a good outcome for Enrique if Gerald's pals joined the fight. Or in extreme circumstances, guns might be drawn.

Men mostly seemed to know when to do that and when not to, but Gerald had been drinking, and even sober he was a hothead.

Cherry pushed her way through to the bar. "Where's Joseph?" The barkeeps kept a sawed-off shotgun under the counter. Often just showing it was enough to cool down a heated situation.

"That's a good question," said the cowboy next to her. "I been trying to get a dang beer all night."

"Now, don't exaggerate, Bart," another man said. "He just went in the back to get more clean glasses."

Somebody started playing the piano.

Cherry didn't know what to do. She looked frantically around the saloon, trying to think.

She saw Garret McCoy. He sipped a beer and was having a casual conversation with the old man who ran the dry goods store. He didn't come in very often, and she could never remember his name.

"Mister McCoy!" She pushed through the crowd toward him. "Mister McCoy!"

McCoy looked up from his beer when he heard someone calling his name.

It was that young redhead Cherry, making her way through the crowd toward him. He started to smile and wave, then stopped himself. Something about the look on her face. Something was wrong.

"Mister McCoy!" Cherry latched on to his arm. "I need your help."

"What's wrong?" he asked.

"You've got to come break up this fight!" Cherry pleaded.

McCoy shook his head and laughed. "Fights happen in a saloon sometimes." It was nice the girl wanted to keep the peace, but that wasn't McCoy's job. "Tell one of the barkeeps. Smitty or Joseph."

"I can't find him," she said desperately. "Please, Mister McCoy. Gerald's been drinking and he's got two of his boys with him and they're going to gang up on my friend."

McCoy's eyes narrowed. "You mean that swaggering dolt that works for Jericho?"

"I guess that pretty much describes him," Cherry said. "He and two of his buddies are about to give Enrique a pounding."

McCoy sighed. "Enrique *Vargas*?"

Her eyes went round with surprise. "How did you know—"

"Mister Miller, can you hold my beer a minute?" McCoy handed his mug to the old dry goods man.

"Oh, uh, certainly," Miller said.

"Show me where they are," McCoy told Cherry.

She grabbed his hand and dragged him along, shouldering her way through the crowd, men stepping out of the way as if she were a brawny circus strongman and not a little saloon gal. McCoy was still hesitant to insert himself into another man's quarrel, but he couldn't deny being curious. They arrived at the scene, and McCoy could see they were moments away from trouble. Gerald and his two sidekicks had Enrique backed up against the wall. The young Mexican looked as if he couldn't decide whether to put up his fists or reach for his six-shooter.

"Gents, this is no way to pass a pleasant evening," McCoy said. "Let's not ruin everyone's good time."

Gerald's lip curled into a sneer. "Get lost, McCoy. This don't concern you."

"Fair enough," McCoy said, voice still calm. "I guess three on one strikes me as a might unfair. Just thought I'd mention it."

"You've mentioned it," Gerald said, voice raised. "Now walk away."

Folks nearby turned their heads, only just realizing something was amiss. The talk died away a little, making the annoying, ragged piano tune seem louder. McCoy couldn't quite place it. Stephen Foster, maybe.

"I can fight my own fights," Enrique said.

"The point was maybe to avoid a fight altogether," McCoy replied.

Gerald growled. "You don't listen good, McCoy. I said take a walk." His hand fell to the six-shooter on his hip.

The sound of glass shattering as a bottle hit the back of Gerald's head. Somewhere one of the saloon gals screamed. Gerald staggered. The men around them backed away.

McCoy looked and saw that Cherry was holding the neck of a broken bottle. It had been her who'd clobbered Gerald.

Gerald shook his head, trying to clear the bells from his ears. His eyes fixed on McCoy, blazing hatred. He somehow missed it had been the saloon gal who'd whacked him with the bottle, and he came at McCoy, hands outstretched like he wanted to rip the man to shreds.

McCoy punched him square in the mouth.

Gerald staggered back, spitting blood, his legs going watery.

McCoy felt a heavy hand suddenly grab his shoulder from behind, one of Gerald's bruisers. McCoy jerked his arm back and caught the man with the point of his elbow in the center of his chest. The man grunted and stumbled back . . .

. . . into a table where four men played a game of draw poker.

The table upended, scattering poker chips and spilling drinks. Men shouted curses and began shoving. McCoy turned to see the entire saloon in an uproar. Someone shoved him from behind.

He went stumbling forward, almost righted himself, but then tripped over a man who went sprawling right in front of him. McCoy went sprawling and landed in a heap next to the piano. He looked up at the piano player, a haggard-looking man with a wooden leg and a battered hat. He attacked the upright piano with vigor, producing a clunky version of "Dixie."

"Can't you play something by the winners?" McCoy asked crossly. "'Lincoln and Liberty Too' maybe."

The piano player frowned. "I didn't leave a leg at Cold Harbor just to play no 'Lincoln and Liberty Too.'"

Fair enough.

McCoy heaved himself to his feet. Everyone in the place seemed to be taking a swing at everyone else, nobody quite sure what they were fighting about. He spotted Enrique. The young Mexican took a punch from Gerald's other bruiser, his head snapping around. McCoy pushed back through the crowd, almost stepping on Cherry.

He reached down and pulled her up. She had a bruise on her cheek.

She blinked at him. "I got knocked over."

"Will you get out of here, please, before you really

get hurt?" He gave her a gentle nudge toward the bar, where the brawl didn't seem so ferocious.

McCoy kept pushing through the crowd until he got to Enrique, who was locked with the bruiser, both dancing around trying to get leverage. He grabbed the bruiser, spun him around, and planted a hard one on his jaw with a loud flesh-on-flesh *smack*. The man stumbled but didn't go down.

McCoy punched him again, and the bruiser's eyes rolled up white. He wilted to the floor.

"Come on!" McCoy grabbed Enrique by the sleeve. "Let's get out of here!"

Enrique looked around frantically. "What about Cherry?"

"She can take care of herself," McCoy said. "Better than you."

They pushed their way to the back door, managing not to be drawn into any more fisticuffs. They erupted out the back door, into the relative cool and quiet of the back alley. Enrique bent double, hands on knees as he panted for breath.

"Not here," McCoy said.

He led them down the street and around a corner, where they stopped under an overhang, the shadows hiding them.

"I was having a nice evening until you showed up," McCoy said.

"I didn't ask for your help." Enrique smiled weakly. "But thanks."

McCoy waved it away. "Forget it."

"I fear you are going to get the wrong impression of

me, *señor*," Enrique said. "Every time I go in there, I seem to be involved in some sort of trouble."

"Maybe don't go in there."

"It has occurred to me," Enrique said. "But this time I didn't start it."

"If you're sweet on a saloon gal, you're going to expect things like that to happen," McCoy told him. "If I was you, I'd see your girlfriend when she's off duty and somewhere else."

"*Señor*, you misunderstand. I did not go there to see Cherry," Enrique said. "I only met her for the first time tonight."

"Then what are you doing here?"

"I came to see you, *señor*."

"*Me*?"

"*Sí!* I have word you have spoken with my brothers," Enrique said. "I'm told that you—"

"Don't talk about it here."

McCoy looked up and down the street. Nobody was around, but voices drifted from the alley around the corner, others making use of Carmen's back door to escape the raucous brawl.

"Go home," McCoy said. "I'll call on you at the right time."

"But, *señor*—"

"Go home and stay there," McCoy said more forcefully. "It's the only way we can be sure to keep you out of trouble."

CHAPTER 12

Garret McCoy waited a full hour. He knew that would be more than enough. Men could only punch each other for so long before running out of steam.

On the way back into Carmen's Place, he passed three cowboys coming out the front door, two dragging a third, unconscious, between them, all three looking battered and bruised. McCoy gave them a curt nod as he passed them and got nothing in return.

Just one of those nights, he reckoned.

The interior of Carmen's saloon had seen better days. Joseph and another barkeep went about the business of righting chairs and tables. The old woman who'd brought the champagne to Carmen swept up broken glass. There was no sign of any of the saloon gals. McCoy presumed they'd gone upstairs . . . with or without clients. He pushed his hat back on his head and whistled at the mess.

"I understand I have you to thank for this, Mr. McCoy."

He turned and saw her sitting in the corner, smoking a cigarette, with a small glass with a long stem and some sort of dark red liquid. It hardly looked more than a swallow, and McCoy wondered why bother.

"I tried to *stop* the fight," he told her.

Carmen frowned. "That's one version of the story, I suppose."

"It's the true version," he insisted. "Naturally, when things got physical, I was obliged to fight back."

"Of course." A blank expression as if she might not believe him and that it didn't really matter anyway. "Join me in a sherry?"

McCoy eyed the tiny glass with its thimbleful of liquid. "I reckon not."

"You've made things difficult," Carmen said. "Gerald's men had to drag him out of here half in a daze. I can't help but think that will taint your meeting tomorrow with Mr. Jericho."

"I don't much care for Gerald, and now that I give it some thought, I didn't much mind punching him in his smart mouth either," McCoy said. "So things have been tainted for a while, leastways from my point of view. I'm paying Jericho a visit tomorrow for one reason only. Because you asked me to."

They glared at each other for a long moment.

Then a crooked smile flickered across her face. "What else will you do if I ask?"

"Depends on what you ask," McCoy said. "And if you ask nice."

Carmen tossed back her sherry, set the glass back on the table, and stood. She kept eye contact with McCoy as she took a log drag on her cigarette, dropped it on the floor, then stamped the butt out with the toe of her boot.

She walked as if to go past McCoy but then paused next to him.

"I'll keep it in mind, Mr. McCoy. In the meantime"—she reached out and tapped his chest with a slender finger, the nail glistening with dark red polish—"behave yourself."

He grinned at her, not sure exactly what game they were playing but enjoying it.

"Sleep well, Mr. McCoy."

He watched her walk away into the back, probably to do some late-night accounting and figure what all this mess would cost her. He sighed and took a last look around. McCoy wouldn't have minded another drink, but the barkeeps were still cleaning, and he doubted they were in the mood to stop what they were doing and fetch him a whiskey.

McCoy went upstairs to his room.

He kicked off his boots and peeled himself out of his clothes. He hung his hat on the bedpost at the foot of his bead and his gun belt around the post at the head. He climbed into bed and closed his eyes.

A moment later, he got up, took the wooden chair, and jammed it under the doorknob.

Coyote Flats was that kind of town.

Nobody downstairs offered him breakfast in the morning, and he wasn't keen to hang around the saloon anyway, so he headed to the slop house where he'd eaten the terrible steak and ordered breakfast.

The coffee, at least, was good and strong.

But the biscuits were hard, the eggs runny, and the bacon burnt.

I really do need to find a different place to eat.

He lingered over another cup of coffee, finally decided he'd stalled enough, and paid for his meal before heading toward the Thirsty Coyote to see Jericho. It was a short walk, and he went inside.

The place was empty. McCoy stood at the entrance and waited to be noticed.

A man came in with a wooden crate of bottles, set them on the bar, and saw McCoy. "Help you?"

"I'm here to see Jericho."

"Oh?"

"I'm McCoy."

The other man frowned. "Oh."

Garret waited. He'd said all that needed saying.

The man cleared his throat, nodded. "Right. Okay, then, wait here. Back in a bit."

McCoy waited.

A few moments later, Jericho entered the room, looking dapper and twirling his walking stick, Gerald swaggering in right behind him.

"Mister McCoy, so good of you to spare me a moment," Jericho said. "Carmen mentioned you'd be around. A drink?"

"A might early for me."

"Coffee then."

McCoy shook his head. "Had some."

"Let's have a seat at least." Jericho took a chair at the center of the room. "We're civilized men, after all."

McCoy wasn't sure about that but took the chair opposite him.

"First, some unfinished business." Jericho twisted in his chair and waved Gerald forward.

Gerald had a fat lip and a purple-green bruise around one eye. He looked embarrassed at having taken a beating and angry that he was embarrassed. He stood there with his thumbs hooked in his gun belt, probably wishing he was anywhere else.

Jericho smiled pleasantly. "Gerald, I believe you have something to say to Mr. McCoy."

Gerald opened his mouth, closed it again, then looked at Jericho. "Boss, do I really have to—"

"Now, Gerald, we rehearsed this." Jericho's voice had gone from pleasant to stern. "You know how I hate to waste time, and repeating myself wastes time. Goading you into something you're going to do anyway wastes time."

Gerald cleared his throat and turned back to McCoy. "Sorry for the . . . uh . . . misunderstanding last night. Sorry to cause that commotion."

McCoy nodded. He'd known men like Gerald and knew it was sticking in his craw to make an apology like that. McCoy was enjoying Gerald's discomfort, but he'd have to be careful. Hotheaded fellas could only be pushed so far. Garret made a point not to turn his back on the man anytime soon.

"Forget it," McCoy said.

A curt nod from Gerald.

"See, and now we're all friends again," Jericho said. "Gerald, if you need to get some air, I'll understand."

"Thanks, Mr. Jericho." Gerald turned and stomped out of the saloon.

Jericho waited until Gerald was gone and then to

McCoy said, "Do you know why I did that? Why I made him apologize like that?"

McCoy shrugged. "You like watching him squirm?"

Jericho laughed. "I must confess it was a source of juvenile amusement for me, but no, I had something more important in mind. I wanted to show there would be no favorites. If you come to work for me, you won't be starting at the bottom of the totem pole. I value your skills, and you would be treated—and paid—with that in mind."

"I appreciate that, Jericho," McCoy said. "But I've been working for myself a long time. The pay's okay, and I like the hours. Also, I've never had a quarrel with the boss."

"You make some fair points, I'll admit. Let me be frank, Mr. McCoy. If you're going to be in Coyote Flats any length of time, it's going to be more and more difficult to sit on the fence when the inevitable conflict comes. I'd prefer it if you were with us." And then Jericho's face and demeanor subtly hardened, barely noticeable but it was there, just enough to show he wasn't all laughs and good manners. "If you were against us, that would be . . . unfortunate."

"I didn't come for your conflict, Mr. Jericho," McCoy said. "I was chasing Larry Prince and just happened to end up in Coyote Flats."

"Yes, but you left after you gunned Prince, didn't you," Jericho reminded him. "So why did you come back? It would sadden me to hear you intended to throw in with Mortimer Lorenzo."

"Maybe I just like it here," McCoy said. "Maybe I came back for a pretty face."

A moment of confusion twisted Jericho's expression, but he recovered quickly and said, "A man's reasons are his own, I suppose, but you're here, and you're handy with a six-gun, and I'd like you on our side."

"As a courtesy, I'll give it serious thought," McCoy said. "But I don't think you'll convince me."

"I'm sorry to hear that, but if I can't convince you, then maybe somebody else can." Jericho looked past McCoy. "How about it, Dwight, want to have a go at convincing your friend?"

McCoy twisted in his chair.

Dwight Combs sat at a table with his feet up, a cup of coffee in a saucer in front of him. His table was all the way in the corner to the right of the door. A good spot, McCoy had to admit, a place where Dwight could watch anyone coming in, but nobody would see him unless they made a point to turn and look.

Which is exactly what McCoy *should* have done upon entering the place. He reminded himself not to get sloppy. His life might depend on it.

"Good Lord, Dwight, you been there the whole time?" McCoy asked.

"Just minding my own business." Dwight sipped coffee.

"In point of fact, Dwight is helping mind *my* business. I put him on the payroll a few days ago. Dwight, tell our friend Mr. McCoy here what a big, happy family we are." Jericho stood. "Speaking of happy families, I suppose I should chase Gerald down and smooth his ruffled feathers. That'll give you gentlemen a chance to talk frankly."

McCoy nodded at Jericho. "Obliged."

"Until later, gentlemen." And Jericho walked out of the saloon.

McCoy stood and went to Dwight's table, gestured at the other chair. "May I?"

Dwight took his feet off the table. "Take a load off."

McCoy sat.

Dwight sipped coffee.

"So are you going to convince me?" McCoy asked.

Dwight shook his head. "Would it do any good?"

McCoy thought about it. "No."

"Okay then."

McCoy chuckled. "But you threw in with him. Why?"

"It ain't so hard to understand, really," Dwight said. "I spent years running around after outlaws. Some I catch. Others I don't. A fella gets tired of running around. Maybe you haven't, but I have."

There was something to that, McCoy had to admit. Laying your head somewhere different every night could weary a man. Some nights he was in a fancy hotel with a soft bed and clean sheets. Other nights, he slept on the cold, hard ground with his saddle for a pillow. He was nearly always alone, and when he wasn't, it was a temporary situation. Garret "Ghost" McCoy didn't belong anywhere. Even proper ghosts usually had a house to haunt.

"And it ain't exactly hard work," Dwight said. "Sitting around looking mean, mostly."

"You know that won't last, Dwight," McCoy told him. "There's a showdown coming, and when it happens, the streets of Coyote Flats will run red with blood."

"I gun half the outlaws I bring in," Dwight said. "So

what's the difference? Blood is blood be it here or somewhere else, and I'm already here."

"The difference is we go after outlaws. We're not killers in some private war. It might be a paper-thin difference, words written on a wanted poster, but it's a difference."

Dwight shrugged. "Maybe. Handling a gun is all I know. I've made my decision. What comes will come. What about you?"

McCoy stood and sighed. "I guess I'll have to think on it."

"Don't think too long."

McCoy headed for the door.

"Ghost."

McCoy paused, looked back at the other gunslinger. "Yeah?"

"If you throw in with Lorenzo, that puts you opposite me."

"I guess that's right," McCoy said. "I wouldn't like it."

"What wouldn't you like?" Dwight asked. "Shooting me, or getting shot?"

A sad smile crossed McCoy's lips. "Neither much appeals. See you around, Dwight."

"See you around, Ghost."

McCoy walked out of the Thirsty Coyote and headed for the other end of town, where Lorenzo waited.

CHAPTER 13

It was a small town and a short walk.

McCoy strolled into Lorenzo's place and found the man himself sitting at a table, tucking into a plate of ham and eggs.

Lorenzo looked up, bit into a biscuit, and said, "I heard you were around." Crumbs fell out of his mouth while he talked. "Come have a seat."

McCoy crossed the room, pulled out a chair, and sat.

Lorenzo looked him in the eye, and again McCoy had that odd feeling that the man wasn't quite looking right at him.

Something strange about this fella's eyes.

"So are you going to work for me or not?" Lorenzo asked.

"Straight to it, huh?"

Lorenzo shrugged. "We both know why you're here. No sense beating around the bush."

McCoy nodded. "Right."

The temptation to draw his Peacemaker and gun Lorenzo where he sat was strong. He'd be justified, wouldn't he? The man had sent killers to do him in, after all.

But . . .

There was something about the man. A mystery. Unanswered questions. It itched at the back of McCoy's brain something fierce. McCoy would make sure Lorenzo got what was coming to him, but not until he had answers to those nagging questions.

"Well, what's it going to be?" prompted Lorenzo.

"I came back to Coyote Flats because I take your offer seriously, Mr. Lorenzo," McCoy said. "But I need to think on it a bit more."

Lorenzo grunted, dropped his fork on his plate. "What is it you need to think about? You need to think about who's going to offer you more money? I know you've been around to see Jericho. What's he offering? Give me a chance to beat it."

"I did talk to Jericho," McCoy admitted. "I told him the same thing I told you. I'm thinking on it. He didn't mention a specific amount of money, but I assume it would be handsome. There's more to something like this than money."

"Is there? Like what?"

"I reckon that's what I need to find out," McCoy said.

Lorenzo gave him that cockeyed look again. "You want to find out how I do things, is that it?"

"I guess that couldn't hurt."

"Big Mike's making a collection this afternoon," Lorenzo said. "Saddle your horse and go with him. You can see what a day's work looks like around here."

* * *

Big Mike didn't see what was so all-fired special about this Ghost McCoy fella and why the boss was so keen to have him join up. Sure, he could handle himself, Mike reckoned, but no better or worse than any other gunslinger. Some called him Ghost. Did that mean something? Was Mike supposed to be impressed?

Because he wasn't.

"We're almost there," Mike said.

McCoy grunted, sat easy in the saddle, seemingly unconcerned.

The two men rode next to one another, south out of Coyote Flats into ranching country. They'd been riding about an hour, and so far, Garret McCoy hadn't been much for conversation.

"Family named Hendershot," said Mike, who then remembered he'd already told McCoy that when they'd set out. "Old man's named Moses. Like in the Bible."

If McCoy gave a dang about that, he didn't let on.

"Why Hendershot?" McCoy finally asked.

"Because he owes us, and it's time to pay," Big Mike explained.

"No, I mean why show me?" McCoy said. "If you're just riding out to pick up some money and then riding back, what do I get out of seeing it firsthand?"

"Oh." Mike thought about it. "Maybe because there might be trouble, and Mr. Lorenzo wants you to see what trouble might look like."

"I've seen trouble in spades."

"I mean our particular flavor of trouble," Mike said. "Folks in town are easily cowed. Jericho thinks he's a hard man because he makes them pay, but these ranchers are a different breed. Takes a man like Lorenzo to keep them in line."

"Then why is Hendershot trouble?"

"*Maybe* trouble," Mike corrected. "Maybe not. Last time old Moses was in town, he was running his mouth and grumbling about having to pay over a tithe of his hard-earned money to the boss, especially when he wasn't getting nothing in return for it."

"He might have a point," McCoy said.

Mike scoffed. "Having a point ain't the point. The boss says pay, and that's the end of it."

"I guess that keeps it simple."

"Dang right," Mike said. "As for what Moses Hendershot gets in return for his money, he gets protection and leadership. Call it a tax, if that makes you feel better. Or a tariff. Or a fee. Don't matter. They pay, or it gets taken out of their hide."

"If there might be trouble, maybe Lorenzo should have sent more men," McCoy said.

Mike shrugged again. "If he pays, we'll take the money and go home. If he doesn't . . . well, we'll call it one of them fact-finding missions. We can always come back later with the rest of the boys. His ranch ain't going nowhere."

The familiar sight of the Hendershot ranch came into view, a long, low house built from heavy timber, a barn and a corral, and then somewhere farther south was a bunch of cows roaming the open range. Mike didn't know much about ranching, and he didn't *want* to know. He just wanted Moses Hendershot to make his usual payment, and then Mike could go back to Coyote Flats for a drink of whiskey.

Mike hoped to catch Moses on his own. Maybe the ranch hands would all be out tending the herd.

His hopes dried up and blew away as he drew nearer to the ranch house. Hendershot stood on the front porch, four men behind him—the ranch hands—all of them cradling rifles in the crooks of their arms.

"I guess they seen us coming," McCoy said.

Mike nodded. "I guess."

"That's close enough!" Moses Hendershot called from the front porch.

Big Mike and McCoy reined in their horses.

"Probably best if you just turn around and ride back," Hendershot said. "Less trouble all around."

"Now, you know that's not how it works, Moses," Mike told him. "It's time for your payment."

Moses came out from under the overhang and down the three steps from his porch. He was in his mid-sixties but stood straight and seemed hale enough. Mike wondered what he'd be doing at that age. Still riding around collecting payments? He hoped not.

Moses levered a shell into his Winchester's chamber and fired into the air. "I said git!"

Mike made to turn his horse around. "I guess we're coming back with the boys."

"Wait," McCoy said. "Let me try."

Mike gave him the fisheye. "Try what?"

"Talking."

Mike gestured toward the old man. "Good luck to you."

He watched McCoy, wondering what he thought he was going to do to dissuade an onery old man with a

Winchester from putting a bullet in him, but that wasn't Big Mike's problem.

"Mr. Hendershot, I'd like to come talk to you." McCoy dismounted from his horse. "I'm going to come over there."

"Come if you want," Hendershot said. "But you'll be talking from a new hole in your face."

McCoy took off his gun belt and draped it across his saddle horn. "I'm unarmed, okay? Don't shoot."

Hendershot hesitated, then let his rifle rest on his shoulder. "Come on then."

McCoy began walking toward the ranch house.

Mike halfway hoped the old man would shoot him. Then the boss would see there was nothing so special about this Ghost McCoy, letting an old man get the better of him. A moment later, the two of them stood talking. Mike wished he could hear what they were saying. Moses got a couple of off looks on his face a few times, as if not understanding—or not believing—what McCoy was saying to him.

Then Moses turned, went back up the stairs to the porch and inside the house. He came back out a minute later and handed something to McCoy. They exchanged a few more words, and Hendershot nodded.

McCoy returned, climbed onto his horse, and tossed a little leather sack to Mike. It clinked with coin when he caught it.

"There's your payment," McCoy said.

"What in the world did you say to him?" Mike asked.

McCoy grinned. "Surprising what a little polite conversation can do."

At first, Big Mike wasn't quite sure if he hated Garret McCoy or not.

Now he was positive.

Nobody had decided to throw a party at Mortimer Lorenzo's place. It just sort of happened. Big Mike had told Lorenzo what had happened, and Lorenzo had slapped McCoy on the back, said it was good to see he had some stones, and broke out a fresh bottle of booze.

Then every time somebody new would walk into the room, Lorenzo would repeat the story just a little more dramatically and pour another round of drinks.

Had the brass to walk right up to the old man and demand the money.

Whiskey.

Wasn't even wearing his guns. Didn't bat an eye.

More whiskey.

Fella has guts, let me tell ya.

Whiskey. Whiskey. Whiskey.

The place was jammed full, the night growing late. McCoy tried to pace himself, but he was starting to feel the whiskey. Then there was food—fried chicken, beans, corn on the cob.

Then more whiskey.

Lorenzo was in a fine mood, and McCoy had to wonder if he'd been looking for an excuse to be in a good mood for a while now, and McCoy just happened along. In spite of the fact Lorenzo had sent men to kill him, McCoy felt he was almost having a good time.

Almost.

Lorenzo put a friendly arm around Big Mike. "Didn't

I tell you this fella would be an asset to the organization? I told you, didn't I?"

"You told me," Mike said, without sounding too happy about it.

Lorenzo talked as if McCoy had already accepted his job offer, even though McCoy had said nothing of the kind. He supposed it was a reasonable assumption, since McCoy had gotten his money for him from Hendershot. He let them think what they liked. McCoy could correct them later if he needed to.

Big Mike turned his gaze on McCoy. "What *did* you say to Moses Hendershot?"

McCoy had thought about that while riding back from the Hendershot ranch, knew he'd be asked about it eventually. He cleared his throat and said, "I just made it clear we'd be back."

A smattering of laughter across the room.

"I think that was already implied," Lorenzo said.

"There's more." McCoy let his voice go flat. "I said he must be brave because surely he knew we'd come back and kill him. When you're an old man maybe you're so close to death it don't bother you. But it wasn't just his life he was putting on the line. Did he have a wife? He said he did. So I said she'd be dead too. And any sons or daughters he had or grandsons and granddaughters. And all the ranch hands too, and any wives they had. And any children. And dogs and cats and chickens. Horses. His entire herd. The flies over the corpses would be so thick, that miles away people would think it was a storm cloud rolling in. And eventually, maybe years from now, long after the names of the dead were forgotten, people would still know the area as a place of death, and they'd ride around miles out of their way just to avoid it."

The room had gone stone silent.

"Dang," Big Mike whispered. "That's dark."

Lorenzo's bark of laughter was so sudden, it made those around him flinch. "I wish I could have seen old Moses's face when you told him that. No wonder he paid up."

Slowly, men picked up their conversations again, but the atmosphere was less jovial than before.

Lorenzo rubbed his eyes as if suddenly fatigued. "Mike, fetch my patch, will ya?"

"Sure, boss." Mike left.

Lorenzo sipped his drink and blew out a long sigh, then leaned forward and lowered his voice. "Some of these boys are downright superstitious. Don't let it bother you. I need men with some meanness in them, men who won't hesitate when the fighting gets down and dirty."

Mike returned and handed something to Lorenzo. "Here you go, boss."

McCoy couldn't quite see what it was, maybe a small piece of black cloth.

"Thanks, Mike." Lorenzo began rubbing his left eye.

As McCoy watched, something peculiar happened. Lorenzo rubbed at his eye a little harder, and then in the next instant, he was digging at the corner of his eye with his thumb, prying out the eyeball. It popped out, and Lorenzo caught it with his other hand.

Lorenzo must have seen the surprise on McCoy's face. He said, "You didn't know, did you?"

McCoy shook his head.

"Glass. I get them from Germany, if you can believe that," Lorenzo said. "Ordered three different ones before I got one that looked real enough. Cost an arm and a leg. It looks all right, but sometimes it begins to pain me by the end of the day."

McCoy watched as Lorenzo slipped the glass eye into his vest pocket. Then he took the cloth Big Mike had given him and began to fasten it around his head. It was an eye patch, covering his left eye.

McCoy blinked at the man . . . Lorenzo's face . . .

In the middle of the muddy road, McCoy's father was on his knees. One of the marauders stood behind him, a six-gun pointed at the back of his head. The marauder was a porky fellow with a greasy sneer. McCoy gasped, eyes widening with growing fear. There was blood on his father's face, at the corners of his mouth, one eye swollen closed, black and blue. His father didn't even look frightened, McCoy thought, just tired, head hanging, shoulders slumped.

McCoy stared at Lorenzo's face, the familiarity flooding back after seeing the man put on the eye patch. He imagined him without the beard.

Another stranger paced back and forth in front of his father, sharp featured, thin but straight, a sneering expression on his face. McCoy had seen the man before. The patch over his left eye had made him memorable.

McCoy swallowed hard, the memory kicking around inside his guts, almost making him sick.

The porky marauder lifted his six-shooter and shot Warren McCoy in the back.

Lorenzo was still talking, but McCoy didn't hear it,

the man's voice had been muffled, cottony and distant. McCoy was dazed. Disbelieving. But he looked again, and saw it was true.

Garret McCoy sat across from the man who'd ordered his father's death.

CHAPTER 14

His mother had chastised him for going into town, even more so than McCoy had. Both had the same message for Enrique Vargas.

Stay home.

Enrique supposed he should listen to McCoy. He was the sort of man who knew how the world worked, and he'd spoken with Enrique's brothers. They had some sort of plan, and Enrique might ruin it if he refused to be patient.

And as for his mother, well she was . . . his mother. He tried to be obedient.

But was he not a man, a full-grown man in charge of his own destiny? Why did he have to listen to other people who always told him what to do and how to act and where to—

Enrique caught himself. He was being foolish. A real man does not slap his chest and shake his fist at the world and shout *I am a man*. A real man calmly goes about the business of doing what men do, and then the world sees he is a man without him having to shout it.

And today a man's business was feeding the chickens and milking the goats and weeding the garden.

At his mother's direction, he did numerous other small chores throughout the day, nothing of much significance, but strung all together, they ate up the day and soon it was dinnertime.

"Wash your hands," his mother told him.

He did as he was told, then sat at the table and bowed his head and his mother offered a brief prayer.

Beans, tortillas, some shredded pork well-spiced.

Dinner came and went with little conversation. His mother turned in early. There was little to do, so even though he was restless, Enrique went to his small room and lay awake on his narrow bed. He tried to sleep but couldn't, and then he stopped trying.

His thoughts drifted to Cherry. He had been enjoying his time with her until that fool Gerald had caused trouble.

Or perhaps it was Enrique who was the fool. What could he and Cherry be to one another? What would his mother say if he brought home a saloon girl?

He let his imagination run wild. Perhaps he could sweep her off her feet, and they could ride off to start a new life together. She could leave the saloon behind, never to be spoken of again. He did not hold that life against her. It was difficult for a woman alone, he supposed. Everyone must eat, must make their way in the world somehow, but he could save her.

And yet . . .

Cherry did not talk or act like someone who needed saving. She seemed happy with herself and her place in life when Enrique had startled her in the alley behind

Carmen's. She'd been curious about him, and Enrique had found it endearing. She was . . .

Ah, but Enrique did not know this woman, not really.

But . . . a feeling. Like perhaps there could be more.

He rolled his eyes. *Idiota. Go to sleep and stop dreaming of things that can never happen.*

He turned on his side and punched his pillow a few times, but he just couldn't get comfortable. No matter how he shifted or adjusted his pillow—

A sound. Something outside.

Enrique sat up in bed and looked through the window at the barn—the moon shone brightly, but he still couldn't see anything. Perhaps it had been his imagination.

But he was awake anyway.

His gun belt hung on the back of a chair. He drew his six-shooter and padded out of the house barefoot, the ground gritty and cool under his feet. Enrique found the barn door cracked open, and he knew for a fact he'd closed it properly before going in for dinner.

He eased into the barn, heart racing, grip tight on his six-gun. He looked around, holding his breath and letting his eyes adjust, waiting and listening for—

There! Movement in the shadows across the barn. Enrique lifted his revolver.

He was grabbed from behind, a hand clamping over his mouth.

"Keep quiet, little brother," a voice whispered in his ear. "Let's not wake Mother."

Carlos!

Juan emerged from the shadows with the Henry rifle resting lazily on his shoulders. "Easy, *hermano*."

Carlos released Enrique and they all exchanged warm embraces and slaps on the back.

"You can't go into town," Enrique said, turning serious. "The bounty killer Dwight Combs is still there. He works for Jericho now, but if he sees you he might remember what you are worth to him dead."

"We're not going into town," Carlos said. "Not until the time is right."

"And when is that?" Enrique asked.

"When *Señor* McCoy tells us," Juan said. "He has a plan."

Enrique raised an eyebrow. "He told you?"

"Only the very basics," Juan said.

"Then tell me," Enrique insisted.

"Can you believe such an inhospitable host?" Carlos asked with mock indignation. "Wants us to talk on an empty stomach."

Enrique laughed. "There are always leftovers. I'll sneak back inside and see what I can bring you."

"And a bottle of something would be nice," Carlos said.

Enrique frowned. "Do you really think Mother would allow Satan's brew in the house?"

Carlos sighed. "Can't win them all."

Smack!

Carmen's head spun around, lights flashing in her eyes.

Jericho hardly ever struck her anymore, but he was furious and had decided to take it out on her. She staggered, bumped into the bed, and fell across it. She pushed herself up on one elbow and prodded the tender spot below her eye with gentle fingertips. There would be an embarrassing bruise, and anger flared within her at the thought of walking around the next day, her girls pretending not to see it.

"I thought I told you to turn on the charm," Jericho said.

Carmen wanted to spit venom at him, but that would do no good. Lashing out would give her a moment of satisfaction, but then he would use his fist instead of an open hand.

She composed herself and said, "He came to see you, didn't he? I can't control what happens after that."

But Jericho wasn't listening. "McCoy's over there right now with that cretinous mouth-breather Lorenzo, whooping it up, celebrating . . . well, I don't know what. Probably welcoming McCoy into the fold."

Probably, Carmen thought, but she didn't say it.

Jericho sat on the bed next to her, grabbed her by the shoulders and pulled her upright. He looked into her eyes. "I'm sorry, darling. That was wrong of me."

Carmen reached out, trailed her fingers down his cheek. "I know you are a man of passion."

"I need your help."

She nodded. "Of course."

Jericho forced something into her hands.

She looked down at it.

A gun.

Not one of the heavy six-shooters all the men carried. A small pistol, easily concealed.

Carmen swallowed hard. "What's this?"

"A single-shot derringer, but don't worry," Jericho

said. "Get close enough and you won't need more than one shot. It's a .22, so hopefully the little pop won't attract too much attention. We'll sort out the details just perfectly to give you the best chance."

She felt suddenly bewildered. "Chance for what?"

"Isn't it obvious?" Jericho asked. "Use your considerable feminine assets to get McCoy alone, lure him up here. Let him think he's about to get what he assuredly wants, because if he has any blood in his veins at all, he wants you, my dear, oh yes. And then . . ."

Jericho grinned, wide and wild.

"And then you kill him," he said.

Mortimer Lorenzo stood and stretched and yawned. It was well past his normal bedtime. He wasn't as young as he used to be.

It had been a good evening, lots of laughs. McCoy had gone quiet toward the end of the festivities, but Lorenzo had seen that sort of thing before. Even the toughest men can drink too much or stay up too late and just shut down. It didn't matter. Lorenzo wasn't hiring McCoy to drink and have a good time.

Lorenzo was hiring McCoy to gun his enemies when the time came.

Anyway, McCoy had gone back to his room at Carmen's Place. He'd sleep it off and be fine.

"See you in the morning, boss," Big Mike said on the way out.

"Hold up."

Mike paused. "Boss?"

"You seen Hank and Rusty?"

Mike scratched his chin and thought about it. "Not since we sent them down to Black Oak."

"Huh."

"You think something's wrong?"

Lorenzo waved away the notion. "They're probably off on a bender or something. They'll turn up."

"Right." Mike nodded. "Well, I'm beat. I'm going to head out and—"

"Still . . ."

Mike waited.

Lorenzo put his hands in his pockets and stood there a moment, tapping one foot. "Tell you what, if they don't turn up tomorrow, pick a couple of the boys to go down there and have a look-see. Either they're lolly-gagging or something's happened to them. Either way, somebody's in trouble."

Chapter 15

It wasn't like McCoy to waste the day away in bed, but when the sun came up and stabbed at him through the crack in the drapes, he grunted, rolled over, closed his eyes, and pretended not to notice a new day had arrived to bother him.

He'd stumbled home from Lorenzo's place in the wee hours of the morning, his mind swimming with jumbled thoughts, his pulse racing with fury and hate. The man who'd killed his father had sat across from him, not three feet away, laughing and drinking like everything was normal. Like he hadn't taken away his whole world when McCoy was a child, murdering his father and brother.

At one point during the evening, McCoy had been forced to sit on his gun hand to keep him from drawing his Peacemaker. The instinct for revenge had been just that strong.

I should have shot him right then. Shot him right through his black heart.

But the place had been full of Lorenzo's men. McCoy would never have made it out of there alive.

The savage fire in his belly, the urge to gun Lorenzo right there had been strong, but not as strong as his levelheaded instinct to come out alive. He'd kill Lorenzo all right, that was never in doubt, but he'd do it in a way that would allow him to escape afterward.

And yet . . .

It didn't seem enough to merely kill the man. When McCoy had lost his father and his brother, he'd lost everything, his whole world. That's what McCoy would do to Lorenzo. He wouldn't just take his life, he'd take everything he ever was or would be or had accomplished. By the time McCoy was done, it would be as if Lorenzo never existed.

And the world would be a better place for it.

But McCoy wasn't going to accomplish much unless he got out of bed first.

He swung his legs over the side with a groan. Pants first. Then he pulled on his boots. He went to the basin and poured it half full of water from the pitcher. He splashed his face, behind his ears, his neck and pits. He finished dressing and strapped on his guns.

Now what?

Coffee was the obvious answer.

Against his better judgment, he went back to the terrible slop house. He fended off any attempt to serve him food. He drank three cups of coffee and thought about what to do next.

Lorenzo was under the impression that McCoy now worked for him. Probably Jericho would hear about it, maybe had already. McCoy doubted Jericho would be friendly next time they crossed paths. He didn't like the notion of Gerald and the boys coming around to pay him a visit.

Since he was sitting at the window, he easily spotted the sleek gig carriage as it came down the street, pulled by a chestnut mare. The driver pulled even with McCoy's window and reined in the horse, and McCoy saw it was Carmen. As always, she looked well put together, a cream blouse held together at the throat by a jade brooch. Leather pants and ankle boots. The flat-brimmed gaucho hat he'd seen her wear before. Black leather gloves. She held the reins in one fist like she knew how to handle the rig.

"Good morning, Mr. McCoy," she called. "Enjoying a hearty breakfast?"

"Just coffee," he replied.

"What are you doing now?"

"Wishing this coffee was a little better," he told her.

Carmen laughed. "Perhaps some fresh air will do you good. Come with me for a ride."

"Where are you going?"

She shrugged. "Just away."

"My favorite place," McCoy said. "Let me settle up, and I'll join you."

He paid for his coffee and went outside.

She scooted over and handed him the reins as he climbed aboard the gig.

"Do the driving, will you?" she asked. "That way I can just enjoy the view."

McCoy took the reins, clicked his tongue, and they headed out of town at an easy trot. They didn't talk for a while. He kept the gig on the narrow road. She sat back with her eyes closed, feeling the wind and the sun on her face.

"Take us along the river," she said after a while.

McCoy took the gig down a side road, and they were at the river within the hour. He reined in the mare, and they sat, looking at the water.

"I have never seen the Mississippi River," Carmen said suddenly.

"Well, it's a lot bigger than this." McCoy gestured at the river in front of them.

She laughed lightly. "I know. But I think I would like to take a trip on a riverboat. I like the idea of rivers and water. The ocean. There is also something to be discovered at the end of a river, or on the other side of the sea. I think I would find traveling by boat more pleasant than traveling by train. Certainly better than a crowded stagecoach."

"You think about traveling a lot?" he asked.

"Sometimes."

"To see new places or to get away?"

Carmen thought about it for a moment. "I think I would know the answer to that once I got wherever I was going. Would I feel homesick, or would I feel free? It would be nice to feel either one, just to have a new feeling."

They lapsed into silence again.

McCoy turned his head and looked down the river, knowing what he'd find if he kept going in that direction. He wondered if it had changed much. He wondered why he should care.

* * *

The little derringer Jericho had given her fit easily into her pants pocket. That was the point of such a small pistol after all—that Carmen could secret it about her person without arousing suspicion.

Still, the weight of it was a constant reminder. It felt like a lumpy, heavy, obvious bulge in her pocket, but she knew that was all in her mind. It almost felt like the thing was pulsing against her hip, thumping in time with her heartbeat, goading her to the dark deed Jericho had set for her.

Carmen went over the instruction in her mind. It was a small-caliber gun, so she'd need to get close. She had only one shot. At the base of his skull would produce the best results. It had been easy to lure him out into the wilderness. Nobody would see or hear. She would put his body into the river and weigh it down with stones, and then the deed would be done. It would be over.

Except would it ever really be over as long as she carried the memory with her? Killing a man. A serious thing. Carmen had no desire to kill anyone, especially not Garret McCoy. He was the sort of man . . . well, if Carmen had been another type of woman, and if things had been different.

But they were not different.

And Carmen had a task that needed doing. Better to get it over with. He was looking at something down the river, the base of his skull right there in front of her like an open invitation. She reached for the gun.

Carmen froze, two fingers just touching the derringer's cool metal.

She felt queasy and swallowed hard.

Just do it.

But she didn't want to.

She took her fingers out of her pocket and felt the queasiness ease. She'd have to face reality sooner or later if she let Jericho down, but . . . not now. She wasn't ready.

Carmen wiped her forehead with the back of her hand. She'd broken out into a sweat.

"What are you looking at?" she asked, simply to break the silence.

"There's a place in that direction," McCoy said. "A place I ain't been to in a long while."

His voice sounded strange, and Carmen could guess why. Men sounded like that sometimes when they dusted off old memories and looked at them with new eyes, as if surprised the memory they thought they knew so well could still surprise them.

"Is it far?" she asked.

He shook his head. "Not far."

"Take us there," Carmen suggested. "See if it's what you remember."

"It won't be," he said. "Nothing ever stays the same."

"Look anyway."

"Okay."

He flicked the reins and the gig rattled along next to the river. A couple hours later, he steered them toward a low hill.

"We'll get a decent view from up there," McCoy said.

A few moments later he reined in the horse under the low, spreading branches of a live oak. He looked down into a narrow gulch, his face tight with tension.

Carmen looked. She didn't notice anything remarkable about the place. A muddy road down the center, shoddy gray houses on either side. A few people coming and going.

"Parson's Gulch it was called," McCoy said.

Carmen hadn't heard of it.

"It's called Blood Gulch now," McCoy explained.

Now *that* Carmen had heard of, not so much in recent years but more as a child. She hadn't realized the place was so close to Coyote Flats, nor did she know why the name had been changed, although as a child she'd been intensely curious.

"Why Blood Gulch?" she asked.

"There was a killing there, a bad one. Way back when—"

His voice caught, and he looked away. Possibly trying to master some emotion he never even expected. Carmen knew what that was like, to have some long-lost feeling she'd thought deeply buried sneak up on her when she least expected it.

"Did you used to live here?" she asked.

McCoy cleared his throat roughly and nodded.

She put her hand on top of his. It was rough and calloused.

"I know what it's like to hurt inside," she told him.

He looked at her, pain and need in his eyes.

"I think sometimes people recognize something in each other." She leaned toward him. "I think when I first saw you, I knew there was some hurt in you."

He leaned toward her.

"Just as there is hurt in me," she said. "And sometimes there is an ease, a . . . relief . . . when two hurts come together."

And then they moved toward each other all at once in a rush, McCoy gathering her in his arms, one of her slender hands going to the back of his neck to pull him close, and then they were kissing, hard and desperate, bodies firm against one another.

It went on and on, time becoming a meaningless blur. She lost herself in his embrace, the world shrinking to just the two of them, everything else vanishing, even as an ugly part of her knew she would use Garret McCoy, that she would make him her tool.

And with his help, she would rid herself of Jericho.

CHAPTER 16

Night fell.

And with it came the restlessness again.

Enrique had been distracted most of the day. It had begun with a tearful reunion over breakfast. Enrique's mother had embraced her other two sons, tearfully fussing over them as she cooked and jabbered at them about any little thing.

He spent the rest of the day catching up with his brothers. They'd spend most of their time hiding from the law. They all lamented the deaths of their two older siblings, but the prevailing thought was that they'd made their beds and now had to lie in them . . . or perhaps had dug their own graves and would now lie in them forever. Such things were discussed out of earshot of their mother. There was no point in needlessly upsetting her.

And then there had been a wonderful family dinner full of love and laughter.

After, Carlos helped his mother with the dishes. Enrique slipped away into the night, went to the barn to saddle his horse.

"Where do you think you're going, *hermano*?"

The voice behind Enrique startled him. He turned to see Juan standing there.

"I just . . . want to go for a ride," Enrique said.

Juan chuckled and shook his head. "Honest men make terrible liars."

Enrique blushed and was glad his brother couldn't see in the dark interior of the barn.

"You're going into town?"

Enrique nodded. "Yes."

"Why?"

Enrique cinched the saddle tight. "It's . . . a long story."

"A girl?"

Enrique grinned despite himself. "I guess the story is not quite as long as I thought."

"You are playing with fire," Juan said. "Stay here with us. Wait until McCoy sends for us. He has a plan."

"If there was a beautiful woman who made your heart nearly beat out of your chest and you couldn't stop thinking about her and I told you to stay here, would you listen to me?" Enrique asked.

Juan thought a moment, then shook his head. "No. We are men, and we have blood in our veins."

"Then you understand."

"But we also have brains in our heads," Juan insisted. "At least say you'll be careful."

"Of course."

Juan sighed and shook his head. "Mother always turns in early. I'll tell her you're out here checking on the animals or something."

"Thank you, Juan."

Juan clapped his brother on the shoulder. "There are moments of passion in which it might seem nothing else in the world matters. This is almost never actually true. Do not die for a pretty face, *hermano*. Come back to us."

A smile and a nod from Enrique. "I will."

Enrique walked his horse the first quarter mile, trying to slip away quietly. Then he mounted and galloped toward Coyote Flats, a heady mix of fear and anticipation churning in his gut.

Carmen clung to McCoy as he drove the gig back to Coyote Flats. They had lingered too long on the hilltop overlooking Blood Gulch, and it would be well after dark when they arrived back in town. McCoy drove by moonlight and was forced to take a slower pace.

She put her head on his shoulder, knowing it would have to end eventually.

Carmen was taking an awful risk. The simpler thing would have been to shoot McCoy in the head as Jericho had asked. But then what? She would still be under Jericho's thumb. Eventually Jericho and Lorenzo would have their stupid, personal war, and who would come out on top? Would Carmen's life be any better under Lorenzo's rule? Would he punish her for being Jericho's woman? There were too many bad answers to all these questions.

But Garret McCoy, ah, now with him there was the possibility to be finished with all of it. To wipe the slate clean in Coyote Flats and live a normal life . . . normal as it could be for a woman like her at least.

A half mile from town, she pushed away from McCoy and sat straight. "Can you walk from here? If Jericho or one of his men were to see us together . . ."

"I understand." McCoy handed her the reins and climbed down from the gig.

"Wait." She reached out, grabbed a fistful of his vest and pulled him toward her.

Their lips mashed together hard, a long kiss filled with promises and questions. A hundred years later they parted.

"When will I see you again?" McCoy asked.

"I don't know," she said. "I don't know anything."

She flicked the reins, and the gig lurched toward Coyote Flats.

Enrique left his horse tied to a tree limb on the edge of town and went the rest of the way on foot, not wanting to be seen. He felt foolish. He wasn't doing anything wrong.

Yet.

It worried him he might run afoul of Gerald and his friends, especially if Enrique was caught in the act of trying to see Cherry. Juan's words came back to him. Enrique had a brain in his head and needed to use it.

So . . . be sneaky, but don't look *like you're trying to be sneaky.*

He circled around the alley behind Carmen's Place and stood in the shadows across from the saloon's back door. Fate had been with him before. Perhaps he would be lucky again, and she'd come out for air. Just to speak with her again for a few moments, to see her face. It would be worth the trip into town. It would be worth all the risk.

But he waited an hour, and nobody came out.

He didn't dare go inside the saloon. That would be asking for trouble.

He stepped back, craned his neck, and scanned the windows on the saloon's second floor. Those rooms belonged to the girls, yes? Some windows were lit, others dark. The roof of the wraparound porch on the first floor would give him a place to stand if he wanted to check most of those windows and see which room was Cherry's.

He sighed and shook his head at his own stupidity. Was he really going to climb up there and peep into windows?

Of course he was.

Cherry thanked the cowboy and pushed him into the hall with promises to *get together again real soon*. As soon as the door clicked shut, her smile fell, and she allowed herself to go numb. She would be expected downstairs eventually. The night was young. But she could linger in her room a few minutes and give herself a short break.

She splashed water on her various parts and dried herself. A spritz of perfume in strategic places. She pulled her stockings back on. Skirt. A green and black bustier. A light robe wrapped around her shoulders, easily dropped to show clear white skin at a strategic moment. She looked at herself in the mirror. Her makeup was smudged. She fixed it.

Cherry took a deep breath, let it out. She smiled. Her reflection showed that the smile didn't touch her eyes. Most men wouldn't notice, might not even realize she had a face at all, their gaze never getting above her neck. But the smart ones would notice, and often it was the smart ones with the money.

She tried again, this time with a happy thought. Fried chicken. She checked the mirror. Better. Was she hungry? She'd only picked at her dinner earlier. The thought of a slice of pie made her smile even wider. Maybe she'd sneak into the kitchen and—

A knock at the window made her gasp and start.

She took three quick steps toward the door, holding her robe closed with one hand. She looked at the window and saw who it was.

"Enrique?"

He waved, then motioned for her to come to the window.

She opened it.

He leaned into the room, hands braced on the windowsill. "I'm sorry. This is ridiculous. I couldn't stop thinking about you and—"

Cherry leaned forward and planted her lips on his, a long, hard kiss meant to last.

She pulled away and gasped for breath. "I didn't know I was going to do that."

"I don't mind."

She kissed him again, then pulled away and said, "I thought Gerald was going to kill you the other night."

A nervous laugh from Enrique. "I was a little worried about that myself."

"You shouldn't be here."

"Can I come in?" he asked.

"No."

"Ah. I thought this was going a little better. I have misjudged."

"I really like you, Enrique," Cherry said.

"And as far as I'm concerned, you are the only woman in the world," Enrique insisted.

"That's maybe a little overboard."

"I don't care," he said. "I love you. My heart is about to explode with it."

Cherry looked pained. "Oh, don't say that, Enrique. Don't say *love*. You can't love me, and I can't love you. You know who I am, what I am. There's no room for love. That's only a path to heartache."

"I can fix it," he said. "I can find a way."

"Don't say that. Don't make me believe it. Don't make me want it if it can't be true. I *order* you not to love me."

"I'm afraid it's out of my hands," he said.

They kissed again.

"Are you sure I can't come in?" he asked.

"Very sure. Get out of here before one of Gerald's boys sees you," she pleaded.

"You want me to go?"

"No."

"Then I'll stay."

"No!" She put a hand against his chest, pushed gently. "Go on. You can't be here."

"When?" he pleaded. "Where?"

"I don't know," she told him. "We'll figure it out. Not now."

One last kiss, and Enrique backed out of the window.

Cherry took a deep breath. Her heart fluttered like a jackrabbit's. Had that really happened?

Stupid boy. Stupid, wonderful, crazy boy.

Cherry had definitely pushed her luck. She needed to get back to work before somebody came looking for her. She headed for the door, paused, looked back at the window. The thought struck her she'd better close it in case Enrique came back. He might get some stupid, romantic notion to crawl inside and wait for her, and boy, oh, boy would *that* be awkward if she brought somebody up to the room.

She went back to close the window.

And then she heard the shouting.

Cherry stuck her head out the window and looked down into the alley. Four men were dragging Enrique away. She recognized them as Jericho's men, friends of Gerald.

Oh, no no no . . .

She rushed from the room. Cherry needed help and needed it now.

Carmen kicked off her boots, then took off her hat and hung it on the bedpost. She was very tired and a little confused. What had she done? What had she started? She'd set something into motion that might be the undoing of all she'd worked for.

But it's too late to second-guess yourself, isn't it, girl? Nothing ventured, nothing gained.

She would worry anew in the morning. Now she only wanted sleep. She'd checked with Joseph before coming up to her room. It was a relatively quiet night, and the barkeeps had everything under control. For once everything was under control.

She began to unbutton her blouse.

A sudden, rapid-fire knock at the door.

Spoke too soon, didn't I?

The knock again, followed by Cherry's voice. "Miss Carmen, please, I need help!"

Carmen crossed the room quickly and threw the door open. "What is it? Are you hurt?"

Cherry babbled it out all in a jumble of smashed-together words. "Miss Carmen they got him and are taking him Lord knows where. I just know they're going to kill him, especially that Gerald who's just crazy, and if somebody don't help him, I just don't know what's going to happen we've got to go help him or—"

"Calm down!" Carmen took Cherry by the shoulders. "I have no idea what you're talking about. Take a deep breath and start at the beginning."

"Enrique came to my window," Cherry said.

Carmen frowned. "That boy that's caused trouble in my place? You let him in your window?"

"No!" Cherry said quicky. "I told him he definitely could *not* come in."

"Cherry, I'm sorry, but this boy sounds like trouble to me," Carmen said.

Cherry's eyes welled with tears. "But . . . but somebody's got to help him! Somebody's got to—"

Carmen took the girl's hand in hers. "Cherry, what is this boy to you?"

Cherry tried to talk, hiccupped, gulped for air.

"Calm." Carmen squeezed her hands gently.

Cherry blew out a ragged breath. "Miss Carmen, was there ever a man, and you know it was stupid, but you couldn't help yourself, and . . ." She sobbed, tears and snot running down her face. "It's so stupid. I didn't even think . . . I didn't . . ."

"It's caught you by surprise, hasn't it, girl?" Carmen said.

Cherry nodded, still sobbing.

Carmen hugged the girl, patted her on the back. "Hush."

Cherry calmed, wiped her nose and eyes with her hand, then wiped her hand on her skirt. "I wish I could be grown-up and smart like you."

Carmen thought about her day in the gig with Garret McCoy, their time atop the hill under the live oak. "You'd be surprised, girl."

"I don't know what to do," Cherry said.

"I'm going to tell you what to do," Carmen said. "Go to your room and stay there. You're not fit to work in this state, and anyway, it will be safer if you go your room and lock the door."

That caught Cherry by surprise. "Safer?"

"Men often get an idea into their heads, and when the idea proves to be wrong, it makes them angry," Carmen explained. "Our young Gerald is one of those, I suspect. He has something in mind about you, and when he finds out it isn't true, it will be your fault. Never mind if that makes sense or not. It doesn't matter. He'll blame you, and he might want to hurt you to make himself feel better."

Cherry shook her head, wiping her eyes again. "That's . . . that's . . ."

"What?" Carmen asked. "Unfair? Even one as young as you knows better. Now go to your room. In fact . . ."

Carmen reached into her pocket and took out the little pistol. She pressed it into Cherry's hand. "Take this."

Cherry looked down at it. "I don't want this."

"I don't blame you." Carmen told Cherry everything Jericho had told her about the derringer. "Keep it close just in case. Now go to your room. Leave Enrique to me. I make no promises, but I'll see what can be done."

They hugged again, and Cherry left.

Carmen paused a moment, her mind racing.

Then she left her room and went to the head of the stairs. From there, she could look down into the saloon. The place wasn't crowded, but it wasn't empty either. The usual mix, including some of Lorenzo's men and, unfortunately, some of Jericho's. Probably, they'd each keep to their own without trouble, respecting neutral ground, but she couldn't risk any of Jericho's men seeing what she was about to do.

She composed herself, forced her voice to sound matter-of-fact. "Joseph, can you send Missy up here, please? I want her to do something for me."

Joseph looked up at her. "Missy's with somebody."

"Claudia then."

"I'll send her right up," Joseph said.

Carmen went back to her room and waited.

There was a knock on the door a minute later.

Carmen opened the door, let Claudia into her room, and quickly closed the door again.

"Joseph said you needed me?" Claudia said.

"Go to Mr. McCoy's room and tell him to come here," Carmen said. "But I don't think he's in. If that's the case, get out of those working clothes and put on a regular drab dress. Scour Coyote Flats until you find him, then send him here."

Claudia frowned. "Is something wrong?"

"No time to explain," Carmen said. "But this must be secret. Do not tell anyone you're looking for McCoy. Tell him to come to my room without being seen. Understand?"

"I understand."

"Good," Carmen said. "And, Claudia, don't dawdle. We're trying to save a man's life."

CHAPTER 17

One of the big guys threw another punch, and Enrique's head snapped around. He didn't fight back at all, mostly because he was tied to a chair, but also because he wasn't conscious anymore. Blood trickled from each corner of his mouth, and one eye was swollen nearly shut.

"It ain't so much fun when he ain't awake for it," Gerald said.

The big bruiser had cranked his fist back for another punch, his sleeves rolled up and a sheen of sweat on his face from the exertion, but he paused when Gerald had spoken. "You want me to stop hitting him, Gerald?"

"Yeah, just for a minute."

Gerald crossed the small back room to a table and grabbed a half-full bottle of whiskey off the table, then went back to stand in front of Enrique. Gerald took a big swig from the bottle, tilted his head back and gargled.

Then spit the whiskey straight into Enrique's face.

Enrique sputtered, his eyes blinking open.

"There he is," Gerald said jovially. "See, boys, our fun ain't over yet. This is one tough kid. I bet he can take lots more punching before he's all worn out."

Enrique spit, a mix of blood, saliva, and whiskey. "You . . . coward."

Gerald put a hand behind his ear. "What was that? Didn't quite catch it!"

"Coward!" Enrique shouted. "You always have your boys with you, don't you? Ever finish a fight yourself?"

"The whole point of being a man in my position is that I *ain't* by myself," Gerald said. "Mr. Jericho is an important man in Coyote Flats, and I'm his next in line."

Gerald actually wondered if that was still true. Jericho seemed to put a lot of faith in the new man, Dwight Combs. Gerald wasn't sure how he felt about that, but he supposed it wasn't relevant to the subject at hand.

"Hit him again," Gerald said.

The bruiser with his sleeves rolled up punched Enrique across the jaw with a loud, flesh-on-flesh *smack*. Enrique winced and groaned, letting his head loll.

"I'm not sure the boss would like this," the other bruiser said. He leaned against the wall next to the door, arms crossed.

Gerald frowned at him. "Why would the boss care?"

The bruiser next to the door shrugged. "We had that trouble at Carmen's Place before, didn't we? With McCoy and this kid."

"We weren't inside the place, were we?" Gerald said.

"I'm just saying."

"We weren't inside the place, so we didn't violate no neutral ground, did we?" Gerald insisted.

But the bruiser wasn't quite ready to concede the point. "We were in the alley out back. Mr. Jericho might think that was close enough. The alley's right next to the place."

"And Texas is right next to Oklahoma," Gerald said irritably. "What, are we supposed to walk on eggshells from one horizon to the other?"

"I'm just saying."

"Well, stop saying," Gerald told him. "What, is this Jericho's favorite Mexican or something? Nobody's going to miss him."

The bruiser kept his mouth shut, but he had that pouty look on his face that Gerald hated so dang much. *Fine, pout then*, Gerald thought. *As long as you do what you're told.*

"Does anyone else want to take a turn hitting this fella?" asked the one with his sleeves rolled up. "I'm getting a might winded."

"Give me ten minutes," Gerald said. "This is getting tiresome anyway. I want to try something new. Bring me a cold beer when you come back. It's hot in here."

The two bruisers left.

Gerald stood a moment looking down at Enrique. The room went stone silent except for the kid's heavy breathing. Gerald crossed the room, his boots clacking sharply on the wooden floor, spurs jingling. He took the room's only other chair and brought it back, setting it in front of Enrique. He sat.

Slowly, he took a tobacco pouch from one pocket and rolling papers from another.

"You don't mind if I have a smoke, do you, Enrique?"

Enrique said nothing.

"Well, you don't object anyway."

He uncinched the tobacco pouch and tapped out

the correct amount onto the rolling paper. Not too much. Gerald didn't like a fat cigarette. Didn't feel right between his lips.

"I suppose it's hard not to take this personally," Gerald said. "Getting dragged into a dark room, and tied up, and beaten and all. I sure as hell would have a few complaints, and that's the truth."

He rolled the cigarette and tucked the ends and licked it. He didn't hurry. If there was one thing he couldn't abide it was a sloppily rolled cigarette. He tucked it into the corner of his mouth and patted his pockets. "Got a light?"

Enrique said nothing.

"I'm just funning you," Gerald said. "I got matches right here."

He took them from his pocket, flicked one to life with his thumbnail, and puffed until he had a nice glow at the end of his cigarette. He waved the match out and tossed it aside.

"Now where was I? Oh, yeah, I get that you might be taking this personally, and I was saying how I sympathize." *Puff, puff.* "But I need you to see this from my point of view."

Enrique made no indication he was going to be seeing the situation any certain way.

"Don't worry, I can keep up both sides of the conversation. I don't mind," Gerald assured him. "Here's the thing. I have dreams and aspirations just like any other man. I know it looks like I've got a good life—and I do—being an important man in Jericho's organization and so on. But I think about the future. And when I squint my eyes looking into the fuzzy uncertain future, one thing I know that I'm going to need is just the right woman by my side. I think most men want that sort of thing, don't you?"

Gerald puffed the cigarette, watched the smoke hang in the air for a moment. He wondered idly if blind people enjoyed smoking as much as them that could see. Was it as pleasant if you couldn't see the smoke?

Deep thoughts for another time.

"I've been going into Carmen's Place for a rock-solid year," Gerald said. "And I see Cherry every single time. I never went with none of the other girls. Only Cherry. Now, I think that's laudable. I think that shows good intent. And I always give her a little something extra because I'm so generous of spirit. Do you understand what I'm saying to you?"

Enrique mumbled something in Spanish.

"Sorry, I'm not too fluent," Gerald said. "*Cerveza por favor* is about as far as I go."

He puffed the cigarette again, watched the smoke make a lazy swirl in midair.

"So there I am, putting in the time, spending the money, and then *you* come along," Gerald said. "Don't misunderstand. I'm no fool. I know what Cherry does to earn a dollar. I know there's other fellas, but there was something about you, something that made her get really upset the other night when I tried to cut in—and I admit that was rude—but I very much didn't like her attitude when it came to you . . . plus you got me into trouble with my boss, so that's *two* reasons I don't like you."

Enrique tried to lift his head and failed. "Please . . . please . . ."

"You got nice manners," Gerald said. "I'll give you that."

He took in a big lungful of smoke from his cigarette and blew it into Enrique's face.

Enrique flinched but said nothing.

"So here's what's going to happen," Gerald said. "You're going to go away. Forever. But I'm going to need satisfaction first. You're going to have to pay for making me look bad. I guess I'm just petty like that, and frankly I'm the sort of fella that handles things like this in a pretty simple way. For example . . ."

Gerald leaned forward and ground out his cigarette on the back of Enrique's hand.

Enrique screamed. On reflex, he tried to jerk away, but he was tied to the arm of the chair, thin rope looped around his wrist. Gerald kept grinding the cigarette until it was nearly flat against Enrique's hand. The smell of tobacco and burnt flesh mixed together, and Gerald was surprised to find he didn't mind it. It smelled sort of bad and good at the same time, which he supposed summed up pretty close exactly what was happening.

"You're gonna be gone." He stood, grabbed the whiskey bottle again and drained it, the booze burning hot down his gullet until the bottle was empty. He burped and wiped his mouth with the back of his hand. "And when you're gone, Cherry will eventually forget you ever existed. I'll probably have to speak some soft words and get back in her good graces. Time is on my side."

Gerald spun the bottle around in his hand until he

held it by the neck. "You, on the other hand, your time is running out."

He brought the bottle down hard and struck Enrique at the base of his skull with a sharp *clank*.

Enrique went limp, head hanging, chin against his chest.

Gerald looked at the bottle and frowned. He'd expected it to shatter dramatically upon impact and felt a vague disappointment that it hadn't.

But Enrique was out, no doubt. Gerald leaned in and checked. Still alive. Good. That meant he could torment him further. There was still plenty of hurt he planned to inflict on the young Mexican.

The door creaked open, and one of the bruisers leaned in. He had a mug of beer in one hand.

"That for me?"

The bruiser handed him the mug. "You said you wanted one."

Gerald took the mug and swigged down half the beer in one go. "Let's go. We'll start in on him again when he wakes up."

The bruiser gave Gerald a look.

Gerald frowned. "What?"

"Maybe we take him out and dump him somewhere," the bruiser said. "He's had enough."

Gerald felt his face go hot. He didn't cotton to being contradicted. "I'll say when he's had enough."

"Okay, okay."

"Come on," Gerald said. "Let's get another beer."

* * *

"What do you have that's not terrible?" McCoy asked.

The old woman blinked at him. "Say what?"

Against his better judgment, McCoy had once again come into the slop house hoping to get a decent meal. "Every time I get food in here, I can barely choke it down. So maybe I thought I'd ask if you got anything good."

She put her hands on her hips and narrowed her eyes. "Well, if you don't like it here you can just get over to the slop house across the street and eat there."

McCoy's eyes widened in surprise. "There's a place across the street?"

"Nope." The old woman cackled laughter, pleased with herself.

McCoy frowned a moment, but then he laughed too. "Okay, you got me."

"Blueberry pie."

"Pie? I wasn't figuring on skipping right to dessert."

"You asked what was good," she said.

McCoy sighed. "Okay then."

"I'll bring you a slice."

"And coffee," he called after her.

She brought the coffee a minute later and set it on the table in front of him and left.

McCoy picked up his fork, said a little prayer, then took a bite.

It was good. Real good. He ate it fast and washed it down with the coffee. McCoy couldn't live solely on blueberry pie the rest of his time in Coyote Flats, but it would do for now. He was swigging down the last swallow of coffee when a tall brunette in a drab farmer's dress and a shawl pulled tight around her shoulders walked past his table. She dropped a beaded clutch, which bounced once and ended up next to McCoy's boot.

He bent and grabbed it, stood and handed it back to her, doffing his hat. "I believe this is yours, ma'am."

She smiled warmly. "How clumsy of me. Thank you so much." Then she whispered, "Meet me out back in two minutes."

McCoy wasn't sure he'd heard her right, and she was already walking away. He paid for his pie, and two minutes later, he rounded the corner to the back side of the building where he spotted her standing in a shadowed doorway.

"Mr. McCoy," she called in a low whisper and waved him over.

As McCoy approached, he realized he recognized her, one of the saloon gals who worked for Carmen. She looked a lot different in regular clothes.

She looked up and down the narrow street before speaking. "I'm not supposed to be seen with you. Miss Carmen needs you. There's been trouble."

McCoy felt his guts go tight. "Is she okay?"

"She didn't tell me why, but she's not hurt or anything like that. She just wants you to come quick but said you can't be seen together, so you need to be sneaky."

"Thanks."

He started to turn, intending to head back to Carmen's as quickly as possible, but her hand on his arm stopped him.

"Help her, Mr. McCoy," she said. "Miss Carmen has always been good to us girls. Help her."

He gave her a grim nod. "That's exactly what I plan to do, ma'am."

CHAPTER 18

Garret McCoy had to stop himself from bursting through the front door of Carmen's Place. She needed him. That's all he knew, but she wasn't hurt. Whatever the emergency was, it wasn't so urgent that he needed to call attention to himself. He walked into the saloon easy and calm just like everything was normal.

He caught Jospeh's eye and flicked him a two-finger salute. Joseph polished the bar with a rag and nodded curtly in reply.

McCoy took his time going up the stairs, and nobody paid him no never mind.

He went down the hall to his room, put his hand on the doorknob but didn't enter. He looked around. He was alone. Nobody saw as he continued down the hall to the end. He knocked.

The door opened immediately, and Carmen grabbed his arm and pulled him in, shutting the door again quickly.

"Are you okay?" he asked.

"It's not me. I'm fine."

He gathered her suddenly in his arms and kissed her

hard, realizing as their lips met how worried he'd been for her. She'd intrigued him the first time he'd set eyes on her, and in a very short time it had become something more. A lot more.

They parted, and she said, "It's Cherry. And that young Vargas boy."

"Enrique?"

"He could not stay away from her," Carmen said. "And she is encouraging him. Gerald and his ruffian friends took Enrique away. My guess is they have him at the Thirsty Coyote. Gerald is cruel and petty. I fear what he might do to the Vargas boy."

McCoy spat a curse.

"Cherry is beside herself," Carmen said. "The boy is young and foolish but not a bad sort. I'm of a mind to help them."

McCoy almost told her not to be stupid. Cherry and Enrique had made this mess for themselves and now they had to live—or maybe die—with the consequences. A day ago, he would have told her exactly that in the coldest, most blunt way possible.

But now . . .

The fact was that Cherry wasn't a bad kid, McCoy could almost think of her as a little sister or a niece or some such. And Carmen was right that Enrique wasn't a bad sort either. So they were good people. So what? Bad things happened to good people every day, and it wasn't Garret McCoy's job to chase after all the good people of the world to make sure they didn't trip over their own shoelaces.

But McCoy couldn't look Carmen in the eye and say any of that.

So this is what it was to get all tangled up with other people. What Ghost McCoy had avoided all his life, showing up places only to vanish again when the job was done. Is this really what Dwight Combs had wanted, to be attached to a place, tethered to the people there?

"What should we do?" Carmen prompted.

McCoy grabbed a chair and plopped into it, rubbing the bridge of his nose between thumb and forefinger. "Let me think."

She put her hand on his back just below his neck. Her way of letting him know she was there, supportive, caring, and McCoy knew he was tethered all right, on a leash he'd put there himself because he'd allowed himself to give a damn about these folks.

About Carmen in particular. He was probably making a mistake, he told himself, but it was a mistake he'd gladly make every day of the week and twice on Sunday.

"I've got a notion what might be done." McCoy stood and took Carmen by the shoulders. "It's a road we'd need to go down sooner or later anyway, but there won't be no half measures with this. We got to go all in or just forget it. And if we're smart and act fast, then maybe we solve a few problems at once. If we're stupid, if we don't do it just right, then we're probably dead. It's all or nothing. What do you say?"

Her arms went around him, and she pulled him against her. "I will do whatever you say. You must know that surely."

And they kissed again.

He could have stayed there a long time. The rest of the night. The rest of his life.

But there was work to be done. He pulled away from her.

"What will you do now?" she asked.

"Now I go see Lorenzo."

McCoy felt like he had lead in his boots as he walked down to Lorenzo's place. He wasn't ready to face the man who'd killed his father.

Or maybe he was too ready, too eager to draw his Peacemaker, point it at the murderer and shoot until the revolver clicked empty.

But McCoy's revenge would have to wait. He needed Lorenzo for what was about to happen next. McCoy wasn't good at pretending, didn't like it because it felt too much like a lie, but he'd have to pretend he didn't hate the man, didn't want to kill him with his own two hands.

McCoy put on a calm face as he walked into Lorenzo's place. A few of the boys offered him a nod or a casual greeting. McCoy had been accepted into the gang. He supposed he could come and go as he pleased now.

He glanced about but didn't see Lorenzo.

A moment later, Big Mike came out of the back room. McCoy waved him down.

"Is Lorenzo back there?" McCoy asked. "It's important."

"I guess I could ask him to come out," Mike said.

McCoy glanced around the room again and lowered his voice. "Maybe better if I go back there."

Mike hesitated, then nodded. "Right. Come on then."

McCoy followed him down a narrow hall to the back room. Mike paused, rapping on the door with a knuckle.

"What?" from the other side of the door.

"It's Mike. I got McCoy with me. Got a minute?"

"Bring him in."

Mike pushed the door open, and McCoy followed him inside.

Mortimer Lorenzo sat at a shabby little desk in a windowless room. Papers in front of him. A whiskey bottle off to one side. Nothing fancy or even inviting about the place at all. The little room reminded him of Carmen's office, functional and drab. Maybe a dark little room was necessary for bosses, someplace without distractions, to take care of the nitty-gritty. Maybe all the grand emperors of Rome had a guy in a little back room who actually ran everything.

"What can I do you for, McCoy?"

Lorenzo wore the eyepatch again instead of the glass eye, and it struck McCoy more than ever how much he wanted to kill the man where he sat. He could see him lording it over his father in the middle of Parson's Gulch's only street, smug look on his face. The scene was so clear in McCoy's mind, as if it had happened only yesterday.

Someone somewhere had said *time heals all wounds*, and maybe that was true most of the time. But then there are those other times when a wound can fester if left untreated, the pain getting sharper and deeper until a man didn't even notice it anymore. Until a sharp reminder came along and the hurt flared up new all over again.

Forget it. You need him. Set it aside. You can kill him another day.

"Your goal is to take out Jericho, isn't it?" McCoy said. "Coyote Flats has one too many bosses, I reckon."

Lorenzo nodded. "That's right."

"Maybe I got a plan for that."

Lorenzo sat back in his chair, blew air out his nose and steepled his hands under his chin. "Well, so do I, but I'm always open to new ideas. Talk."

"Sometimes, with a complicated enterprise like this, the thing to do is plan and bide your time and put in a lot of effort to arrange circumstances just right," McCoy said. "But other times, circumstances change on their own, fall into place unexpected like, and present you with an opportunity."

Lorenzo nodded. "You saying circumstances have changed on us?"

"That's what I'm saying."

Lorenzo raised an eyebrow. "And so we now need to take advantage of these circumstances and strike sooner?"

"You're reading me just right," McCoy said.

"How soon?" Lorenzo asked.

"Tonight."

Lorenzo and Mike exchanged glances.

Then they both started laughing.

McCoy said nothing. *Let them laugh it out.*

"I do appreciate the enthusiasm, son," Lorenzo said.

At the word *son*, McCoy's hand twitched toward his Peacemaker.

Not now. Not yet.

"I think you're maybe a might ambitious," Lorenzo

said. "Hiring you was a step in the right direction, but I'd hoped to hire ten more like you before having a go at Jericho."

"You hire ten, and he hires ten," McCoy said. "Then where are you? Square one. I have a way to take him right now."

"Okay then, let's hear it."

McCoy glanced at Big Mike.

"We're all glad to have you on board," Lorenzo said. "But Mike was here before you, McCoy, so you can either talk in front of him or don't bother talking at all."

The slightest hesitation, and then McCoy offered Big Mike a curt nod.

Mike nodded back.

McCoy spelled it out as quickly and as accurately as possible—Cherry, Enrique Vargas, Carmen.

"I don't see how none of that helps me," Lorenzo said. "Some Mexican kid got himself in trouble. So what? Some working girl is heartbroke. Too bad. You're not convincing me, McCoy."

"You ever heard of a Trojan horse?" McCoy asked.

Lorenzo frowned. "No."

"From an old Roman story," Big Mike said.

"Greek."

Mike raised an eyebrow. "What?"

"Greek, not Roman," McCoy told him.

"Whatever," Mike said. "It's about sneaking your men into an enemy camp."

Lorenzo scratched his chin. "Let's hear it then."

McCoy explained his plan, highlighting the boldness of it and the element of surprise and glossing over the hundred ways it could all go wrong. He made up a good bit of it as he went along.

The three of them lapsed into silence. McCoy could see Lorenzo was thinking about it, conflicting notions making the man's face twist with indecision. This was it, McCoy realized. If Lorenzo didn't go for it, then it was over. McCoy didn't have a backup plan.

Lorenzo looked up as if just remembering McCoy was standing there waiting for an answer. He reached for the whiskey bottle. "Drink?"

McCoy shook his head. "No thanks."

Lorenzo pulled the cork and took a long swig right from the bottle.

More silence.

"What about Carmen?" Lorenzo asked.

"What about her?"

"I trust that brothel trash about as far as I can throw her one-handed," Lorenzo said. "Why would she go along with anything we cook up? She's Jericho's woman."

McCoy puffed out his chest and lifted his chin. "Not anymore."

It took Lorenzo a moment to get it. Then he barked out a laugh. "So that's how it is, eh? Get a load of this slick customer, Mike."

"He's slick all right, boss." Although Mike's face remained blank.

Lorenzo took another swig from the bottle, still thinking. Then he slammed an open palm down on his desk. "To hell with it. Let's do it!"

McCoy wasn't quite sure if he was glad or not. It didn't matter. The war started tonight.

"You need to round up all your boys," McCoy said.

"Where are they?" Lorenzo asked Mike.

"Some here, others at their homes," Mike said. "Some at Carmen's, I reckon."

"Send somebody to wake up everyone at their homes and bring them here," Lorenzo told him. "And be subtle. Don't all come marching down Main Street in a mob. You go yourself over to Carmen's and gather any of ours and bring them back here."

"And get a head count of any of Jericho's men," McCoy said. "We need to know how many are at Carmen's and how many are elsewhere."

"That's good thinking," Lorenzo said. "Okay, Mike, get to it."

"Right, boss."

Big Mike left Lorenzo and McCoy alone in the little office.

Lorenzo took another swig of whiskey. "So lay it out for me. How exactly is this horse thing going to work?"

McCoy explained what he had in mind.

"Bold and brash," Lorenzo said. "I guess this time tomorrow, I'll either be king of Coyote Flats, or we'll all be dead. Well, life is risk, ain't it? Go tell your woman to get ready. I'll organize things here."

McCoy left, took the alley back to Carmen's Place and entered through the back door. He lingered in the back a moment, letting his eyes go to every part of the saloon. Big Mike had been there already and done his job. None of Lorenzo's men were left in the place.

A handful of Jericho's boys talked and laughed and drank, seemingly unaware anything was afoot.

McCoy headed up the stairs again, doing his best to look casual. The upstairs hall was empty. He passed rooms, laughter and talk and other noises on the other side of closed doors, business as usual in Carmen's Place. He arrived at Carmen's door and took one more look to make sure the coast was clear before knocking.

The door opened, and she quickly ushered him in, and in the next instant, they held one another, lips meeting. She pulled away, searched his eyes and must have seen that something had changed.

"Tell me."

"Lorenzo's with us," McCoy said. "We do it tonight."

Her eyes widened. "Tonight?"

"What did you think?" he asked. "How long do you think Enrique will last with Gerald?"

"I . . . suppose you're right," she said. "It's just so sudden."

"I need you," McCoy told her. "This won't work without you. I need you to be brave."

She nodded. "Tell me what to do."

He told her.

And he could see in her face that she was frightened.

"You can do this," he said. "You can do anything. You're the strongest woman I've ever met."

She held him tightly, her face against his chest.

Then she abruptly pulled away, her expression stone.

"I will tell Cherry," she said. "Don't worry. We'll be ready."

CHAPTER 19

"No crying," Carmen said. "This has got to seem like normal business, or it won't work."

Cherry sniffed and nodded. "Sorry."

"Don't be sorry." Carmen dabbed at the corners of Cherry's eyes with a handkerchief. "But get control of yourself."

Cherry breathed in through her nose and then blew it out slowly. "I'll be okay."

Carmen looked her over. She'd thought about telling the girl to change into a normal dress but then reconsidered. It would be helpful to remind Jericho that Cherry was a working girl, an asset, and that Carmen had a business to run. So Cherry wore the same saloon outfit she'd had on earlier with the addition of a shawl to cover her exposed shoulders. They weren't going to Jericho's to drum up business, after all.

Carmen put on her gaucho hat and breathed out a ragged sigh. She was doing her best not to look as nervous as she felt.

*Nervous? What a ridiculous understatement. I'm
petrified.*

"Ready?"

Cherry nodded.

"Good. Follow me."

They went downstairs and crossed the saloon to the
front door, not hurrying but walking with purpose. They
drew a few looks, but there was nothing out of the ordinary about that. The next moment they were outside and
walking at a brisk pace toward the Thirsty Coyote.

Carmen put her hand on Cherry's arm and gave it a
reassuring squeeze. "Don't worry."

Cherry swallowed hard and said nothing.

They arrived at the Thirsty Coyote. Carmen took a
deep breath, and they entered.

They place was crowded, and all heads turned to
regard the two women.

Carmen's heart beat so hard, she thought it might
burst from her chest, but her face was calm as her cool
gaze went from one side of the room to the other, expression aloof and commanding. She was no ordinary,
meek woman, but Miss Carmen, owner and operator of
Carmen's Place and known to all—although it wasn't
spoken aloud—as Jericho's woman.

"Would it be possible to have a word with Mr. Jericho?" Carmen's voice was steady and businesslike.

"Carmen?"

Jericho stood. He'd been sitting at a table in the rear
with his back to the door, so Carmen hadn't been able
to spot him. He came toward her, looking confused.
She didn't usually show up at the Thirsty Coyote, and
she could see Jericho didn't like it.

He forced a smile as he took Carmen's hand. "My dear, this is a surprise." He glanced at Cherry, then led Carmen away a few feet, pitching his voice low. "Have you come to tell me you've taken care of that little matter we discussed?"

She knew what he meant. Jericho had given her the derringer and had asked her to use it on Garret McCoy. "That's still a work in progress."

"Disappointing," Jericho said. "I would have thought it a simple matter."

"Don't worry, I'll attend to it," Carmen assured him. "In the meantime, there is another issue we must discuss."

Jericho raised an eyebrow. "Oh?"

"There has been . . . an incident," she said. "Involving your man Gerald."

His eyes went to the bar where Gerald and those two lunkheads he went around with sat and drank beer. "I see."

"I wanted to talk to you in person," she said. "To make sure we're clear on what the boundaries are."

Jericho's face went hard. "You forget yourself, my dear. I say what the boundaries are, and if I change my mind tomorrow and decide they're different, then you just have to live with that."

She pitched her voice low to match his. "Of course, darling. I would not have it any other way. But do all of your men know which lines they cannot cross? Does Gerald?"

Jericho's eyes narrowed as he looked back at his henchman, Gerald still sitting with his two pals, oblivious to the fact his future was being decided at that very moment.

"Tell me what he did," Jericho said.

"Perhaps this is not the best place. It is not my intention to embarrass you, darling," Carmen said. "Is there somewhere private?"

Jericho thought about it, tapping his walking stick irritably on the floor. "Gerald, come here a moment."

Carmen's eyes went to Cherry. The girl looked worried.

"Sure thing, boss." He hopped down off his barstool and came toward Jericho, slowing suddenly when he spotted Carmen and Cherry.

Carmen's gut pinched. This isn't quite how she'd pictured this happening. She'd planned to get Jericho alone to sell him on her version of the story. If Gerald was around to contradict her, it would complicate matters.

Never mind. She'd improvise.

"Gerald, these ladies tell me you've maybe not been on your best behavior," Jericho said.

"Now, hold up, boss, I don't know what they told you but—"

"Is he here?" Carmen interrupted. "Or is he dead by now?"

"He ain't dead!" Gerald said hurriedly.

"I'm growing tired of being the only person in this conversation that has no idea what's going on," Jericho said, a dangerous edge in his voice.

Gerald held up his hands. "Hey, I can explain."

"Not here," Jericho said.

"But, boss, you've got to listen to me. I'd never—"

Jericho took a menacing step toward him, the muscles in his jaw working. "Not. Here."

Gerald took a step back and shut his mouth.

"Is there something you'd like to show me, Gerald?" Jericho's grin was more predatory than friendly.

"Okay, okay, this way." Gerald motioned for them to follow. "But you've got to let me explain."

They followed Gerald past the bar to a door in the back, down a hall to another door, then went inside.

Carmen heard Cherry gasp behind her.

Enrique Vargas sat tied to a chair, unconscious, head hanging, face swollen and bloody.

"What's this?" Jericho demanded.

"It's a personal dispute with me and him," Gerald said. "It's nothing to do with anyone else."

"That is not true," Carmen said calmly and—she hoped—with authority. "He was at my place. He did not like Cherry giving this boy her attention."

Jericho's face went the color of a tomato. "You stupid son of a—"

Carmen watched Gerald wilt beneath the torrent of obscenities Jericho heaped upon him. She would almost have been amused if she hadn't known what was about to happen next.

Lorenzo's place was full of armed men ready for war.

McCoy grudgingly admitted to himself he was impressed. The men had gathered quickly and were ready to go.

"You got men at Carmen's?" Lorenzo asked Big Mike.

"Front and back," Mike said. "My guess is they'll

high-tail it to the Thirsty Coyote when they hear all the shooting, and when they spill out of the door, our boys will be waiting to gun them down."

Lorenzo nodded his satisfaction. "Good. Okay, McCoy, this is your show."

McCoy raised his voice for everyone to hear. "Okay, this is the real thing, so look sharp. Surprise is key, and that means keeping quiet until all hell breaks loose. So no talking on the way. This ain't some dang Indian raid with a bunch of whoopin' and hollerin'. Mouths shut and ears open. When we get close, some of you are going to break off and circle around front. I spoke to you earlier, so you know who you are. Don't be seen. The rest with me and Lorenzo around back. Any questions?"

There were none.

McCoy looked at each man in the room, nodding his head. "This is one tough-looking bunch of hombres. I almost feel sorry for Jericho and his boys. Almost."

Grins from the men in the room, some elbow-nudging others in the ribs, but no shouts or cheers. They had their orders to keep quiet and were taking it seriously.

"Let's go," McCoy said.

They filed out the back door in an orderly way, still remaining as silent as possible.

Halfway to the Thirsty Coyote, Big Mike and a dozen men broke off from the main group to head down a side alley, sticking to the shadows. McCoy had instructed to either gun anyone coming out once the shooting started or to go in blazing depending on the situation. A lot would depend on Mike's ability to assess the situation and decide the right thing to do. Lorenzo had assured McCoy that Mike was up to the job.

The rest of them went down the narrow alley to the Thirsty Coyote's back door.

McCoy suddenly threw up a hand, bringing them all to a halt.

Dwight Combs leaned in the doorway, looking about as unconcerned as a man could get. He stuck a cigarette in his mouth, struck a match on the wall next to him, and lit his smoke. His Colt Walker loomed big on his hip.

"Hang back," McCoy told Lorenzo. "Keep the boys still, will you? I'll handle this."

McCoy moved forward, stopping ten feet from the gunman. "Dwight."

Combs touched the brim of his hat. "Garret."

"You called me *Garret* instead of *Ghost*," McCoy noticed. "You must be looking to keep it friendly."

"Wouldn't mind."

"So how do you want to do this?" McCoy asked.

Combs took a long drag on the cigarette, tilted his head back, and blew a long stream of smoke at the sky. "I guess that's up to you. We could start shooting, I reckon, but a lot of people would hear that, probably wouldn't work out how either of us wants."

"And what *do* you want?"

"What I did want was for the gravy train to go on a little longer," Combs said. "I thought it would be a while before the shooting part of this started. I was hoping to sort of ease along and collect a paycheck for a while. I guess that ship sailed."

"Looks like it."

"I haven't worked for Jericho long enough to grow

fond of him," Combs said. "Surely not long enough to kill for him . . . or die for him."

"Understandable," McCoy said. "You got something else in mind?"

"I wouldn't mind taking a stroll over to Carmen's Place, maybe get a bottle," Combs told him. "There's a pretty blonde over there too. Might try to strike up a conversation."

"Talk with your wallet," McCoy suggested. "The conversation will go faster."

Combs laughed.

"Want some advice?" McCoy asked.

Combs puffed his cigarette and nodded. "Always."

"The main event is here," McCoy told him. "But there's a sideshow brewing at Carmen's. You might wait until the smoke clears before you get that bottle."

"That's good advice." Combs started walking. "I'll take the long way."

McCoy turned to the men behind him. "Let him through."

Combs paused as he passed McCoy and winked. "Good luck."

McCoy grinned. "Good luck with that blonde."

When Combs had gone, McCoy nodded to Lorenzo. "It's time."

CHAPTER 20

"I specifically told you not to cause any more trouble in Carmen's Place." Jericho's eyes were daggers of fire burying themselves in Gerald's face. "I guess I'm wondering why you would so cavalierly disregard my direct and very specific orders."

Jericho had always found Gerald useful, but the idiot could be exhausting. He was growing less and less tolerant of these constant irritations.

Gerald's hands flew up in a *let me explain* gesture. "Now, I wasn't *inside* Carmen's Place. I was in the alley out back."

"Is that supposed to be some kind of joke?" Jericho demanded. Did Gerald really think he'd put up with such tedious hair-splitting? "What is it you have against this man anyway?"

Gerald pointed an accusing finger at Enrique. "He was talking to Cherry all lovey-dovey . . . he was at her *window*."

"This is ridiculous!" Carmen said. "Do your men not know what my girls do for a living? It is their *job* to talk to men in such a way. Cherry entertains many men, and only this Gerald person causes trouble. He skirts your orders by ambushing my customers in the back alley as if such a technicality can free him from obeying you. How am I supposed to run my business?"

"Easy, Carmen."

"You must do something."

"I will discipline my men in my own way," Jericho said heatedly. Honestly, the woman tried his patience. She was right, of course, but that didn't mean he should always tolerate her strong-willed nature. It wouldn't do for it to appear as if he took orders from the woman.

Carmen tugged at her collar. "How can you stand it in here?"

Jericho frowned. "What now?"

"It stinks of blood and man sweat in here." She was breathing through her mouth and looked like she might be sick, the expression on her face distressed. "I need air."

"Just take it easy."

"I'm going to be sick if I don't get some fresh air."

Jericho made an irritated noise in his throat. If it wasn't one thing, it was another. He gestured at the back door across the room. "Go out back and get some fresh air then."

Carmen dabbed at her mouth and forehead with a handkerchief. "Thank you." She slowly walked toward the back door.

Jericho pointed at Gerald. "I'm not done with you. Stay here. I'm going to go get her a glass of water."

He walked past Cherry on his way out of the room. Yes, a pretty girl certainly, but was she really worth this much fuss? Honestly, the utter nonsense he had to put up with on a daily basis.

He went back down the hall to the saloon and told the man behind the bar to give him a glass of water.

"And a whiskey," he said. "Make it a double."

Jericho wasn't about to put up with all this foolishness without a good, stiff drink.

Carmen unlocked the back door, unhooked the latch, and glanced once over her shoulder, then stepped out into the alley. The sight of so many men with guns startled her. She'd known they'd be there—that had been the plan, after all—but they stood with such quiet menace, she found it unnerving.

"Who's in there?" McCoy whispered.

"Cherry and Gerald—and Enrique, but he's unconscious."

"But alive?"

She nodded.

"That's something then," McCoy said. "Cherry knows what to do?"

Carmen nodded again.

"And she's up to it?"

Carmen had no idea. She'd thought it cruel to make her do it, one so young, but McCoy had said it would be better if it was her. Cherry would be able to get closer to Gerald. It had worked out better than Carmen had hoped, Jericho leaving to get her a glass of water. That left only Gerald to be disposed of as quickly and quietly as possible.

But Jericho wouldn't be gone for long.

"Stay right next to the door," she told McCoy. "Be ready. I'm going back in."

Carmen composed herself, went back in, pulling the door shut behind her but leaving it unlocked, and letting the latch hook dangle.

She caught Cherry's eye and nodded.

The girl swallowed hard, composed herself, and turned to Gerald.

"Why did you have to do that to Enrique?" she asked. "That's just going to get you in trouble, and if Mr. Jericho doesn't let you come over to Miss Carmen's then how are we going to see each other?"

Gerald blinked. "What?"

Cherry moved toward him, nothing obvious, just somebody closing the distance for a more intimate conversation. "You know you're my best customer, Gerald."

Gerald's face softened for a moment before anger flared again. "I heard what you said to him! All that lovey-dovey stuff."

Cherry put a hand on his shoulder. "It's like Miss Carmen said. It's my job to talk to men like that, but of course, you're my favorite. Everybody knows that."

He blinked. "They do?"

"Didn't you know that?" Cherry pressed against him. "Honey, you've just got to calm down. You have to know it's always been me and you."

One of Gerald's arms snaked around Cherry's waist, and he held her tight. "Well, I did really want to hear you say that. And it just drove me crazy the way he was looking at you and, well, it seemed like you was liking it a little too much, so, yeah, I reckon maybe I did take things too—"

Cherry pressed the barrel of the derringer against Gerald's chest and pulled the trigger.

A sharp *pop*. They'd hoped the small caliber would be quiet enough not to draw attention, but the suddenness of it made Carmen flinch and gasp.

Gerald's eyes popped wide, and he staggered back, a strangled animal sound caught in his throat, anger and shock and bewilderment all mixed together.

Carmen saw that Cherry had missed the heart, the spreading blood stain in Gerald's shirt a little too high and to the right. Cherry took two steps back from him, mouth hanging open, the derringer drooping from her limp hand as if she couldn't decide whether to drop it or not.

The scuff of boots behind Carmen. She was aware Garret McCoy and Lorenzo's men were filling the little room, but she couldn't take her eyes away from Gerald.

He took short, halting steps until he hit the far wall, all the time pawing at the wound on his chest as if it was only something on his shirt he could wipe away. He looked at his own blood, wet and red on his fingertips.

And then he looked at Cherry.

Gerald's face twisted with hate. A trembling hand fell to the six-shooter on his hip, he fumbled it a bit, trying to pull it free.

Cherry pointed at him and screamed.

Gerald's gun finally cleared the holster, and he lifted it, eyes furious and eager for Cherry's blood.

McCoy drew and fired twice, the shots like roaring thunder compared to the little derringer.

Gerald twitched and died, firing his pistol harmlessly into the ceiling.

Well, Carmen thought, her ears ringing from the pistol fire. *So much for the element of surprise.*

Jericho finished his whiskey and asked the barkeep for another. He wasn't especially eager to return to the back room to face Carmen and Gerald.

Carmen was rapidly becoming too big for her britches. An alluring woman, yes, but often not quick to obey. Yes, that was part of her charm, but it could be tiresome also. Perhaps when Jericho had finally dealt with Lorenzo, he'd consider a change of ownership for Carmen's Place. Yes, he quite liked that idea.

As for Gerald, well, the man was an idiot in some ways but still useful. Naturally, he'd need to be punished, but Jericho would probably use a light hand. Good men were harder to come by than pretty faces.

As for Cherry . . . well, she was young and would do as she was told.

He brought the shot glass to his lips and froze.

Had he heard something? A sort of *pop*. He glanced around. Nobody else seemed to be taking notice. Jericho shrugged it off. There was no point in worrying about every little—

A women screamed.

Now some of the others did take notice, although most of the men in the saloon carried on with their conversations.

Two pistol shots. Loud and close. Then a third.

Everyone went quiet, then started talking all at once. Jericho drew his six-gun. *Something's happening.*

Glass from the big front windows shattered inward.

Two lanterns had been tossed through by somebody outside. They landed, oil and flames spreading over a couple tables. Men jumped back from the flames. Others drew pistols.

Jericho saw the flashes of gunshots beyond the smoke, and lead streaked through the shattered windows. Some of his men caught lead and fell, clutching their bloody guts. Others returned fire.

Jericho coughed. The smoke was getting bad. All of his boys were too busy trading gunfire to put out the flames.

Time to retreat to a more hospitable environment.

He headed back down the back hallway but froze in his tracks when he saw the door at the far end fly open, armed men pouring in.

Jericho turned and ran. His office had a window. If he could get past the flames, he'd get out that way.

"They heard those shots for sure!" McCoy shouted. "Let's hit them before they can get organized!"

There was a mad rush for the door on the other side of the room, McCoy leading the way. As a bounty hunter, McCoy had worked mostly alone. Now he was in a press of men again, and he flashed on a bayonet charge from his war days, the heady confusion of it all, only seeing bits and pieces of a battle, images here and there, and now the same thing happened as he was carried along through the room.

Cherry and Carmen's frightened faces.

Enrique, tied to a chair, head hanging.

Gerald, slumped limp to the floor, a long streak of blood on the wall where he'd slid down it.

The racket of numerous gunshots out in the saloon.

The stink of something burning.

Suddenly he was through the door and into the hallway. At the other end of the hall a man stood silhouetted against smoke and flame. He turned to run, and McCoy caught a glimpse of his face.

Jericho!

McCoy ran after him, Lorenzo and his boys following close behind.

The saloon was a blazing wreck, tables and chairs burning. Flames climbing the wall, the bodies of dead men strewn everywhere. McCoy waved smoke away from his face. They wouldn't be able to stay in here for long.

Two men rose from the smoke, leveling their six-shooters at McCoy.

He fired once, caught the first man in the chest, sending him spinning back into the flames. He pivoted, fired again and killed the second man, who pitched forward, landed on his face, and never moved again.

McCoy saw a man vanish through a door all the way across the saloon. He'd only glimpsed him, but McCoy was sure it was Jericho.

"Get everyone out of here!" McCoy shouted back at Lorenzo. "I'm going after Jericho."

"Right. Be careful."

McCoy headed toward the door, flames crawling up the walls on both sides of him. He heard the crack of timber, looked up, and saw one of the ceiling beams come loose and fall right at him.

He dove forward and rolled away just as the beam crashed to the floor where he'd been a split-second earlier, flames and sparks flying. McCoy scrambled to his feet and through the door after Jericho.

The hall was filled with smoke, but the flames had yet to engulf this part of the building.

McCoy tried the nearest door. Locked.

He kicked it in and started to enter and spotted Jericho with one leg out the window.

Jericho lifted his six-shooter.

McCoy ducked back just as Jericho fired, hot lead chewing up the wall opposite the door. McCoy ducked back in and fired twice. The second shot caught Jericho in the forearm, blood splattering. He dropped his revolver as he fell the rest of the way out of the window.

McCoy raced to the window and saw Jericho fleeing down the street, his walking stick in one hand, the other arm hanging limply. McCoy awkwardly ducked his head through the window, climbed through and landed on the ground just in time to see Jericho duck around the corner of a building across the street.

People had spilled into the street now, gawkers in robes and dressing gowns, flames casting their alarmed faces in a hellish red-orange. They gasped as the Thirsty Coyote's roof fell in on itself with a catastrophic clamor, sparks spiraling into the air.

McCoy ignored them and ran after Jericho.

He rounded the corner and found himself behind what must have been a cooper's shop, stacks of barrels in front of him. McCoy eased between the stacks, palm sweaty on the grip of his Peacemaker. He held his breath, listening for movement.

He slowly rounded another stack of barrels and—

Movement in the corner of his eye.

He darted left, and there was Jericho ahead of him, trying to squeeze between two stacks of barrels. One arm dripping blood, he looked back, saw McCoy and tried to run in a different direction, tripped over his own feet and fell into the dirt.

And in the next instant, McCoy stood over him, Peacemaker aimed at Jericho's chest.

Jericho's eyes darted in every direction, the tension leaking out of him with a sigh as the obvious truth hit him plain and obvious. He was caught.

"Guess I should have tried a little harder to hire you onto my side." Jericho chuckled and it sounded tired. "I guess Lorenzo won that one."

McCoy nodded. "I reckon so."

"Did he offer more money?" Jericho asked. "Did he say he'd make you a partner?"

"Nope. Nothing like that," McCoy said.

"Then what?"

McCoy shrugged, bored with it now. He just wanted this night to be over. "Let's just say I've got my own long-term plans, and this is how it has to happen."

"So you weren't on my side or Lorenzo's side," Jericho said. "You were always on your own side."

"That's every man I ever met."

"You're not just going to shoot me in cold blood are you, lying here in the dirt?" Jericho said it like a challenge. "You're better than that, McCoy."

"Am I?"

"I think so," Jericho insisted. "You're no saint. I'm

not trying to sell that, but you've got some sense of honor."

"If I take you to Lorenzo, he'll shoot you anyway," McCoy said.

"Sure, but ten minutes from now." Jericho grinned. "Ten minutes is a long time to a man about to die."

McCoy hated to admit it, but Jericho was right about one thing. He wasn't keen on shooting a defenseless man. "Stand up then. I'll take you to Lorenzo." Sure, Lorenzo would kill him, but then that would be on Lorenzo. McCoy's hands wouldn't exactly be clean, but not so dirty either.

Jericho grinned. "I knew it. Deep down, you're a good man, McCoy. Tough as nails, yes, but good."

"Uh-huh." McCoy shook the Peacemaker at him. "Less talk. More getting up."

"Of course."

Jericho grunted as he tried to stand, the bloody arm useless, the other hand gripping his walking stick tightly as he used it to push himself to his feet. He was sweating and trembling slightly. No surprise. McCoy had been shot before and knew it was no picnic.

Jericho panted, leaning heavily on the walking stick. "Thank you for your patience. You're not exactly catching me at my best right now."

"Can you walk or not?"

"I can, not fast, but I can," Jericho said. "Oh, and one more thing."

"Yeah, what's that?"

Jericho twisted the silver ram's head at the top of his walking stick. There was an audible *click* and a trigger released just below the ram's head. "Say hello to the devil for me."

Instinct and reflex took over, and McCoy dodged to one side just as Jericho lifted the cane and fired, a pop and flash from the cane's tip. McCoy felt pain, hot and wet on his right ear. He lifted his Peacemaker and squeezed the trigger, thunder booming.

Jericho took the shot right through the heart and staggered back, knocking over a stack of barrels. He lay there, not moving. McCoy kicked him in the side, but Jericho didn't move, didn't make a noise.

Dead.

McCoy holstered his six-shooter, turned, and left the corpse where it was, heading back the way he came. His hand went to his ear. Blood. He winced as he felt around, discovering the extent of his wound.

Well, what's a man need an earlobe for anyway?

He walked back to the street, where a few men had organized a bucket brigade and were tossing water onto the blaze, but anyone could see it was useless. At least none of the adjacent buildings had caught.

McCoy turned his head to see Lorenzo coming toward him.

"You've looked better," Lorenzo said.

A weak smile from McCoy. "You should see the other fella."

Lorenzo raised an eyebrow. "Jericho?"

"Dead."

Lorenzo nodded. "That's a clean sweep then. Jericho's boys are all dead. Well, a few made it to their horses, but they'll still be running this time next week. We won't see them again. We won the war, McCoy."

Lorenzo gave him a pat on the shoulder. "You won it for us."

Right.

"Get some rest," Lorenzo said as he turned to get back to his place. "We'll celebrate tomorrow with a proper shindig. A victory celebration."

McCoy stood there and watched him walk away.

The bucket brigade had thrown down their buckets and had called it quits. The only thing to do was let it burn.

Another figure broke loose from the crowd, a woman's silhouette against the flames. McCoy stood and let her come. When Carmen stood directly in front of him, they looked at each other for a moment.

"Jericho's dead," he told her.

"You're hurt." She started to reach for his ear, then drew her hand back.

"I'm okay."

But was he? He was alive. That wasn't the same.

"How's Cherry?" he asked.

"She'll be okay."

"And Enrique?"

"Roughed up pretty badly," Carmen said. "But he'll be okay too."

"And you?"

Carmen shrugged. "I'm indestructible."

And then they fell into each other's arms, kissing long and hard as the flames rose behind them.

CHAPTER 21

Three days later, McCoy started to feel human again.

He'd been hurt plenty worse a time or two and had been in bigger battles during the war. But there was something in a big action that took it out of a man. That frantic rush of death and the blood pumping and the confused tumult of emotions—fear, rage, fury, and confusion. And then the cool flood of relief at the end that you've made it.

Lorenzo's men must have felt something similar, for the victory party the next night was a subdued affair, drinking and food and congratulatory slaps on the back, but not a raucous, whooping, all-night party. Which suited McCoy just fine. Everyone was just glad it was over.

But it wasn't over, not really. In a way, it was just beginning. The next day, Lorenzo had sent his men around Coyote Flats to explain the new world order to the townsfolk. Payments would continue, but now they would go into Lorenzo's coffers instead of Jericho's.

The king was dead. Long live the king.

McCoy buttoned up his shirt as he looked at himself

in the mirror. The bandage on his ear looked odd. He'd probably feel lopsided for a while.

Behind him, Carmen slipped out of bed and shrugged into a sheer, silky robe. "You slept well, darling?"

"Once you let me sleep."

She grinned.

He ran a hand along his jaw, still looking in the mirror. "I need a shave again."

"Don't," she said. "Like I told you before. I like my man a little bit rough."

"Maybe I should go for the full beard then."

Her face scrunched up in displeasure. "I said a little bit rough, not Yukon fur trapper."

McCoy laughed.

"What will you do today?" she asked.

"I thought I might ride out to the Vargas place and see how Enrique is healing," he told her.

"That is nice of you," she said. "When you return, I would like to discuss . . . a concern."

"Oh?"

"But it can wait."

"Don't keep me in suspense," he said. "Out with it."

"Very well." A sigh. "With Jericho's death, I am somewhat worried now. Carmen's Place used to be neutral ground. You have to have opposing sides to have neutral ground."

He turned and looked at her. "I thought you were glad Jericho was gone."

"Yes, for personal reasons," she said. "For business reasons, I am concerned. There is no longer a need for neutral ground. Lorenzo might decide I should pay along with everyone else in town."

"I guess I hadn't thought of that," McCoy admitted. "We'll cross that bridge when we come to it. Anyway, I'm Lorenzo's golden boy. I won his war for him. If I need to, I can have a word with him."

She crossed the room and wrapped her arms around him. "As you say. We will cross that bridge when we come to it."

They kissed.

McCoy grabbed his guns. "I'll say hello to Enrique for you."

She smiled. "Tell him Cherry says hello. That will mean more to him."

McCoy winked. "Will do."

He left the saloon, went to the livery stable, and saddled his horse. He passed the ruined remains of the Thirsty Coyote. There was still a burnt smell in the air. Eventually the charred debris would be cleared away. Somebody would build a new building. The town would forget Jericho had ever been there.

Not soon, but eventually.

He'd gotten directions to the Vargas place from Juan and Carlos when he'd met them in Black Oak, knowing he'd likely be riding out there for one reason or another sooner or later. McCoy hadn't forgotten who Lorenzo was and what he'd done. McCoy's plans for revenge had not been forgotten. He was enjoying his time with Carmen.

But sooner or later it would be time.

The Vargas place was not extravagant but neat and orderly, the ground well taken care of. Somebody hailed McCoy from the barn as he dismounted. McCoy turned to see Juan walking toward him, a big smile on his face.

"*Señor* McCoy!" Juan said. "I wondered when we might see you."

"Juan."

The two men shook hands.

"I thought I might see how Enrique was doing?" McCoy said.

"Oh, he will be glad to see you," Juan said. "Please, follow me."

In the house, McCoy shook hands with Carlos and was introduced to their mother. The old woman spoke a lengthy bit in Spanish, and McCoy caught every twentieth word—if that much.

"She says she is most grateful for returning her boy to her," Juan translated. "He is young and foolish and has not the guidance of a father." He rolled his eyes. "He would be foolish anyway, if you asked me, especially for a pretty face."

Carlos laughed.

"Ask her if it's okay if I say hello to him," McCoy said.

Juan exchanged words with his mother, then told McCoy, "She says it is fine but not to disturb him for too long. He needs his rest. She babies him. Come, I will show you this lazy boy and how he lies around all day pretending to be hurt."

Juan led McCoy to a small room where Enrique lay sprawled on a narrow bed.

The young Mexican sat up quickly when he saw McCoy. "*Señor* McCoy!"

"Just rest easy," McCoy told him. "You look better."

There were still numerous bruises all over Enrique's face, but the swelling had gone down considerably.

"He was never very good-looking anyway." Juan tousled Enrique's hair.

Enrique swatted his older brother's hand away. "*Idiota*."

"Miss Carmen and Miss Cherry send their regards," McCoy said.

Enrique smiled. "Tell Cherry I will come and see her soon!"

"No, you will not," Juan said. "Every time you go into town there is trouble. The last time an entire building burned to the ground."

"That was not my fault!"

The two brothers went at each other in Spanish.

"Okay, enough," McCoy said. "You two can do this after I leave, can't you?"

"Don't worry, *Señor* McCoy," Juan said. "We'll keep him home and safe."

"Juan, I want to talk to you and Carlos," McCoy said. "But let me have a word with Enrique first."

"Okay, *señor*. Come out to the barn when you are ready." Juan left.

"Okay, seriously, feeling stronger?" McCoy asked.

"Oh, yes. Mother fusses, but I am fine."

"Cherry will be glad to hear that."

Enrique grinned.

"And she'll be glad to see you too," McCoy told him. "But not soon. Your brother's right. It wouldn't do for you to go back into Coyote Flats anytime soon. Jericho and Gerald are gone, but there's going to be a new sort of trouble starting soon. That's what I'm here to talk to Juan and Carlos about. They'll fill you in after I'm gone. In the meantime, stay home. Got it?"

Enrique looked crestfallen, but nodded. "I understand."

McCoy turned to go, then stopped himself. "There's . . . one more thing."

"Yes?"

"I don't usually care to butt into other people's personal business. Maybe because I don't take it well when people butt into mine," McCoy said. "But I'll speak my mind because maybe it'll do you some good. Cherry's a sweet kid, but nothing's different. She still is who she is. She still works for Miss Carmen. There's always going to be men like Gerald who couldn't get his mind right about that reality. I'd hate to see you turn into that sort of fella. I guess you could marry her, away from Carmen, but wives can be expensive, and mothers are often right picky when it comes to what kind of a woman marries her son. Personally, I think you'd be lucky, but I'm not your mother."

Enrique nodded slowly, letting McCoy's words sink it. "There is much to what you say. Much for me to think about."

"Get rest, kid. Tomorrow's another day."

McCoy left the little house and entered the barn.

"Sorry to make you come out to the barn," Carlos said. "Mother knows more English than she lets on, and anything she heard us say would only worry her."

"Well, let's not do that," McCoy said.

Juan held out an earthen jug toward McCoy. "Refreshment, *señor*?"

McCoy took the jug, sniffed it, and winced. "You stripping paint off a wagon?"

The brothers laughed.

"It is something we brew ourselves," Juan said.

"Mother does not keep strong drink in the house, and we haven't been to town. So we have been forced to get creative. It is made with—"

"No, no, don't tell me," McCoy said. "I'd only worry."

He took a big swig, and it burned going down. He coughed and handed back the jug.

"There's plenty if you want more," Juan said.

McCoy waved him away. "I'd better not push my luck."

"We have been waiting to hear your plan," Carlos urged.

"We've gotten rid of one boss in Coyote Flats," McCoy said. "It's time to get rid of the other."

Juan and Carlos looked at each other.

Then Juan cleared his throat and asked, "Why?"

McCoy blinked, taken aback. The obvious, straightforward question had caught him completely by surprise.

He composed himself and said, "Lorenzo is a bad man. The people of Coyote Flats would be better off without him. Doesn't it bother you Lorenzo takes hard-earned money from them that he doesn't deserve? That he throws his weight around and threatens people?"

"It does not sound very nice, I will admit," Carlos said.

"I'm sure the town would like to be rid of Lorenzo," Juan said. "He is a bad man, as you say. But the world is full of bad men. Do we chase them all endlessly until there are no bad men left? If we lived a hundred lifetimes, we would never accomplish such a thing."

Juan was right. There was no way around it. And anyway, McCoy wasn't quite being totally honest, was he? Yes, he was fond of some of the people in Coyote Flats—Carmen, obviously, but that wasn't why he had it in for Lorenzo. The image of his father kneeling in the mud in Parson's Gulch would forever be seared into McCoy's mind. It was unlikely McCoy's desire for revenge would move the two brothers to action.

But that was the answer: not McCoy's revenge, but that it had to be personal to Juan and Carlos.

"Isn't Coyote Flats your home?" McCoy asked.

Carlos shrugged and looked at Juan.

"We have no home anymore," Juan said. "We are wanted men and doomed to wander."

McCoy thought about that for a moment. "I know a few federal marshals. You meet them in my line of work. Not all of them like me. Some do. I can put in a word. We can find out how to clear your names. Maybe you can have a home again instead of wandering."

Juan scratched at his sparse beard, eyes narrowed in thought.

"I would like to have a home again," Carlos said to his brother. "Or at least not have to worry about visiting Mother, so we can come visit and not bring a posse after us, or so we can leave her here and not worry about what Lorenzo will do. And what about Enrique? Do we not want him to live in a peaceful, happy place where he can marry his girl, Cherry, and bring up a family?"

Juan put his hands on his hips, looked away and sighed, shaking his head.

McCoy kept his mouth shut. Carlos was doing a good job of convincing his brother without McCoy's help.

Juan looked at McCoy. "Can you guarantee that one

of your marshal friends can help us? I do not want to go to prison, *Señor* McCoy. Can you promise to clear our names?"

McCoy thought carefully before answering. This was no time to give up on honesty. He shook his head. "Nope. There are no guarantees. No promises except this one. I'll try my best. I'll stick up for you, and I'll keep trying. But I can't see the future. I can't guarantee it's all going to work out."

Juan and Carlos went back and forth in Spanish for a minute.

Then they looked at McCoy, faces serious.

"We will help you," Juan said.

"A man cannot always be running," Carlos added. "There must come a day when he will stand, when he will try."

"Thank you both." McCoy offered his hand.

They shook.

"I've got to get back into town," he said. "I'll send word when it's time. Be ready."

CHAPTER 22

Mortimer Lorenzo stood at the counter of Miller's Dry Goods and counted money. Big Mike stood behind him looking big. Sometimes a reminder like that was a good idea. It was a simple way to ensure cooperation. *This big fella can hurt you real good if you don't cooperate.*

But so far, everyone had cooperated. No fuss. No bother. Lorenzo had to admit Jericho had his sheep trained well.

"Looks like it's all here," Lorenzo said. "You understand everything is the same, yes. It'll just be a different fella coming around to collect."

"I understand." Miller's face was carefully neutral, not friendly, but no scowls or frowns to give offense.

Lorenzo could respect that. Honest but not stupid.

He left the dry goods store, Big Mike right behind him. He'd barely taken two steps when he heard somebody calling his name.

"Mr. Lorenzo!"

Lorenzo turned his head to see Froggy Morton running toward him.

Although *running* was maybe being generous. He

was called Froggy for the obvious reason that he looked like a frog, short and very fat with a big, bloated frog sack of flesh hanging under his chin. He had dark little eyes in his pillowy face. He stopped in front of Lorenzo, huffing and puffing. He took off his hat, wiped his bald head with a handkerchief. "Been looking for you, Mr. Lorenzo."

"Well, you've been looking a long time," Lorenzo said. "Where the hell were you the other night when we raided Jericho? I don't remember seeing you anywhere."

Big Mike leaned in from behind and said, "You asked me to send a couple boys down to Black Oak to see where Hank and Rusty got themselves, remember? I sent Froggy and Bill Bachman to ask around."

"Oh, right. Sorry about that, Froggy," Lorenzo said. "What've you got for me?"

Froggy looked one way then another, lowered his voice. "Maybe best we talk in private, sir."

Lorenzo groaned inwardly. In the history of private conversations, nobody had ever told him good news. "Come on then."

They went back to the club, and Lorenzo plopped into a seat at the center table. "Thirsty, Froggy?"

Froggy nodded eagerly. "A cold beer would do me."

"Beers for everyone," Lorenzo told the man behind the bar.

They all drank beers.

"Now," Lorenzo said. "Where's Hank and Rusty?"

"Ah." Froggy took another gulp of beer. "Me and Bill are still a little bit fuzzy on that."

Lorenzo frowned. "What? Fuzzy?"

"Where is Bill, anyway?" Mike asked.

"Ah. See, that's part of the story," Froggy said.

"Story? Who wants a dang story?" Lorenzo demanded. "Did you find them or not?"

"It might be best if I start from the beginning," Froggy suggested.

"You're going to make me listen to your dang story, aren't you?" Lorenzo said.

"It might be best."

"Fine." Lorenzo waved at the barkeep. "Gonna need a lot more beer over here."

"And one of them pickled eggs out the jar," Big Mike said.

"Can we get on with the story, please?" Lorenzo asked.

Froggy cleared his throat. "Okay, here's what happened."

It was already after dark when Froggy Morton and Bill Bachman rode into Black Oak.

"Where to first?" asked Bill.

"Food and a drink," Froggy said.

"Shouldn't we ask around about Hank and Rusty?"

"You don't think Hank and Rusty like to eat and drink?" Froggy asked. "We'll start in the saloon. Nobody says we got to have a lousy time just because we're on the job."

"And maybe some of them pretty saloon gals know what happened to Hank and Rusty," Bill said. "We could spend a lot of time asking them."

Bill grinned big, and Froggy winced. Bill was not a handsome fella, not that it was his fault. He'd been kicked in the head by a mule as a kid, and one side of his face was sort of all caved in, three missing teeth on one side of his smile, and a nose bent to one side.

They dismounted in front of a place called Herman's Saloon, tied up their horses, then went inside to the bar.

"Hello, strangers," said the man behind the bar. "What can I do for you?"

"You Herman?" Froggy asked in a friendly way.

"No sir. Herman died back in sixty-eight. Man named McGregor bought the place off Herman's window. I'm the senior barkeep. Call me Franklin."

"Bought it off his widow, eh? That's interesting, Franklin." Froggy didn't think it was interesting at all, but he wanted to get some talk going. "How 'bout a couple whiskeys?"

Franklin poured the drinks.

"Franklin, as the senior man, I imagine you're in here a lot," Froggy said.

"That I am, sir, that I am."

"Then maybe you've seen a couple friends of ours. We're hoping to meet up with them."

"I don't catch many names, but I see plenty of faces," Franklin said. "You describe them, and I'll say if they've been through."

Franklin hadn't seen anyone of Hank Blevins's description, which was understandable since Froggy could hardly picture Hank in his head to describe him. Hank was probably the most dull-looking man Froggy had ever laid eyes on.

Rusty Calhoun, on the other hand, was a different kettle of fish.

"Goofy looking red-haired fella with a big gap between

his front teeth," Franklin said. "Had an odd way about him."

"That's him," Froggy confirmed.

"Yeah, I remember him," Franklin said. "Came through a few days ago."

Froggy and Bill downed their drinks.

"Fill us up again," Froggy told the barkeep. "And pour one for yourself."

"Thank you, sir. That's right neighborly." Franklin refilled the first two glasses and a third for himself.

"Sounds like we missed them." Froggy said. "Maybe they'll come back. You seen them since that first time?"

"Nope. I'd have remembered that red-haired fella," Franklin said. "Of course, they might've stopped through when one of the other barkeeps was on duty."

"Hmmmm. I'm not sure what to do now," Froggy admitted. "Move on or hang around here a while to see if they come back. Did they talk to anyone else around here, maybe say where they was going or what they was going to do?"

"I saw the one fella talking to a few of the girls," Franklin said. "After that, I couldn't say. Can't really keep track of every single person when it starts to get busy in here."

"Maybe I can talk to a few of the girls," Froggy suggested. "Ask them."

Franklin winced as if sorry for what he had to say next. "Well, if you're spending time with any of the ladies, you're supposed to buy them a drink."

"That's not a problem," Froggy assured the man. "Always happy to play by the rules."

"Thanks, friend," Franklin said apologetically.

"You know how it is. The boss catches me letting things slide . . ."

"Say no more," Froggy told him.

He bought a bottle and asked for another glass and moved to the end of the bar where one of the saloon gals had been giving him the eye. She was a little long in the tooth, but there was something to be said for experience as far as Froggy was concerned. He poured her a drink and made small talk, turning the subject quickly to Rusty Calhoun. Yes, she'd seen him. No, she hadn't been impressed.

Then Froggy had bought a drink for a freckled girl with light brown hair.

Then a drink for a leggy blonde.

A shot of whiskey for a chubby gal with hair almost purple, some kind of dye job gone awry.

They all had more or less the same story. Rusty had been there, talked to most of the girls, his hands going everywhere except into his wallet. He hadn't said anything about his future plans, and he hadn't been back since that first night, which suited all the ladies just fine.

Not a single one of the saloon gals remembered Hank Blevins.

"Well, they was here, that's for sure," Froggy told Bill. "But nobody's seen 'em since."

"Huh." Bill had been drinking whiskey nonstop and looked a little bleary-eyed.

"Listen, I think Penelope uh, might have more information," Froggy said. "So I'm going to take her upstairs and question her a little more closely."

That woke up Bill some. "Hey, I got questions I want to ask too."

"You ain't paid for one drink all night," Froggy scolded. "Find your own girl and question her. If you want to be useful, go to the hotel across the street and see if there's vacancy."

When Froggy came back downstairs forty minutes later, Bill was still sitting in the exact same spot, drinking whiskey.

"Did you get us a room?" Froggy asked.

Bill hiccupped. "What?"

Froggy rolled his eyes. "Thanks for nothing. Come on."

The hotel had one room left but only with one bed, so Froggy and Bill had to share. They kicked off their boots and fell into bed. Bill stole the covers, and Froggy stole them back. They spent most of the night trying to out-snore each other.

They slept too late the next morning.

Bill rolled out of bed, hit the floor and groaned.

"You drank too much last night," Froggy told him.

Bill groaned again. "I feel like something that came out the wrong end of a mule. A sick mule."

"That's nice," Froggy said flatly. "Very nice. You think I want to hear that?"

They dressed, found a place for coffee, and sat there, Froggy trying to think what to do next and Bill groaning and looking green, doing his level best to keep the coffee down.

"We should talk to the sheriff," Froggy said.

"You want to go to the law?" Bill asked, incredulous. "I don't like that."

"We're not asking him which bank to rob, fool," Froggy chided. "We're just asking if he's seen some fellas. He's a public servant."

"Public?"

"The public," Froggy said. "Us."

"I still don't like it."

"Too bad." Froggy stood and left money on the table for the coffee. "Come on. We'll see if he's in his office."

They walked down the street to the jailhouse, and Froggy knocked on the door.

No answer.

"Any more big ideas?" Bill asked.

Froggy frowned at him. "Shut up and let me think."

"You fellas looking for the sheriff?"

They turned and saw a man walking toward them, one of his arms in a sling.

"That's right," Froggy said.

"I'm the sheriff." He walked past them, a ring of keys jangling in his good hand. "Bryson Tate. Come on in."

The sheriff opened the door, and Froggy and Bill followed him inside.

Tate tossed the keys onto the desk. "Can I help you fellas with something?"

"Looking for a couple fellas," Froggy told him. "Figured since you're the law, your eyes might be sharp for strangers coming through."

"These fellas wanted for something?"

"No, nothing like that," Froggy said. "Just a couple of acquaintances."

Froggy described Hank and Rusty.

The sheriff shook his head immediately. "Nope. Nobody like that."

Froggy's shoulders sagged. "Well, it was worth a try."

"Sorry, boys. Have a good day."

Froggy left the jailhouse, Bill right behind him, and they headed for the livery stable to get their horses. Something about the sheriff wasn't sitting right with Froggy, but he couldn't quite put his finger on it.

The Mexican kid at the stable brought out the horses.

"Did you notice how fast that sheriff said he hadn't seen Rusty or Hank?" Froggy asked Bill.

Bill shrugged. "So what? If he ain't seen 'em, then he ain't seem 'em."

"But he didn't even pause and think about it," Froggy said. "Every single person in Herman's remembered seeing Rusty. He stands out. Hard to miss him with the way he looks with that bright orange hair and buck teeth and the loud way he's always talking, but the sheriff is the only guy that doesn't know who we're talking about. Just seems odd."

"I have seen this man also, *señor*," said the Mexican kid. "You are right. He is a very odd-looking man. Anyone who saw him would remember."

Froggy squinted at the kid. "What's your name?"

"Jorge," he said brightly.

"And you saw Rusty, huh?"

"*Sí, señor*, with another man. I see many people coming and going," Jorge explained. "Many strangers in town bring their horses here."

Froggy scratched the stubble on his throat, thoughtful. "If you seen so much then maybe you seen something helpful. Might be two bits in it for you."

"Are these two men bounty hunters?" Jorge asked.

Froggy frowned. "Why would you think that?"

"I saw one of the men—not the funny-looking one, but the other one—I saw him talking to *Señor* McCoy, who is a famous bounty hunter."

Froggy's ears perked up at McCoy's name. "You saw Hank talking to McCoy?"

The kid shook his head. "I do not know his name, *señor*."

"The friend of the funny-looking one," Froggy clarified.

"Oh, yes," Jorge said. "After Hank talked to *Señor* McCoy, he met up with the funny-looking one. And then *Señor* McCoy went to talk to the sheriff. They all rode out of town in the same direction. Not at the same time, but all the same direction. I thought if they were bounty hunter friends of *Señor* McCoy, then maybe they were all chasing an outlaw together for the reward!"

"And did they all come back?" Froggy asked.

Jorge's face scrunched up like he was thinking hard about it. "The sheriff came back, and his arm was hurt."

"Wait," Froggy interrupted. "His arm wasn't hurt before?"

"No, he was fine, then he left town, but when he came back, he was hurt," Jorge said.

"Go on then."

"And then later *Señor* McCoy came back into town."

"Was he hurt?" Froggy asked.

Jorge shook head. "No . . . but he was very dirty."

"Dirty, huh? What about Hank and the funny-looking one?"

"I did not see them come back, *señor*."

"Not at all?"

"I never saw them again," Jorge said.

Froggy thought about that.

And then he thought some more.

Then Froggy gave Jorge a serious look. "How would you like to earn five dollars?"

Jorge's eyes shot wide. "So much?"

"That's right, but there's a condition," Froggy told him. "You know what *no questions asked* means?"

"It means . . . not to ask questions?"

"No," Froggy said. "I mean, yes, but it's more serious than that. It means it's nobody's business. It means if somebody asks you about it, you don't know a thing because it ain't *their* business. You understand? It's just a private business transaction between men."

Jorge stood straight. "I understand, *señor*."

"Then listen close, and I'll tell you exactly what to do," Froggy said. "And if you do it right, I'll give you five dollars . . . no questions asked."

Sheriff Bryson Tate hadn't liked the look of those two men, and he liked their questions even less. When he'd left Garret McCoy to bury two dead men, Tate had thought that would be the end of it. Just a couple of no-goods. Who'd miss them?

But apparently the no-goods had some no-good friends. That might be trouble.

He tried to guess what they might find out, and the answer always came back the same: Nothing. Only two people knew where those bodies were buried, and McCoy had left town.

And Tate was for dang sure not telling anybody. The secret was safe.

Still . . .

He wandered over to Herman's and found Franklin behind the bar, asked if there was anything new going on, tried to be subtle, and found out those same two guys had been over here to ask around about their friends. As far as Franklin could tell, they hadn't had any luck.

Tate thanked him and strolled back to the jailhouse, sat behind his desk and drummed his fingers on the surface. He was being paranoid. Them two fellas had looked for their friends, crapped out, and now they'd leave none the wiser. It was as simple as that. He put the whole thing out of his mind.

He tidied up around the jailhouse even though it wasn't really needed. It had been a while since he'd had any customers, not even a couple of unruly drunks to slam into the cells. He put the coffeepot on the potbelly stove, deciding he needed a pick-me-up. It was a little awkward one-handed, but he managed.

That's when the Mexican kid from the stables walked in.

"What's going on, Jorge?"

Jorge swept his hat off his head, held it to his chest. "Sheriff, I thought you should know something?"

"Oh? Let's hear it then." Tate used his handkerchief to grab the coffeepot handle and fill a mug.

"You know those two strangers in town? The ones asking about their friends?"

Tate was reaching to return the pot to the stove and froze, head turning slowly to look at the boy. "A short, fat fella? The other one with half his face sort of smashed in?"

"*Si*, Sheriff. Those are the two."

Tate blew a long breath out of his nose and set the pot on the stove. "What about 'em?"

"I heard them talking as they were saddling their horses," Jorge said. "They did not see me and spoke freely. They said they had discovered where their friends were but were worried something bad had happened to them. They were going to the place to see."

Tate's eyes narrowed. "What place?"

"I do not know exactly," Jorge said. "A place out of town."

Tate forced an easygoing demeanor. "You did the right thing coming to me, but you shouldn't worry about it. I'll check it out. Thanks, Jorge."

The boy nodded and left.

Damn. Tate sipped coffee. *Damn. Damn. Damn.*

Those graves were still fresh. A blind man could find them. Heck, maybe McCoy hadn't even buried them. He might have just left them to rot in the sun and ridden away. Tate didn't take McCoy to be that sort. To Tate, McCoy seemed like the kind of man to do things right. No loose ends.

But Tate didn't *know*. He just had to hope it was true.

And it would keep nagging at him if he didn't look. That was it, wasn't it? He was gonna have to look. He had to be sure.

He grumbled out some curses as he set his coffee mug down, and fifteen minutes later, he was on his horse, riding out of town toward the abandoned ranch house.

"That's him."

Bill burped, still looking a little green. "You sure?"

"Yeah."

Froggy and Bill sat astride their horses amid a cluster of scrub oaks and watched the sheriff ride out of town.

"I guess that Mexican kid sold him the story," Bill said.

"Seems like it." Froggy spurred his horse. "Let's get after him."

They followed at a safe distance, and when they arrived at the ranch house, Froggy spotted the sheriff's horse tied up out front. He and Bill dismounted and took a look at the place. Didn't seem like anyone had lived here for a long time.

Bill burped then turned his head and spit. "Oh, man . . . I don't . . . don't feel so good."

Froggy drew his pistol. "Pull yourself together."

Bill spit again. "Right."

"Go through the house," Froggy said. "I'll circle around."

Froggy went around the house to the back, grip tight on his pistol, ready to shoot anything that moved.

He spotted two mounds of dirt. Fresh. Graves.

Then Froggy heard the *click-click* of a hammer being thumbed back on a six-shooter.

"Don't move." Tate's voice.

Froggy didn't move.

"Toss that shooter away."

Froggy tossed his gun.

"Turn around."

Froggy turned around.

Tate came out from behind a tree, six-shooter in his good hand. "Where's the other one?"

"In the house."

"Call him out," Tate said. "Tell him nobody's out here."

Froggy hesitated.

Tate pointed his six-shooter straight at Froggy's face. "Do it."

Froggy raised his voice. "Hey, Bill. Come out. Sheriff's gone. I think we missed him."

Noise from within the house.

Then the screen door slammed open, and Bill came out. "Then whose horse is out front if the sheriff—"

Tate pointed his gun at him. "Drop that gun belt."

But that's not what Bill did.

He went for his gun, and Tate fired, hitting Bill's shoulder, staggering him, but Bill didn't go down.

Froggy reached behind his back for the knife on his belt.

Tate fired again, this time catching Bill right in the middle of his chest. Bill fell over dead.

Tate tried to bring his gun back around on Froggy, but Froggy was already moving.

He threw himself on the sheriff, and both of them went over, Tate landing on his back with a whuff of air, Froggy landing right on top of him.

Froggy thrust the knife up under his ribs, pulled it

out, and thrust again. Tate made a ragged shuddering sound, bucked once, then went limp.

Froggy rolled off him, panting, the hand holding the knife hot and red with blood. He lay there a moment to catch his breath, then lurched to his feet and went to check on Bill.

He looked around. What a mess. Dead sheriff. That would bring trouble, wouldn't it? You weren't supposed to kill lawmen. He cursed and went to fetch the horses, came back, and heaved Bill's body over his horse before mounting his own.

He took a last look around. Time to get out of there before somebody saw him.

Froggy headed for Coyote Flats with bad news and a dead body.

CHAPTER 23

"You didn't dig them up?"

Froggy blinked. "What?"

"Hank and Rusty," Lorenzo said. "You didn't dig them up?"

Froggy gawked at Lorenzo, then looked into his empty beer mug as if there might be help there, then back at Lorenzo. "Dig them up? But . . . why?"

Lorenzo sighed like he was trying to have patience with an especially dull-witted child. "Because, Froggy, if I'm going to kill a man over this, I want to make dang sure I have all my facts straight."

McCoy strolled into Carmen's, feeling good about his visit to the Vargas brothers. There were still a few gaps in his plan, but it was all coming together.

He spotted Dwight Combs at the bar and bellied up next to him. "Dwight."

Combs nodded. "Ghost."

McCoy sighed. "You know I'm not keen on being called that."

Combs grinned. "I know."

McCoy spied Combs's empty beer mug. "Spot you a refill."

"Obliged."

McCoy waved at the barkeep. "Two beers."

The barkeep brought the beers, and the two bounty hunters drank.

"Maybe I've got something for you," McCoy said.

"Work?"

"That's right."

"Somewhere out of town, chasing after outlaws?" Combs asked. "Or business here in Coyote Flats?"

"Local," McCoy said.

Combs shook his head. "Sorry."

"You got something better lined up?"

Combs shook his head again, more slowly this time. "Nope. That's what I'm trying to figure out right now. Coyote Flats is too . . . complicated. I should never have thrown in with Jericho. I'm making a point not to get involved the rest of my time here."

McCoy finished his beer and set the empty mug on the bar. "Come find me if you have a change of heart."

"Will do."

McCoy headed toward the stairs.

"Ghost."

McCoy paused, looked back.

"Lorenzo," Combs said. "He's not sore at me for throwing in with Jericho, is he?"

"You stepped aside before the shooting started,"

McCoy reminded him. "You're probably in the clear, but I'll ask him if it's worrying you."

"Obliged."

McCoy went upstairs and knocked on Carmen's door but didn't get an answer.

What now? Get food.

He went back downstairs, glanced at the bar, and saw that Dwight Combs was gone. McCoy wondered when and where he'd see the other bounty hunter again, if at all.

He left Carmen's and went to the slop house.

The old woman came to his table, frowning. "You again."

"Sorry."

"Blueberry pie?"

"Man cannot live by pie alone," McCoy said.

"What then?" she asked.

"You pointed me in a good direction with the pie last time," McCoy said. "Anything else I can keep down?"

"Hold on."

The old woman left and came back with a plate, set it on the table in front of him. "Chicken and dumplings."

He picked up a fork and tried some. "Not as good as the pie but not bad."

"Such high praise."

"What's your name?" McCoy asked.

"Cordelia."

"Good to make your acquaintance, Cordelia," he said. "I'm McCoy."

"I know." She turned away to let him eat in peace. "Everybody knows you."

McCoy finished the chicken and dumplings, paid, and walked outside.

He spotted a familiar face across the street. Moses Hendershot and a couple of his ranch hands were bringing sacks out of the feed store and loading them onto a buckboard. The feed store was two doors down from Miller's Dry Goods, and McCoy suddenly had an idea.

He crossed the street and entered the dry goods store.

Miller looked up from his ledger. "Mr. McCoy, what can I do for you today?"

McCoy looked around the store and saw it was empty of customers. "Do you know Moses Hendershot?"

"I do," Miller said. "He shops here on occasion."

"He's down at the feed store," McCoy told him. "Do me a favor and fetch him here, would you?"

"But why?"

"Because I'd like us all to have a chin-wag," McCoy said. "But I don't want all three of us seen together on the street."

Miller licked his lips nervously. "Well, okay."

He left his store and came back a minute later with Hendershot.

Hendershot saw McCoy and frowned. "You. Last time I saw you, I was handing over my hard-earned money."

"And do you remember what I told you at the time?" McCoy asked.

Hendershot hooked his thumbs into his belt and lifted his chin, defiance in his eyes. "I remember . . . and I'm still waiting."

"Miller, lock the door," McCoy said.

Miller hesitated a moment, then did as McCoy asked.

"The waiting's over," McCoy said. "I take it you don't like making payments to Lorenzo."

"Why would anyone like it?" he said as if it were the stupidest question ever.

"How about you, Miller?" McCoy asked the dry goods man. "Paying off Lorenzo sit well with you?"

"Well, he doesn't take any more than Jericho did," Miller said tentatively. "But no, can't say as I like it."

"That's settled then. He takes your money, and you don't like it." McCoy looked each man in the eye, then crossed his arms. "So let's do something about it."

Lorenzo and Big Mike watched Froggy Morton ride out of town, a shovel resting on his shoulder, and a pack mule in tow.

"I dunno, boss," Mike said. "I'm sort of with Froggy on this one. It's got to be Hank and Rusty in them graves. It all adds up."

Lorenzo gave Mike a hard look. "You didn't say anything."

Mike shrugged. "Not like I got to go dig 'em up."

"I think you're both right," Lorenzo admitted. "Otherwise, why ain't they come home? It's them, but we're going to be absolutely, one hundred percent sure."

"And when we're sure?"

Lorenzo's grin was pure evil. "Then we jump on Ghost McCoy with both feet."

CHAPTER 24

"Such a lazy man. Are you going to sleep all day?" But there was a smile in her voice when she said it. She liked having Garret McCoy around. She liked it very much, and it wasn't just that he was more palatable than Jericho.

She looked over her shoulder, saw McCoy pull the blanket over his head, and laughed softly before turning back to the mirror, buttoning her red blouse to the throat, then donning her gaucho hat, tilting it to a jaunty angle. She applied a modest amount of dark red stain to her lips, then stood back, looked at herself, turning her head one way and then the other.

Good. She was ready to meet the world.

"I'm going," she said.

McCoy grumbled. "So early?"

"Unlike some layabouts, I have a business to run."

Another grunt.

"One more thing." She went to the bed and stood there, waiting for him to pay attention.

McCoy sat up and rubbed his eyes. "Yeah?"

"Cherry doesn't want this anymore. Bad memories, I suppose." She handed him the single-shot derringer.

He handed it back to her. "Keep it. I'll feel better knowing you have a little something. Jericho's gone, but you never know."

She raised an eyebrow. "Lorenzo?"

"It's no secret we're keeping company," McCoy said. "I doubt he'll bother you."

"So?"

"So I might not always be around."

"You plan on going somewhere?" The thought he might leave bothered her.

And it bothered him that it bothered her.

"A man in my line of work stops looking too far ahead," McCoy said. "It too often leads to disappointment."

Carmen slipped the derringer into her clutch. "As you say. A little something."

"You'll need more ammunition for it."

"I suppose you're right," she said. "I'll stop by Miller's."

She left the room and went downstairs to find Joseph sweeping the floor. He gave her a friendly nod. "Morning, Miss Carmen."

"Good morning, Joseph. Have we received that new shipment of shot glasses yet?" The saloon went through an alarming number of shot glasses on a monthly basis. When the saloon got rowdy, the patrons especially seemed to drop them, throw them, or sometimes take them into the street to throw into the air for target practice with their six-shooters.

"No, ma'am," Joseph said. "Supply wagon ain't been through yet."

"When it comes, make sure they don't short us on beer again," Carmen said. "Explain to Leonard I intend to get what I'm paying for."

"Yes, ma'am."

Carmen left the saloon to begin her errands.

She went to see the wainwright first to negotiate a good price for taking a look at the loose wheel on her gig. Then to the greengrocer and the butcher. Carmen's Place didn't routinely serve meals, but she'd found it easier over the years to feed the girls in-house rather than sending out, and anyway, Carmen had always been partial to a well-stocked kitchen.

Her next stop was to the old woman who was in charge of cleaning. She and her two daughters came in twice a week to clean. Carmen could not abide filth and asked the old woman to come three times a week instead. Carmen would, of course, pay her more.

Then to the seamstress to have some clothes altered. She'd ordered two elegant dresses all the way from Boston, and they'd finally arrived after months and months. They were slightly too large and needed to be taken in.

A few more stops, routine errands, then finally, she went to Miller's.

Carmen looked around, making sure the place was empty before taking the derringer out of her clutch and setting it on the counter for Mr. Miller to see. "I need a bullet for this."

He grinned. "A bullet? They come in boxes of fifty."

"Oh? Well, yes, of course. That will be fine."

He took a box from under the counter, opened it, and took out a single round. "Never mind. Go on and take it. You've given me lots of business these past years." He held the little bullet out to her between thumb and forefinger.

Carmen took it and smiled. "You're very kind, Mr. Miller."

"I'm just in a good mood," he said. "It's nice to know that nasty rat Gerald will never come around again to ask me for money. I suppose it's unchristian to delight in another man's death, but those are the times we live in, I'm afraid."

"But now Lorenzo takes your money," Carmen reminded him.

"True. But at least it's not Gerald."

She thanked him again and left the store.

And almost ran right into Dwight Combs on the sidewalk.

"My apologies, Mr. Combs," she said. "How clumsy of me."

Combs tipped his hat. "No worries, Miss Carmen. No harm done. And how are you finding life in Coyote Flats, sans Jericho?"

"More peaceful," Carmen said. "For the moment."

"Mind if I walk with you a ways?"

"Not at all."

She started down the wooden sidewalk, and he fell in next to her.

"You said *for the moment*," Dwight reminded her. "Lorenzo?"

"Who else?"

"Oh, I dunno. Takes two to fight," Combs said.

"Without Jericho around, who's going to ruffle Lorenzo's feathers? Might end up being more peaceable around here than you think."

The slightest of shrugs from Carmen, almost indifference. "Perhaps. But it has been my experience that men like Lorenzo will always find displeasure with something. Feathers like his are self-ruffling."

Combs chuckled. "You might have a point there. I reckon the best thing is to just stay out of his way all together."

"You're a pragmatic man, aren't you, Mr. Combs?"

He thought a moment before answering. "I guess that's right. Pragmatism can keep a man alive in the long term. On the other hand, folks ain't going to hoist me up on their shoulders for it. Not a lot of praise and glory for the pragmatic man."

"And you want praise and glory?"

"I don't know. Maybe? I'm only human, after all," Combs said. "But then I can't help feeling pretty silly about it. You can't eat glory. Can't pay the rent with praise."

A pragmatic man indeed. Carmen considered him for a moment. He was cut from the same cloth as Garret McCoy. Perhaps that was why the two men seemed to understand one another so well. If McCoy left Coyote Flats, and Combs remained . . .

And she suddenly hated herself for what she was about to think. She despised thinking of every man she met as part of a calculation. It had been necessary for survival, but that didn't mean she liked it. She'd thought her feelings for McCoy were different, but then his comment about not always being around had gotten to her. The calculations began anew.

"You okay, ma'am?" Combs asked.

She looked up, met his eyes. "I'm sorry?"

"A sudden disagreeable look crossed your face," Combs said. "I hope I didn't say anything out of line."

She forced a smile. "Of course not. It's just that I have so much to do. If you'll excuse me, Mr. Combs."

And she quickly walked away down the sidewalk.

McCoy sat at his usual table in the slop house.

Cordelia brought him coffee. "Back in a moment."

"No rush."

McCoy saw Dwight Combs walk in and waved him over.

"Have a seat," McCoy said.

"Thanks." Combs took off his hat, hung it on the back of the chair next to him, then sat. "What's good?"

"That's always the question in this place," McCoy said. "Hold on. Here she is."

Cordelia returned to the table and said, "What can I get you fellas?"

"Roast chicken and mashed potatoes?" Combs said.

McCoy looked at Cordelia.

She scrunched up her face and shook her head.

Combs frowned. "I reckon I guessed wrong."

"What do you suggest?" McCoy asked her.

"Eggs are real fresh," Cordelia said. "And my old man just took out a ham."

"Ham and eggs then." McCoy said.

"Make it two," Combs chimed in.

"You'll want biscuits with that," she said.

"Any chance for gravy with those biscuits?" Combs asked.

"Sure," Cordelia said. "If you want to spend the rest of the day in the outhouse."

"Never mind."

"I'll bring jam for the biscuits," she told them.

"And coffee," Combs said.

"Right." She went away.

"Ordering a meal in this place is a tricky business," Combs said.

"Remember to order what's good and not what you want, and you'll be okay," McCoy told him.

"I traded pleasantries with your woman a few minutes ago," Combs said.

McCoy shook his head. "She's her own woman. She just tolerates me hanging around. I didn't figure you for still being in Coyote Flats."

"Still trying to work out my next job."

"Want me to ask Lorenzo to put you on?"

"I reckon not," Combs said. "That would just be like working for Jericho. And I already quit that."

McCoy nodded. "Probably for the best, to be honest."

Cordelia brought the food, and both men tucked in.

"Good ham," Combs said. "Not too salty."

They ate seriously and in silence, only pausing to slurp coffee.

Combs finished first and pushed his plate away. "Not bad."

"Come back to Carmen's Place with me and wash it down with a beer," McCoy suggested.

Combs shook his head. "Nope. Gotta go someplace and think. Gotta get my life together."

"Don't think too long." McCoy leaned forward and lowered his voice. "Things are about to heat up around here."

Combs thought about that for a moment. "Understood." He pushed away from the table and stood, paused before turning away. "Thanks for the heads-up, Ghost."

"Keep it to yourself."

McCoy turned his attention back to his coffee.

CHAPTER 25

"McCoy!"

McCoy leaned against the bar in Carmen's Place, where he'd been nursing a beer, and turned his head to see who was calling him.

Big Mike came toward him, a bounce in his step like he was in a good mood.

He gave McCoy a friendly slap on the back. "Life treating you right, McCoy?"

"Can't complain," McCoy said. "What's got you in a good mood?"

"Why wouldn't I be?" Mike said. "The sky is blue, the sun is shining, and Coyote Flats has one hundred percent less Jericho than it did a few days ago."

"We're still celebrating that, are we?"

"Well, actually, no," Mike said. "I came to fetch you because the boss wants to have a meeting. Looks like he's got some work for us. Jericho might be gone, but there's always something to do."

McCoy didn't like the sound of that, but he needed to play along. As far as everyone knew, Garret McCoy was a loyal employee of the Lorenzo outfit.

"Right now, huh?"

Mike shrugged. "Right now."

"Okay then." McCoy chugged his last swallow of beer, then set the mug on the bar. "Let's go."

McCoy followed Mike to Lorenzo's place, and then went inside. As usual, a few of the boys sat around gabbing or playing cards. McCoy spotted someone he'd never seen before at the bar, chugging a cold beer. A short man and fat, but what was unusual about him was that he was filthy, covered head to toe in dirt.

"Who's that?" McCoy asked.

"Froggy Morton," Mike said. "Never mind him."

McCoy shrugged. It wasn't like he was looking to make new friends anyway.

Mike opened the door and gestured for McCoy to enter, a dumb grin on his face. "Ladies first."

Hilarious.

McCoy strode into the middle of the room and stopped, his face twisting momentarily with confusion. A man sat in a chair on the other side of the room, sort of listing to one side and as filthy with dirt as Froggy Morton. His eyes were open and strangely glassy, buck teeth and red hair so familiar –

McCoy went for his Peacemaker.

He felt something slam hard across his back, he staggered, grunted in pain, hunching his shoulders as he tried to right himself. The next blow sent him to the floor.

McCoy rolled over, saw the men crowding in around him, one nearly as big as Big Mike, holding an axe handle tight in his grip.

McCoy went for the Peacemaker again.

The big fella brought the axe handle down hard across his wrist with a sharp *crack*.

McCoy howled in pain.

"Get his guns." Lorenzo's voice from somewhere.

His gun belt was taken. He didn't see where it went.

Then they were kicking him. Hard. McCoy did the only thing a man can do when half a dozen fellas are kicking hell out of you. He curled into a ball and took it.

Was it a minute or a day later when Lorenzo spoke up? "Okay, lay off him."

McCoy let out a sigh and held in a whimper. He held his wrist up next to his body and moved it back and forth to see how bad it was hurt. Pain flared. Maybe broken, maybe not. A crack anyway in one of the bones, maybe. Hurt like the devil to move it.

"Okay, everybody out," Lorenzo said. "Not you, Mike. You stay."

A curt nod from Big Mike. "Right, boss."

The rapid shuffle of boots. The click of a door closing.

McCoy lay there, gathering himself, trying to slow his breathing and his heartbeat. His whole body throbbed, but the wrist was the worst. He'd have to use his left hand when it came time to make a play.

But at that moment, making a play was the farthest thing from his mind. All he wanted to do was lie there and hurt and wait for it to stop.

"I suppose you understand what this is all about," Lorenzo said.

McCoy lifted his head to look. It took effort. Lorenzo leaned against a tall wooden cabinet, arms crossed, a smug look on his face. Big Mike stood next to him, face hard as stone as he rolled up his sleeves.

"You sent men to kill me," McCoy said. "What was I supposed to do? Stand there and let that giggling, red-haired idiot shoot me?"

"I would have expected you to defend yourself like any man," Lorenzo told him. "But there's more to it."

McCoy let his head flop back down to the floor, but his eyes stayed on the two men. "More to what?"

"I told Rusty to kill you. I admit it. You shot him fair and square," Lorenzo said. "But I told him to kill you *only if* you didn't come back to work for me. So I had to ask myself . . . why did you come back? You could have ridden off anywhere, but you came back to Coyote Flats. I been thinking real hard on that ever since Froggy came back from Black Oak. I thought about what I'd do if I was in your place."

"Oh? And what would you do, Lorenzo?" McCoy asked.

"If somebody ordered my death, I'd find the man, and I'd kill him," Lorenzo said. "Wouldn't have to think twice about it. I'd kill him."

"But I ain't killed you, have I?" McCoy pointed out.

Lorenzo wagged a finger at him. "Now *that's* an interesting point. In fact, it's why you aren't dead right this very minute. You could have killed me a dozen times. You could have shot me in the back and ridden off into the night." A shrug. "But you didn't. Why not?"

"Maybe you're underestimating my love for the splendor or Coyote Flats," McCoy said.

Lorenzo chuckled. "Funny fella, ain't he, Mike?"

"Hilarious," Mike said flatly.

"So, I know you're up to something. You haven't killed me yet, so there's something else cooking. You've got some plan," Lorenzo said. "And you're going to tell me what it is. Frankly, I'm a curious fella, and I just don't think I could stand it if I didn't know what scheme you were hatching."

"So this is where I start singing?" McCoy asked.

Lorenzo shook his head. "Nope. Not yet. First, we need you in the right frame of mind."

McCoy didn't like the sound of that.

Lorenzo nodded at Big Mike. "Let the lesson begin."

Mike took off his gun belt, opened the cabinet, and hung it from a hook inside. McCoy glimpsed the interior of the cabinet before Mike closed it, and saw other gun belts hanging there, including his own.

Big Mike crossed the room, bent over, grabbed a fistful of McCoy's shirt, and hauled him to his feet. McCoy wobbled on his boots, trying to stay upright.

He needn't have bothered.

Mike's enormous fist came around as fast as a steam locomotive and collided with McCoy's jaw. His head snapped around, and he felt himself floating and floating until the sensation suddenly ended when the floor flew up to slam into him.

He blinked stars. The sensation of being lifted, and McCoy realized Big Mike was hauling him up again. McCoy blinked his vision clear just in time to see the fist flying at him again. He turned with the punch, but it still landed with enough force to set the bells off. He staggered across the room, hit the far wall and went down.

And then Mike must have gotten tired of picking him up because he just kicked for a bit.

"Work the ribs some," Lorenzo suggested.

McCoy curled into a ball again and waited it out.

Somewhere around the change of seasons, he heard Lorenzo's voice say, "That's enough."

McCoy let out a long, ragged sigh of relief as the kicking stopped.

"That was pretty basic," Lorenzo said. "Hitting and kicking. Hurts but probably nothing new for you. But if I don't get the answers I want, I can get real creative. Don't doubt me."

"Just tell me what you want to know," McCoy said.

"Why'd you come back?" Lorenzo asked. "What's your plan?"

McCoy's mind groped for something plausible.

"You would have figured out I killed your men, eventually. I didn't want you to come looking for me," McCoy said. "Figured if I came back to Coyote Flats, you wouldn't suspect me."

"Thought you could hide in plain sight, huh?"

McCoy tried to shrug, but it hurt too much. "Something like that. Then eventually I'd think of a reason to go my own way."

"Maybe." Lorenzo rubbed the back of his neck. "But I don't buy it. You're not that kind of fella."

"A man could be just about any kind of fella if he has the need."

"I don't figure you for a man who runs or hides," Lorenzo said. "The way you just told it, coming back to Coyote Flats was just a tricky way to hide. Nope. You're not here to hide. You're here to make something happen. Not something I'll be keen on, I reckon."

"You're giving me too much credit," McCoy said.

"Or you ain't been softened up enough. Mike."

McCoy didn't get his hands up in time to ward off the kick, and Big Mike's bootheel caught him square in the mouth. McCoy tasted blood and spit.

"This is getting boring," Lorenzo said. "Let's try something different."

Lorenzo and Mike conferred in hushed tones, Mike nodding along. McCoy tried to listen but couldn't catch anything. Probably nothing he would have enjoyed hearing anyway.

"Watch him," Lorenzo told Mike. "I'll be back in a bit."

Mike nodded. "Right."

Lorenzo left, and Mike moved to stand over McCoy, looking down at him with all the menace he could muster. This might be the best chance McCoy would get with just Mike in the room. He tried to figure a way to take him, distract him so McCoy could make some move, but nothing reasonable came to mind. Not only was Mike a big, strong man, but he was surprisingly fast.

And McCoy could barely move. There wasn't a place on his body that wasn't bruised. Bruises on top of bruises.

Mike cracked his knuckles and sneered down at McCoy. "I'm glad I didn't waste a lot of time getting to like you."

"I've been told I'm slow to grow on people."

"Well, time's up," Mike said. "So don't bother growing anymore."

"What if I said I had ten thousand dollars stashed away?" McCoy told him. "Saved up all those bounties over the years. I'll tell you where it is if you let me slip out the back door."

"There ain't no back door." Mike pointed across the room. "There's a window."

"The window then."

"You should have said five thousand," Mike suggested. "That's more believable."

The door swung open, and Lorenzo walked in. "Everything all right in here?"

Big Mike nodded. "All good."

"Then I'll bring in our guest." Lorenzo stood aside.

Carmen walked into the room. Her eyes shot wide when she saw McCoy on the floor, bruised and bloody.

"I ain't blind to the fact that you and Miss Carmen here have been keeping company," Lorenzo said. "Well, Jericho's gone, so I guess I don't blame you."

Carmen rushed to McCoy and knelt down next to him. "Darling, what have they done to you?"

"Looks worse than it feels," McCoy lied.

"I thought you and she might like a last word together," Lorenzo said solemnly.

McCoy met her eyes, saw her eyes go glassy with tears he knew she'd never let fall. She wasn't the sort to show her weakness. But it hit him hard. This was it. This was goodbye.

"Poor darling." She gathered one of his rough hands between hers and—

He felt something cold and hard press into his palm and immediately recognized the shape of the little derringer.

"Just tell Lorenzo what he wants to know," she pleaded.

"Listen to her, son." Lorenzo took her under one arm

and hauled her to her feet. "That's enough goodbyes, I reckon. Mike, tell Freddy to come in here."

Mike opened the door and mumbled some words into the hall.

McCoy had curled back into a ball, his closed fist concealing the derringer up against his chest. One shot, and left-handed. He'd have to wait for the perfect opportunity to make it count.

A few moments later, the large man with the axe handle entered the room.

"Watch him, Freddy," Lorenzo said. "We'll be back in a moment."

"What about him?" Carmen asked, meaning McCoy.

"His fate is sealed," Lorenzo told her. "But you . . . well, that all depends on Ghost McCoy. A lot can happen to you once he's not around to look after you. A lot of bad things. You think on that for a bit, McCoy. You think of all the things that might happen to this pretty little *señorita* if I feel like taking my frustration with you out on her."

"You're a damn coward," McCoy said.

Lorenzo chuckled. "I been called plenty worse."

He and Big Mike left, dragging Carmen along with them.

Freddy pointed the axe handle at McCoy. "You just stay right there and don't move, mister, and we'll get along just fine."

"What do you plan to do to me?" Carmen demanded.

"Rest easy," Lorenzo said. "You're a fine-looking

woman. When Jericho was gone, you replaced him with McCoy. I reckon when McCoy's gone, you'll be looking for a replacement again. I wouldn't mind putting in for the job, but I won't force the issue. Not my style."

Carmen lifted her chin, a hint of defiance. "How gentlemanly."

"But you and I are definitely going to have a talk soon," Lorenzo said. "When there were two sides in this town, it was useful to have a place that was neutral, and that was your place, but we don't need that no more. There's only one way of doing things now in Coyote Flats, and that's my way. You run a successful business, and I think it's about time you paid your share like everyone else."

Carmen didn't care for that notion at all, but she wasn't surprised. In fact, she'd seen it coming. "Very well. We can discuss it at your convenience."

"At my convenience is exactly what I had in mind."

"What about Mr. McCoy?"

Lorenzo's face grew hard. "You need not trouble yourself about him anymore."

"I see." Carmen cleared her throat. "If I'm no longer needed, I'll be going."

"Mike, walk the lady back," Lorenzo said.

Carmen shook her head. "There's no need to—"

"Mike will walk you back."

Ah.

"What're you gonna do here, boss?" Mike asked.

"I'm going to give McCoy a while to stew, let him wonder what's happening to his lady friend," Lorenzo said. "I suppose I might have a shot or two of whiskey while I'm waiting."

"What about some water?" McCoy asked with a croak.

"What about shutting your mouth?" Freddy replied.

McCoy didn't know how long Lorenzo and Big Mike would leave him alone with Freddy, so whatever McCoy was going to do, he'd better get a move on.

"Can I level with you?" McCoy asked.

"You're not talking your way out of this," Freddy said. "Anyway, I just do what I'm told. What happens to you ain't up to me."

"It could be."

"Well, it's not."

"You could let me crawl out that window," McCoy said. "That's all I'm asking. Just let me crawl out and make my own way."

"Why in the hell would I do that?" Freddy asked.

"Mercy and kindness and your generous nature?"

Freddy laughed.

"No, I didn't think so," McCoy said. "How does ten thousand dollars sound?"

"Sounds like you think I'm a dang fool."

"What do you think I do with all those bounties I collect?" McCoy asked. "Two hundred bucks here, five hundred bucks there. It adds up over the years. What do I spend it on? Some fancy mansion with servants? No, I've been stashing it away to retire young and put my feet up somewhere. Maybe buy a ranch. But retiring doesn't do me no good if I don't live long enough to do it."

"That's a lot of money, and that's for sure," Freddy said. "But anyone could *say* they got ten thousand dollars. You could say a hundred thousand or a million. Saying is cheap."

"It's true."

"Maybe shut up now," Freddy suggested.

"It's right here." McCoy made a show of trying to reach inside his vest with his injured hand, playing it up, hand curled and twisted like every bone was broken. He grunted and gave up. "I can't reach it."

"I'm not an idiot! You ain't got no ten thousand dollars in your vest pocket," Freddy said.

"Of course not." McCoy tried to sound irritated and desperate at the same time. "Nobody walks around with that kind of money. I got a bank statement."

"A what?"

"Come on, you've heard of banks, haven't you?" McCoy asked. "It's where people keep their money."

"Just watch your tone," Freddy warned. "I know what a bank is."

"Then start acting smart!" McCoy said heatedly. "I'm trying to buy my life, and I can't even get you to believe I got the money."

Freddy narrowed his eyes. "You really got ten thousand dollars?"

"That's what I'm trying to tell you. Look at the dang statement."

Freddy shook his head. "Even if you do have it, so what? It's in the bank."

"We'll figure it out," McCoy insisted. "First thing I got to do is prove I have it."

Freddy started forward, then stopped himself, raised

the axe handle, and shook it at McCoy. "You'd better not be wasting my time, or I'll take this to your kneecaps, you hear me?"

McCoy tried to reach into his vest again, the pain of his injured hand making him wince. "I . . . can't."

"I'm going to look because I'm curious." Freddy bent down to reach inside McCoy's vest. "But it still don't mean I'm helping you."

Freddy's hand went into McCoy's vest.

McCoy brought his left hand up fast, clutching the little derringer in a tight grip, shoved the barrel under Freddy's chin, and squeezed the trigger.

Freddy's eyes went wide a split-second before the pop of the derringer sent a little chunk of lead up through his mouth to lodge in his brain. He shot straight to his feet and stood there rigidly, eyes rolling up, mouth working like a trout's. He staggered a half step sideways, mouth still opening and closing, blood dripping red over his bottom lip as he made gurgling, choking sounds. Then he froze.

And toppled over like a felled redwood.

The thud of his body hitting and rattling the floorboards seemed louder to McCoy than the pop of the little derringer, and he worried the racket would bring somebody. He needed to get away before that happened, but his body let him know immediately that moving fast wasn't an option.

He winced and stifled a groan as he got up to one knee and then to his feet. Halting steps to the cabinet. Opened it with his left hand, the injured right still up against his body. He grabbed his gun belt, but it took two hands to buckle it on, hot pain lancing up his right arm, McCoy gritting his teeth the whole time.

Then he limped to the window, opened it with a grunt. One leg through. A deep breath and then he toppled out, landing with another grunt on the hard ground outside. He lay there a moment, catching his breath and listening but heard no sign anyone was on to him.

McCoy got up again and took a route to the livery stable he thought might give him the best chance not to be seen. He made it inside and found his horse. Getting the saddle on was nearly impossible with his injured wrist, but somehow he did it and heaved himself onto the horse's back, his heart pounding, shirt sticking to him with his own sweat, his head swimming, his whole body vibrating with pain.

He headed out of town in no particular direction.

CHAPTER 26

Lorenzo hadn't been wrong, not completely.

Carmen hated to admit it, but it was true. As unpleasant as she'd often found her association with Jericho, the man had served a purpose. Lorenzo had been right that she'd traded one man for another when it had suited her. As fond as Carmen had grown of Garret McCoy, he too served a purpose, a shield against ill winds.

Who will be your shield now, stupid girl?

The answer was obvious.

Mike had escorted her back to her place, and she'd gone immediately upstairs to her room.

She knelt in front of her dresser, opened the bottom drawer, and reached all the way in the back under some heavy winter clothing. She pulled out the revolver and held it in her hand. She knew little of weapons but this particular gun fired a slightly larger bullet than the derringer. A .32 if Carmen remembered correctly.

She went to her bed and slipped it under her pillow. She wanted it handy. Under the pillow would do for now, but eventually she'd have to find a better place for it. She'd prefer to carry it with her everywhere she went, but it was just a tad too large to fit into her clutch.

Carmen left her room and went to the head of the stairs. A quick glance told her the saloon was not busy yet.

"Joseph," she called down.

He looked up. "Ma'am?"

"Go down to the cellar and bring up that wooden box, the one with the padlock," Carmen said. "Horace can mind the bar for a moment."

"Yes, ma'am."

She went back to her room and searched for the key, finding it in the middle drawer of the vanity. Joseph arrived a minute later with a small crate.

"On the table, please," she instructed.

Jospeh set the box down and left.

Carmen went to Cherry's room and found the girl brushing her hair.

"Are any of the girls busy?"

Cherry shook her head. "Still too early."

"Gather them and bring them to my room," Carmen said. "Try not to look obvious about it."

A few minutes later they were all in Carmen's room, crowded around the table with the crate on it. Carmen held the key in a tight fist.

"Ladies, things are rapidly changing in Coyote Flats," Carmen said in a businesslike fashion. "And that means we'll have to change how we do things too."

She inserted the key and turned, and the lock fell open with a slight *click*. Slowly she opened the lid, and all the girls leaned in to have a look.

An assortment of revolvers, at least a dozen, some rusted beyond use, but others looking almost new. The collection had grown over the years. A drunk cowboy would leave his gun belt hanging from a girl's bedpost. Or they'd find them under tables. Or someone couldn't pay his tab and had traded his guns. A different story for each pistol.

"Anyone shoot a gun before?" Carmen asked.

"Me," Cherry said.

But of course. The girl had shot Gerald the night they'd raided Jericho's.

"What about loading them?" Carmen asked.

Missy, a stunning blonde, raised her hand. "I been shooting with my father and brothers. It's been a few years, but I remember."

Carmen gestured to the weapons. "Pick one and show us."

He was so thirsty.

He knelt next to the stream, kept scooping handfuls of water into his mouth, but no matter how much he drank, he couldn't quench the thirst. His tongue was so dry. His throat ached. It became maddening to the point that—

He hit hard, the air knocking out of him. A cold, gritty feeling against his left cheek.

Slowly, McCoy opened his eyes. Night. He'd passed out and had fallen out of his saddle.

Embarrassing.

He rolled over and groaned, felt the horse nudge the top of his head with its nose.

"Give me a minute, will ya?"

He stood and leaned against the horse. He found his

thirst wasn't just a dream. His mouth and throat were parched. He took the canteen from where it hung on the saddle and emptied nearly half of it. He touched a spot above his left ear, and his fingertips came away sticky. One of Big Mike's bootheels must have caught him on the side of the head. He blinked his eyes a few times.

The moonlight was bright, and he looked around to get his bearings, surprised to see he was near the river and had evidently ridden along the same path he'd taken in the gig toward Parson's Gulch when he'd been out with Carmen. That day seemed a million years ago. Had some part of his brain chosen to come this direction, or had it been chance?

Wait. Carmen. Lorenzo had made some sort of threat toward her, hadn't he? A way to force McCoy to answer Lorenzo's questions. Was she in danger? Should McCoy go back?

He could barely stand. What help could he offer the woman?

McCoy tried to get back on the horse and failed. He felt dizzy.

He found himself walking again, leading the horse. He had no recollection of deciding to do that, but again, he was headed toward Parson's Gulch.

Was it an hour later that he saw the lights?

Time meant nothing to him anymore. Houses ahead on either side of a narrow road. He plodded toward them, the horse dutifully following. This place looked familiar. A buzzing in his ears all coming in a rush. His face felt so hot, and his gut churned like he might be sick. What was this place? He'd been here before, hadn't he? He tried to make himself remember even as his head grew lighter and lighter . . .

. . . and . . .

. . . lighter.

The sun had been up an hour, and Mortimer Lorenzo forked scrambled eggs into his face.

The eggs were pretty dang good, way better than usual, which was a shame because Lorenzo was in a right foul mood and in no mood to enjoy a delicious breakfast. He ate out of habit, scowling at the old man who came with the pot to refill his coffee, and pushed the plate away, not even bothering with the slab of ham, disdain for his toast.

And his glass eye was giving him an ache, earlier in the day than usual, which annoyed him to no end. Worthless chunk of glass.

He'd sent two men out to bury Freddy someplace— he didn't give a damn where—and they returned now looking dirty and sweaty.

"Seen Big Mike?" Lorenzo asked one of them.

He shook his head. "Not back yet."

Lorenzo nodded. "Right."

He waited an hour and then another.

Finally, Big Mike walked through the door with a handful of the boys. He didn't look happy.

Which meant Lorenzo wasn't going to be happy.

Lorenzo drained the last of his coffee and set the cup aside. "Well?"

Mike shook his head. "No sign of him."

"No sign of him!" Lorenzo flared. "What do you mean, no sign of him? He's got to be somewhere."

Mike threw up his hands, exasperated. "We looked all over town. Then I split the boys into four groups— north, south, east, and west, and we rode out. We looked. I promise you, we looked, but we ain't no Indian trackers. He could be anywhere."

Lorenzo grumbled a curse. "The man was beat to pudding, with Freddy standing guard over him, and he just waltzes out of here? And where in the hell did McCoy get a gun to shoot Freddy with?"

"Maybe hidden in his boot or something?" Mike said.

"And nobody thought to search him?"

Mike looked sheepish and wisely remained silent.

"Normally, killing the man who messed up would make me feel better, but Freddy's already dead."

Lorenzo abruptly snatched his coffee cup off the table and flung it across the room, where it shattered into a hundred pieces. He sat drumming his fingers, shaking his head, and muttering all the bad words he'd ever heard in his life.

"Well, that didn't make me feel better, and now I'm down a coffee cup," Lorenzo said.

"What do you want us to do, boss?" Mike asked.

"I'm thinking on it."

He wanted to think of something clever, but Lorenzo had to admit—even if only to himself—that he was not a clever man. Sharp in certain ways, and possessing a sort of animal cunning, but not clever like a great scholar or some robe-wearing Greek philosopher.

So. Time to play to his strengths.

And Mortimer Lorenzo's strengths were being mean and pushing people around.

He stood and cleared his throat. "Gather all the boys, Mike. It's time we taught the folks of Coyote Flats a valuable object lesson."

CHAPTER 27

Enrique Vargas cinched the saddle tight and put one foot into the stirrup, preparing to mount.

"And where do you think you are going, *hermano*?"

Enrique took his foot from the stirrup and put on his most innocent expression. "Oh, hello, Juan. I thought I would go for a ride. It's a nice day."

Juan nodded. "Oh, yes, so very nice. I notice that you've bathed, and your hair is combed. You must want this to be a very special ride indeed."

Enrique frowned. "There's nothing wrong with taking a bath. Something you might want to try yourself one day."

Juan leaned in and sniffed. "And the expensive soap. My goodness, you smell just like a beautiful flower."

Enrique swatted him away. "Stop that."

Juan ducked out of the way and laughed. "Do you think I'm so easily fooled? You're trying to sneak away to see sweet, sweet Cherry."

"*Cierra el pico!*"

"Enrique." Juan's face grew serious. "You know

Señor McCoy wanted us to stay out of sight, not draw attention to ourselves."

"Trust me, Juan, I will be careful," Enrique assured him. "But I must see her. I need to tell her I'm thinking of her. What if she's forgotten me? I need to know."

"Patience, *hermano.*"

"Patience." Enrique rolled his eyes. "That is something the old tell the young. And then suddenly the young are old and they've had nothing all their lives except a bunch of patience. I need to see her *now.*"

Juan sighed and shook his head. "Just promise me you will be careful."

A huge grin split Enrique's face. "I will, and I'll be back before you know it."

Juan clapped Enrique on the shoulder. "Give her a kiss for me."

Enrique laughed, climbed onto his horse, and was off like a shot.

He finally felt good again, partly because his bruises had healed—not completely but enough—but mostly because he was on his way to see the woman he loved.

Again, he left his horse on the outskirts of Coyote Flats, approaching the same way he did when he'd climbed up to Cherry's window the first time. There was a decent chance he would not be seen, at least not by anyone who would care. This time there was no Gerald to inflict his jealous fury upon Enrique. Who could object if he paid a short visit to Cherry?

He supposed Miss Carmen might not want to see him, not because she had anything against him personally, but he had caused disturbances in her place that were, understandably, bad for business. He decided it would be best to stay out of the saloon. Going to her window again seemed the smartest option.

Enrique skulked through back alleys and in short order found himself behind Carmen's Place. He remembered her window and climbed. What if she wasn't there? Should he wait? No, of course not. He could not perch all day on the roof of Carmen's Place like some lonely buzzard. That would surely draw attention. If she wasn't there, he'd simply have to come back later.

He reached the roof of the wraparound porch, then began scooting sideways past the second-floor windows until he reached Cherry's.

And there she was!

Cherry sat on the edge of the bed, slipping on a stocking, toes pointed as she rolled it up a smooth, white leg to her knee.

Enrique knocked on the window.

Cherry looked up, startled, but her surprised expression immediately shifted to a huge smile when she recognized who it was. She ran to the window and threw it open.

"I'm sorry but I had to see you," Enrique said. "It's probably stupid to come to your window again like this but—"

She grabbed the sides of his face, pulled him close, and planted a huge, wet kiss square on his lips. His heart tried to beat through his chest. She pulled away and looked at his face, frowning with sympathy.

"You're still so bruised." But then she brightened, trailing a thin finger down the side of his face. "But you look a lot better than when you were tied to that chair. I was so worried about you that I could hardly stand it."

He took both of her cool, soft hands in his. "I'm sorry about Gerald . . . that you had to. . ."

"I did it for you. For us."

They kissed again.

Enrique began to climb through the window. "I'll come in."

"No!" She put a hand against his chest.

"No?"

"Someone might see you," Cherry said. "There's a lot going on right now. Miss Carmen might come by at any minute."

"But I want to be with you!"

She leaned out, craned her neck to look up. "The roof."

He followed her gaze. "Up there?"

"Can you make the climb?" she asked.

"You'll meet me up there?"

"Yes."

Enrique nodded, his face determined. "Then I can make the climb."

"You got it?" Lorenzo asked.

Froggy Morton held up the iron triangle. "Got it off a chuck wagon."

"Good. Where's Mike?"

"In the street," Froggy said. "He's got all the boys assembled."

"Let's get to it then."

Lorenzo went outside, Froggy right behind him.

Mike was there with two dozen men behind him,

some with rifles, others with shotguns, the rest standing ready with deadly iron on their hips. Mike held a Winchester in his hands

"You know what to do," Lorenzo told Mike.

Mike looked back at the rest of his men and shouted, "Let's go!"

They marched down the street as a mob, Froggy Morton banging the heck out of the iron triangle, the *clang clang clang* echoing along the street. Lorenzo's men went into the shops, shouting for people to get into the street. Frightened townsfolk emerged, wondering what on Earth was happening.

Lorenzo strolled into Carmen's Place, all smiles and good nature.

Carmen appeared at the top of the stairs. "What is going on outside?"

"Sorry for the disturbance, but it'll all be over soon enough." Lorenzo looked at the man behind the bar. "You're Joseph, right?"

"That's right."

"Step outside with me a moment, will you? I just need your help with something," Lorenzo said. "Please don't worry. It won't take long."

Jospeh looked up at Carmen.

She nodded quickly.

"Okay, sure," Joseph said. "Always glad to lend a hand."

"Good man. Follow me."

Lorenzo exited the saloon with Joseph right behind him.

The street had rapidly become crowded with all the people who lived and worked up and down the street.

Froggy was still beating the triangle for all he was worth.

"You can knock off that racket now, Froggy," Lorenzo said. "I think we've got their attention."

"Right. Sorry, boss." Froggy lowered the triangle.

Lorenzo raised his voice. "Ladies and gentlemen, your attention."

The murmuring crowd quieted.

"I appreciate that we all have to make an adjustment," Lorenzo said. "Jericho's gone, but I'm still here. I think most of you understand that things will go on as normal except there's one boss now instead of two; however, I'm concerned that not everyone might be taking this new situation seriously, so today we're going to make it very clear where we all stand and what I expect in terms of your complete cooperation."

Concern crossed the faces of the men and women in the crowd.

"You all know Garret McCoy," Lorenzo said loudly. "Turns out he ain't as loyal as we thought. He managed to slip away from us, something I don't plan to let happen again. He's hurt, and he probably needs help. That's where you folk need to guard against being kind-hearted, because if you protect him or help him, then you're in just as much hot water as he is. You have this one time—and *only* this one time—to step forward and tell me if you know where he is or if you've got him hidden in your attic or something, because Lord help anyone who's holding out on me."

Lorenzo made a slow turn as he talked, trying to look directly into the eyes of as many townsfolk as possible. Some looked away, not wanting to meet his eye.

He was surprised to see Dwight Combs sitting on the front porch of Carmen's Place, leaning back in a chair, boots up on the railing. He didn't seem alarmed by the proceedings at all and looked on with mild interest. Perhaps the man might be useful, Lorenzo thought.

"If anyone has a notion as to Garret McCoy's whereabouts, speak now!" Lorenzo shouted.

Everyone looked at everyone else, but nobody spoke up.

Lorenzo nodded, still making his slow turn to look at everyone. "So here's the thing. Nobody's speaking up. The simplest explanation is 'cause there's nothing to tell. You ain't seen McCoy. That fella could be anywhere. Or . . ."

Lorenzo thrust a finger into the air for emphasis.

"Or, you're not taking me serious," Lorenzo said. "You think I'm all talk, and that's a shame because I really need you people to understand that I mean what I say."

Lorenzo gestured at the barkeep from Carmen's Place. "What's your name again, son?"

"Joseph, sir."

"Oh, yeah, that's right." Lorenzo raised his voice for everyone else. "Folks, Joseph here is going to help me with a brief demonstration. You know him. He's probably served you a drink or two at Carmen's Place. Joseph, you ready to lend me a helping hand?"

Joseph looked confused but said, "Uh . . . sure. I mean, whatever you need, Mr. Lorenzo."

"Fantastic. I appreciate it."

Lorenzo drew his six-shooter, thumbed back the

hammer, and aimed it at a spot directly between Joseph's eyes.

Enrique anxiously waited on the roof for Cherry to arrive. Butterflies in his gut. Heart thumping like mad. But she'd kissed him. She was coming to see him. It was the best day of his life.

The hatch in the roof was thrown open and Cherry scrambled through. She ran to Enrique, face beaming, and threw herself into his arms. They kissed hard and long before breathlessly pulling away from one another.

"I can't believe it," Cherry said.

"What?"

"Why you? Why now?" she said. "There's no reason for it, but I can't stop thinking about you, and I don't get it. I hardly know you. What's so special?"

"I understand," Enrique said, grinning. "You can do much better."

She threw her head back and laughed, overflowing with unfettered joy.

They kissed again.

"I want to marry you," Enrique said. "I want to take you away and make you my wife."

Cherry sobered. A wan smile. "Oh, Enrique."

"I mean it."

"I know." She put a hand against his chest and hung her head. "I know you do."

"Then why not?"

She shook her head, then sank into him, arms going around him. "It's all so messed up right now. Lorenzo is terrorizing the whole town, and nobody knows where Mr. McCoy is, and Miss Carmen is worried that—"

Enrique took Cherry by the shoulders. "What? Something has happened to *Señor* McCoy?"

"You didn't know?"

"Tell me."

"Lorenzo found out Mr. McCoy double-crossed him or something, so he set an ambush for him," Cherry said. "They caught him by surprise and beat him bad, kicking him and hitting him with an axe handle. Busted him up so he could hardly move."

Enrique felt himself go cold and leaden as Cherry spoke.

"He got away, but Miss Carmen doesn't know if he got very far," Cherry said. "He was injured pretty bad."

Enrique let that sink in. If McCoy was dead, then what? Would all their plans to free Coyote Flats from Lorenzo's iron grip be for nothing? Everything suddenly seemed hopeless.

No. Don't jump to conclusions, idiota. *Señor McCoy might still be alive out there, watching and waiting.*

"Don't worry, Cherry," Enrique said with more calm than he felt, pulling her close again. "I will think of something."

She laughed, her face against his chest. "Oh, Enrique, the world is bigger than the two of us put together."

He stroked her hair. "I say it's not."

A commotion. Shouts from the street. The relentless *clang* of an iron triangle.

Cherry turned her head. "Something's happening."

They went to the edge of the roof and looked down. It took a few moments for Enrique to understand what was going on. Lorenzo had his men with him, they were forcing people from the shops to gather outside. He wanted them all to hear what he was saying, some announcement.

"What is he doing?" Enrique asked.

"Hush," Cherry said. "Listen."

Lorenzo went about the business of telling the townsfolk what he expected of them, reminding everyone he was the boss of the place and so on. Then he was talking about McCoy, telling people they'd better not help him. Telling people they'd better tell if they saw him.

Enrique felt himself tighten all over, jaw clenching. Who was this man to tell others what they must do? Who made him god ruler of Coyote Flats? Unconsciously, Enrique's hand went to his six-shooter.

It was as if Cherry read his mind. She grabbed his arm, pulled him close. "You're not going down there, Enrique."

His back stiffened.

"You're *not*," she said firmly. "I've already seen you bloodied and bruised. I'm not going to see you dead in the street. What do you think you'll do against all them fellas?"

He let out a long breath, some of the tension leaking out of him. She was right, of course, but it galled him to see what was happening.

Then he saw Lorenzo pull his gun and point it at another man, one of the barkeeps from Carmen's Place.

Enrique felt his gut twist. *Oh, no*.

* * *

Lorenzo squeezed the trigger, the crowd flinching at the sudden, sharp, *bang*. The slug punched a bloody hole through Joseph's forehead, exploded out the back in a spray of blood and bone and flesh.

Ladies in the crowd screamed. Men cried alarm and protest.

Lorenzo turned to look at everyone, holding his gun over his head. "If you think I don't mean it, if you think this can't happen to you, now you know. I'm not playing. I want Garret McCoy's head on a stick, and I won't put up with helping or hiding him."

Lorenzo holstered his six-shooter. "I think I've made my point that crossing me is a bad idea, but there's another side to this. Getting on my good side can be profitable for you. I got a thousand dollars real money to anyone that brings me Garret McCoy's corpse. Shoot him in the back. Shoot him in the front. Cut his throat with a kitchen knife. I don't care. Kill him and show me the body, and I'll hand you a thousand dollars."

He looked at everyone, watching it sink in. Men murmured to one another, and Lorenzo could guess what they were thinking. A thousand dollars was nothing to sneeze at.

"I've said my piece," Lorenzo told the crowd. "Go on now. Back to what you were doing."

Big Mike and the rest of Lorenzo's boys shooed people back inside.

Lorenzo stepped over Joseph's body and walked to Carmen's front porch, leaned on the railing, and gave Dwight Combs a wry look. "Enjoy the show?"

"Can't say I ever enjoy seeing a man's brains spread all over the street," Combs said. "But it was instructive."

"My money's on you to collect that thousand dollars." Lorenzo gestured at the dissipating crowd behind him. "These folks, shop owners and the like, most men don't have it in them to kill. Even if a fella got it into his head he could do it for the money, it's a different thing when it comes time to pull the trigger. You're different. You're a professional."

"The first rule of being a professional is to pick your battles. Otherwise, a fella won't stay a professional for long. I don't fancy going up against Ghost McCoy." Combs sighed and looked away, as if seeing something interesting in the distance. "On the other hand, I could probably find a use for that much money."

"Think about it," Lorenzo suggested. "He's going to be dead anyway. Might as well get paid."

CHAPTER 28

Garret McCoy had the vague notion that he felt better.

But still not good.

His eyes creaked open, grit in the corners. He blinked a few times, his blurry vision slowly clearing. He tried to sit up, and his head throbbed, so he gave it up and stayed put. Where was he? He looked around, turning his head slowly.

A barn. Daylight seeped in through the cracks in the walls, igniting dust motes floating on a lazy draft. The snorting shuffle and smell of animals nearby. McCoy lay in a nest of dry hay, itching his back a little but a better bed than the cold ground. He touched his head. A bandage. Oh, yeah. He'd been kicked a lot, and part of his head was bloody.

"You're awake. Good."

McCoy tried to turn to see who'd spoken, but moving caused him to go dizzy.

But the man came into view a second later, arms full of tack and harness. He was more or less McCoy's age, thin brown hair, burly without being fat, and a friendly, open face. He hung the tack and harness on a row of wooden pegs as he spoke.

"You had a long night," he said. "Lots of moaning and groaning and sweating. We were a might worried about you for a time."

"Where—" His voice caught, throat thick with gunk. He cleared it, coughed a few times. "Where am I?"

"Parson's Gulch. My barn, specifically. We found you face down in the mud. Hope that hay was comfortable. Sorry we didn't bring you into the house, but I've got three young'uns and you're a stranger. You know how it is."

"I don't blame you." He touched the bandage on his head again. "Thanks for patching me up."

"Thank my wife when you see her," he said. "I don't have the healing touch, but she's good at it."

"Who are you?"

"Oh, where are my manners?" he said, a note of apology in his voice. "I'm Grant Colby. And you are?"

"I'm . . ." McCoy hesitated. Would anyone remember his name in Parson's Gulch? He'd never thought to come back, but now that he was here, this wasn't how he'd pictured his homecoming, knocked cold and found in the mud. All things considered, he'd probably rather slip away anonymously as soon as he could stand.

"I can't quite recall my name," McCoy lied.

"Oh? Well, I've heard that can happen with a head injury," Grant said. "By the way, I fed your horse and gave her a brush down."

"I guess I owe you."

"Just the Christian thing to do," Grant said. "If somebody found me in trouble, I would hope they'd help."

"Still, I've been in your way enough." He tried to push himself up again. "I'll be on my way before—"

A wave of nausea hit him. Dizzy. He lowered himself back into the hay.

"If I were you, I'd stay right there," Grant suggested. "I'll go into the house and see about wrangling you some grub."

McCoy opened his mouth to say don't bother, but he was already being pulled down into cottony silence, eyelids getting heavy, darkness taking him like warm water flooding in and rising above his head.

When McCoy opened his eyes again, the light was different.

Sunlight replaced by the low glow of a lantern.

He looked up into the face of the woman mopping his brow with a damp cloth and recognized her immediately.

Mary Jane Potts.

The childlike softness in her face had hardened, and there was a sharp intelligence in her eyes now. Hair tied back. She wore men's work clothes.

"The mystery man is awake." She smiled.

"Mystery man?"

"Grant told me you'd forgotten your name."

"Grant?"

"My husband."

So not Potts anymore. Mary Jane Colby. Grown up and married with three children.

McCoy realized she didn't recognize him. Maybe because his face was swollen from the beating. Or maybe just the years. He was simultaneously relieved and disappointed.

"There's soup," Mary Jane said. "It's a little cold now."

"Thanks. Maybe in a minute."

"Have you been to Parson's Gulch before?"

McCoy realized she was trying to make conversation. He didn't want to admit who he was, that he'd lived here, but he didn't want to lie either, so he changed the subject.

"I hear it's called Blood Gulch now."

"We don't call it that," Mary Jane said a little too quickly.

"I didn't mean to give offense."

"Sorry," she said. "You didn't. There was blood here at one time, a real bad thing. Lots of sorrow. But that's years behind us. We're just good, normal people living normal lives."

"Sounds good."

She shook her head and looked away, a wan smile. "I'm just being silly, I guess. I was just a little kid when it happened. I only remember bits and pieces. But the bad feelings . . . I can still feel them, like it all happened yesterday. It's just hard to connect them feelings to actual events. That's why I hate to think about it, I guess. Just a bunch of feelings I don't know what to do with."

"Sorry I mentioned it," McCoy said. "Parson's Gulch sounds better."

She brightened. "Doesn't it? I like living here. Good people. Nothing fancy, but good, nice people."

"If everyone here is as nice as you, then it must be

Heaven," McCoy said. "It's not everyone that would help a stranger."

And that coaxed a genuine, warm smile out of her. "Now, you know I'm married, mystery man, so mind your sweet talk."

McCoy laughed. "I'd better just have the soup then."

She helped him sit up, and he was pleasantly surprised not to be hit with a wave of dizziness. The soup had gone tepid, but it was good, and he found he was starving. Chicken, carrots, potatoes, onion. It was all gone in a matter of a minute and a half.

"Somebody's feeling better," Mary Jane said. "A healthy appetite is a good sign."

She set the bowl aside, and McCoy leaned back into the hay, sighing, and letting his eyelids go heavy. Already he was feeling the fatigue again, the simple exertion of talking and eating a bowl of soup sapping his strength.

Mary Jane must have seen it. "Go back to sleep, mystery man. You're on the mend."

He opened his mouth to tell her something. He wasn't sure what, but the words never made it past his lips anyway. Once again, sleep took hold and pulled him under.

Daylight.

McCoy sat up, bits of hay covering him from head to foot. His body ached in a dull, distant sort of way, except for his wrist. The strike from the axe handle still hurt sharply. He flexed the wrist to test it out. Pain. Not terrible but not insignificant. It would hamper his ability to draw the Peacemaker.

He stood. Weak. But he didn't fall over.

McCoy went to the barn door, pushed it open just enough to slip through to the outside, one hand going up to shade his eyes from the sudden, bright sun.

There was a small house on the other side of a little pig pen. He was looking at the back. It wasn't much, but it wasn't shabby, well kept, a fresh coat of white paint maybe only a few years old. Poor, but proud poor.

Off to one side, Mary Jane hung clothes on a line. Two children played at her feet, maybe two years old, not much more, pulling grass out of the ground and cooing at each other, girls in simple dresses, twins maybe. Another child, a boy perhaps six years old, wearing faded overalls, took clothes from a basket, handed them to his mother so she could hang them on the line. Grant was probably off somewhere doing chores.

Hardworking people and honest.

McCoy and never intended to return to Parson's Gulch, yet in his dazed stupor, something had brought him back here. What did he think? That a man like him could live a normal life among simple folk again? Garret McCoy was a hardened bounty hunter with blood on his hands. The twelve-year-old boy who'd lived here long ago no longer existed. He was a memory, a ghost.

He looked at Mary Jane with children and knew he couldn't stay, not permanently, and not even for another day. Mortimer Lorenzo wasn't the type to forgive and forget. If he came through Parson's Gulch looking for McCoy, then his presence here would only bring down trouble on these simple folk, and they'd already had enough for a lifetime.

McCoy went back into the barn and saddled his horse. By the time he finished, he was breathing hard. He was a long way from healed.

He took the horse's reins and led the animal out of the barn.

Mary Jane stood waiting for him, hands on hips. "Going somewhere, mystery man?"

"I've put you folks out too long already," McCoy said.

"You ain't in nobody's way sleeping on the hay in our barn," she said. "And you could probably use some more rest."

"Obliged, but I'd best be going."

"Just wait here a minute then. Make sure the children don't wander off, will you?"

She went into the house.

McCoy watched the children play.

She came back out a moment later with a gun belt in her hands.

McCoy looked down at his waist. No guns. He hadn't even realized he'd been walking around naked.

Mary Jane handed him the gun belt. "You'll probably need these . . . although I hope you don't."

"Thanks."

He strapped on the guns, wincing at the pain in his wrist.

McCoy put his foot in the saddle, tried to hoist himself into the saddle with a grunt and went back to the ground. He stood a moment, catching his breath.

"My worry is you won't get a mile before falling out of the saddle again," Mary Jane said.

"I'll make it."

McCoy tried again and this time managed to make it into the saddle.

He caught Mary Jane giving him a funny look. "What is it?"

"Just something about you," she said.

McCoy shrugged. "I'm just one of those kind of fellas, I guess."

"Are you sure you won't stay?"

"Things to do, and I'm burning daylight. Thanks again," McCoy told her. "Tell Grant thanks for me."

"I will."

He waved, turned the horse, and spurred the animal to a trot, again leaving Parson's Gulch behind him.

He hoped Carmen was safe. She was a smart woman and had taken care of herself for years without McCoy, but the urge was still strong to ride straight back to Coyote Flats. He talked himself out of it. There wasn't much he could do alone against Lorenzo and his entire gang, and anyway, whatever Lorenzo might do to Carmen he could have done plenty already in the last few days. He just had to hope everything was okay for the time being.

Instead, McCoy rode toward a place where he hoped he could find a friend.

He rode hard all day—as hard as he could manage in his condition—and arrived at the arroyo just after dusk. He wasn't keen to ride at night, but he was too close to stop now, and the moon was still shining light good enough for him to make his way.

McCoy entered the arroyo, taking it slowly, the banks rising on either side as he went. He twisted and turned and soon saw an orange glow ahead, obviously a campfire, nothing big to draw attention from far away, but plain enough now that he was getting close.

He rounded another corner and rode into a part of the arroyo that widened a bit, and spotted the little camp. A circle of stones with a small blaze in the middle. A makeshift shelter made from sticks and a horse blanket, just enough for a man to duck under and get out of the sun. He squinted into the darkness just beyond the fire and made out a horse, saddle off and tethered to a small boulder.

McCoy heard the sound of a lever working a shell into a rifle chamber and froze.

"Just hold it right there, mister. No sudden moves, okay?"

McCoy raised his hands, turned slowly and smiled. "Is that any way to treat an old pal?"

Rufus Lee lowered his rifle. "McCoy? I'd almost given up on you. Been waiting here for days."

"Sorry," McCoy said. "I meant to meet you sooner, but . . . things happen."

Lee gave McCoy the once-over. Even in the dim, flickering light of the campfire, the bruises were plain to see. "Looks like things happened all over your face."

"It was a near thing." McCoy flexed and wiggled the fingers of his bad hand, the ache in his wrist getting better but still not good enough to quick-draw his Peacemaker. "I need a place to lay up a few days."

"You're welcome to share my campfire," Lee told him.

McCoy looked at the camp again with little relish. "I'm not keen to sleep on the ground."

Lee laughed. "I don't exactly love it myself."

"We need a place where nobody's likely to see us."

Lee scratched his chin, eyes narrowed as he thought about it. "I maybe know someplace."

CHAPTER 29

"One bag of flour and one bag of sugar," Moses Hendershot told Walt Miller. "Mrs. Hendershot has a notion to bake a cake. Oh, and vanilla extract."

Miller nodded and put the items on the counter. "Never a bad time for cake."

Hendershot paid, then lowered his voice and asked, "Any sign of McCoy?"

Miller shook his head.

"A shame," Hendershot said. "My boys are all loaded for bear. And I was hoping to get my money back."

Miller raised an eyebrow. "Money?"

Hendershot related the story of the day Big Mike came out with McCoy to collect payment. McCoy had asked Hendershot to go along with it, promising the money would be returned later.

"I'm not a man who relishes violence," Hendershot said. "But I do like to have things settled." He gave Miller a hard look. "What if we just handle this ourselves?"

Miller swallowed hard. "It's not easy for a man to stick his neck out. I'm just a simple dry goods man."

Hendershot grumbled and gathered up his things. "At some point, the folks of this town will stop waiting for somebody else to come along and save them."

"He just shot him. In cold blood," Enrique said bitterly. "The man never had a chance. Lorenzo is a monster."

Juan nodded. "Nobody is arguing that."

The three brothers stood in the barn, as had become their habit when discussing anything that might worry their mother. Recently, that seemed to be nearly every conversation.

"We should wait for *Señor* McCoy before doing anything," Carlos said.

"Did you not hear what I said?" Enrique asked, an edge of fury creeping into his voice. "Lorenzo and his men have hurt McCoy. He might be off somewhere licking his wounds, but he could also be dead. We can't wait."

"Why not?" Juan asked.

"Because . . . because . . ." Enrique waved his hands in frustration.

"Because you are angry," Juan said. "Because you feel the need to do something, but what will change if you wait calmly to see what happens? Will Lorenzo go mad and kill the whole town? No. Wait for McCoy."

"And what if McCoy is dead?" Enrique asked.

Juan looked away. He didn't have an answer.

"I do not want this Lorenzo fellow in charge of Coyote Flats," Carlos said. "But I am no leader. McCoy has a plan. Without him . . . I don't know. I don't want to ask for more trouble than we can handle."

"Sometimes a man has to stand up!" Enrique insisted.

"And what if you stand up like a man, get killed like a man? What if we bury you in a man's grave?" Juan asked. "Is that what you want us to tell Cherry? That it is okay if she cries a river because her tears are for a real man?"

Enrique opened his mouth to protest, then closed it again, his turn to look away now. The thought of never seeing Cherry again was a powerful deterrent before haphazardly going up against Lorenzo. She would be the first to tell him not to be foolish.

"Fine," Enrique said. "We will wait for McCoy. But we can't wait forever. At some point, we will have to decide if we're going to do anything or not."

Carlos nodded. "This is reasonable."

Enrique let out a long, tired sigh. *Where are you, Señor McCoy? We need you.*

A week after Lorenzo had made his speech to the folks of Coyote Flats and aired out the back of Joseph's head, there had still been no sign of Garret McCoy. Lorenzo was disappointed. He figured surely somebody would have wanted to collect that thousand dollars. He'd hoped Dwight Combs would step up and do the job.

Or maybe McCoy was dead already. He'd been bashed up pretty good. Anything could have happened. He could have fallen off his horse and hit his head on a rock or drowned in the river. Lorenzo didn't like the idea of being deprived of his revenge. He didn't want McCoy *maybe* dead. He wanted to see a corpse.

The place was nearly deserted, but he knew that's because some of the boys were making collections and the rest were searching for McCoy. He walked to the front window and looked out on the street, just standing there quietly with his hands behind his back.

Coyote Flats wasn't much, but it could be something. Maybe one day. It could grow. Lorenzo understood what people thought about him, that he was just a greedy man who wanted money and was willing to do violence to get it.

And . . . well . . . he *did* want money, and he *was* willing to do violence to get it.

But with Jericho now out of the way, there was a feeling of power Lorenzo had never felt before. What if he could leave his mark, some legacy? No man is bigger than death, but what if the idea of him could live on? Lorenzo wondered if there was a way to legitimize himself, make himself mayor, call the money he collected *taxes* or *fees*. The idea that decades from now people might look at him as a founder instead of a criminal had a certain appeal. He didn't know why, really, he'd be long dead and buried.

Still . . .

He shook his head and laughed the notion away. He was thinking foolishness in his old age.

Through the window, he saw Big Mike ride up with a few of the boys and dismount. They came into the place grumbling and calling for beers. Big Mike saw him and came over.

"Well?" Lorenzo prompted.

"Looked all over, boss," Mike said. "No sign of McCoy."

Lorenzo spat a curse. "He's got to be *somewhere*."

Mike shrugged. "I mean, by now, who knows how far he could have gotten. We could search Austin or Dallas or all of Texas. What good would it do? He could be halfway to California. We gave him a good pasting. I doubt he wants to show his face around here again."

Lorenzo grumbled some more, then said, "Well, get a beer for yourself then. It's thirsty work riding all over."

"Thanks, boss."

Lorenzo sighed. Maybe this was why they called the man *Ghost* McCoy. He'd done a pretty good job of disappearing. Maybe he was dead. Or maybe Big Mike was right that he'd taken off for parts unknown never to show his face again, in which case what did it matter? Out of sight, out of mind. In a week or a month or a year, everyone would stop asking *Where's Garret McCoy?*

CHAPTER 30

"**W**here in the hell are we?" Garret McCoy had asked.

That had been a week ago. Rufus Lee had packed up his meager camp the next morning after McCoy had found him in the arroyo and had led him nearly due west all day and half the next. They'd stayed off the road, slipping through sparse woods and riding along narrow streams.

The farm had sprung up out of nowhere in a shallow, wooded valley, a gray clapboard house, a barn, chicken coop, and pigpen. The wide fields had gone to seed, with only a patch off to one side kept for a large garden.

Lee's answer to McCoy's question had been, "Someplace where nobody will look for us."

When Rufus Lee had originally come down to Texas, he'd been worried the law might be tailing him, so he hadn't gone straight to Austin. Instead, he'd zigged and zagged through the wilderness, staying away from roads and towns and settlements. He'd stumbled upon the farm without meaning to. It wasn't near anything that resembled civilization, but the three old women who'd lived there were happy for a strong back and eager hands to do some chores, and in exchange they let Lee stay in the barn and fed him regular meals. Eventually he'd moved on.

The old ladies were ready to offer the same deal again, and McCoy had learned recently that a warm, dry nest of hay was better for sleeping than the cold ground.

McCoy helped with simple things at first so as not to aggravate his injured wrist. He weeded the garden and picked tomatoes while Lee mended a fence. As the ache in his wrist faded, he took on more strenuous tasks, hauling buckets of water from the well, patching a hole in the roof, chopping wood. There seemed to be a never-ending list of chores associated with farm life, and the ladies weren't as spry as they used to be.

Abigail was the oldest, frail and thin with a face like tree bark. She took her place in a rocking chair on the front porch each morning, a blanket on her lap, and didn't budge until dinnertime.

McCoy walked past her, hauling water with his shirt off, sweat glistening in his chest hair.

"If I was a few years younger," she said to him with a gleam in her eye and then cackled laughter.

McCoy didn't take his shirt off after that.

Matilda was a few years younger and did most of the cooking, and at one point it seemed like her goal was to make McCoy and Lee as fat as possible. There seemed to be no end to butter and biscuits and slabs of ham and potatoes and fluffy flapjacks in the morning.

"Old hens like us just peck at our food," Matilda told him. "It's good to have men to cook for again."

At first, McCoy thought the women were sisters, but casual conversation revealed they'd all been young widows who'd lost their husbands in the first year of the Second Seminole War. Upon discovering they each had no other family, the three of them decided to pull together and head to Texas.

Blanche was the youngest of the three and thus did the majority of the heavy chores.

"You can say no if you like," Blanche told McCoy. "You're not slaves, you know."

McCoy grinned. "Then how would we earn our biscuits?"

Blanche waved the comment away and shook her head. "Just try to stop Matilda feeding you."

"I'm not going to try," he told her. "Just tell Matilda to keep the food coming, and Rufus and I will do whatever you like."

Blanche laughed, then turned serious, giving McCoy a searching look. "You boys hiding from something, ain't ya. None of my business, and it don't make no never mind to me, but I guess curiosity got the best of me. I meant to ask Rufus Lee the same question the first time through but never quite got up the gumption."

McCoy took off his hat and wiped the sweat off his forehead with the back of his hand, pondering how to answer. He decided to play it straightforward. "We're hiding."

"From the law?"

Rufus was, in fact, hiding from the law, but that situation was more complicated than a yes or no answer. "We're hiding from men who want to do a lot of people wrong. And they want to kill me for standing up to them. I'm hiding now, but I won't be hiding long." He looked down at his right hand, wiggled the wrist back and forth and flexed the fingers. "Now that I'm on the mend, I'll be ready to face them."

"Well, don't hurry off and get killed on my account," Blanche said. "You're welcome here, you and Rufus both, but I understand there's things a man has to do."

"Obliged for that, Blanche."

That night after dinner, Rufus Lee and Garret McCoy stood next to each other and leaned on the fence of the pigpen.

"I sure am going to miss Matilda's biscuits," McCoy said.

"Is that your way of saying it's time to go?" Lee asked.

McCoy blew out a sigh. "I reckon."

"A shame."

McCoy raised an eyebrow. "Oh?"

"It's not bad here. Good honest work. Simple. Nothing to twist a man's thoughts around and worry him at night." A wide grin split Lee's face. "If only Blanche was thirty years younger."

Both men laughed.

But then the laughter died away.

"Time to face the music," McCoy said.

Lee nodded. "Right."

"First thing in the morning?"

Lee nodded again. "No sense putting it off."

"Then let's tell the ladies."

They found the three women waiting for them on the front porch, Abigail in her rocker, Matilda sitting on a bench next to her, and Blanche leaning in the doorway with her arms crossed.

The men climbed the steps to the porch and took off their hats.

"Ladies, we need to tell you something," McCoy announced.

"Let me guess," Blanche said. "You're both back on the road first thing in the morning."

A sheepish grin from McCoy. "That obvious?"

"I spent many years learning to read faces and postures and moods," Blanche told him. "I could tell at dinner there was a sort of tension in you, like maybe you was pondering a decision."

"I guess you got it figured."

"Well, you don't think we'd let you go without a proper send-off, do you?" Blanche said.

Abigail pulled a bottle of whiskey out from under her blanket and cackled. "Saving it for a special occasion."

Matilda handed out tin cups. Blanche took the bottle from Abigail and filled each cup. Then they raised the cups to toast.

"To our boys," Blanche said. "May they find whatever they're looking for."

And they drank.

They stayed up later than usual, laughing and telling stories. Abigail knew an alarming number of dirty jokes. When the bottle was finally empty, they all went to bed, McCoy and Rufus Lee flopping into their nests of hay.

They awoke with the dawn the next morning, saddled their horses, and were ready to go. There were hugs all around, and the ladies waved them goodbye.

"That wasn't a bad place to be," Lee said. "To live quiet and simple for a while."

"No argument here," McCoy said.

"But I guess a man can't hide forever."

McCoy shook his head. "Nope."

"Back to Coyote Flats?" Lee asked.

"We need to make a stop or two first," McCoy said. "But then, yeah, Coyote Flats. I think being away for a while was good. Not just so I could heal up, but also to let things quiet down. Might work to our advantage."

"It would be nice if something did," Lee said.

They rode back the way they'd come, the streams and the woods and the fields all the same but looking different from a new direction and a new perspective. They'd been getting away from something before.

Now they were headed toward it.

Campfires and beans and strong coffee and little talk. They missed Matilda's biscuits and Abigail's mad laugh and Blanche's easygoing wisdom.

Never mind. There was a job to do.

It was midmorning when they came to the Vargas place.

Enrique Vargas was walking from the barn to the house when he saw the two riders approaching and paused to watch them come.

McCoy and Lee reined in their horses ten feet from him.

McCoy touched the brim of his hat. "Sorry I'm late."

Enrique grinned. "So many people are saying Ghost had become a ghost for real, but I never believed it. Who's your *amigo*?"

"Rufus Lee, meet Enrique Vargas. Enrique, this is Rufus Lee."

Lee nodded. "Good to make your acquaintance."

Enrique returned the nod.

"Lee and your brothers have something in common," McCoy told Enrique.

"Oh?"

"The law wants them all for something they didn't do," McCoy said.

"Actually, I *did* do it," Lee corrected. "It's just that it was self-defense."

"Don't split hairs."

"The important thing is that we are all together," Enrique said triumphantly. "Now we shall vanquish that filthy creature Lorenzo, free Coyote Flats from his tyrannical rule, and then I will sweep my sweet Cherry away into the eternal bonds of matrimony!"

"That's a full day," Lee said. "We're not trying to fit all that in before lunch, are we?"

McCoy shook his head. "Not yet, we ain't. We're making another stop first."

"I'll get my brothers!" Enrique ran for the barn, youthful glee spurring him on.

CHAPTER 31

"Let's go to Carmen's Place and get a drink," Big Mike said.

Froggy Morton looked up and gestured at the interior of Lorenzo's place. "We can drink here."

"But there ain't no women here."

Froggy stood and followed Mike. "Let's go."

They took the short walk from Lorenzo's to Carmen's in no particular hurry. Mike had noticed that recently. No need to hurry. No need to rush or worry. No looking over his shoulder for Jericho's men lurking in the shadows.

"You ever worry about being out of a job?"

Froggy blinked. "Huh?"

"Think about it," Mike said. "The boss was always trying to hire more men to keep up with Jericho, but now there ain't no Jericho. And then he had us all running around looking for McCoy, but he's cooled on that now too."

"Good," Froggy said. "The boss was acting weird and obsessed. McCoy's long gone. Better for all of us to move on."

"That ain't the point," Mike told him. "The boss's got a lot of guys on the payroll now with nothing to do. Might be that he figures out eventually that don't make the best economic sense."

Froggy gave Mike an odd look.

"A bad way to spend money," Mike clarified.

Froggy scratched his head. "Huh."

"I'm just saying, don't be surprised if there's some changes coming," Mike said. "I don't know what exactly . . . but something."

They walked in and spotted Mortimer Lorenzo standing at the bar, scowling, a bottle of whiskey in his hand. Everyone was giving him plenty of room.

"Should we join him?" Froggy asked.

Mike watched Lorenzo for a moment. The boss was muttering to himself and seemed in a foul mood. "We'd best steer clear."

"He's changed," Froggy said.

"He'll be fine."

"It's like with Jericho gone . . ." Froggy shrugged. "I don't know. Like he doesn't know what to do with himself now."

"I said he'll be fine," Mike insisted. "Everyone needs time to adjust to the new normal. Still . . . let's stay out of his way for now. Let's grab that corner table and get a bottle."

Froggy Morton shook his head, his sigh the saddest sound in the west. "Strange days have come to Coyote Flats."

* * *

"Coyote Flats could really be something." Mortimer Lorenzo punctuated each word by thrusting his finger at the man behind the bar. "We have singular leadership now. Anything's possible, right? Is this America or not?"

"That's right!" the man behind the bar agreed.

Lorenzo poured more whiskey into his shot glass, spilled some on the bar. "Oh, I know what you're thinking . . . uh . . . what's your name again?"

"Barney, sir."

"I know what you're thinking, Barney," Lorenzo said. "Kansas City has the river. That makes a big difference for commerce, but we've got a river close by. We could expand in that direction. And if we could get the railroad to come through . . ." Lorenzo winked. "Well, sky's the limit, don't you think?"

"Sound good to me, Mr. Lorenzo."

"Dang right."

Lorenzo's eye socket had begun to pain him again. The glass eye had cost an arm and a leg, and they still couldn't get the fit right, but he wasn't about to send all the way to Germany for another one. Not like he couldn't make do with the eyepatch. Vanity, he supposed, which was a laugh since he wasn't exactly some handsome type all the ladies swooned over. Anyway, the whiskey had numbed the pain to a distant ache, the mere memory of discomfort.

"Barney, is Carmen upstairs?" Lorenzo asked.

"I reckon so, sir."

Lorenzo grabbed the bottle. "I'm going to go up and talk to her. She's a woman that understands ambition."

"Sir, I don't—" Barney closed his mouth, and when he opened it again said, "Yes, sir, Mr. Lorenzo."

Lorenzo knew the barkeep had been about to object. Carmen didn't allow just anyone to wander upstairs and disturb her.

But Lorenzo wasn't just anyone.

He was the man in charge of this town. More specifically, he was the man who'd splattered the brains of Barney's predecessor all over the street. It was understandable the new barkeep wasn't about to tell Lorenzo where he could and couldn't go.

Lorenzo headed for the stairs, head feeling like it was floating on a cloud. He knew he'd had more to drink than usual. So what? A man was entitled to let loose now and again. Who'd earned it more than he had?

Nobody. That's who.

The stairs tilted one way and then another, and he was obliged to quickly latch on to the banister to keep himself from tumbling backward. He righted himself, took a couple of deep breaths, then finished the climb to the second floor.

He pounded on the first door he came to.

"Occupied!" came a feminine voice from within.

Lorenzo banged on the door with his fist.

"Didn't you hear the lady?" A man's voice. "Get lost!"

Lorenzo pounded on the door with renewed aggression.

A second later, the door flew open, and a stunning blonde stood there with a cross expression, holding a blanket over her nudity. "Didn't you hear what I said, you stupid son of a—"

She blinked. "Oh. Mr. Lorenzo."

"Which room is Carmen's?"

She hesitated only a moment and then told him, pointing down the hall.

"Thanks." He moved away, hearing the door click shut behind him.

He arrived at Carmen's door and lifted his fist to pound again, hesitated, musing that maybe going in too loud wasn't the best way to approach the woman. He took a deep breath, removed his hat, and ran his fingers through his hair. A polite rap on the door with one knuckle.

The door creaked open. Carmen stood there, eyelids heavy, chin up, a cool reception if not exactly hostile, which Lorenzo reckoned was about the best he could hope for under the circumstances.

"I thought I might speak with you." Lorenzo felt the words tumble lazily out of his mouth, the clumsy syllables of a slow-witted drunk. This had been a bad idea, not the idea he wanted to pitch to her, but coming late at night like this, all full of whiskey.

Too late to take it back now. He'd started this. He'd finish it.

"Of course," Carmen said primly. "I'm listening."

She didn't invite him in nor step aside, but be damned if he'd be kept standing in the hall like some tinhorn traveling salesmen. He gently pushed his way in, and her choices were to move aside or get walked on.

Carmen frowned and elected to move.

He entered and closed the door behind him, pausing a moment to look around. He spotted a chair near the window. He hadn't been asked to sit, but he hadn't been asked to come in either.

In for a penny, in for a pound.

He crossed the room and plopped into the chair, setting his hat on a cedar chest under the window. He held up the half-empty bottle of whiskey. "Drink?"

"No . . . thank you."

Lorenzo took a slug and smacked his lips. "I've been thinking."

"About?"

"The future."

That gave her pause. "The future of what exactly."

"The town and everybody in it," Lorenzo said. "And the town that will still be here when all of us are gone."

"I'm afraid I don't understand."

He didn't really know how to start explaining. Part of that was the drink. He was getting more and more muddleheaded but couldn't really find the motivation to stop taking little swigs from the bottle, as if the constant working of his arm to bring the bottle to his mouth was the only thing keeping the clunky machinery of his brain working.

Lorenzo told her about the town growing and expanding. Businesses being built, and homes. The money he collected wouldn't be extortion if they called it taxes. He'd get the railroad to come through. That meant building a station, laying track. Jobs. The place would boom. Men and women would come to Coyote Flats because they *wanted* to, not just because it was the place they ended up. People would settle and raise families. They'd have to build a school.

"Schools?" Carmen raised a suspicious eyebrow. "I did not know you care so much for children."

Lorenzo almost told her he didn't give a tinker's

damn about children, but was that really true? Any sons he had would have sons of their own. The family name would live on.

"Legacy," he said. "Don't you want to leave something behind? You don't even have a sign out front telling folks this is Carmen's Place."

"They all know it's Carmen's Place," she said. "It's a small town."

Lorenzo sat forward in his seat. "That's the point. It's small now. But in a hundred years? People will walk by and see this place and wonder who built it. Don't you want . . ." He groped for the right words, the right thought. "Don't you want them to *know*?"

Carmen narrowed her eyes, regarding him with strange curiosity.

Then she threw back her head and laughed.

There was a moment he considered taking offense, but he let it go. He reckoned he did sound ridiculous. "Let me in on the joke, why don't you?"

"It is always the way of men who reach a certain age," she said. "You fear death."

He scoffed. "I've been shot at more times than I can count."

"I don't mean the sudden death of a bullet through your heart," she said. "Anyone can die without warning. I can be hit by a runaway wagon in the street tomorrow. That is not what I'm talking about."

"Then talk plain!"

"I'm talking about seeing the grim reaper standing on the horizon, his dark, tattered cloak flapping in a cold wind," she said, ice in her tone. "He's always there and always getting closer. And one day the slow withering will start, and you'll realize it had actually started long ago. We all start dying the moment we're born. One day you realize it, and it occurs to you how *late* you've realized it, so then there is a mad scramble for it all to mean something, to show the world you matter. But the clock ticks and tocks, and time runs out at last. Did you put your names on enough buildings? Did you have enough sons? Did the city fathers build enough statues of you? But . . . well . . . someday all of that will be dust too. Just dust."

Lorenzo sat back in his chair. He brought the bottle to his lips again, not another little nip this time, but a long, thoughtful swallow.

"You paint a bleak picture," he said. "But I must admit I wouldn't mind a few statues."

She laughed again, but sadly. "Why tell me all of this? Is this not something Big Mike wants to hear?"

"Because I need you," Lorenzo said.

"If I had a dollar for every man who told me that, I'd have—"

"Not like that," Lorenzo said. "You run this place. You have a sense of details. I need that. I need us to work together."

"What? A partnership?"

"More than that," Lorenzo said. "More like . . . a union."

Another suspicious look. "What are you saying, Mortimer Lorenzo?"

"You could be queen of Coyote Flats," Lorenzo said. "Queen of what this place could become."

"Good Lord," Carmen said. "You are not seriously proposing marriage to me."

He shook his head and took a swig from the bottle. "No. More like trying to gauge how open you might be to such an arrangement."

"You killed Jericho. I didn't like him, but he was still mine, in a sense. You've disposed of Garret McCoy—either dead or run off—and I *did* like him. You blew my best barkeep's brains out the back of his head. How would any woman in my position possibly answer such a proposition?" Carmen asked. "Obviously I'll think about it."

CHAPTER 32

Froggy Morton hopped around on one foot, trying to pull off his other boot.

Claudia sat perched on the edge of the bed and giggled.

Froggy looked over at her and grinned, still hopping. "Don't worry, darlin'. I'll be with you in a moment."

She giggled again as she rolled her stockings down, pulled them off and tossed them across the room. Claudia had thick, black hair, and long, long legs. There was a graceful way about her.

In short, she was everything Froggy Morton wasn't.

Which suited Froggy just fine.

Froggy and Big Mike had finished a bottle and then had turned their attentions to some pretty young things. Claudia had captured Froggy's attention utterly, and he'd lost track of Mike, which was fine because Mike was a big boy and could take care of himself. Froggy had money burning a hole in his pocket, and at that moment, he could not think of a better way to spend it, not that he was trying too hard. Claudia had led him upstairs to her room, her smile full of promises.

He pulled off the other boot with a grunt. "Finally." He panted and looked around the room to give him a second to gather himself. A small fireplace, cold. A small vanity. A second door which lead to . . . *who knows?* The bed took up most of the small room

Froggy unbuckled his belt, pulled down his pants, one leg getting caught. He found himself hopping again before getting tangled and toppling over onto the rag rug.

Claudia's giggle became full-throated laughter. "Sugar, you're going to hurt yourself before you've even had a chance to—"

The sharp *pop* from the next room startled a gasp out of her.

Froggy looked up, still on his hands and knees. He knew a gunshot when he heard one, and it had gone off right on the other side of the door, not the door to the hall, but the other one across the room. Not the big *boom* of something like a Colt Walker. A .32 maybe.

"Cherry!"

Claudia sprang from the bed and was across the room in three strides, pushing the door open without knocking. A blather of hushed voices from the other room, female voices, Froggy thought. He grunted and groaned to one knee. Man, he was in bad shape. He thought, not for the first time, he should do something about that.

Later.

He lurched to his feet, pulled up his pants, and shuffled to the doorway. He was in his socks, so he didn't make any noise. He looked into the other room.

Three of the working girls stood at the foot of a bed in the middle of a frantic hushed discussion. One of them was Claudia—obviously—and right next to her was the girl Froggy recognized as Cherry. The third girl Froggy didn't know. Brown skinned and curvy with huge, dark eyes. Short. He was surprised he didn't recognize her. There wasn't much going on in a place like Coyote Flats, and a new girl at Carmen's was usually something all the fellas would be talking about. Maybe if he came back in another night, he could get to know—

His eyes fell to the bed and the small collection of pistols spread out on the quilt.

That . . . didn't seem right.

"It just went off, okay?" Cherry whispered frantically.

"What are you doing messing with them anyway?" Claudia asked.

"I'm trying to figure which one to pick," Cherry shot back.

The brown-skinned girl babbled a string of words in Spanish, gesticulating wildly.

"I don't speak that!" Cherry said.

"Just calm down!" Claudia told them. "I don't think anyone heard, so just—"

All three looked up at the same time and saw Froggy Morton standing in the doorway.

"Uh . . . what's going on?" he asked.

"Nothing." Cherry shook her head, face blank. "Nothing's going on."

"Nothing's going on," Claudia echoed.

"*Todos bueno*," the new girl said.

"Oh." Froggy's eyes shifted to the pistols on the bed again. "What's with the guns?"

"Nothing," Cherry said. "There's nothing with the guns."

Claudia shrugged. "What guns?"

Froggy's eyes narrowed. Even booze-addled, it seemed to him that something was obviously going on. "What are you doing with those?"

"Froggy, honey, it's nothing." Claudia came around the bed, took him by the arm, and steered him back into her room. "It's nothing. There's nothing going on. Let's get back to me and you, baby. Come on."

He pulled his arm away from her. "I think something *is* going on."

"No, baby—"

"I need to tell Mr. Lorenzo." Froggy bent to grab his boots off the floor. "There is definitely something going on with you girls and them guns." He straightened and turned. "If you ladies know what's good for you, you'll wait right here while I—"

The ceramic pitcher came toward his face at lightning speed, cracking across the bridge of his nose and breaking into heavy pieces. Stars and bells went off and the room spun and in the next instant, he was face down on the rug.

Cherry held the handle of the busted pitcher, eyes wide at what she'd done. "Is he dead?"

She'd killed Gerald, and now she'd killed Froggy Morton. Cherry couldn't honestly say she felt bad about either man being gone. They weren't nice people. But killing wasn't a pleasant thing. The feeling of smashing the heavy pitcher against Froggy's face, the heavy crack, and the vibrations up her arms. It had all been so physical.

Cherry blinked. "He's dead, isn't he?"

A groan. Froggy Morton tried to push himself up.

Claudia rushed to the cold fireplace and snatched up the poker. She brought it down hard on the back of Froggy's head, Cherry flinching at the sickening crack of the heavy iron poker against the base of Froggy's skull. He twitched once and then didn't move again.

"*Now*, he's dead," Claudia said.

"Good Lord." Cherry blinked down at the corpse. "What do we do now?"

Claudia went to the other door, opened it just enough to stick her head out into the hall and look both ways. "I don't think anyone heard." She came back in and closed the door.

The new girl looked down at Froggy's body and shook her head. "*Qué lástima*."

Cherry wished the girl would speak American.

"We can't just leave him there," Claudia said.

Cherry rolled her eyes. "Ya think?"

"We could hide him in the cellar," Claudia suggested.

"He can't be found on the property. Miss Carmen will get in trouble. Anyway, he can't stay down there forever. He'll get pretty ripe sooner or later." Cherry turned to the new girl. "Gabriela, go down to the livery and hook up Miss Carmen's wagon. Not the little two-seater but the buckboard she uses to haul stuff around. Bring it to the back door in the alley. If anyone sees you and asks what you're doing, just pretend you don't understand."

"*Qué?*"

"Exactly. Now go on. Hurry!"

Gabriela left quickly.

"Get his arms," Cherry said.

Claudia bent and grabbed Froggy's wrists. Cherry took him by the ankles. They both lifted—or tried to, grunting until their faces went red and then finally letting go.

"He's so fat!" Claudia panted. "We need to get some help."

"No!" Cherry said quickly. "The less people know about this the better."

"What then?"

Cherry appraised the situation. "He's on that rag rug. We can slide him."

Claudia nodded. "Okay. The back stairway?"

"Right."

Cherry took his ankles again, and Claudia grabbed his wrists. They spun Froggy to line him up with the doorway, the rag rug moving easily over the smooth wooden floor.

"It's working," Claudia said.

She pulled while Cherry pushed and steered. They slid Froggy into the hall after checking if it was clear, then turned toward the back stairs, the whisper of the rug on the wood floor the only sound as they passed a half dozen rooms to the end of the hall.

Claudia opened the door to the back stairs.

"Move out of the way," Cherry said.

Claudia stepped aside.

Cherry lifted Froggy's ankles and pushed. Froggy tipped over the edge, then went tumbling, bouncing down the stairs with a thudding racket and landing in a heap at the bottom, arms and legs at an awkward angle.

"That was louder than expected," Cherry said.

Claudia frowned. "You tossed a dead body down a flight of stairs. What did you expect?"

"Just grab the rug."

At the bottom of the stairs, they maneuvered Froggy back onto the rug and slid him to the back door. Cherry stuck her head into the alley just in time to see Gabriela rein in the buckboard. They dragged the body outside, and Cherry realized both she and Claudia were still barefoot, the ground cold and gritty. She hoped she didn't step on a stone. The three ladies grunted and groaned and broke into sweat trying to load Froggy into the back.

Cherry grunted and heaved. "Like . . . trying to . . . load . . . a dang . . . buffalo."

They finally managed to get Froggy's corpse into the back of the buckboard. Cherry threw the rug over him. The three ladies leaned against the wagon, panting, hearts racing.

"What you ladies doing?"

They all flinched.

Cherry looked up and saw the outline of a huge person against the pale moonlight. His face was in shadow, but Cherry didn't need to see it to know it was Big Mike. He swayed where he stood, and she could smell the whiskey.

"Hey, Mr. Mike." She tried to sound friendly. Her voice shook only a little. "Out for a stroll?"

"Looking for my pal, Froggy." Mike hiccupped.

"You seen him? We was having a few drinks, and then I spent some time with one of your friends upstairs. Sort of lost track of him."

All three ladies vehemently shook their heads at the same time.

"Nope."

"Haven't see him."

"*No he visto a nadie.*"

"Oh." He took a halting step toward the buckboard. "Whatcha got there?"

Claudia moved quickly to stand in front of him. "Potatoes!" she blurted.

Cherry winced at the terrible lie.

Mike frowned. "Potatoes?"

Claudia nodded with enthusiasm. "That's right. Potatoes."

"Potatoes," Cherry echoed.

"*Las patatas son el fruto de la vida.*"

"What are you doing with potatoes this time of night?" Mike asked.

"Planting them," Claudia said.

Cherry winced again. *Oh, my God, stop talking.*

Mike raised an eyebrow. "At night?"

"Uh . . ." Claudia glanced at Cherry for help.

"Because it's not so hot at night," Cherry said.

"Way too hot during the day," Claudia agreed.

"*La noche fresca es un alivio del implacable asalto del sol.*"

Mike leaned in, eyes narrowing. "You know what I think?"

Cherry swallowed hard. "What?"

Mike leaned in farther still, threatening to topple

over, his face only three inches from Cherry's. "I think that's . . . *smart.*"

Cherry felt relief wash over her. "Right?"

"Dang right," Mike said. "Why don't farmers do that? Way cooler at night."

A shrug and a nervous laugh from Cherry. "I guess us working gals are just a little more clever than farmers."

Big Mike tossed her a wave as he kept walking. "Well, I've had enough. If you see Froggy, tell him I went to bed."

"Will do," Cherry said brightly.

They watched Mike walk down the alley, zigging and zagging in his inebriated state. When he turned the corner and vanished from view, the ladies blew out the breath they'd been holding and sank against the buckboard.

"This is not what I expected to be doing tonight," Claudia said.

Cherry climbed up and sat on the buckboard's bench next to Gabriela. She took the reins. "Just get on. We need to pick up some shovels."

Claudia climbed into the back with Froggy. "Shovels?"

"So we can bury these potatoes," Cherry said. "Somewhere out of town."

A faraway look glimmered in Gabriela's eyes. "*Supongo que era un hombre malvado, pero es triste cuando se quita una vida humana. Se apaga otra luz en el mundo.*"

Cherry flicked the reins, and the buckboard lurched forward. "You can say that again."

CHAPTER 33

Moses Hendershot's dinner table was long and crowded, stretching the length of the long dining hall in his sprawling ranch house. Circular iron chandeliers hung over each end of the table, holding a ring of fat candles which gently illuminated the room. Antlers from some long-ago hunt guarded the doorways at each end. The house had grown as the family had gotten bigger over the years, and Moses himself seemed to rule the ranch like some benevolent, old-style European baron.

Hendershot, his wife and grown daughters, and the ranch hands all sat along the table with the wives of a few of the senior ranch hands and several of Hendershot's grandchildren. They'd been more than happy to make room for McCoy, Rufus Lee, and the Vargas brothers.

Dinner was a loud affair, dishes and pitchers being passed back and forth every which way—mashed potatoes and a huge pork roast and carrots and brown bread with butter, and purple cabbage

"I was ready to do battle that day you and Big Mike

came out to collect," Hendershot confided. "A man could only put up with so much."

Hendershot had a half dozen hard-looking ranch hands ready to go to war, so McCoy wasn't surprised the old man had been tempted to take on Lorenzo.

"But it's a good thing you talked me out of it and told me to wait," Hendershot admitted. "I've got young'uns here to think of, and even if I succeeded in taking down Lorenzo, there was Jericho to think of. That's too much for me and my boys, but you cleverly figured out how to get rid of Jericho for us. I reckon that makes our remaining task a bit more manageable, eh?"

"I saw an opportunity, that's all," McCoy said. "If you want to give credit to somebody for getting rid of Jericho, I guess that would be Lorenzo. All I did was encourage him."

Hendershot turned to Rufus Lee. "You should have heard this fella. Big Mike comes out to collect, and I tell him where to go. Then McCoy comes over, and I'm expecting more threats, but you know what he says? He says, *Mr. Hendershot, how would you feel about never paying another cent to this dirty Lorenzo son of a—*"

"Moses! No foul language at the table." His wife shot him a stern look.

Hendershot cleared his throat. "Well, you get the gist."

They finished the meal, and just when McCoy was sure he couldn't possibly push one more bite of food into his face, Mrs. Hendershot emerged from the kitchen with a chocolate cake the size of a barn.

McCoy somehow found room for a small slice.

When they'd all finally had enough, Hendershot

stood. "Another fine meal. My thanks to all involved. Now, it's time for some of us to talk business. I've been saving a bottle of good brandy, and I've got a box of cigars too. If our guests would like to join me on the front porch." Hendershot nodded at a man across the table. He was burly, with a thick beard and ruddy cheeks. "Lonnie, I want you to join us."

They adjourned to the porch. Hendershot poured brandy and handed out cigars.

Enrique looked at the cigar in his hand, then looked at McCoy.

"Like this." McCoy bit a chunk out of the rounded end of the cigar then spit it over the railing before lighting the cigar.

Enrique followed his example.

Soon the porch was engulfed in a thick, gray cloud.

"This is your show, McCoy," Hendershot said. "You talk and we'll listen."

McCoy fortified himself with a large swig of brandy, then said, "I wish I could tell you there was some clever, tricky way to accomplish what we're trying to do, but there isn't. We want Lorenzo gone. He'll see it different. It comes down to shooting and killing. When the smoke clears, the winners will be alive, and the losers will be dead. That's about as final as it gets. Lorenzo dead is the only way to solve this problem."

"Then maybe one of us follows him out to the outhouse late one night and bushwhacks him," Rufus Lee suggested. "Not exactly my style. Seems a sort of low-down way to go about it, but it would get the job done."

"And then Big Mike would step in and take over," Garret said. "And then somebody else if we killed Big

Mike. The folks of Coyote Flats will keep being fleeced by some outlaw or another because everyone knows the people here will sit still for it. Time to show all them bad men out there it ain't true no more, that the people here will stand up.

Hendershot nodded agreement. "A clean sweep."

"So that's what we're signing up for," McCoy said. "A gunfight."

"Lonnie, you're the senior hand," Hendershot said. "We're talking about killing and dying. There won't be one harsh word if anyone wants to bow out."

"The boys and I had a chin-wag about this very subject, and I can speak for them," Lonnie said. "You took those men, paid 'em good, put a roof over their heads. When they was sick or laid up with busted ribs because they'd been kicked by a mule or some dang thing, you still paid 'em. You treat us like family. If you say mount up, we'll mount up."

"Thank you, Lonnie," Hendershot said. "And thank the boys for me."

"I'll let the boys know it's on," Lonnie said.

"One more thing, Lonnie."

"Sir?"

"You and Ray are sitting this one out," Hendershot said.

Lonnie frowned. "Mr. Hendershot, you heard Mr. McCoy. This is going to get bloody. You need every man."

"I know you hate to hear it, but you and Ray are the senior men," Hendershot said. "We've got women and children here. Somebody's got to mind the store."

It was clear Lonnie didn't like it, but he nodded. "You're the boss."

"Okay then," Hendershot said. "McCoy, how should we go about it?"

"You and your people should go in first," McCoy told him. "Take your buckboard and go into town like you're picking up routine supplies. Get into position. Me and Rufus and these Vargas boys will be along later."

Hendershot nodded. "Sounds right."

"Now we just need to work out all the details," McCoy said.

"And then what?" Hendershot asked.

McCoy's face went hard as stone. "And then blood."

The morning after Mortimer Lorenzo's audacious proposition, Carmen found herself still thinking about it. Was it such a bad offer? The notion of them together as husband and wife was off-putting, that they would share a marital bed together or conduct themselves as a normal man and woman in such a situation. No, the idea repulsed her.

But that's not really what Lorenzo was offering, not completely. He was simply offering the most binding partnership he could think of.

And his proposal was not without appeal. She liked running her place, liked being the boss, liked having the girls listen to her, liked that the barkeeps jumped when she snapped her fingers. And she was good at it. The place ran smoothly under her management and was profitable. Could she do the same for Coyote Flats?

Could they become the county seat? Carmen could be a powerful person of respect in Texas.

But, no. Even if Lorenzo appointed himself mayor, Carmen would only be the *wife* of the mayor, adjacent to the real power.

Still . . . a start. A stepping stone.

There was much to think about.

It was barely after dawn, but Carmen was too restless to sleep any longer. Might as well make a start to the day. She dressed and went downstairs to inspect the saloon. The early morning light slanted in, dirty and orange, through the front windows.

The barkeeps cleaned up each night after closing, as a matter of routine, but there were often surprises or something missed—broken glass, a spilled bottle of whiskey, a knocked-over spittoon. Once, she'd even found a cavalry corporal sound asleep under one of the corner tables. Carmen thought she could not be surprised anymore, not running a saloon.

She'd seen it all.

The door creaked open and three filthy beggars walked in, shuffling with fatigue, shoulders slumped, two of them holding shovels.

I stand corrected, Carmen thought.

Cherry, Claudia, and Gabriela were covered in dirt, bedraggled, and barefoot.

"Oh," Cherry said when she saw Carmen. "We didn't think anybody would be up this early."

"Do I want to know?"

The three girls looked at each other.

"I reckon not," Cherry said.

Carmen pointed up the stairs. "Baths and clean clothes. Now."

Cherry frowned. "We're pretty tired, Miss Carmen."

"Laundry is not until the end of the week," Carmen said. "If you think you're going to dirty your sheets, then it's your brain that's tired. Now go do as I say."

"Yes, ma'am."

They dragged themselves upstairs, muttering as they went.

Carmen inspected the saloon and the kitchen and found nothing amiss. She checked the supplies and was pleased to find they were not currently short of anything. She made a pot of coffee, poured herself a cup, and took it to the front porch to sip slowly and watch the town awaken.

This can be a good place, Carmen thought. *It can prosper and grow.* With Jericho gone and Lorenzo tamed, there could be . . . possibilities.

She heard the clatter of a buckboard coming up the street and saw Moses Hendershot sitting on the bench, a handful of his ranch hands with him. Hendershot reined in the horse in front of Miller's Dry Goods. A bit early to be coming into town for supplies, but if Carmen could get a head start on the day, then why not old man Hendershot?

Hendershot twisted on the bench to say something to the hands riding in the bed, pointing this way and that. They nodded and climbed out of the buckboard. Two went to Miller's front door, stood on either side of it, leaning there, thumbs hooked into belts. The other two ranch hands crossed to the sidewalk on the other side of the street and stood there.

Hendershot climbed down from the buckboard and went to the dry goods store. Miller came out to meet him. Both men shook hands and wore stern expressions. Miller and Hendershot went inside, and the two hands waited, still flanking the front door.

Carmen's gaze drifted back to the two hands who'd crossed the street. They hadn't moved, just stood there waiting.

Waiting for what?

Carmen's eyes slowly widened. Perhaps it was some instinct, or maybe because she knew what sort of man Moses Hendershot was. She turned slowly and went back inside.

She stood at the foot of the stairs and raised her voice. "Cherry!"

The girl appeared at the top of the stairs, clean, her hair wet. She wore a plain, cream-colored blouse, and a light-weight, dark green skirt. Nobody would look at Cherry and think she was a working girl at Carmen's Place.

"Gather the girls and get them down here," Carmen said.

"Some are still sleeping."

"Get them down here," Carmen repeated. "And bring the guns and ammunition."

Cherry's eyes widened. "The guns?"

"You heard me, Cherry," Carmen said calmly. "Go on."

Carmen went to the front door and locked it. She went down the back hall to make sure that door was locked too. Less than ten minutes later, all the girls had gathered in the saloon. They'd put all the guns and ammunition on the center table. Ones too old or rusty had been discarded for obvious reasons of safety.

"Missy, you've shown everyone how to load these?" Carmen asked. "The basics of point and shoot?"

"Yes, ma'am," the blonde said.

Carmen nodded.

"Good. Has anyone had any trouble loading them?"

Claudia shot a sideways glance at Cherry. "*Most* of us have got the hang of it."

Cherry glared back at her.

Carmen almost asked but stopped herself. *I don't want to know. I don't want to know. I don't want . . .*

"Load them," Carmen told the girls. "Get ready."

"What're we getting ready for?" Claudia asked.

"For fighting," Carmen said. "For the finale. If I'm wrong, then we'll call it a drill."

She watched Cherry load the .32 with exaggerated care. Carmen knew the girl had picked the gun because it was the shiniest and the newest looking. The other girls had different revolvers of various calibers. They all seemed to have basic competency and knew what they were doing.

Gabriela's Colt Army looked huge in her slender hands. "*Es muy pesado. No necesito acortarlo. Puedo golpear a alguien en la cabeza.*"

"Miss Carmen, there ain't enough guns for you to have one," Cherry said.

"I see." Carmen circled behind the bar where she knew the barkeeps kept a double-barreled twelve-gauge. She broke the gun, checked to see there were indeed two shells, then snapped the barrels back into place and leaned the shotgun on one shoulder. "I will use this one."

"Now what?" Claudia asked.

"Keep watch in the window," Carmen said. "Maybe nothing will happen, but if it does, we're ready.

"I learned guns from my brothers and my pa, but I never shot no living person before," Missy said. "I never killed nobody."

Carmen's eyes went hard as dark river stones. "Just remember what Joseph's brains looked like splattered all over the street, and you'll know what to do."

Big Mike walked through the front door of Lorenzo's place and said in a loud, boisterous voice, "Anyone seen that dang fool lazy Froggy Morton anywhere?"

Mortimer Lorenzo sat at a back table with a cup of black coffee in front of him and held both sides of his head. "Would you stop that shouting?"

Mike frowned. "You okay?"

"Did a lot of important thinking last night," Lorenzo said. "And a lot of drinking to go along with it."

"Thinking about what?"

Lorenzo waved the question away. "I'll tell you after I've got it all figured. What's this about Froggy Morton?"

"We separated last night and each spent some time with one of Carmen's girls," Mike said. "We were supposed to meet up again after, but I haven't seen hide nor hair of him."

"He's probably sleeping it off somewhere," Lorenzo said.

"You know anything about potatoes?" Mike asked.

"Potatoes?"

"I had a dream last night somebody told me it was better to plant potatoes at night because it wasn't so hot." Mike took off his hat and rubbed the top of his head. "Sort of fuzzy now. It seemed like a good idea to me, farming at night. You ever have that happen in a dream? Something seems like a good idea, and then when you wake up, you realize how dumb it is?"

"I feel like I'm going to wake up and realize how dumb this conversation is," Lorenzo said.

"Well, don't get sore. I mean, it sort of maybe *is* a good idea. Really hot planting crops under the harsh sun."

Lorenzo leaned over his coffee and shook his head. "I'm done talking about this."

"You never want to hear anything interesting I have to say," Mike grumbled.

If you ever say anything interesting, I'll eat my hat, Lorenzo thought.

Somebody walked in through the front door. A short man at the tail end of his fifties, pot belly and a clean-shaved and deeply lined face. He took off a battered hat and held it in front of him. "Mr. Lorenzo, is this a bad time?"

Lorenzo squinted at the newcomer. "Who are you?"

"I'm Chester Cobb," he said. "I have a fish camp at the bend in the river."

"Oh, that's right," Lorenzo said. "I know you. You have some business with me?"

"No, sir." Cobb shifted awkwardly, fussing with the brim of his hat. "Which is to say not yet, but I hope we do."

"Out with it, man."

"Are you still offering that thousand dollars for shooting Garret McCoy?" Cobb asked.

Lorenzo's eyes narrowed. "Are you trying to tell me that *you* shot Ghost McCoy?"

"Oh, no-no-no." Cobb laughed nervously. "I could never shoot nobody. But I thought if you were offering a thousand to shoot him, you might could part with a lesser amount for some information on him."

"Like what kind of information?"

"Well, I seen him," Cobb said. "Fit the description perfectly, even had a little piece of his ear shot off."

"Tell me what you know, and I'll tell you what it's worth," Lorenzo said.

"Well, I saw him coming this way," Cobb told him. "I was taking a load of smoked fish over to the Ferguson place to trade for eggs and saw McCoy come through the Mission del Aguila Crossroads. And he had friends with him."

"How many?"

"Him and four others," Cobb said.

A wicked grin twisted Lorenzo's face. He looked at Big Mike. "Looks like McCoy wants to settle the score. He thinks he can get the drop on us with a few of his pals. Probably going to bust in here and start slinging lead while we're all sitting comfortable having coffee, but we'll be ready. Mike, get everybody together, but do it on the sly. When McCoy and his buddies ride into town, we'll be ready for 'em."

Cobb cleared his throat, shifting from one foot to the other. "I hope my information has been worth something, Mr. Lorenzo."

Lorenzo made a shooing motion. "Go on, Cobb. We'll sort you out after the dust settles."

"Oh." Cobb backed away, putting his hat back on. "Okay, then." He failed to keep the disappointment off his face but knew better than to argue.

When Cobb had gone, Lorenzo turned back to Big Mike. "There's no playing this time, Mike. He's going to come in shooting, but we're going to have him out-gunned. Simple as that. Let the boys know. Ghost McCoy dies today."

Garret McCoy sipped coffee from a tin cup and watched the rider come. Behind him, Rufus Lee and the Vargas brothers huddled around a small fire, not because it was cold. What else was a fella supposed to do with a fire? Stare into it. Drink coffee. Twiddle thumbs. McCoy didn't like waiting, but there was nothing else to do.

A few minutes later, the rider took shape, came into focus.

Rufus Lee moved to stand next to McCoy. "That him?"

"I think so."

"You trust him?" Lee asked.

"I don't know him," McCoy said. "But Miller vouched for him."

"And you trust Miller?"

"I reckon so," McCoy said. "A man's got to trust somebody sometime."

The rider approached and reined in his horse ten feet from McCoy. "You Garret McCoy?"

"That's right."

"Miller described you just right. I'm Cobb."

"Well?"

"I reckon he's taken the bait all right," Cobb said. "He told Big Mike to gather all the boys . . . and that's a lot of guns. Could be you're biting off more than you can chew."

McCoy sighed. "We'll see, I guess."

"Okay, then. I've done my part," Cobb said. "I'm not much for shooting."

McCoy nodded. "Obliged."

"Good luck to you." Cobb turned his horse and headed toward the river at a trot.

"Now what?" Lee asked.

McCoy turned over his tin cup and let the contents spill on the ground. The coffee had gone cold.

"Now we mount up."

CHAPTER 34

They rode in a line toward Coyote Flats, Garret McCoy in the middle, Enrique and Rufus Lee on one side of him, Juan and Carlos on the other. Each man's thoughts were his own, but McCoy reckoned they all ran in a similar vein.

I could die today.

Why am I doing this?

McCoy knew why he was doing this. The man who'd killed his father and brother was in Coyote Flats, and today that man would die. Or maybe McCoy would die.

Either way, it would be finished.

They stopped at the edge of town and dismounted.

"Straight down the street," McCoy told the others. "Eyes right and left. Let's bring 'em out."

Thumbs hooked into their gun belts, hats pulled low, they began to walk.

"They're coming," Cherry said.

Carmen raised an eyebrow. "They?"

"McCoy's got some fellas with him. Some men I

never see before and—" Cherry gasped, her slender hand going to the surprised O of her mouth. "Enrique's with them."

"Never mind that," Carmen said. "He's a big boy, and he's made his choice. Look the other way and tell me what you see."

Cherry turned her head, face pressed to the window glass. "Mr. Lorenzo and his men are coming from the other direction. Oh . . . there's at least twenty of them. Maybe more."

"Get back from the window now, Cherry," Carmen said.

"What's going to happen?" Claudia asked.

"Killing."

The girls blanched, some swallowing hard.

"We're not going to get involved, but we are going to protect ourselves if they come in here and try to do us harm," Carmen said. "Some of you position yourselves along the stairway, high up so you can shoot down at them. The rest of you duck behind the bar with me."

The girls moved into position.

Carmen gripped her shotgun tightly, palms sweaty on the stock.

Mortimer Lorenzo marched down the street surrounded by his boys. It was difficult to keep the grin off his face. The idea that McCoy might be alive and kicking somewhere out in the world had been an itch Lorenzo had been unable to scratch. Now, he'd turn the page on that chapter, the last act of the old outlaw Mortimer Lorenzo before the new civic-minded man he vowed to become. *Mayor of Coyote Flats* had a nice ring to it.

He spotted McCoy at the other end of the street. Coming toward him. He had men with him, but Lorenzo wasn't worried in the least. He had McCoy and his men outnumbered five to one. Lorenzo chuckled, thinking McCoy was probably staining his britches at the sight of what he was up against.

But McCoy wouldn't run. He wasn't that sort. Lorenzo almost respected him for it.

Almost.

The street was empty. The townsfolk must have sensed trouble was brewing and were staying low. Probably for the best. Truth be told, Lorenzo felt sort of bad about shooting that Joseph fella. He'd been trying to make a point, of course, but that's not how he wanted to do things anymore. He was going to be different.

After he killed McCoy.

The two groups stopped twenty feet from each other.

"I ain't exactly glad to see you, McCoy," Lorenzo said. "But I am glad for the opportunity to tie up a loose end. I guess this is your chance for last words, but keep it short. I ain't as patient as I used to be."

"I only got two words for you, Lorenzo." McCoy raised his voice for all to hear. "Let's go!"

People on both sides of the street spilled out of the front doors of their businesses, carrying rifles and pistols.

Lorenzo saw the dry goods man—Miller—lift a shotgun. Moses Hendershot stood right next to him, drawing a six-shooter.

You dirty sons of—

"Slap leather, boys!" Lorenzo shouted.

Everyone drew.

Dozens of guns exploded all at once and the air filled with lead. Lorenzo's gun was in his hand, but he was more worried about dodging lead than he was in dishing it out. The man next to him twitched and dropped, blood pouring from his temple. The pops and blasts continued unabated, everyone shooting at somebody else.

Time to grab some cover!

He ran left, hunching and ducking, a handful of his men following, maybe thinking the boss knew a safe spot. He hit the wooden sidewalk and saw two men coming toward him, guns up and ready.

Lorenzo fired three times, hitting nothing, but sending the men scrambling.

He saw Carmen's Place right next to him and decided it was time to get inside. "Follow me, boys!"

Lorenzo slammed into the front doors, shoulder first. He felt and heard the lock and door frame crack as he tumbled inside the saloon, four of his men right on his heels.

Carmen saw the shapes hurtling toward the front door through the frosted glass and braced herself, grip tightening on the twelve gauge.

A split second later, Mortimer Lorenzo came crashing through, a handful of his men stumbling in behind.

Carmen saw her chance and made a snap decision. "Shoot!"

The gunfire started immediately from the stairs. The girls were not good shots but made up for it with their seeming intent not to save any of their ammunition for future use. Lorenzo's men convulsed in a shower of blood as a storm of lead ripped into them, red splashes blooming on shoulders, across backs, and down legs. They fell across each other in a quivering, bloody heap. Gunsmoke hung in the air.

Lorenzo had been ahead of them and had somehow escaped the hail of gunfire. He ran for the back hallway, obviously thinking to flee to the alley out back.

He saw Carmen and paused. "Carmen, hide me!"

And in that instant, she knew. None of his talk about a partnership mattered. Nothing about them marrying and being the future power brokers of Coyote Flats and beyond meant a thing to her. Upon seeing his cowardly face, she wanted nothing more than to lift the shotgun and pull the trigger and watch his head vanish in a red mist of destruction.

But she was unpracticed with the weapon. In the heat of battle, it was heavier than expected. She raised it too slowly and squeezed the trigger too quickly. The right barrel thundered and belched fire. The shotgun bucked in her hands, a mule kick to the shoulder.

Lorenzo's right sleeve turned wet and red, and he howled in pain. The arm hung limp as he turned away and ran for the back.

Carmen fired again, but it was too late. The shotgun pellets blistered the wall behind the spot where Lorenzo had stood a moment before.

It went suddenly quiet in the saloon, although scattered gunshots could still be heard outside. Corpses littered the floor.

"Is everyone okay?" Carmen asked.

All the girls nodded.

"I don't think anyone else will come in here," Carmen said. "But reload just in case."

If that scattergun hadn't been loaded with birdshot, it would have taken Lorenzo's arm clean off. He tried to be grateful for that, but it hurt like the devil. He could barely move the arm and flex his fingers.

Lorenzo staggered out the back door of Carmen's Place, headed down the alley before putting his back against the wall of the nearest building. He leaned there, panting, trying to gather himself. He could still hear smatterings of gunfire here and there, but nobody was chasing him at the moment. He desperately wanted to slide down the wall into a sitting position, but he doubted he'd get back up again.

Carmen had shot him. Of all people. After what he'd offered her. He muttered every bad thing a man could call a woman. He'd be back—oh, yes, he'd find a place to lay low and heal up, and in a month or two or a year he'd be back and Carmen would pay.

The whole town would pay. McCoy had put them up to it, of course.

Lorenzo heard more gunfire, some of it a little too close for comfort. He wondered who was winning.

No, he couldn't risk it. He'd need to get out of town fast and come back for revenge later. He needed a horse, but the livery stable was in the other direction, back through the fighting.

He'd give his glass eye for a horse.

Lorenzo pushed away from the wall and staggered

away as quickly as possible from the sound of gunfire. He headed toward his place, thinking that was a bad idea since surely they'd look for him there, but he didn't know what else to do. He decided to turn away instead, heading for the far corner of town, not that it was really so far. Coyote Flats was a small place, after all.

He headed down a narrow street, dripping blood all the way. He was starting to feel a bit queasy. A drink of cool water would have been nice.

Later, fool. Drink a whole river later if you want. Right now, you've got to get out of here.

He turned the corner and saw the freight wagon near the Harry's Carpenter Shop. A pair of horses were hitched to the wagon. It was full of logs that hadn't been unloaded yet. Harry was probably about to head to the sawmill when all the shooting started. Maybe he found a place to hide.

Or maybe he'd joined in.

Lorenzo added Harry's name to the vengeance list.

He tried to climb up to the wagon's bench but had to pause, dizziness washing over him. He took a few deep breaths, tried again, pain lancing all up and down his right side, but finally managed to get himself seated.

He took the reins in one hand and gave them a flick, the wagon lurching forward.

I'll be back, Coyote Flats, Lorenzo thought. *And then there will be hell to pay.*

CHAPTER 35

Everything slowed.

It was a trick of the mind, something that had saved Garret McCoy over and over again back during the war, a way to make sense of the roiling chaos of a big battle. Charging a Confederate bayonet line, for example, had been terrifying, bullets whizzing past, artillery rounds exploding on all sides, the flanks on either side falling behind, leaving McCoy's unit out front all alone. But everything slowed, and McCoy had been able to see it, the individual elements of the battle, how they fit together or came apart.

Now it was happening again on the streets of Coyote Flats.

Gunfire had erupted on both sides, and by the time McCoy pulled his Peacemaker, chaos ruled.

He lost sight of Lorenzo almost immediately as the man ducked into a crowd of his men, ducking and dodging across the street toward Carmen's Place, and then McCoy lost sight of him, his attention drawn back to the men in the street in front of him, some of whom drew their pistols, eyes on McCoy. Others died bloody in the crossfire coming from both sides of the street.

McCoy fanned the hammer of his Peacemaker, moving the six-shooter from left to right, one of Lorenzo's men clutching a bloody chest or gut wound with each shot. McCoy moved as he fired, crossing the street to duck down behind Moses Hendershot's buckboard.

He was still aware of the battle, each piece of it unfolding like the choreography of some violent ballet. Lorenzo's men broke into groups of three or four, scattering this way or that. Others died where they stood in the street before they could return fire. The townsfolk huddled in doorways or behind posts as they poured on the lead from rifles or six-guns.

McCoy had emptied his Peacemaker, and in the time it took him to holster it and draw the Colt Navy from his belly holster, one of Lorenzo's men came around the other side of the buckboard and . . .

. . . everything . . .

. . . went slow, slow, slow.

McCoy saw the man lift the six-shooter.

His thumb on the hammer, cocking it back with a *click-click*.

The cylinder spinning around.

The man had McCoy dead to rights.

Behind McCoy a shotgun thundered.

The man who'd gotten the drop on McCoy was thrown back, chest suddenly a mess of blood. McCoy looked behind him and saw Cordelia. She'd come out of the slop house, apron flapping in the breeze, gray smoke oozing from the barrel of a single-barrel shotgun.

"Get up, McCoy!" The old woman broke the shotgun,

took out the spent shell, threw it over her shoulder, and replaced it with a fresh one. "There's still work left to do!"

"Obliged, ma'am." McCoy ducked his head and ran across the street toward Carmen's Place.

In the corner of his eye, McCoy saw Rufus Lee backing into the dubious cover of a doorway, trading fire with Lorenzo's men. He glanced the other way and saw the Vargas brothers ducking into an alley, guns blazing, no idea if they were winning or losing. They'd have to fend for themselves.

Like the lady said, there was work left to do.

Enrique and his brothers fired at Lorenzo's men, and Lorenzo's men fired back, lots of shooting and ducking and dodging and running sideways and shouting and nobody hitting anything. Finally, three of Lorenzo's men must have figured this whole thing wasn't going to come out well, turned, and ran down a side alley.

"After them!" Enrique shouted, pursuing at a full run, his brothers right behind him.

They came around the corner of the burnt pile of rubble that used to be Jericho's place to see that Lorenzo's men had turned to take a stand, crouching behind the corner of the ruined building. Enrique dove to the ground just as one of the men fired, the shot passing over him.

And striking Carlos in the chest. He stumbled in mid-stride and went sprawling into the dirt.

"Carlos!" Juan lifted his Henry rifle and fired.

The shot caught Carlos's killer in the center of his forehead. His eyes rolled back, and he went down.

The other two opened up with their six-shooters.

Enrique rolled over and fired from his place on the ground, fanning the hammer of his six-gun until it clicked empty, three shots, catching the first man once in the throat, the next two catching the second man in the chest. They twitched and fell across each other in the ashen remains of Jericho's place.

"Carlos!"

Juan tossed aside his rifle and went to his knees next to his brother. He turned Carlos over. His chest was soaked with blood, eyes lifeless.

"Oh, no," Juan said. "No, no, no."

Enrique let the spent shells drop to the ground and replaced them with new rounds from his gun belt. "Dead?"

Juan nodded slowly.

"Then let's go."

Juan looked momentarily confused. "Go?"

"We're going to kill the rest," Enrique said. "We're going to kill them all."

Dwight Combs had been in Miller's Dry Goods when the shooting started. He was gearing up to leave Coyote Flats and had an armload of merchandise—coffee, flour, saddle oil, and a new blanket.

Miller had left the store a moment, then came back in with an old cowboy. The shopkeeper suddenly didn't seem so interested in taking Combs's money. He went behind the counter, bent down, and when he came back up again, he was holding a rifle.

Combs sighed. *Another fifteen minutes and I'd have been out of this town.*

Raised voices in the streets. Was that McCoy?

Combs peered through the window. A bunch of fellas out there, and they looked like they were about to scrap.

An old woman who'd been looking at a bolt of fabric shifted over to stand next to him at the window. "Oh my. Is something going on?"

"Looks like it."

McCoy raised his voice another notch. "Let's go!"

Miller and the old cowboy rushed from the store out to the sidewalk, and an instant later all hell broke loose, the street erupting in a storm of gunfire. Men dropped dead. Combs saw McCoy nearly get his head blown off, but the old woman from the slop house saved him. The next moment he was running toward Carmen's Place, lead buzzing by him like angry hornets.

"That McCoy fella better be careful," the old woman said. "There's too many bad men looking to collect that thousand dollars. That's a lot of money."

Combs nodded slowly, thinking. "Yep. A lot of money." He went to the counter and set down his items. "If Miller don't get himself killed, tell him I'll be back to buy those things."

Combs let his hand rest on the grip of his Walker and stepped outside.

At least a dozen men lay dead in the streets. Others had run for cover. Miller and the old cowboy squatted behind a buckboard. He could hear shooting in the next street over and elsewhere. The fighting was all over the place.

He hunched his shoulders as he ran across the street, knowing a stray bullet would hit him any second, but luck was with him. He made it across without getting hit and burst into Carmen's Place.

Every woman in the saloon pointed a gun at him.

"Whoa!" Combs threw his hands up. "I'm not your enemy."

"Ladies, don't shoot Mr. Combs," Carmen said.

"Obliged." Combs lowered his hands. "I saw McCoy come in here."

"He was looking for Lorenzo," Carmen said. "Both went out the back."

"Then I guess I am too."

He headed for the back door, and Carmen grabbed his arm as he passed. "Mr. Combs, what are you going to do?"

Combs drew the Walker and cocked the hammer back with his thumb. "Something I should have done before now."

Carmen let her hand drop, and Dwight Combs was out the back door three seconds later.

Garret McCoy stood to one side, eased open the front door to Lorenzo's place, and stuck his head inside for a quick look. At a glance, the place seemed empty. He went inside, stepping lightly, trying to remain as quiet as possible, the Colt Navy in his hand, up and ready.

If Lorenzo had escaped this way, he might be back in his office, grabbing important personal effects before making an escape. McCoy hadn't stayed to see the end of the gunfight in the street, but Lorenzo's men were getting shot up pretty good. Also, Carmen had said the man was hurt. McCoy guessed the man would take off, find a place to lay low and lick his wounds and then come back when he was ready to—

The flash of movement behind the bar kicked McCoy's instincts into high gear, and only quick reflexes saved him. He dove to one side just as Big Mike squeezed the trigger, and the shot meant for McCoy's heart ripped a bloody gash in his left shoulder instead.

McCoy felt the hot sting and landed hard, the Colt Navy knocked out of his hand. It slid across the floor just out of reach. He scrambled for it on his belly, reached.

"Oh, no you don't!" Big Mike scrambled over the bar and raised his six-gun.

"Don't do it, Big Mike," came a voice from behind him. "I'll kill you where you stand."

Mike froze, then slowly turned his head to see that Dwight Combs had emerged from the back hall, his enormous Colt Walker pointed right at Mike's face.

"Ease that hammer down," Combs said.

Mike did as he was told.

"Now put the gun on the table."

Moving with exaggerated care, Mike slowly set the gun on the table, then took a step back from it.

McCoy grinned. "I thought you decided not to get involved."

"That's right," Combs said. "But that decision never did sit well. Kept bugging me like a bad case of heartburn."

McCoy retrieved his Colt Navy and stood. "Better late than never."

"What do you want to do with him?" Combs still had his six-gun trained on Big Mike.

"Coyote Flats needs to be rid of him," McCoy said.

"So you're just going to shoot me in cold blood?" Mike said. "Is that how you do things?"

"I don't think you'd hesitate for a second to shoot *me* in cold blood," McCoy said. "But, no, that ain't my way."

Mike's brow furrowed with confusion. "So . . . you're just going to let me go?"

"No. Can't do that either."

"Then what?"

McCoy slipped the Colt back into the belly holster. "Then I guess we have to do it the hard way."

Mike's eyebrow went up. "You're giving me a chance?"

McCoy shook his head. "I wouldn't say that, but you get to die fair."

Mike's eyes shifted to Combs. "What about him?"

"Dwight, if Big Mike wins fair and square, let him go," McCoy said.

Combs shrugged. "If that's what you want. Mike, take your gun and holster it. Try anything before it's time, and I'll gun you myself."

Mike took a hesitant step toward his gun, pausing to look at the other men, clearly wondering if he were being tricked. Finally, he took his gun and slid it into the holster.

"Give each other some room," Combs said.

McCoy and Mike took a few steps back from each other.

"What me to count it off?" Combs asked.

McCoy nodded, his eyes never leaving Mike's. "Go ahead."

"On three then," Combs said. "One . . ."

McCoy stood motionless.

Big Mike licked his lips nervously.

"Two . . ."

Mike went for his gun.

It was only halfway out of its holster when McCoy drew and fired.

The shot hit Mike right between the eyes, knocking his head back. He didn't go down right away, took two staggering steps sideways as his eyes crossed, mouth working, strangled croaking sounds coming out. He reached for something invisible in front of him. Finally his legs got the message it was all over. His knees buckled and he went crashing into a table, scattering chairs.

"Did you know he was going to cheat and go on two?" Combs asked.

McCoy reloaded his guns. "They always cheat."

"By the way," Combs said. "You're bleeding, in case you hadn't noticed."

"Let it bleed."

"Now what?" Combs asked.

"Now we get Lorenzo."

They searched the place quickly, but nobody else was there.

McCoy paused in Lorenzo's small office when something caught his attention on the desk. Lorenzo's eye patch. McCoy couldn't say what motivated him, but he grabbed the patch and shoved it in his pocket before meeting Combs again in the main room.

"Well?"

"Ain't nobody here," Combs said.

McCoy mumbled a few choice obscenities. To go through all of this only to have Lorenzo escape stuck in his craw.

Moses Hendershot burst through the front door, followed closely by Walt Miller.

"It's over," Hendershot said. "We finished them."

"But we didn't get Lorenzo," McCoy informed them.

"That's what we came to tell you," Miller said. "He was seen high-tailing it out of town on a freight wagon. He was headed toward the river."

McCoy's eyes narrowed. "Get my horse."

CHAPTER 36

The wagon hit a rock, and the bump sent white-hot agony lancing through Mortimer Lorenzo's arm. His shirtsleeve was soaked red. Sooner or later, he'd need to look at the wound and was afraid it would look like hamburger.

He looked over his shoulder for the hundredth time but saw no pursuit. Lorenzo wished the wagon could go faster, but it was loaded down with lumber. He thought about stopping to offload it, but with one arm, it would take him forever and a day.

Lorenzo would need to get to a doctor, although he did not relish sitting there while he pried all that bird shot out of his arm. He'd need a few slugs of good whiskey to sit still for it. Then when he was all patched up, he'd hatch his scheme for getting back at that skunk McCoy and all the ungrateful townsfolk of Coyote Flats.

Out of habit, he looked behind him, not really expecting to see much. By now, he'd probably shed himself of anyone who might want to come after him.

He was wrong.

In the distance behind him. No more than a dot but definitely a man on a horse.

Lorenzo flicked the reins one-handed. "Go faster. You stupid animals."

The horses picked up speed, but not much and not for long. The nags were old and tired. Lorenzo looked back again to see that the rider was closer. He cursed and flicked the reins again, shouting at the animals to no avail.

He scanned the terrain, but the open country didn't offer very good hiding places.

Lorenzo knew this area and also knew there was a patch of woods on the other side of the river. He might be able to get out of sight among the trees and throw off his pursuit. He tugged the reins, nudging the team toward the river.

By the time he reached the river's edge, the rider behind him had gotten close enough that he could see who it was.

McCoy!

Lorenzo spat out every curse word he'd ever heard and invented a few new ones.

He shouted at the horses and urged them into the water. The river was never very high, especially this time of year, and he made it halfway across, no problem. Then the wagon lurched to a stop, tilted so violently to one side, it almost tossed him off the bench and into the water. One of the wheels must have been caught on something below the surface.

Lorenzo looked back. McCoy was fast closing the distance.

He screamed at the horses until he was red in the face, but the wagon wouldn't budge.

Lorenzo would have to run for it.

He slid off the bench and into the river. The current was stronger than he'd anticipated, and his legs were swept away and he went under. He quickly found his footing and resurfaced, coughing and sputtering, the water up to his waist. He trudged toward the shore, one foot in front of the other, the process agonizingly slow, but finally he made it to the far bank.

Lorenzo was too afraid to look back now. Surely McCoy had reached the river. The woods were a hundred yards ahead of him, maybe a little more. If he could make it to the tree line, he might have a chance. He could hide himself, maybe even find a good spot for an ambush, although he wasn't confident about how well he could shoot left-handed.

He tried to run, but it was more of a staggering lope. *Just keep going. Don't look back.*

McCoy slowed the horse from a gallop to a trot as he approached the river.

It was plain for anyone to see that the big freight wagon was hung up on something. McCoy watched Lorenzo go into the water, then go under, and for a moment, he wondered if the man might drown, but a second later he was back up again, heading for the far bank, evidently giving up on the wagon and its team.

Lorenzo wasn't moving fast, one limp arm bouncing against his side. McCoy would catch him easily.

He encouraged his horse into the water and reined in next to the wagon team. He leaned over to the nearest horse and got a firm grip on the collar, trying to coax the team one way and then another. The horses pulled the wagon past the unseen obstruction, and soon the wagon was moving again.

By the time McCoy and the wagon reached the other side of the river, he saw Lorenzo heading for the trees. He left the team. He'd tell somebody later where to come fetch it. Right now, McCoy had bigger fish to fry.

He galloped toward the fleeing man. Lorenzo must have heard the pounding of hooves. He looked back over his shoulder, fear plain on his face. He stopped, turned, and fumbled awkwardly with his left hand at the six-shooter on his belt.

McCoy drew the Peacemaker and pointed it at his face. "Don't."

Lorenzo froze.

"Take it out nice and slow," McCoy told him. "Thumb and forefinger."

Lorenzo pinched the pistol's grip between thumb and forefinger and eased it out of the holster.

"Toss it."

Lorenzo flung the gun, and it landed ten feet away. "Now what? Gonna shoot me? Get on with it then."

"Start walking," McCoy said. "Back toward the river."

"What for?"

"Walk or get shot," McCoy said. "You choose."

Lorenzo started walking. "Well, you ain't shot me

yet, so you must want something. Money? We can work that out."

"I don't want your money, Lorenzo."

"Where are we going?"

"You'll see."

Lorenzo soon gave up trying to bribe him or get information. Lorenzo trudged along ahead, with McCoy right behind on his horse. They crossed back to the other side of the river, then followed the bank. It was slow going, and eventually Lorenzo tried conversation again.

"You got blood down one of your arms too," Lorenzo observed. "It would take two of us to row a boat."

"Mine looks worse than it is," McCoy said.

It was a shallow wound, but it had been bleeding freely the whole time. He'd need a stitch or two.

Later.

Lorenzo gestured to his limp arm. "Mine hurts like the devil. Are we going to walk forever? I'm in a bad way. If I don't get a rest, I'll drop."

"You drop, and I'll make sure you never get up again," McCoy told him. "Keep walking."

When Parson's Gulch came into view, Lorenzo turned and squinted up at McCoy. "I know this place. What are we doing here?"

"You'll find out. Now shut up and walk."

They made quite a sight walking down the center of the gulch, a bleeding man on a horse and another bleeding man marching in front of him. People came out of their houses to gawk.

McCoy raised his voice. "Listen to me, everybody. Gather 'round!"

More people spilled from their shabby houses, faces curious. McCoy saw Mary Jane step onto her front porch, eyes wide, her husband, Grant, right next to her.

"Listen up, everyone," McCoy said. "This is important."

He dismounted and let the horse wander away. Then he went to Lorenzo and said, "On your knees."

Lorenzo frowned. "What are you talking about?"

McCoy kicked him hard in the knee with the heel of his boot.

Lorenzo howled in pain and sank to the ground.

"The people of Parson's Gulch were hurt a long time ago." McCoy spoke loud enough for everyone to hear. "This place became known as Blood Gulch. It's time to heal that wound. It's time for justice."

Mutters rolled through the crowd.

"This is the man responsible." McCoy gestured at Lorenzo.

Lorenzo scowled. "Now wait just a damn minute."

McCoy drew his Peacemaker, cocked the hammer back with a thumb, and pointed the barrel at Lorenzo's head. "I'm talking now. You keep shut."

Lorenzo swallowed hard.

"Maybe you don't recognize him."

McCoy reached towards Lorenzo's face. He dug a thumb into Lorenzo's eye socket. People in the crowd gasped, and Lorenzo tried to jerk away, but McCoy had a tight grip on him, dug the thumb in harder. The glass eye popped out. McCoy tossed it over his shoulder and heard it bounce and roll across somebody's porch.

"Maybe this will jog your memory."

McCoy circled behind the man on his knees and took the eyepatch from his front pocket. He tied it around Lorenzo's head.

A woman in the crowd grabbed the arm of the man next to her. "It's him." She had gray in her hair and tired eyes. "That's him."

Others in the crowd recognized him too.

"This man murdered good people," McCoy said. "Murdered the heart of a community. He thought there was gold here, and when there wasn't, he forgot about this place, but I can see a lot of you haven't forgotten him."

McCoy pointed the Peacemaker at Lorenzo's head again.

"Come on now," Lorenzo said, voice trembling. "Don't do this."

"It don't seem like blood can wash away blood," McCoy said, a hitch in his own voice. "But sometimes that's all you can do. Blood for blood."

Lorenzo's eye had grown big as a dinner plate. "Please."

The whole gulch had gone stone quiet.

"You don't get to walk around living when good people are dead," McCoy said.

"Please."

McCoy's gun hand was steady, but inside he was shaking to pieces. He realized he was lightheaded. It had been a long, violent morning. A long ride to Blood Gulch. He'd lost so much blood, and now, so close to the end of it all, he felt like he might not last another minute, like he was all used up in heart and soul and body.

"Please."

He had one more thing to do. Pull the trigger. And then it would be over.

"Please."

He saw the horrible scene play over again in his mind, so clear, like it was yesterday. His brother murdered. His father. Killed without a chance. His father died on his knees. McCoy could see it and hear it like it was happening all over again.

All he had to do was pull the trigger.

But he couldn't.

Not any more than he could shoot Big Mike in cold blood.

He took a step back from Lorenzo, but he didn't lower the gun. He pointed it at his head, willing himself to pull the trigger. Told himself it was justice. That nobody would blame him. That the world would be a better place without Mortimer Lorenzo in it. One squeeze of the trigger would be all it would take. Just one—

A shotgun blast shook the gulch, and half of Mortimer Lorenzo's face vanished in an explosion of red mist, bone, and flesh.

Screams.

The remains of Lorenzo fell over into the mud.

McCoy turned, eyes searching.

Mary Jane stood there, smoke wafting from the shotgun in her hands. Her eyes were wide and unblinking, face haunted.

Grant came up behind her and very gently put a hand

on her shoulder. She looked at him, still unblinking, as if in a trance. Grant slowly took the shotgun out of her hands. He put one arm around her shoulder, and they turned and went back into their house.

McCoy looked around at the dumbfounded people of Parson's Gulch.

He went to his horse, tried to mount, but a wave of dizziness washed over him, a hot buzzing in his ears. He took a few deep breaths, gathered himself, then hoisted himself up and into the saddle.

Garret McCoy turned the horse and headed back to Coyote Flats.

EPILOGUE

McCoy opened his eyes.

He was in a bed with clean sheets.

"Have yourself a good nap?"

Rufus Lee sat in a chair, his boots resting on the corner of the bed.

"You been sitting with me?" McCoy asked.

"It was my turn."

"Where am I?" McCoy wanted to know.

"Spare room over the slop house," Lee told him. "Cordelia was worried about her best customer."

"What happened?"

"You rode back into town, got off your horse, and fell over," Lee said. "Doc said too much blood coming out and not enough water going in. He stitched your arm and said to let you rest."

"I'm hungry."

"I'll bet." Lee stood and went to the door. "I'll let them know you're awake."

McCoy sighed and closed his eyes.

When he opened them again, Carmen was there.

"Well," she said. "You've had something of an adventure."

"I think I'll lay off adventures for a while," McCoy told her. "Hard on a man's health."

"Glad you're still with us," she said.

"What did I miss?"

Carmen filled in the gaps. McCoy was sorry to hear that Enrique's brother Carlos had been killed along with two of Moses Hendershot's ranch hands. Two of the townsfolk had also been killed, and there were a handful of wounded who were already on the mend.

"We've paid a price," Carmen said. "But I suppose it could have been much worse."

"Nothing like this ever comes cheap."

"And what of Lorenzo?" Carmen asked.

McCoy considered how much to say about that. "Nobody needs to worry about him anymore. He's not coming back."

Carmen was obviously curious to hear more but didn't ask. "Good. Then it truly is over."

"Except your town needs a new leader now, I reckon," McCoy said.

"We have already taken steps in that direction," Carmen told him. "Miller and Hendershot and a few other prominent men are forming a town council. They asked me to be part of it. I said yes."

"Good. They need you."

A wan smile. "Perhaps we all need each other."

An awkward silence.

"You might have told me," Carmen said.

"Told you what?"

"That you were organizing the townsfolk against Lorenzo," she said.

"Sometimes knowing something like that can be . . . a burden."

Her smile was playful this time. "Meaning you didn't trust me."

"You're the kind of woman that needs to look out for herself," McCoy said. "I don't mean that in a bad way. I didn't want to saddle you with a difficult decision."

Carmen let out a long sigh. "I feel that you and I are saying goodbye to one another."

"I reckon so. I've got things to do."

"Yes. As do I."

Later that day, Cordelia brought him a tray of food from the slop house, and it was the best thing McCoy had ever eaten. People came in one or two at a time to say hello or shake McCoy's hand.

Coyote Flats was going to be just fine.

The next morning, he found Rufus Lee and Juan Vargas mounted and waiting for him. They'd saddled McCoy's big black horse for him. Dwight Combs and Enrique Vargas were also there, standing and chatting with the others.

"You fit to ride?" Lee asked when he saw McCoy.

McCoy mounted. "Right as rain."

Combs grinned up at him. "Take care of yourself, Ghost."

"Glad you picked a side in the end," McCoy said. "What are your plans now?"

"Nobody told you?" Combs reached into his pocket for something. He pinned the tin star on his vest. "I figure it's steady work."

McCoy grinned. "You gonna bring law and order to Coyote Flats all on your own."

"I got some help." He patted Enrique on the shoulder.

"Are you sure you want to be a deputy sheriff, little brother?" Juan asked.

"I need gainful employment if I'm going to marry Cherry away from Miss Carmen," Enrique said.

Juan laughed. "I expect to see bambinos by the time I return."

Enrique blushed.

"Don't be in a hurry with that sort of thing," McCoy said.

They made their final goodbyes, then rode away.

McCoy reined in his horse on the edge of town. "Gentlemen, I made you a promise and I aim to make good on it. We need to clear your names. In the meantime, would you mind if we took a slight detour?"

"I ain't in no hurry," Rufus Lee said.

"Do what you need to do, *amigo*," Juan agreed. "The world will still be waiting for us."

He'd come down the narrow path this time behind the row of houses so as not to draw so much attention to himself and reined in his horse at the edge of the barn when he saw her.

Mary Jane was back to hanging laundry. The children were nowhere to be seen this time. A gentle breeze lifted her hair. She looked peaceful, and not at all like a woman who'd just blown half a man's head off. McCoy didn't know what he'd expected to see. He almost turned the horse around to go when she looked up, her eyes meeting his.

"Oh. It's you."

"I didn't mean to startle you," McCoy said.

"You didn't."

He dismounted and went to her, leading the horse. "Where's Grant?"

"He took the children to see their grandma," Mary Jane said. "What are you doing here?"

"I guess I was just worried. I just wanted to see if you were okay. After what happened."

She picked up a piece of laundry, a man's shirt. She looked at it a moment, then sighed and let it fall back into the basket. "It don't seem real. Like a faded memory. Like it was almost somebody else that done it. Can you believe that?"

"You shouldn't have had to do it," McCoy said. "If I'd had more courage . . ."

"No." She shook her head. "All the hard deeds in the world can't always fall to the same man. The world would grind you down. Sometimes others need to do the hard things."

"Is that why you did it?"

A sad laugh. "I don't know why. I just did it. I recognized that face and just . . . did it."

"I'm sorry."

"We're all a little sorry these days."

They stood quietly for a moment.

"Well." McCoy cleared his throat. "I'll get out of your hair."

He turned his back on her, made ready to mount, putting his foot in the stirrup.

"Goodbye, Garret."

He froze at the sound of his name. He wasn't sure if he was glad she remembered or sad. Then he hoisted himself into the saddle, looked down at her and touched the brim of his hat.

"Goodbye, Mary Jane."

Garret McCoy left Blood Gulch behind and rode to catch up with his new traveling companions. Juan Vargas was right. The world was still out there.

Time to go meet it.

**TURN THE PAGE
FOR A RIP-ROARING PREVIEW**

**The Wildest Western You'll Ever Read—
Believe It or Not**

In this rollicking novel from the bestselling
Johnstones, fact and fiction collide
in the jaw-dropping story of Jesse James's
little-known, disaster-prone brother.
They call him Calamity—for a reason . . .
Calvin Amadeus James, aka Calamity, isn't an outlaw
like his notorious brothers Jesse and Frank.
He's worse—due to the bad luck that follows him
everywhere he goes. Every job he takes—from army
scout to gambler to cowboy and rail worker—ends in
catastrophe. No matter what he does, Calamity James
always seems to be on the wrong side of history . . .

The Great Chicago Fire of 1871?
Calamity placed the lantern next to the cow that
kicked it over. The gunfight at O.K. Corral?
Calamity stirred up trouble in Tombstone right before
it all went down. The fateful saloon shooting of
Wild Bill Hickock? Blame it on Calamity James.
Some folks say he's even responsible for Custer's last
stand at Little Big Horn—but Calamity swears it ain't
true. He's just a magnet for bad luck who's trying to
find his good luck charm—a pretty little dancehall girl
known as Clumsy Catherine. But somewhere along
the way, he foolishly joins the James-Younger Gang
with his outlaw brothers. And that's when Calamity's
infamous bad luck gets a whole lot worse . . .

**National Bestselling Authors
William W. Johnstone
and J.A. Johnstone**

CALAMITY JAMES

The Unbelievable, Untold Story of Jesse James's
Other Brother

FIRST IN A NEW SERIES!
On sale now, wherever Pinnacle Books are sold.

Live Free. Read Hard.
williamjohnstone.net
Visit us at kensingtonbooks.com
Western

CHAPTER 1

He was born in the cabin his father's congregation built. It burned down that night.

At least his mother was used to hard luck. Anyone who came to this earth in Kentucky, even those born into money and good stock, knows all too much about misfortune. As a child, Zerelda Cole's father broke his neck in a riding accident, her brother would kill himself in 1895, and between her birth and her brother's demise, she would witness more torment and tragedy, more brutality and beastliness, than a writer of myriad penny dreadfuls could dream up. Giving birth to an illegitimate child fathered by a soon-to-be minister just continued Zerelda's string of foul luck.

This is not to say that Calvin Amadeus James was born out of wedlock. Even those who could not fill a flush at a table or bet on the right horse to win at Kansas City's agricultural fair eventually will see something work out. No, Cal was born on January 28, 1842, one month after Robert James married Zerelda, whose daddy had been dead since she was two years old, and her mama, after remarrying, had left that young but tough girl with her grandpa Cole. And even though the fire that left the new cabin in ashes and just about everything the newlyweds owned was consumed in the blaze, one of the blessings was that Robert James's family Bible was lost, too. The parents of Cal, a pink lad of five pounds, seven ounces, would not realize this at first—indeed, there were many tears and questions to the Lord of why, why, *why?*—but well before Cal reached the age for schooling, both Robert and Zee—Zee being what most folks called Cal's mama—realized that the loss of the cabin, and the family Bible, was a blessing from the Almighty.

That Bible was the only written documentation to prove that Calvin James was ever born into this family. Zee didn't even call for a midwife to birth her first baby. That was all left to Zee and her praying husband, and the baby entered the world bawling and pink and healthy.

Yes, sympathy should be given to Cal, for his father and mother decided, since Robert was about to graduate from Georgetown College and enter the ministry—though he was already practicing his sermoning, but not his baptisms, at the cabin those settlers had put up—that they would be better off giving up the infant. Robert paid a young couple to take the newborn as their own. It would work out for the best, all parties agreed, because the woman, Charity Marmaduke, just lost her own infant child to an outbreak of diphtheria, and, more importantly, she and her husband, Obadiah, were headed west.

Robert wiped his eyes and did some serious praying and begging for forgiveness as the Marmadukes rolled down the pike with the sleeping infant in his new mama's lap, but Zerelda was of sterner stock, and she just spit the juice from her snuff into the grass. As fate would have it, Zerelda would get in the family way again and give birth to a strapping young fellow. By then, the Reverend Robert James was preaching the gospel. They named him Alexander Franklin James, who entered this world on January 10, 1843, on their farm near Centerville, Missouri—which eventually changed its name, as towns were fond of doing in those times (especially when it came time to get a post office), to Kearney.

But we shall come back to the James family in due time.

Obadiah and Charity Marmaduke were, like Cal's true parents, natives of Kentucky. Blue grass ran through their veins. Their grandparents, if you believe the stories Obadiah told in the taverns and after barn-raisings, had traveled to Kentucky with Daniel Boone. And even if the closest the Marmadukes ever got to Daniel Boone was following the trails he had blazed, Obadiah did have a case of the wanderlust that afflicted Dan'l and other explorers of our wondrous western frontier.

The Marmadukes settled in Iowa, and, oh, how Charity doted on that baby boy, even though he had a habit of crying and keeping both new mother and new father awake all night. Charity once confided to a friend that she hardly slept a wink on the journey by wagon from Kentucky. But she was a young woman with a baby boy to hold and she was not one to complain. At least, for the first couple of years.

They kept his name, at least Calvin, which, as most Calvins will tell you, got shortened to Cal. They even told the Jameses they would keep his middle name, Amadeus, and it was penciled into their Bible, too, but the lead faded, and worsened after the roof leaked and soaked that Good Book.

We should point out that by the time the boy was five years old, calamity followed young Cal with such frequency that not only friends of the Marmadukes, but the Marmadukes themselves, thought there might be some truth to the rumor quickly spreading that a Kickapoo woman put a curse on the newborn—despite the fact that it's hard to find a Kickapoo in Kentucky. Or Iowa. In fact, after years of investigation, we have never found proof that any Kickapoo ever set foot in the state that has given us Daniel Boone, Jim Bowie, Kit Carson, and Hunter S. Thompson.

And certainly not Iowa.

Folks started calling young Cal, a tall, good-looking and fairly smart lad, Calamity, because bad luck just seemed to follow him; though, more often than not, bystanders—and that strapping youngster—seemed to get the worse of things.

Like the horseshoe-pitching contest on the Fourth of July, when Cal was five or six years old and all the boy had to do was come close and he would have won the fat sow for a prize. Instead, he busted out the windowpane at the Market House—which was behind Cal. The owner of the Market House, a generous sort, shrugged it off, even though glass was right scarce around Flint Hill.

Iowa on the Mississippi River was a fine place to be in the 1840s. The pig market was sound, and cholera was kept in check, at least more than it was down south in St. Louis and New Orleans, where folks boarded steamboats all the time to escape that infernal plague. There were tanners and hunters, coopers and grocers, merchants dealing in dry goods, queensware, boots, nails, iron, stone, steel, nails, Jewett's Patent Ploughs, medicines, dyes, putty, saddles, tin. There were more lawyers than one could shake a stick at. There was a Congregational church on Columbia Street, but Mr. Partridge often opened up the hall above his store for other religious services. And the *Burlington Hawk-Eye* came out at least once a week, most times. In fact, Mr. Marmaduke read about the war against Mexico in that newspaper, and considered going, but decided against it.

There wasn't a dentist, the nearest one being a steamboat ride down to St. Louis, but you could get a tooth pulled by just about anyone who had a keg of whiskey and a pair of pliers.

"Maybe I should have gone to Mexico," Obadiah was heard to say at Drury's groggery in the dreary winter of 1846–47, when Iowa was still celebrating its admittance into the Union. "I could have died a hero at the Alamo."

"That wasn't the Mexican war, feller," the man next to him said.

"Sure it was," Obadiah said. "Mexicans slaughtered Crockett and Bowie and all them others."

"That was the war for Texas," the stranger said. "Then Mexico and Santee Annie got riled and that's why we marched to Mexico. To free Texas ag'in and get all the rest of 'em places. Like Californy."

"You don't know nothin', mister. So quit yer brayin'."

That resulted in Obadiah having to work his way to St. Louis and back as a stevedore to get a busted tooth pulled.

Obadiah could have kept on stevedoring but complained that the work was too hard and that the Mississippi River was a right frightening place to be traveling. And sometimes the river stunk worser than a pig farm.

In short, the Marmadukes had landed in a place that was full of opportunities, for this was the West (at least at that time), and a fellow could make his mark in this wild, new, free country.

Unless your name happened to be Obadiah Marmaduke.

Especially after Obadiah gave up on being a stevedore. Well, that job did require a willingness to sweat for hours and you ought to be able to carry a fifty-pound keg down the plank and up the bank without dropping the keg three times.

Speaking of dropping, a pail of nails slipped out of Obadiah's hand and fell on the construction boss's right foot, and so Obadiah was unemployed as soon as Mr. Clavean stopped hopping around and cussing up a storm. The nails didn't weigh anywhere near fifty pounds, but five pounds on your big toe when you're not expecting it hurts just the same.

Old Fullerton gave him a chance at selling dry goods, but Obadiah was color-blind and couldn't tell a bolt of blue gingham from the pink one, and he broke two silk parasols trying to show Mrs. Bettie McDowell how to open one. Those were the five-dollar parasols, mind you, not the fifty-cent ones.

He tried selling bottles of Wistar's Balsam of Wild Cherry, which, he said, reading from the slip of paper he was given and twenty-seven cents in advance, could prevent consumption, which killed fifty thousand folks a year, and also remedy any liver afflictions, and asthma and bronchitis, not to mention things like chronic coughs and weak lungs or even bleeding lungs. Problem was, Obadiah realized he liked the taste of the wild cherry and drunk up three bottles without selling a one. Chillicothe George, who was running that deal, broke one of the empty bottles over Obadiah's head.

Thing was, Obadiah Marmaduke had been quite successful back in Kentucky. That's how come he could afford a wagon and mules to take his family all the way to the Mississippi and cross it into Iowa Territory, which entered the Union on December 28, 1846.

So poor Obadiah took to drink and then, as so often can be the case, he took to cards.

Glory be, for a while he thought his luck had changed.

Obadiah Marmaduke won a sternwheeler in a poker game, and everyone said that the Marmadukes had it made now, for the *Hawkeye* was one of the finest vessels on the Mississippi, a double-engine mastered by the able and fine Christian captain, Silas S. Throckmorton. Two nights later, bound for Oquawka, New Boston, Bloomington, Rock Island, Davenport, Galena, Dubuque, and Potosi, the *Hawkeye* went up in flames just like the James's cabin. Some folks said they had seen young Cal poking at a fire near the boat landings—though he might have just been warming himself as it was February and the temperature was well below zero—but most just chalked it up to a stevedore who had been careless with pipe or cigar.

This was about the time that Obadiah began to think about his son who really wasn't his son, and began to believe that either the Almighty had turned His back on this poor, struggling, kindhearted and hardworking (at least in his mind) soul who had a lovely wife, who had been distraught over losing a young son, and now was disheveled, dismayed, and disillusioned.

Once, after Cal had been playing with a dog, and either canine or kid had torn up half the butter bean plants, Obadiah had sighed, found the jug of Carmichael's corn liquor, and said, "I swan, Charity, but that boy is a jinx or a curse."

"Hush your mouth, husband!" Charity barked back, and Obadiah obeyed.

But later, after Charity stepped on a nail and had to find the Indian woman who could cure such injuries, and the Indian woman—who was not Kickapoo, but Otoe—would not treat Charity unless that boy of hers was out of sight, so Charity told Cal to go to the river and fish. The nail wound was treated, no fish were caught, but Grover Denton drowned in the Mississippi that day, though his boat capsized a good two hundred yards downstream from where Cal was wetting his line.

"Maybe," Charity suggested to Obadiah, "t'ain't Cal whose causin' us this mess of bad luck. Maybe it's just Iowa is a curse to us."

Which got them to thinking.

After all, it wasn't like Burlington, Iowa, was some sort of paradise, not after struggling to survive for nigh a dozen years. Charity conceded that she missed Kentucky. She even told her husband she could settle for Missouri.

Little did she know that Missouri was about to come to their home.

CHAPTER 2

Charity Marmaduke was putting out the fire when, over the towering flames and popping of grease in the skillet in the chimney, she heard a man's voice call out, "Halllooooo, the cabin."

She had just screamed at young Cal because when the skillet got all blazing, she asked for the flour, and the young lad, about seven years old, handed her the sugar by mistake. Fire, in case you are not much at cooking, reacts to sugar a whole lot differently than it does to flour. Much shrieking and some profanity followed as flames leaped toward the roof and smoke caused both mother and child to cough a bit and shriek in alarm a lot more. Charity found the flour herself, thus tragedy was averted.

Strangers were uncommon at the Marmaduke cabin— a little ways out of town—but not unheard of. Still, Charity, fanning herself with a smoky-smelling towel, left the fireplace, which served as the winter and summer kitchen, since the summer setup had been destroyed by an angry cow Cal had been trying to milk.

"Don't open that door, boy!" Charity snapped when

she realized what her son, her adopted son, was about to do. She dunked the towel into a bucket of water—which Cal had brought in to throw on the fire in the skillet before his mother had screamed, "No!" and later would teach him that oil fires and water do not mix well at all, same as oil fires and sugar, and such an act might could have burned down the entire cabin and, possibly, mother and son with it.

A muzzleloading rifle leaned in the corner near the door, but Charity did not go for it. She simply looked through the peephole in the door, pulled back, rubbed her eyes, then tried for a better view.

Recognition was slow to come, but come it did, and Charity stepped back.

"Who is it, Mama?" Cal asked, then coughed, because smoke remained heavy. The fireplace had never drawn worth a fig even when it was burning oak, not grease.

Well, she needed to open the door anyway to let that rancid smoke out of their home. Rubbing her eyes, she looked at Cal, then peered through the hole again. Maybe she had been seeing things.

She hadn't.

"Stay—" No, she couldn't let the boy stay inside this smoky cabin that stunk of burned grease and scorched bacon.

So she opened the door.

"Come along, Cal," she said. "Leave the door open so the smoke'll go out. And . . ." She stepped outside. "Company's here."

The man held the reins to a good horse. He removed his black hat and bowed slightly. The wind blew the linen duster.

"Preacher," she said softly. "How are things in . . . ?" She almost said Kentucky, but Robert James had written every Christmas. The letters were always signed by him, not his wife. They were short, simple, usually with a verse or two of Scripture.

"Missouri?" Charity finished.

The Reverend Robert Sallee James bowed, and put his flat black hat atop his head.

"Fine, Missus Marmaduke," the preacher said. His eyes quickly moved from the woman to the boy.

God was good, he thought with a smile. The kid looked more like his daddy than he did his ma. The preacher's wife was a good woman, a fine mother, worked harder in gardens than anyone the preacher had known, and could milk a cow without complaint. And was fat and mean and ugly.

"Cal," Charity said, turning to the tall, strapping, handsome kid. "This is . . . this is . . . a preacher we knew back in Kentucky. The Reverend James."

"Preacher." Cal nodded.

"Calvin," the preacher said. He must have gotten some smoke in his eyes, the boy thought, because he brought a knuckle to his right eye, then his left, and sniffed a bit before his Adam's apple went up and down.

"Why don't you bring your horse to the corral?" Charity suggested. "Cal, go fill a bucket with water from the well, and then get some grain for the preacher's hoss."

Cal did as he was told, and with the horse drinking and snorting up some grain, he walked over to the stump that served as a thinking chair in the front yard. The preacher was sitting, but Cal, without even being

ordered, drug the rocking chair off the porch and brought it so his mother could rest. Then he put his hands behind his back and just stood there like that knot on a log folks was always talking about.

The stranger, Cal learned, was the minister at New Hope Baptist Church in Clay County, Missouri. He had two sons, Frank being the oldest, seven years old, "Just about a year older than you, Calvin." The man's clear eyes smiled at young Cal, who thought this preacher was a real preacher and knowed things better than anyone who didn't know the gospel from cover to cover because most folks thought Cal was a good year or two older than he actually was.

"A young son—Jesse—he'll be three when September comes along. And a precious little girl, Susan Lavenia. She's just a couple of months old now." He looked around. "Is this strapping young lad your only child?"

"Yes, Reverend," was all Cal's mama said, and she changed the subject. "What brings you so far from your congregation—and your family?"

The preacher sipped water Cal had brought him.

"I'm called to preach," he said. "We have a fine new church at New Hope—made of brick—but I ride the circuit for the Lord."

He preached on and on about all he had done in Missouri. Luring some Baptist college to the nearby town of Liberty; it had just opened this year of 1850. He had married many young couples, saved hundreds of souls, preached far too many funerals, and shown the unenlightened the Light.

"And my family has a fine cabin on a creek in Clay County. We have a fine farm. Growing hemp for cash.

And food to eat. They'll be fine without me. The Lord called me to Missouri, and I've preached and saved many souls. But now . . ." He pointed west. "Now there is a great migration to California. Gold fever is luring many folks westward. Gold can bring deviltry with it, and I must fight the devil with all my might. So I am bound for California. For how long, I do not know."

"How far away is Californy?" Cal asked.

The preacher smiled. "As far as it takes us to get there."

"You goin' alone?" Charity asked.

"I go with the Lord." Smiling, he pointed south and west. "I'm to join a party in Independence, Missouri."

Charity stared at the reverend for a long while. After glancing at her son, she looked Preacher James in his sparkling clear eyes.

"Ain't this a fer piece out of your way?"

This time, the preacher did not answer.

"Cal," Charity said, "go get that skillet and take it to the crick and wash it good. We don't want the preacher to think we'll serve him burnt bacon on his journey west to save souls and such."

The boy didn't want to go, but he did.

"Scrub that skillet good," she told him, and then waited for the Reverend James to speak his piece.

Which Charity related to her husband when the worthless oaf came home that evening.

Obadiah Marmaduke's mouth stayed open.

He was sober, bringing home all of his twelve and a half cents he had earned doing a few odd jobs in town.

He scratched the stubble on his cheeks. He was sure he was sober. He didn't recall going into any saloon, and, besides, most of the grog shops wouldn't let him inside anyway.

"Say that ag'in," he requested of his wife.

"The preacher wants to take Cal with him."

That's what it had sounded like the first time.

The man's sore head shook slowly. He found the cup of coffee, which wasn't really coffee but was all they could afford, and drank about a quarter of it down.

"There's a train—wagon train—they are to join in Independence. A number of Missourians are going."

"We ought to go!" Obadiah sang out.

"We're not going to California," she told him. "I'm too far from Kentucky as it is, and there are wild Indians between here and that gold—if there's any gold left by the time we could get there—and California is full of Mexicans, I hear, who don't speak a word of English."

"Like Kentuckians do!" Laughing at his joke, Obadiah slapped his knee.

Charity's eyes left him groveling and staring at his worn-out boots.

"What's the preacher want with Cal?"

The woman sighed. "Forgiveness," she whispered.

"Huh?"

"He feels he committed a sin. Which"—she shrugged—"I guess he did. I guess we all did. And he wants to get to know his son. That's the best I could get out of what he was saying. He'd say this, then bawl for thirty or forty seconds, then spout out some Scripture, then cry some more, and then he would talk about that woman he married."

Obadiah leaned forward. This might be something worth hearing.

"Well, between tears and torment," Charity said, "what I taken from his talkin' is that this Zerelda James ain't the most forgivin' and kindly Christian woman you'd expect to be a preacher's wife. She yells and threatens. She don't like him runnin' off here and there all the time to preach—even though that's what a preacher does."

"Maybe he just wants gold," Obadiah suggested. "I heard on the riverfront that the newspapers say that the gold won't never run out. That it's like pickin' apples off an apple tree. That there's more gold than there is ants in California, and a body can't help but get rich there. Maybe we should—"

"We're not going anywhere," she told him. "Till they run you out of town."

He pouted. She sighed after two minutes, and leaned over and patted his hand.

Looking into his wife's eyes, Obadiah whispered, "Do you think he'll tell Cal the truth?"

"Do you think he should?"

He studied his feet, then looked around the cabin, then stared at his wife again. "He's handy to have around, ain't he?"

Charity sighed and shook her head.

"We were young and foolish and heartbroke." Her head bowed, and she sniffled. "But he is a good boy. Handsome. He's just . . ."

"Unlucky."

Her head shook. "To us." Her eyes met his again. "He almost burned down the cabin this morn."

"Did the preacher mention . . . ummmm . . . you know . . . maybe . . . offering some . . . money . . . for getting his son back?"

She would have slapped him, but she recalled the Reverend James's words about forgiveness and charity and love.

The hard part, of course, was telling Cal the truth.

Which is why they lied.

California was the land of dreams and gold, and the future—their future—lay in that wondrous place. It would be an adventure. Riding—though from what Charity had heard, it was a whole lot more walking than riding to get to California—across the great West, seeing those never-ending plains and then the greatest spectacles in all of America—the mountains, the glorious Rockies and Sierras so high they touched the clouds. Waterfalls and rapids. Sunsets with every color on the palette stretching across a never-ending sky. And the Pacific Ocean, blue and calm and wondrous.

Cal's eyes brightened at his future. In California, no one would know how much bad luck he brought with him. He would have friends. And maybe he would keep friends. Maybe his luck would change in California. He probably could find some gold, too. He'd be helpful, for once.

"When do we leave?" he shouted.

"Well . . ." His mother reached out and patted his hand.

"You're going out with the Reverend James," she

said, and waved her hand around the cabin. "We have to sell our place, you see."

He saw. He saw his mother's eyes. He said, "I see."

But he told himself that California would be an adventure. And there was something about the preacher that he liked and respected. Cal's ma had taken him to services, maybe not every Sunday, but lots of times, and he had enjoyed the singing. He could belt out "Rock of Ages" like everyone else, and there was much satisfaction in saying *amen*. And he sure liked that concept of forgiveness.

So he forgave his mother, silently, and asked the Almighty to do the same. Then he climbed up to his bed to pack up his clothes and such, and get ready for the trip west.

Visit our website at
KensingtonBooks.com
to sign up for our newsletters, read
more from your favorite authors, see
books by series, view reading group
guides, and more!

Become a Part of Our
Between the Chapters Book Club
Community and Join the Conversation